The Tale of Genji

The Tale of Genji

Lady Murasaki Shikibu

MINT EDITIONS

The Tale of Genji was first published in the early 11th century.

This edition published by Mint Editions 2023.

ISBN 9798888970119 | E-ISBN 9798888970263

Published by Mint Editions®

 MINT
EDITIONS

minteditionbooks.com

Publishing Director: Katie Connolly
Design: Ponderosa Pine Design
Production and Project Management: Micaela Clark
Translated by: Arthur Waley
Typesetting: Westchester Publishing Services

To
Beryl De Zoete

Contents

Preface

Readers of the *Diaries of Court Ladies of Old Japan*, translated by Madame Omori and Professor Doi, will remember that the second of the three diaries is that of a certain Murasaki Shikibu. The little that is known of this lady's life has been set forth by Miss Amy Lowell in her introduction to that book. A few dates, most of them very insecure, will be found in Appendix I of this volume. It is, however, certain that Murasaki was born in the last quarter of the tenth century, that she lost her husband in 1001, and that a few years later she became lady-in-waiting to the Empress Akiko. We know that she was chosen for this post on account of her proficiency in Chinese, a subject which the young Empress was anxious to study. Akiko was then about sixteen, so that Murasaki's position in the house was what, in our parlance, we should call that of "governess" rather than of lady-in-waiting. Akiko, though officially espoused to the Emperor, was still living at home, and her father soon began to pay somewhat embarrassing attentions to the new governess. From the Diary we know that on one occasion at any rate his solicitations were refused.

Was the *Tale of Genji* or any part of it already written when Murasaki came to Court? We only know that in a passage of the Diary which apparently refers to the year 1008 she speaks of her novel having been read out loud to the Emperor. His majesty's comment ("This is a learned lady; she must have been reading the *Chronicle of Japan*") shows that what was read to him must have been the opening chapter of the tale. For in the whole work there is only one sentence which could possibly remind any one of the *Nihongi* ("*Chronicle of Japan*"), and that is the conclusion of Chapter I. So though we may be certain that the first few books were already written in 1008, it is quite possible that the whole fifty-four were not finished till long afterwards. But from the *Sarashina Diary*, the first of the three contained in the *Court Ladies of Old Japan*, we know that the *Tale of Genji* in its complete form was already a classic in the year 1022. The unknown authoress of this diary spent her childhood in a remote province. Her great pleasure was to read romances; but except at the Capital they were hard to come by. She prays fervently to Buddha to bring her quickly to Kyoto, and let her read "dozens and dozens of stories."

In 1022 she at last arrives at Court and her wildest dreams are fulfilled. Packed in a big box her aunt sends round "the fifty-odd chapters of *Genji*" and a whole library of shorter fairytales and romances. "Are there really such people as this in the world? Were Genji my lover, though he should come to me but once in the whole year, how happy I should be! Or were I Lady Ukifune in her mountain home, gazing as the months go by at flowers, red autumn leaves, moonlight and snow; happy, despite loneliness and misfortune, in the thought that at any moment the wonderful letter might come. . ."

Such were the *rêveries* of one who read the *Tale of Genji* more than nine hundred years ago. I think that, could they but read it in the original, few readers would feel that in all those centuries the charm of the book had in any way evaporated. The task of translation in such a case is bound to be arduous and discouraging; but I have all the time been spurred by the belief that I am translating by far the greatest novel of the East, and one which, even if compared with the fiction of Europe, takes its place as one of the dozen greatest masterpieces of the world.

List of Most Important Persons
(Alphabetical)

Aoi, Princess	Genji's wife.
Asagao, Princess	Daughter of Prince Momozono. Courted in vain by Genji from his 17th year onward.
Emperor, The	Genji's father.
Fujitsubo	The Emperor's consort. Loved by Genji. Sister of Prince Hyōbukyō; aunt of Murasaki.
Genji, Prince	Son of the Emperor and his concubine Kiritsubo.
Hyōbukyō, Prince	Brother of Fujitsubo; father of Murasaki.
Iyo no Suke	Husband of Utsusemi.
Ki no Kami	Son of Iyo no Kami, also called Iyo no Suke.
Kiritsubo	Concubine of the Emperor; Genji's mother.
Kōkiden	The Emperor's original consort; later supplanted by Kiritsubo and Fujitsubo successively.
Koremitsu	Genji's retainer.
Left, Minister of the	Father of Aoi.
Momozono, Prince	Father of Princess Asagao.
Murasaki	Child of Prince Hyōbukyō. Adopted by Genji. Becomes his second wife.
Myōbu	A young Court lady who introduces Genji to Princess Suyetsumuhana.
Nokiba no Ogi	Ki no Kami's sister.
Oborozukiyo, Princess	Sister of Kōkiden.
Ōmyōbu	Fujitsubo's maid.
Right, Minister of the	Father of Kōkiden.
Rokujō,	Princess Widow of the Emperor's brother, Prince Zembō. Genji's mistress from his 17th year onward.
Shōnagon	Murasaki's nurse.

Suyetsumuhana, Princess	Daughter of Prince Hitachi. A timid and eccentric lady.
Tō no Chūjō	Genji's brother-in-law and great friend.
Ukon	Yūgao's maid.
Utsusemi	Wife of the provincial governor, Iyo no Suke. Courted by Genji.
Yūgao	Mistress first of Tō no Chūjō then of Genji. Dies bewitched.

Genealogical Tables

Prince Zembō, *m*. Lady Rokujō, and died young.
└ Vestal Virgin of Ise.

The Emperor.
└ Heir Apparent (his mother was Kōkiden).
   │ San no Miya.
   ├ └ Kaoru Genji.
   └ Genji (his mother was Kiritsubo).

Prince Momozono.
└ Princess Asagao.

Princess Ōmiya, *m*. the Minister of the Left.
│ Aoi.
│ └ Yūgiri.
├ Tō no Chūjō.
└ └ Kashiwagi.

Minister of the Right.
├ Kōkiden (eldest daughter).
└ Oborozukiyo (sixth daughter).

A Former Emperor.
├ Prince Hyōbukyō.
│ └ Murasaki (Genji's second wife).
└ Fujitsubo.
   └ Child (supposed to be the Emperor's, really Genji's).

Iyo No Kami (husband of Utsusemi).
├ Ki no Kami (by a former marriage).
└ Nokiba no Ogi (by a former marriage).

I

KIRITSUBO[1]

A t the Court of an Emperor (he lived it matters not when) there was among the many gentlewomen of the Wardrobe and Chamber one, who though she was not of very high rank was favoured far beyond all the rest; so that the great ladies of the Palace, each of whom had secretly hoped that she herself would be chosen, looked with scorn and hatred upon the upstart who had dispelled their dreams. Still less were her former companions, the minor ladies of the Wardrobe, content to see her raised so far above them. Thus her position at Court, preponderant though it was, exposed her to constant jealousy and ill will; and soon, worn out with petty vexations, she fell into a decline, growing very melancholy and retiring frequently to her home. But the Emperor, so far from wearying of her now that she was no longer well or gay, grew everyday more tender, and paid not the smallest heed to those who reproved him, till his conduct became the talk of all the land; and even his own barons and courtiers began to look askance at an attachment so ill-advised. They whispered among themselves that in the Land Beyond the Sea such happenings had led to riot and disaster. The people of the country did indeed soon have many grievances to show: and some likened her to Yang Kuei-fei, the mistress of Ming Huang.[2] Yet, for all this discontent, so great was the sheltering power of her master's love that none dared openly molest her.

Her father, who had been a Councillor, was dead. Her mother, who never forgot that the father was in his day a man of some consequence, managed despite all difficulties to give her as good an upbringing as generally falls to the lot of young ladies whose parents are alive and at the height of fortune. It would have helped matters greatly if there had been some influential guardian to busy himself on the child's behalf. Unfortunately, the mother was entirely alone in the world and sometimes, when troubles came, she felt very bitterly the lack of anyone

---

[1] This chapter should be read with indulgence. In it Murasaki, still under the influence of her somewhat childish predecessors, writes in a manner which is a blend of the Court chronicle with the conventional fairytale.

[2] Famous Emperor of the T'ang dynasty in China; lived A.D. 685–762.

to whom she could turn for comfort and advice. But to return to the daughter. In due time she bore him a little Prince who, perhaps because in some previous life a close bond had joined them, turned out as fine and likely a man-child as well might be in all the land. The Emperor could hardly contain himself during the days of waiting.[3] But when, at the earliest possible moment, the child was presented at Court, he saw that rumour had not exaggerated its beauty. His eldest born prince was the son of Lady Kōkiden, the daughter of the Minister of the Right, and this child was treated by all with the respect due to an undoubted Heir Apparent. But he was not so fine a child as the new prince; moreover the Emperor's great affection for the new child's mother made him feel the boy to be in a peculiar sense his own possession. Unfortunately she was not of the same rank as the courtiers who waited upon him in the Upper Palace, so that despite his love for her, and though she wore all the airs of a great lady, it was not without considerable qualms that he now made it his practice to have her by him not only when there was to be some entertainment, but even when any business of importance was afoot. Sometimes indeed he would keep her when he woke in the morning, not letting her go back to her lodging, so that willy-nilly she acted the part of a Lady-in-Perpetual-Attendance.

Seeing all this, Lady Kōkiden began to fear that the new prince, for whom the Emperor seemed to have so marked a preference, would if she did not take care soon be promoted to the Eastern Palace.[4] But she had, after all, priority over her rival; the Emperor had loved her devotedly and she had born him princes. It was even now chiefly the fear of her reproaches that made him uneasy about his new way of life. Thus, though his mistress could be sure of his protection, there were many who sought to humiliate her, and she felt so weak in herself that it seemed to her at last as though all the honours heaped upon her had brought with them terror rather than joy.

Her lodging was in the wing called Kiritsubo. It was but natural that the many ladies whose doors she had to pass on her repeated journeys to the Emperor's room should have grown exasperated; and sometimes, when these comings and goings became frequent beyond measure, it would happen that on bridges and in corridors, here or there along the way that she must go, strange tricks were played to frighten her or

---

[3] The child of an Emperor could not be shown to him for several weeks after its birth.

[4] I.e. be made Heir Apparent.

unpleasant things were left lying about which spoiled the dresses of the ladies who accompanied her.[5] Once indeed someone locked the door of a portico, so that the poor thing wandered this way and that for a great while in sore distress. So many were the miseries into which this state of affairs now daily brought her that the Emperor could no longer endure to witness her vexations and moved her to the Kōrōden. In order to make room for her he was obliged to shift the Chief Lady of the Wardrobe to lodgings outside. So far from improving matters he had merely procured her a new and most embittered enemy!

The young prince was now three years old. The Putting on of the Trousers was performed with as much ceremony as in the case of the Heir Apparent. Marvellous gifts flowed from the Imperial Treasury and Tribute House. This too incurred the censure of many, but brought no enmity to the child himself; for his growing beauty and the charm of his disposition were a wonder and delight to all who met him. Indeed many persons of ripe experience confessed themselves astounded that such a creature should actually have been born in these latter and degenerate days.

In the summer of that year the lady became very downcast. She repeatedly asked for leave to go to her home, but it was not granted. For a year she continued in the same state. The Emperor to all her entreaties answered only, "Try for a little while longer." But she was getting worse everyday, and when for five or six days she had been growing steadily weaker her mother sent to the Palace a tearful plea for her release. Fearing even now that her enemies might contrive to put some unimaginable shame upon her, the sick lady left her son behind and prepared to quit the Palace in secret. The Emperor knew that the time had come when, little as he liked it, he must let her go. But that she should slip away without a word of farewell was more than he could bear, and he hastened to her side. He found her still charming and beautiful, but her face very thin and wan. She looked at him tenderly, saying nothing. Was she alive? So faint was the dwindling spark that she scarcely seemed so. Suddenly forgetting all that had happened and all that was to come, he called her by a hundred pretty names and weeping showered upon her a thousand caresses; but she made no answer. For sounds and sights reached her but faintly, and she seemed dazed, as one that scarcely remembered she lay upon a bed. Seeing her thus he knew

---

[5] She herself was of course carried in a litter.

not what to do. In great trouble and perplexity he sent for a hand litter. But when they would have laid her in it, he forbad them, saying "There was an oath between us that neither should go alone upon the road that all at last must tread. How can I now let her go from me?" The lady heard him and "At last!" she said; "Though that desired *at last* be come, because I go alone how gladly would I live!"

Thus with faint voice and failing breath she whispered. But though she had found strength to speak, each word was uttered with great toil and pain. Come what might, the Emperor would have watched by her till the end, but that the priests who were to read the Intercession had already been dispatched to her home. She must be brought there before nightfall, and at last he forced himself to let the bearers carry her away. He tried to sleep but felt stifled and could not close his eyes. All night long messengers were coming and going between her home and the Palace. From the first they brought no good news, and soon after midnight announced that this time on arriving at the house they had heard a noise of wailing and lamentation, and learned from those within that the lady had just breathed her last. The Emperor lay motionless as though he had not understood.

Though his father was so fond of his company, it was thought better after this event that the Prince should go away from the Palace. He did not understand what had happened, but seeing the servants all wringing their hands and the Emperor himself continually weeping, he felt that it must have been something very terrible. He knew that even quite ordinary separations made people unhappy; but here was such a dismal wailing and lamenting as he had never seen before, and he concluded that this must be some very extraordinary kind of parting.

When the time came for the funeral to begin, the girl's mother cried out that the smoke of her own body would be seen rising beside the smoke of her child's bier. She rode in the same coach with the Court ladies who had come to the funeral. The ceremony took place at Atago and was celebrated with great splendour. So overpowering was the mother's affection that so long as she looked on the body she still thought of her child as alive. It was only when they lighted the pyre she suddenly realized that what lay upon it was a corpse. Then, though she tried to speak sensibly, she reeled and almost fell from the coach, and those with her turned to one another and said, "At last she knows."

A herald came from the palace and read a proclamation which promoted the dead lady to the Third Rank. The reading of this long proclamation by the bier was a sad business. The Emperor repented bitterly that he had not long ago made her a Lady-in-Waiting, and that was why he now raised her rank by one degree. There were many who grudged her even this honour; but some less stubborn began now to recall that she had indeed been a lady of uncommon beauty; and others, that she had very gentle and pleasing manners; while some went so far as to say it was a shame that anybody should have disliked so sweet a lady, and that if she had not been singled out unfairly from the rest, no one would have said a word against her.

The seven weeks of mourning were, by the Emperor's order, minutely observed. Time passed, but he still lived in rigid seclusion from the ladies of the Court. The servants who waited upon him had a sad life, for he wept almost without ceasing both day and night.

Kōkiden and the other great ladies were still relentless, and went about saying "it looked as though the Emperor would be no less foolishly obsessed by her memory than he had been by her person." He did indeed sometimes see Kōkiden's son, the first born prince. But this only made him long the more to see the dead lady's child, and he was always sending trusted servants, such as his own old nurse, to report to him upon the boy's progress. The time of the autumn equinox had come. Already the touch of the evening air was cold upon the skin. So many memories crowded upon him that he sent a girl, the daughter of his quiver-bearer, with a letter to the dead lady's house. It was beautiful moonlit weather, and after he had despatched the messenger he lingered for a while gazing out into the night. It was at such times as this that he had been wont to call for music. He remembered how her words, lightly whispered, had blended with those strangely fashioned harmonies, remembered how all was strange, her face, her air, her form. He thought of the poem which says that, "*real things in the darkness seem no realer than dreams,*" and he longed for even so dim a substance as the dream-life of those nights.

The messenger had reached the gates of the house. She pushed them back and a strange sight met her eyes. The old lady had for long been a widow and the whole charge of keeping the domain in repair had fallen upon her daughter. But since her death the mother, sunk in age and despair, had done nothing to the place, and everywhere the weeds grew high; and to all this desolation was added the wildness of the autumn gale. Great clumps of mugwort grew so thick that only the moonlight could penetrate them. The messenger alighted at the entrance of the house. At first the mother could find no words with which to greet her, but soon she said: "Alas, I have lingered too long in the world! I cannot bear to think that so fine a messenger as you have pressed your way through the dewy thickets that bar the road to my house," and she burst into uncontrollable weeping.

Then the quiver-bearer's daughter said, "One of the Palace maids who came here, told his Majesty that her heart had been torn with pity at what she saw. And I, Madam, am in like case."

Then after a little hesitation she repeated the Emperor's message: "For a while I searched in the darkness of my mind, groping for an exit from my dream; but after long pondering I can find no way to wake. There is none here to counsel me. Will you not come to me secretly? It is not well that the young prince should spend his days in so desolate and sad a place. Let him come too!"

This he said and much else, but confusedly and with many sighs; "and I, seeing that the struggle to hide his grief from me was costing him dear, hurried away from the Palace without hearing all. But here is a letter that he sent."

"My sight is dim," said the mother. "Let me hold his letter to the light." The letter said:

> I had thought that after a while there might be some blurring, some slight effacement. But no. As days and months go by, the more senseless, the more unendurable becomes my life. I am continually thinking of the child, wondering how he fares. I had hoped that his mother and I together would watch over his upbringing. Will you not take her place in this, and bring him to me as a memory of the past?

Such was the letter, and many instructions were added to it together with a poem which said, *"At the sound of the wind that binds the cold dew on Takagi moor, my heart goes out to the tender lilac stems."*

It was of the young prince that he spoke in symbol; but she did not read the letter to the end. At last the mother said, "Though I know that long life means only bitterness, I have stayed so long in the world that even before the Pine Tree of Takasago I should hide my head in shame. How then should I find courage to go hither and thither in the great Palace of a Hundred Towers? Though the august summons should call me time and again, myself I could not obey. But the young prince (whether he may have heard the august wish I know not) is impatient to return, and, what is small wonder, seems very downcast in this place. Tell his Majesty this, and whatever else of my thoughts you have here learnt from me. For a little child this house is indeed a sorry place. . ."

"They say that the child is asleep," the quiver-bearer's daughter answered. "I should like to have seen him and told the Emperor how he looks; but I am awaited at the Palace and it must be late."

She was hastening away, but the mother: "Since even those who wander in the darkness of their own black thoughts can gain by converse a momentary beam to guide their steps, I pray you sometimes to visit me of your own accord and when you are at leisure. In years past it was at times of joy and triumph that you came to this house, and now this is the news you bring! Foolish are they indeed who trust to fortune! From the time she was born until his death, her father, who knew his own mind, would have it that she must go to Court and charged me again and again not to disappoint his wishes if he were to die. And so, though I thought that the lack of a guardian would bring her into many difficulties, I was determined to carry out his desire. At Court she found that favours only too great were to be hers, and all the while must needs endure in secrecy the tokens of inhuman malice; till hatred had heaped upon her so heavy a load of cares that she died as it were murdered. Indeed, the love that in His wisdom He deigned to show her (or so sometimes it seems to me in the uncomprehending darkness of my heart) was crueller than indifference."

So she spoke, till tears would let her speak no more; and now the night had come.

"All this," the girl answered, "He himself has said; and further: 'That thus against My will and judgment I yielded helplessly to a passion so reckless that it caused men's eyes to blink was perhaps decreed for the very reason that our time was fated to be so short; it was the wild and vehement passion of those who are marked down for instant separation. And though I had vowed that none should suffer because of my love, yet in the end she bore upon her shoulders the heavy hatred of many who thought that for her sake they had been wronged.'

"So again and again have I heard the Emperor speak with tears. But now the night is far spent and I must carry my message to the Palace before day comes."

So she, weeping too, spoke as she hurried away. But the sinking moon was shining in a cloudless sky, and in the grass-clumps that shivered in the cold wind, bell-crickets tinkled their compelling cry. It was hard to leave these grass-clumps, and the quiver-bearer's daughter, loth to ride away, recited the poem which says, *"Ceaseless as the interminable voices of the bell-cricket, all night till dawn my tears flow."*

The mother answered, "Upon the thickets that teem with myriad insect voices falls the dew of a Cloud Dweller's tears; for the people of the Court are called *dwellers above the clouds*."

Then she gave the messenger a sash, a comb and other things that the dead lady had left in her keeping,—gifts from the Emperor which now, since their use was gone, she sent back to him as mementoes of the past. The nursemaids who had come with the boy were depressed not so much at their mistress's death as at being suddenly deprived of the daily sights and sensations of the Palace. They begged to go back at once. But the mother was determined not to go herself, knowing that she would cut too forlorn a figure. On the other hand if she parted with the boy, she would be daily in great anxiety about him. That was why she did not immediately either go with him herself or send him to the Palace.

The quiver-bearer's daughter found the Emperor still awake. He was, upon pretext of visiting the flowerpots in front of the Palace which were then in full bloom, waiting for her out of doors, while four or five trusted ladies conversed with him.

At this time it was his wont to examine morning and evening a picture of The Everlasting Wrong,[6] the text written by Teiji no In,[7] with poems by Ise[8] and Tsurayuki,[9] both in Yamato speech, and in that of the men beyond the sea, and the story of this poem was the common matter of his talk.

Now he turned to the messenger and asked eagerly for all her news. And when she had given him a secret and faithful account of the sad place whence she had come, she handed him the mother's letter:

> His Majesty's gracious commands I read with reverence deeper than I can express, but their purport has brought great darkness and confusion to my mind.

---

[6] A poem by the Chinese writer Po Chü-i about the death of Yang Kuei-fei, favourite of the Emperor Ming Huang. *See* Giles, *Chinese Literature*, p. 169.

[7] Name of the Emperor Uda after his retirement in A.D. 897.

[8] Poetess, 9th century.

[9] Famous poet, 883–946 A.D.

All this, together with a poem in which she compared her grandchild to a flower which has lost the tree that sheltered it from the great winds, was so wild and so ill-writ as only to be suffered from the hand of one whose sorrow was as yet unhealed.

Again the Emperor strove for self-possession in the presence of his messenger. But as he pictured to himself the time when the dead lady first came to him, a thousand memories pressed thick about him, and recollection linked to recollection carried him onward, till he shuddered to think how utterly unmarked, unheeded all these hours and days had fled.

At last he said, "I too thought much and with delight how with most profit might be fulfilled the wish that her father the Councillor left behind him; but of that no more. If the young Prince lives occasion may yet be found. . . it is for his long life that we must pray."

He looked at the presents she had brought back and he cried, "Would that like the wizard you had brought a kingfisher-hairpin as token of your visit to the place where her spirit dwells," and recited the poem: "*Oh for a master of magic who might go and seek her, and by a message teach me where her spirit dwells.*"

For the picture of Kuei-fei, skilful though the painter might be, was but the work of a brush, and had no living fragrance. And though the poet tells us that Kuei-fei's grace was as that of "the hibiscus of the Royal Lake or the willows of the Wei-yang Palace," the lady in the picture was all paint and powder and had a simpering Chinesified air.

But when he thought of the lost lady's voice and form, he could find neither in the beauty of flowers nor in the song of birds any fit comparison. Continually he pined that fate should not have allowed them to fulfil the vow which morning and evening was ever talked of between them,—the vow that their lives should be as the twin birds that share a wing, the twin trees that share a bough. The rustling of the wind, the chirping of an insect would cast him into the deepest melancholy; and now Kōkiden, who for a long while had not been admitted to his chamber, must needs sit in the moonlight making music far on into the night! This evidently distressed him in the highest degree and those ladies and courtiers who were with him were equally shocked and distressed on his behalf. But the offending lady was one who stood much upon her dignity and she was determined to behave as though nothing of any consequence had taken place in the Palace.

And now the moon had set. The Emperor thought of the girl's mother in the house amid the thickets and wondered, making a poem of the thought, with what feelings she had watched the sinking of the autumn moon: "*for even we Men above the Clouds were weeping when it sank.*"

He raised the torches high in their sockets and still sat up. But at last he heard voices coming from the Watch House of the Right and knew that the hour of the Bull[10] had struck. Then, lest he should be seen, he went into his chamber. He found he could not sleep and was up before daybreak. But, as though he remembered the words "*he knew not the dawn was at his window*" of Ise's poem,[11] he showed little attention to the affairs of his Morning Audience, scarcely touched his dried rice and seemed but dimly aware of the viands on the great Table, so that the carvers and waiting-men groaned to see their Master's plight; and all his servants, both men and women kept on whispering to one another "What a senseless occupation has ours become!" and supposed that he was obeying some extravagant vow.

Regardless of his subjects' murmurings, he continually allowed his mind to wander from their affairs to his own, so that the scandal of his negligence was now as dangerous to the State as it had been before, and again there began to be whispered references to a certain Emperor of another land. Thus the months and days passed, and in the end the young prince arrived at Court. He had grown up to be a child of unrivalled beauty and the Emperor was delighted with him. In the spring an heir to the Throne was to be proclaimed and the Emperor was sorely tempted to pass over the first born prince in favour of the young child. But there was no one at Court to support such a choice and it was unlikely that it would be tolerated by the people; it would indeed bring danger rather than glory to the child. So he carefully concealed from the world that he had any such design, and gained great credit, men saying, "Though he dotes on the boy, there is at least some limit to his folly." And even the great ladies of the Palace became a little easier in their minds.

The grandmother remained inconsolable, and impatient to set out upon her search for the place where the dead lady's spirit dwelt, she soon expired. Again the Emperor was in great distress; and this time the boy, being now six years old, understood what had happened and

---

[10] 1 A.M.

[11] A poem by Lady Ise written on a picture illustrating Po Chü-i's *Everlasting Wrong*.

LADY MURASAKI SHIKIBU

wept bitterly. And often he spoke sadly of what he had seen when he was brought to visit the poor dead lady who had for many years been so kind to him. Henceforward he lived always at the Palace. When he became seven he began to learn his letters, and his quickness was so unusual that his father was amazed. Thinking that now no one would have the heart to be unkind to the child, the Emperor began to take him to the apartments of Kōkiden and the rest, saying to them, "Now that his mother is dead I know that you will be nice to him."

Thus the boy began to penetrate the Royal Curtain. The roughest soldier, the bitterest foeman could not have looked on such a child without a smile, and Kōkiden did not send him away. She had two daughters who were indeed not such fine children as the little prince. He also played with the Court Ladies, who, because he was now very pretty and bashful in his ways, found endless amusement, as indeed did everyone else, in sharing his games. As for his serious studies, he soon learnt to send the sounds of zithern and flute flying gaily to the clouds. But if I were to tell you of all his accomplishments, you would think that he was soon going to become a bore.

At this time some Koreans came to Court and among them a fortuneteller. Hearing this, the Emperor did not send for them to come to the Palace, because of the law against the admission of foreigners which was made by the Emperor Uda.[12] But in strict secrecy he sent the Prince to the Strangers' quarters. He went under the escort of the Secretary of the Right, who was to introduce him as his own son. The fortune teller was astonished by the boy's lineaments and expressed his surprise by continually nodding his head: "He has the marks of one who might become a Father of the State, and if this were his fate, he would not stop short at any lesser degree than that of Mighty King and Emperor of all the land. But when I look again—I see that confusion and sorrow would attend his reign. But should he become a great Officer of State and Counsellor of the Realm I see no happy issue, for he would be defying those kingly signs of which I spoke before."

The Secretary was a most talented, wise and learned scholar, and now began to conduct an interesting conversation with the fortune teller. They exchanged essays and poems, and the fortuneteller made a little speech, saying, "It has been a great pleasure to me on the eve of my departure to meet with a man of capacities so unusual; and though

---

[12] Reigned 889–897. The law in question was made in 894.

I regret my departure I shall now take away most agreeable impressions of my visit." The little, prince presented him with a very nice verse of poetry, at which he expressed boundless admiration and offered the boy a number of handsome presents. In return the Emperor sent him a large reward from the Imperial Treasury. This was all kept strictly secret. But somehow or other the Heir Apparent's grandfather, the Minister of the Right, and others of his party got wind of it and became very suspicious. The Emperor then sent for native fortunetellers and made trial of them, explaining that because of certain signs which he had himself observed he had hitherto refrained from making the boy a prince. With one accord they agreed that he had acted with great prudence and the Emperor determined not to set the child adrift upon the world as a prince without royal standing or influence upon the mother's side. For he thought, "My own power is very insecure. I had best set him to watch on my behalf over the great Officers of State."

Thinking that he had thus agreeably settled the child's future, he set seriously to work upon his education, and saw to it that he should be made perfect in every branch of art and knowledge. He showed such aptitude in all his studies that it seemed a pity he should remain a commoner and as it had been decided that it would arouse suspicion if he were made a prince, the Emperor consulted with certain doctors wise in the lore of the planets and phases of the moon. And they with one accord recommended that he should be made a Member of the Minamoto (or Gen) Clan. So this was done.

As the years went by the Emperor did not forget his lost lady; and though many women were brought to the Palace in the hope that he might take pleasure in them, he turned from them all, believing that there was not in the world any one like her whom he had lost. There was at that time a lady whose beauty was of great repute. She was the fourth daughter of the previous Emperor, and it was said that her mother, the Dowager Empress, had brought her up with unrivalled care. A certain Dame of the Household, who had served the former Emperor, was intimately acquainted with the young Princess, having known her since childhood and still having occasion to observe her from without.

"I have served in three courts," said the Dame, "and in all that time have seen none who could be likened to the departed lady, save the daughter of the Empress Mother. She indeed is a lady of rare beauty."

So she spoke to the Emperor, and he, much wondering what truth there was in it, listened with great attention. The Empress Mother heard of this with great alarm, for she remembered with what open cruelty the sinister Lady Kōkiden had treated her former rival, and though she did not dare speak openly of her fears, she was managing to delay the girl's presentation, when suddenly she died.

The Emperor, hearing that the bereaved Princess was in a very desolate condition, sent word gently telling her that he should henceforward look upon her as though she were one of the Lady Princesses his daughters. Her servants and guardians and her brother, Prince Hyōbukyō, thought that life in the Palace might distract her and would at least be better than the gloomy desolation of her home, and so they sent her to the Court. She lived in apartments called Fujitsubo (Wistaria Tub) and was known by this name. The Emperor could not deny that she bore an astonishing resemblance to his beloved. She was however of much higher rank, so that everyone was anxious to please her, and, whatever happened, they were prepared to grant her the utmost licence: whereas the dead lady had been imperilled by the Emperor's favour only because the Court was not willing to accept her.

His old love did not now grow dimmer, and though he sometimes found solace and distraction in shifting his thoughts from the lady who had died to the lady who was so much like her, yet life remained for him a sad business.

Genji ("he of the Minamoto clan"), as he was now called, was constantly at the Emperor's side. He was soon quite at his ease with the common run of Ladies in Waiting and Ladies of the Wardrobe, so it was not likely he would be shy with one who was daily summoned to the Emperor's apartments. It was but natural that all these ladies should vie eagerly with one another for the first place in Genji's affections, and there were many whom in various ways he admired very much. But most of them behaved in too grown-up a fashion; only one, the new princess, was pretty and quite young as well, and though she tried to hide from him, it was inevitable that they should often meet. He could not remember his mother, but the Dame of the Household had told him how very like to her the girl was, and this interested his childish fancy, and he would like to have been her great friend and lived with her always.

One day the Emperor said to her, "Do not be unkind to him. He is interested because he has heard that you are so like his mother. Do not think him impertinent, but behave nicely to him. You are indeed so like him in look and features that you might well be his mother."

And so, young though he was, fleeting beauty took its hold upon his thoughts; he felt his first clear predilection.

Kōkiden had never loved this lady too well, and now her old enmity to Genji sprang up again; her own children were reckoned to be of quite uncommon beauty, but in this they were no match for Genji, who was so lovely a boy that people called him Hikaru Genji or Genji the Shining One; and Princess Fujitsubo, who also had many admirers, was called Princess Glittering Sunshine.

Though it seemed a shame to put so lovely a child into man's dress, he was now twelve years old and the time for his Initiation was come. The Emperor directed the preparations with tireless zeal and insisted upon a magnificence beyond what was prescribed. The Initiation of the Heir Apparent, which had last year been celebrated in the Southern Hall, was not a whit more splendid in its preparations. The ordering of the banquets that were to be given in various quarters, and the work of the Treasurer and Grain Intendant he supervised in person, fearing lest the officials should be remiss; and in the end all was perfection. The ceremony took place in the eastern wing of the Emperor's own apartments, and the Throne was placed facing towards the east, with the seats of the Initiate to-be and his Sponsor (the Minister of the Left) in front.

Genji arrived at the hour of the Monkey.[13] He looked very handsome with his long childish locks, and the Sponsor, whose duty it had just been to bind them with the purple filet, was sorry to think that all this would soon be changed and even the Clerk of the Treasury seemed loath to sever those lovely tresses with the ritual knife. The Emperor, as he watched, remembered for a moment what pride the mother would have taken in the ceremony, but soon drove the weak thought from his mind.

Duly crowned, Genji went to his chamber and changing into man's dress went down into the courtyard and performed the Dance of Homage, which he did with such grace that tears stood in every eye. And now the Emperor, whose grief had of late grown somewhat less insistent, was again overwhelmed by memories of the past.

It had been feared that his delicate features would show to less advantage when he had put aside his childish dress; but on the contrary he looked handsomer than ever.

---

[13] 3 P.M.

His sponsor, the Minister of the Left, had an only daughter whose beauty the Heir Apparent had noticed. But now the father began to think he would not encourage that match, but would offer her to Genji. He sounded the Emperor upon this, and found that he would be very glad to obtain for the boy the advantage of so powerful a connection.

When the courtiers assembled to drink the Love Cup, Genji came and took his place among the other princes. The Minister of the Left came up and whispered something in his ear; but the boy blushed and could think of no reply. A chamberlain now came over to the Minister and brought him a summons to wait upon His Majesty immediately. When he arrived before the Throne, a Lady of the Wardrobe handed to him the Great White Inner Garment and the Maid's Skirt,[14] which were his ritual due as Sponsor to the Prince. Then, when he had made him drink out of the Royal Cup, the Emperor recited a poem in which he prayed that the binding of the purple filet might symbolize the union of their two houses; and the Minister answered him that nothing should sever this union save the fading of the purple band. Then he descended the long stairs and from the courtyard performed the Grand Obeisance.[15] Here too were shown the horses from the Royal Stables and the hawks from the Royal Falconry, that had been decreed as presents for Genji. At the foot of the stairs the Princes and Courtiers were lined up to receive their bounties, and gifts of every kind were showered upon them. That day the hampers and fruit baskets were distributed in accordance with the Emperor's directions by the learned Secretary of the Right, and boxes of cake and presents lay about so thick that one could scarcely move. Such profusion had not been seen even at the Heir Apparent's Initiation.

That night Genji went to the Minister's house, where his betrothal was celebrated with great splendour. It was thought that the little Prince looked somewhat childish and delicate, but his beauty astonished everyone. Only the bride, who was four years older, regarded him as a mere baby and was rather ashamed of him.

The Emperor still demanded Genji's attendance at the Palace, so he did not set up a house of his own. In his inmost heart he was always thinking how much nicer *she* [16] was than anyone else, and only wanted

---

[14] These symbolized the unmanly life of childhood which Genji had now put behind him.
[15] The *butô*, a form of kowtow so elaborate as to be practically a dance.
[16] Fujitsubo.

to be with people who were like her, but alas no one was the least like her. Everyone seemed to make a great deal of fuss about Princess Aoi, his betrothed; but he could see nothing nice about her. The girl at the Palace now filled all his childish thoughts and this obsession became a misery to him.

Now that he was a "man" he could no longer frequent the women's quarters as he had been wont to do. But sometimes when an entertainment was afoot he found comfort in hearing her voice dimly blending with the sound of zithern or flute and felt his grown-up existence to be unendurable. After an absence of five or six days he would occasionally spend two or three at his betrothed's house. His father-in-law attributing this negligence to his extreme youth was not at all perturbed and always received him warmly. Whenever he came the most interesting and agreeable of the young people of the day were asked to meet him and endless trouble was taken in arranging games to amuse him.

The Shigeisa, one of the rooms which had belonged to his mother, was allotted to him as his official quarters in the Palace, and the servants who had waited on her were now gathered together again and formed his suite. His grandmother's house was falling into decay. The Imperial Office of Works was ordered to repair it. The grouping of the trees and disposition of the surrounding hills had always made the place delightful. Now the basin of the lake was widened and many other improvements were carried out.

"If only I were going to live here with someone whom I liked," thought Genji sadly.

Some say that the name of Hikaru the Shining One was given to him in admiration by the Korean fortuneteller.[17]

---

[17] This touch is reminiscent of early chronicles such as the *Nihongi*, which delight in alternative explanations. In the subsequent chapters such archaisms entirely disappear.

II

The Broom-Tree

Genji the Shining One. . . He knew that the bearer of such a name could not escape much scrutiny and jealous censure and that his lightest dallyings would be proclaimed to posterity. Fearing then lest he should appear to after ages as a mere good-for-nothing and trifler, and knowing that (so accursed is the blabbing of gossips' tongues) his most secret acts might come to light, he was obliged always to act with great prudence and to preserve at least the outward appearance of respectability. Thus nothing really romantic ever happened to him and Katano no Shōshō[1] would have scoffed at his story.

While he was still a Captain of the Guard and was spending most of his time at the Palace, his infrequent visits to the Great Hall[2] were taken as a sign that some secret passion had made its imprint on his heart. But in reality the frivolous, commonplace, straight-ahead amours of his companions did not in the least interest him, and it was a curious trait in his character that when on rare occasions, despite all resistance, love did gain a hold upon him, it was always in the most improbable and hopeless entanglement that he became involved.

It was the season of the long rains. For many days there had not been a fine moment and the Court was keeping a strict fast. The people at the Great Hall were becoming very impatient of Genji's long residence at the Palace, but the young lords, who were Court pages, liked waiting upon Genji better than upon anyone else, always managing to put out his clothes and decorations in some marvellous new way. Among these brothers his greatest friend was the Equerry, Tō no Chūjō, with whom above all other companions of his playtime he found himself familiar and at ease. This lord too found the house which his father-in-law, the Minister of the Right, had been at pains to build for him, somewhat oppressive, while at his father's house he, like Genji, found the splendours somewhat dazzling, so that he ended by becoming Genji's

---

[1] The hero of a lost popular romance. It is also referred to by Murasaki's contemporary Sei Shōnagon in Chapter 145 of her *Makura no Sōshi*.
[2] His father-in-law's house, where his wife Princess Aoi still continued to live.

constant companion at Court. They shared both studies and play and were inseparable companions on every sort of occasion, so that soon all formalities were dispensed with between them and the inmost secrets of their hearts freely exchanged.

It was on a night when the rain never ceased its dismal downpour. There were not many people about in the palace and Genji's rooms seemed even quieter than usual. He was sitting by the lamp, looking at various books and papers. Suddenly he began pulling some letters out of the drawers of a desk which stood near by. This aroused Tō no Chūjō's curiosity.

"Some of them I can show to you," said Genji, "but there are others which I had rather. . ."

"It is just those which I want to see. Ordinary, commonplace letters are very much alike and I do not suppose that yours differ much from mine. What I want to see are passionate letters written in moments of resentment, letters hinting consent, letters written at dusk. . ."

He begged so eagerly that Genji let him examine the drawers. It was not indeed likely that he had put any very important or secret documents in the ordinary desk; he would have hidden them away much further from sight. So he felt sure that the letters in these drawers would be nothing to worry about. After turning over a few of them, "What an astonishing variety!" Tō no Chūjō exclaimed and began guessing at the writers' names, and made one or two good hits.

More often he was wrong and Genji, amused by his puzzled air, said very little but generally managed to lead him astray. At last he took the letters back, saying, "But you too must have a large collection. Show me some of yours, and my desk will open to you with better will."

"I have none that you would care to see," said Tō no Chūjō, and he continued: "I have at last discovered that there exists no woman of whom one can say 'Here is perfection. This is indeed she.'"

There are many who have the superficial art of writing a good running hand, or if occasion requires of making a quick repartee. But there are few who will stand the ordeal of any further test. Usually their minds are entirely occupied by admiration for their own accomplishments, and their abuse of all rivals creates a most unpleasant impression. Some again are adored by overfond parents. These have been since childhood guarded behind lattice windows[3] and no knowledge of them

---

[3] Japanese houses were arranged somewhat differently from ours and for many of the terms which constantly recur in this book (*kichō*, *sudare*, *sunoko*, etc.) no exact English

is allowed to reach the outer-world, save that of their excellence in some accomplishment or art; and this may indeed sometimes arouse our interest. She is pretty and graceful and has not yet mixed at all with the world. Such a girl by closely copying some model and applying herself with great industry will often succeed in really mastering one of the minor and ephemeral arts. Her friends are careful to say nothing of her defects and to exaggerate her accomplishments, and while we cannot altogether trust their praise we cannot believe that their judgment is entirely astray. But when we take steps to test their statements we are invariably disappointed."

He paused, seeming to be slightly ashamed of the cynical tone which he had adopted, and added, "I know my experience is not large, but that is the conclusion I have come to so far."

Then Genji, smiling: "And are there any who lack even one accomplishment?"

"No doubt, but in such a case it is unlikely that anyone would be successfully decoyed. The number of those who have nothing to recommend them and of those in whom nothing but good can be found is probably equal. I divide women into three classes. Those of high rank and birth are made such a fuss of and their weak points are so completely concealed that we are certain to be told that they are paragons. About those of the middle class everyone is allowed to express his own opinion, and we shall have much conflicting evidence to sift. As for the lower classes, they do not concern us."

The completeness with which Tō no Chūjō disposed of the question amused Genji, who said, "It will not always be so easy to know into which of the three classes a woman ought to be put. For sometimes people of high rank sink to the most abject positions; while others of common birth rise to be high officers, wear self-important faces, redecorate the inside of their houses and think themselves as good as anyone. How are we to deal with such cases?"

At this moment they were joined by Hidari no Uma no Kami and Tō Shikibu no Jō, who said they had also come to the Palace to keep the fast. As both of them were great lovers and good talkers, Tō no Chūjō handed over to them the decision of Genji's question, and in the

---

equivalents can be found. In such cases I have tried to use expressions which without being too awkward or unfamiliar will give an adequate general idea of what is meant.

discussion which followed many unflattering things were said. Uma no Kami spoke first.

"However high a lady may rise, if she does not come of an adequate stock, the world will think very differently of her from what it would of one born to such honours; but if through adverse fortune a lady of highest rank finds herself in friendless misery, the noble breeding of her mind is soon forgotten and she becomes an object of contempt. I think then that taking all things into account, we must put such ladies too into the 'middle class.' But when we come to classify the daughters of Zuryō,[4] who are sent to labour at the affairs of distant provinces,—they have such ups and downs that we may reasonably put them too into the middle class.

"Then there are Ministers of the third and fourth classes without Cabinet rank. These are generally thought less of even than the humdrum, ordinary officials. They are usually of quite good birth, but have much less responsibility than Ministers of State and consequently much greater peace of mind. Girls born into such households are brought up in complete security from want or deprivation of any kind, and indeed often amid surroundings of the utmost luxury and splendour. Many of them grow up into women whom it would be folly to despise; some have been admitted at Court, where they have enjoyed a quite unexpected success. And of this I could cite many, many instances."

"Their success has generally been due to their having a lot of money," said Genji smiling.

"You should have known better than to say that," said Tō no Chūjō, reproving him, and Uma no Kami went on:

"There are some whose lineage and reputation are so high that it never occurs to one that their education could possibly be at fault; yet when we meet them, we find ourselves exclaiming in despair 'How can they have contrived to grow up like this?'

"No doubt the perfect woman in whom none of those essentials is lacking must somewhere exist and it would not startle me to find her. But she would certainly be beyond the reach of a humble person like myself, and for that reason I should like to put her in a category of her own and not to count her in our present classification.

"But suppose that behind some gateway overgrown with vine-weed, in a place where no one knows there is a house at all, there should be

---

[4] Provincial officials. Murasaki herself came of this class.

locked away some creature of unimagined beauty—with what excitement should we discover her! The complete surprise of it, the upsetting of all our wise theories and classifications, would be likely, I think, to lay a strange and sudden enchantment upon us. I imagine her father rather large and gruff; her brother, a surly, ill-looking fellow. Locked away in an utterly blank and uninteresting bedroom she will be subject to odd flights of fancy, so that in her hands the arts that others learn as trivial accomplishments will seem strangely full of meaning and importance; or perhaps in some particular art she will thrill us by her delightful and unexpected mastery. Such a one may perhaps be beneath the attention of those of you who are of flawless lineage. But for my part I find it hard to banish her. . ." and here he looked at Shikibu no Jō, who wondered whether the description had been meant to apply to his own sisters, but said nothing.

"If it is difficult to choose even out of the top class. . ." thought Genji, and began to doze.

He was dressed in a suit of soft white silk, with a rough cloak carelessly slung over his shoulders, with belt and fastenings untied. In the light of the lamp against which he was leaning he looked so lovely that one might have wished he were a girl; and they thought that even Uma no Kami's "perfect woman," whom he had placed in a category of her own, would not be worthy of such a prince as Genji.

The conversation went on. Many persons and things were discussed. Uma no Kami contended that perfection is equally difficult to find in other spheres. The sovereign is hard put to it to choose his ministers. But he at least has an easier task than the husband, for he does not entrust the affairs of his kingdom to one, two or three persons alone, but sets up a whole system of superiors and subordinates.

But when the mistress of a house is to be selected, a single individual must be found who will combine in her person many diverse qualities. It will not do to be too exacting. Let us be sure that the lady of our choice possesses certain tangible qualities which we admire; and if in other ways she falls short of our ideal, we must be patient and call to mind those qualities which first induced us to begin our courting.

But even here we must beware; for there are some who in the selfishness of youth and flawless beauty are determined that not a dust-flick shall fall upon them. In their letters they choose the most harmless topics, but yet contrive to colour the very texture of the written signs with a tenderness that vaguely disquiets us. But such a one, when we have at last secured a meeting, will speak so low that she can scarcely be heard, and the few faint sentences that she murmurs beneath her breath serve only to make her more mysterious than before. All this may seem to be the pretty shrinking of girlish modesty; but we may later find that what held her back was the very violence of her passions.

Or again, where all seems plain sailing, the perfect companion will turn out to be too impressionable and will upon the most inappropriate occasions display her affections in so ludicrous a way that we begin to wish ourselves rid of her.

Then there is the zealous housewife, who regardless of her appearance twists her hair behind her ears and devotes herself entirely to the details of our domestic welfare. The husband, in his comings and goings about the world, is certain to see and hear many things which he cannot discuss with strangers, but would gladly talk over with an intimate who could listen with sympathy and understanding, someone who could laugh with him or weep if need be. It often happens too that some political event will greatly perturb or amuse him, and he sits apart longing to tell someone about it. He suddenly laughs at some secret recollection or sighs audibly. But the wife only says lightly, "What is the matter?" and shows no interest. This is apt to be very trying.

Uma no Kami considered several other cases. But he reached no definite conclusion and sighing deeply he continued: "We will then, as I have suggested, let birth and beauty go by the board. Let her be the simplest and most guileless of creatures so long as she is honest and of a peaceable disposition, that in the end we may not lack a place of trust. And if someother virtue chances to be hers we shall treasure it as a godsend. But if we discover in her some small defect, it shall not be too closely scrutinized. And we may be sure that if she is strong in the virtues of tolerance and amiability her outward appearance will not be beyond measure harsh.

"There are those who carry forbearance too far, and affecting not to notice wrongs which cry out for redress seem to be paragons of misused fidelity. But suddenly a time comes when such a one can restrain herself no longer, and leaving behind her a poem couched in pitiful language and calculated to rouse the most painful sentiments of remorse, she flies to some remote village in the mountains or some desolate seashore, and for a long while all trace of her is lost.

"When I was a boy the ladies-in-waiting used to tell me sad tales of this kind. I never doubted that the sentiments expressed in them were real, and I wept profusely. But now I am beginning to suspect that such sorrows are for the most part affectation. She has left behind her (this lady whom we are imagining) a husband who is probably still fond of her; she is making herself very unhappy, and by disappearing in this way is causing him unspeakable anxiety, perhaps only for the ridiculous purpose of putting his affection to the test. Then comes along some admiring friend crying 'What a heart! What depth of feeling!' She becomes more lugubrious than ever, and finally enters a nunnery. When she decided on this step she was perfectly sincere and had not the slightest intention of ever returning to the world. Then some female friend hears of it and 'Poor thing' she cries; 'in what an agony of mind must she have been to do this!' and visits her in her cell. When the husband, who has never ceased to mourn for her, hears what she has become, he bursts into tears, and some servant or old nurse, seeing this, bustles off to the nunnery with tales of the husband's despair, and 'Oh Madam, what a shame, what a shame!' Then the nun, forgetting where and what she is, raises her hand to her head to straighten her hair, and finds that it has been shorn away. In helpless misery she sinks to the floor, and do what she will, the tears begin to flow. Now all is lost; for since she cannot at every moment be praying for strength, there creeps into her mind the sinful thought that she did ill to become a nun and so often does she commit this sin that even Buddha must think her wickeder now than she was before she took her vows; and she feels certain that these terrible thoughts are leading her soul to the blackest Hell. But if the *karma* of their past lives should chance to be strongly weighted against a parting, she will be found and captured before she has taken her final vows. In such a case their life will be beyond endurance unless she be fully determined, come good or ill, this time to close her eyes to all that goes amiss.

"Again there are others who must needs be forever mounting guard over their own and their husband's affections. Such a one, if she sees in him not a fault indeed but even the slightest inclination to stray, makes a foolish scene, declaring with indignation that she will have no more to do with him.

"But even if a man's fancy should chance indeed to have gone somewhat astray, yet his earlier affection may still be strong and in the end will return to its old haunts. Now by her tantrums she has made a rift that cannot be joined. Whereas she who when some small wrong calls for silent rebuke, shows by a glance that she is not unaware; but when some large offence demands admonishment knows how to hint without severity, will end by standing in her master's affections better than ever she stood before. For often the sight of our own forbearance will give our neighbour strength to rule his mutinous affections.

"But she whose tolerance and forgiveness know no bounds, though this may seem to proceed from the beauty and amiability of her disposition, is in fact displaying the shallowness of her feeling: 'The unmoored boat must needs drift with the stream.' Are you not of this mind?"

Tō no Chūjō nodded. "Some," he said, "have imagined that by arousing a baseless suspicion in the mind of the beloved we can revive a waning devotion. But this experiment is very dangerous. Those who recommend it are confident that so long as resentment is groundless one need only suffer it in silence and all will soon be well. I have observed however that this is by no means the case.

"But when all is said and done, there can be no greater virtue in woman than this: that she should with gentleness and forbearance meet every wrong whatsoever that falls to her share." He thought as he said this of his own sister, Princess Aoi; but was disappointed and piqued to discover that Genji, whose comments he awaited, was fast asleep.

Uma no Kami was an expert in such discussions and now stood preening his feathers. Tō no Chūjō was disposed to hear what more he had to say and was now at pains to humour and encourage him.

"It is with women," said Uma no Kami, "as it is with the works of craftsmen. The woodcarver can fashion whatever he will. Yet his products are but toys of the moment, to be glanced at in jest, not fashioned according to any precept or law. When times change, the carver too will change his style and make new trifles to hit the fancy of the passing day. But there is another kind of artist, who sets more soberly about his work, striving to give real beauty to the things which men actually use and to give to them the shapes which tradition has ordained. This maker of real things must not for a moment be confused with the carver of idle toys.

"In the Painters' Workshop too there are many excellent artists chosen for their proficiency in ink-drawing; and indeed they are all so clever it is hard to set one above the other. But all of them are at work on subjects intended to impress and surprise. One paints the Mountain of Hōrai; another a raging sea-monster riding a storm; another, ferocious animals from the Land beyond the sea, or faces of imaginary demons. Letting their fancy run wildly riot they have no thought of beauty, but only of how best they may astonish the beholder's eye. And though nothing in their pictures is real, all is probable. But ordinary hills and rivers, just as they are, houses such as you may see anywhere, with all their real beauty and harmony of form—quietly to draw such scenes as this, or to show what lies behind some intimate hedge that is folded away far from the world, and thick trees upon some unheroic hill, and all this with befitting care for composition, proportion, and the like,—such works demand the highest master's utmost skill and must needs draw the common craftsman into a thousand blunders. So too in handwriting, we see some who aimlessly prolong their cursive strokes this way or that, and hope their flourishes will be mistaken for genius. But true penmanship preserves in every letter its balance and form, and though at first some letters may seem but half-formed, yet when we compare them with the copybooks we find that there is nothing at all amiss.

"So it is in these trifling matters. And how much the more in judging of the human heart should we distrust all fashionable airs and graces, all tricks and smartness, learnt only to please the outward gaze! This I first understood some while ago, and if you will have patience with me I will tell you the story."

So saying, he came and sat a little closer to them, and Genji woke up. Tō no Chūjō, in wrapt attention, was sitting with his cheek propped upon his hand. Uma no Kami's whole speech that night was indeed very much like a chaplain's sermon about the ways of the world, and was rather absurd. But upon such occasions as this we are easily led on into discussing our own ideas and most private secrets without the least reserve.

"It happened when I was young, and in an even more humble position than I am today," Uma no Kami continued. "I was in love with a girl who (like the drudging, faithful wife of whom I spoke a little while ago) was not a full-sail beauty; and I in my youthful vanity thought she was all very well for the moment, but would never do for the wife of so fine a fellow as I. She made an excellent companion in times when I was at a loose end; but she was of a disposition so violently jealous, that I could have put up with a little less devotion if only she had been somewhat less fiercely ardent and exacting.

"Thus I kept thinking, vexed by her unrelenting suspicions. But then I would remember her ceaseless devotion to the interests of one who was after all a person of no account, and full of remorse I made sure that with a little patience on my part she would one day learn to school her jealousy.

"It was her habit to minister to my smallest wants even before I was myself aware of them; whatever she felt was lacking in her she strove to acquire, and where she knew that in some quality of mind she still fell behind my desires, she was at pains never to show her deficiency in such a way as might vex me. Thus in one way or another she was always busy in forwarding my affairs, and she hoped that if all down to the last dew drop (as they say) were conducted as I should wish, this would be set down to her credit and help to balance the defects in her person which meek and obliging as she might be could not (she fondly imagined) fail to offend me; and at this time she even hid herself from strangers lest their poor opinion of her looks should put me out of countenance.

"I meanwhile, becoming used to her homely looks, was well content with her character, save for this one article of jealousy; and here she showed no amendment. Then I began to think to myself 'Surely, since she seems so anxious to please, so timid, there must be some way of giving her a fright which will teach her a lesson, so that for a while at least we may have a respite from this accursed business.' And though I knew it would cost me dear, I determined to make a pretence of giving her up, thinking that since she was so fond of me this would be the best way to teach her a lesson. Accordingly I behaved with the greatest coldness to her, and she as usual began her jealous fit and behaved with such folly that in the end I said to her, 'If you want to be rid forever of one who loves you dearly, you are going the right way about it by all these endless poutings over nothing at all. But if you want to go on with me, you must give up suspecting some deep intrigue each time you fancy that I am treating you unkindly. Do this, and you may be sure I shall continue to love you dearly. It may well be that as time goes on, I shall rise a little higher in the world and then. . .'

"I thought I had managed matters very cleverly, though perhaps in the heat of the moment I might have spoken somewhat too roughly. She smiled faintly and answered that if it were only a matter of bearing for a while with my failures and disappointments, that did not trouble her at all, and she would gladly wait till I became a person of consequence. 'But it is a hard task,' she said, 'to go on year after year enduring your coldness and waiting the time when you will at last learn to behave to me with some decency; and therefore I agree with you that the time has come when we had better go each his own way.' Then in a fit of wild and uncontrollable jealousy she began to pour upon me a torrent of bitter reproaches, and with a woman's savagery she suddenly seized my little finger and bit deep into it. The unexpected pain was difficult to bear, but composing myself I said tragically, 'Now you have put this mark upon me I shall get on worse than ever in polite society; as for promotion, I shall be considered a disgrace to the meanest public office and unable to cut a genteel figure in any capacity, I shall be obliged to withdraw myself completely from the world. You and I at any rate shall certainly not meet again,' and bending my injured finger as I turned to go, I recited the verse, *'As on bent hand I count the times that we have met, it is not one finger only that bears witness to my pain.'* And she, all of a sudden bursting into tears. . . 'If still in your heart only you look for pains to count, then were our hands best employed in parting.' After a few more words I left her, not for a moment thinking that all was over.

"Days went by, and no news. I began to be restless. One night when I had been at the Palace for the rehearsal of the Festival music, heavy sleet was falling; and I stood at the spot where those of us who came from the Palace had dispersed, unable to make up my mind which way to go. For in no direction had I anything which could properly be called a home. I might of course take a room in the Palace precincts; but I shivered to think of the cheerless grandeur that would surround me. Suddenly I began to wonder what she was thinking, how she was looking; and brushing the snow off my shoulders, I set out for her house. I own I felt uneasy; but I thought that after so long a time her anger must surely have somewhat abated. Inside the room a lamp showed dimly, turned to the wall. Some undergarments were hung out upon a large, warmly-quilted couch, the bed-hangings were drawn up, and I made sure that she was for some reason actually expecting me. I was priding myself on having made so lucky a hit, when suddenly, 'Not at home!'; and on questioning the maid I learnt that she had but that very night gone to her parents' home, leaving only a few necessary servants behind. The fact that she had till now sent no poem or conciliatory message seemed to show some hardening of heart, and had already disquieted me. Now I began to fear that her accursed suspiciousness and jealousy had but been a stratagem to make me grow weary of her, and though I could recall no further proof of this I fell into great despair. And to show her that, though we no longer met, I still thought of her and planned for her, I got her some stuff for a dress, choosing a most delightful and unusual shade of colour, and a material that I knew she would be glad to have. 'For after all,' I thought 'she cannot want to put me altogether out of her head.' When I informed her of this purchase she did not rebuff me nor make any attempt to hide from me, but to all my questions she answered quietly and composedly, without any sign that she was ashamed of herself.

"At last she told me that if I went on as before, she could never forgive me; but if I would promise to live more quietly she would take me back again. Seeing that she still hankered after me I determined to school her a little further yet, and said that I could make no conditions and must be free to live as I chose. So the tug of war went on; but it seems that it hurt her far more than I knew, for in a little while she fell into a decline and died, leaving me aghast at the upshot of my wanton game. And now I felt that, whatever faults she might have had, her devotion alone would have made her a fit wife for me. I remembered how both in trivial talk and in consideration of important matters she had never once shown herself at a loss, how in the dyeing of brocades she rivalled the Goddess of Tatsuta who tints the autumn leaves, and how in needlework and the like she was not less skilful than Tanabata, the Weaving-lady of the sky."

Here he stopped, greatly distressed at the recollection of the lady's many talents and virtues.

"The Weaving-lady and the Herd boy," said Tō no Chūjō, "enjoy a love that is eternal. Had she but resembled the Divine Sempstress in this, you would not, I think, have minded her being a little less skilful with her needle. I wonder that with this rare creature in mind you pronounce the world to be so blank a place."

"Listen," replied Uma no Kami, "About the same time there was another lady whom I used to visit. She was of higher birth than the first; her skill in poetry, cursive writing, and lute-playing, her readiness of hand and tongue were all marked enough to show that she was not a woman of trivial nature; and this indeed was allowed by those who knew her. To add to this she was not ill-looking and sometimes, when I needed a rest from my unhappy persecutress, I used to visit her secretly. In the end I found that I had fallen completely in love with her. After the death of the other I was in great distress. But it was no use brooding over the past and I began to visit my new lady more and more often. I soon came to the conclusion that she was frivolous and I had no confidence that I should have liked what went on when I was not there to see. I now visited her only at long intervals and at last decided that she had another lover.

"It was during the Godless Month,[5] on a beautiful moonlight night. As I was leaving the Palace I met a certain young courtier, who, when I told him that I was driving out to spend the night at the Dainagon's, said that my way was his and joined me. The road passed my lady's house and here it was that he alighted, saying that he had an engagement which he should have been very sorry not to fulfil. The wall was half in ruins and through its gaps I saw the shadowy waters of the lake. It would not have been easy (for even the moonbeams seemed to loiter here!) to hasten past so lovely a place, and when he left his coach I too left mine.

"At once this man (whom I now knew to be that other lover whose existence I had guessed) went and sat unconcernedly on the bamboo skirting of the portico and began to gaze at the moon. The chrysanthemums were just in full bloom, the bright fallen leaves were tumbling and tussling in the wind. It was indeed a scene of wonderful beauty that met our eyes. Presently he took a flute out of the folds of his dress and began to play upon it. Then putting the flute aside, he began to murmur 'Sweet is the shade'[6] and other catches. Soon a pleasant-sounding native zithern[7] began to tune up somewhere within the house and an ingenious accompaniment was fitted to his careless warblings. Her zithern was tuned to the autumn-mode, and she played with so much tenderness and feeling that though the music came from behind closed shutters it sounded quite modern and passionate,[8] and well accorded with the soft beauty of the moonlight. The courtier was ravished, and as he stepped forward to place himself right under her window he turned to me and remarked in a self-satisfied way that among the fallen leaves no other footstep had left its mark. Then plucking a chrysanthemum, he sang:

> *Strange that the music of your lute,*
> *These matchless flowers and all the beauty of the night,*
> *Have lured no other feet to linger at your door!*

---

[5] The tenth month.

[6] From the *saibara* ballad, *The Well of Asuka*: "Sweet is the shade, the lapping waters cool, and good the pasture for our weary steeds. By the Well of Asuka, here let us stay."

[7] The "Japanese zithern"; also called *wagon*. A species of *koto*.

[8] As opposed to the formal and traditional music imported from China.

and then, beseeching her pardon for his halting verses, he begged her to play again while one was still near who longed so passionately to hear her. When he had paid her many other compliments, the lady answered in an affected voice with the verse:

Would that I had some song that might detain
The flute that blends its note
With the low rustling of the autumn leaves.

and after these blandishments, still unsuspecting, she took up the thirteen-stringed lute, and tuning it to the *Banjiki* mode[9] she clattered at the strings with all the frenzy that fashion now demands. It was a fine performance no doubt, but I cannot say that it made a very agreeable impression upon me.

"A man may amuse himself well enough by trifling from time to time with some lady at the Court; will get what pleasure he can out of it while he is with her and not trouble his head about what goes on when he is not there. This lady too I only saw from time to time, but such was her situation that I had once fondly imagined myself the only occupant of her thoughts. However that night's work dissolved the last shred of my confidence, and I never saw her again.

"These two experiences, falling to my lot while I was still so young, early deprived me of any hope from women. And since that time my view of them has but grown the blacker. No doubt to you at your age they seem very entrancing, these 'dew-drops on the grass that fall if they are touched,' these 'glittering hailstones that melt if gathered in the hand.' But when you are a little older you will think as I do. Take my advice in this at least; beware of caressing manners and soft, entangling ways. For if you are so rash as to let them lead you astray, you will soon find yourselves cutting a very silly figure in the world."

Tō no Chūjō as usual nodded his assent, and Genji's smile seemed such as to show that he too accepted Uma no Kami's advice.

"Your two stories were certainly very dismal," he said, laughing.

And here Tō no Chūjō interposed: "I will tell you a story about myself. There was a lady whose acquaintance I was obliged to make

---

[9] See *Encyclopedia de la Musique*, p. 247. Under the name Nan-lü this mode was frequently used in the Chinese love-dramas of the fourteenth century. It was considered very wild and moving.

with great secrecy. But her beauty well rewarded my pains, and though I had no thought of making her my wife I grew so fond of her that I soon found I could not put her out of my head and she seemed to have complete confidence in me. Such confidence indeed that when from time to time I was obliged to behave in such a way as might well have aroused her resentment, she seemed not to notice that anything was amiss, and even when I neglected her for many weeks, she treated me as though I were still coming everyday. In the end indeed I found this readiness to receive me whenever and however I came very painful, and determined for the future to merit her strange confidence.

"Her parents were dead and this was perhaps why, since I was all she had in the world, she treated me with such loving meekness, despite the many wrongs I did her. I must own that my resolution did not last long, and I was soon neglecting her worse than before. During this time (I did not hear of it till afterwards) someone who had discovered our friendship began to send her veiled messages which cruelly frightened and distressed her. Knowing nothing of the trouble she was in, although I often thought of her I neither came nor wrote to her for a long while. Just when she was in her worst despair a child was born, and at last in her distress she plucked a blossom of the flower that is called 'Child of my Heart' and sent it to me."

And here Tō no Chūjō's eyes filled with tears.

"Well," said Genji, "and did she write a message to go with it?"

"Oh nothing very out-of-the-ordinary," said Tō no Chūjō. "She wrote, 'Though tattered be the hillman's hedge, deign sometimes to look with kindness upon the Child-flower that grows so sweetly there.' This brought me to her side. As usual she did not reproach me, but she looked sad enough, and when I considered the dreary desolation of this home where every object wore an aspect no less depressing than the wailing voices of the crickets in the grass, she seemed to me like some unhappy princess in an ancient story, and wishing her to feel that it was for the mother's sake and not the child's that I had come, I answered with a poem in which I called the Child-flower by its other name 'Bed-flower,' and she replied with a poem that darkly hinted at the cruel tempest which had attended this Bed-flower's birth. She spoke lightly and did not seem to be downright angry with me; and when a few tears fell she was at great pains to hide them, and seemed more distressed at the thought that I might imagine her to be unhappy than actually resentful of my conduct towards her. So I went away with an easy mind and it was some while before I came again. When at last I returned she had utterly disappeared, and if she is alive she must be living a wretched vagrant life. If while I still loved her she had but shown some outward sign of her resentment, she would not have ended thus as an outcast and wanderer; for I should never have dared to leave her so long neglected, and might in the end have acknowledged her and made her mine forever. The child too was a sweet creature, and I have spent much time in searching for them, but still without success.

"It is, I fear, as sorrowful a tale as that which Uma no Kami has told you. I, unfaithful, thought that I was not missed; and she, still loved, was in no better case than one whose love is not returned. I indeed am fast forgetting her; but she, it may be, cannot put me out of her mind and I fear there may be nights when thoughts that she would gladly banish burn fiercely in her breast; for now I fancy she must be living a comfortless and unprotected life."

"When all is said and done," said Uma no Kami, "my friend, though I pine for her now that she is gone, was a sad plague to me while I had her, and we must own that such a one will in the end be sure to make us wish ourselves well rid of her. The zithern-player had much talent to her credit, but was a great deal too light-headed. And your diffident lady, Tō no Chūjō, seems to me to be a very suspicious case. The world appears to be so constructed that we shall in the end be always at a loss to make a reasoned choice; despite all our picking, sifting and comparing we shall never succeed in finding this in all ways and to all lengths adorable and impeccable female."

"I can only suggest the Goddess Kichijō,"[10] said Tō no Chūjō, "and I fear that intimacy with so holy and majestic a being might prove to be impracticable."

At this they all laughed and Tō no Chūjō continued: "But now it is Shikibu's turn and he is sure to give us something entertaining. Come Shikibu, keep the ball rolling!"

"Nothing of interest ever happens to humble folk like myself," said Shikibu; but Tō no Chūjō scolded him for keeping them waiting and after reflecting for a while which anecdote would best suit the company, he began:

"While I was still a student at the University, I came across a woman who was truly a prodigy of intelligence. One of Uma no Kami's demands

---

[10] Goddess of Beauty.

she certainly fulfilled, for it was possible to discuss with her to advantage both public matters and the proper handling of one's private affairs. But not only was her mind capable of grappling with any problems of this kind; she was also so learned that ordinary scholars found themselves, to their humiliation, quite unable to hold their own against her.

"I was taking lessons from her father, who was a Professor. I had heard that he had several daughters, and some accidental circumstance made it necessary for me to exchange a word or two with one of them who turned out to be the learned prodigy of whom I have spoken. The father, hearing that we had been seen together, came up to me with a wine-cup in his hand and made an allusion to the poem of 'The Two Wives.'[11] Unfortunately I did not feel the least inclination towards the lady. However I was very civil to her; upon which she began to take an affectionate interest in me and lost no opportunity of displaying her talents by giving me the most elaborate advice how best I might advance my position in the world. She sent me marvellous letters written in a very far-fetched epistolary style and entirely in Chinese characters; in return for which I felt bound to visit her, and by making her my teacher I managed to learn how to write Chinese poems. They were wretched, knock-kneed affairs, but I am still grateful to her for it. She was not however at all the sort of woman whom I should have cared to have as a wife, for though there may be certain disadvantages in marrying a complete dolt, it is even worse to marry a blue-stocking. Still less do princes like you and Genji require so huge a stock of intellect and erudition for your support! Let her but be one to whom the *karma* of our past lives draws us in natural sympathy, what matter if now and again her ignorance distresses us? Come to that, even men seem to me to get along very well without much learning."

Here he stopped, but Genji and the rest, wishing to hear the end of the story, cried out that for their part they found her a most interesting woman. Shikibu protested that he did not wish to go on with the story, but at last after much coaxing, pulling a comical wry face he continued: "I had not seen her for a long time. When at last some accident took me to the house, she did not receive me with her usual informality but spoke to me from behind a tiresome screen. Ha, Ha, thought I foolishly, she is sulking; now is the time to have a scene and break with her. I might have known that she was not so little of a philosopher as to sulk

---

[11] A poem by Po Chü-i pointing out the advantages of marrying a poor wife.

about trifles; she prided herself on knowing the ways of the world and my inconstancy did not in the least disturb her.

"She told me (speaking without the slightest tremor) that having had a bad cold for some weeks she had taken a strong garlic-cordial, which had made her breath smell rather unpleasant and that for this reason she could not come very close to me. But if I had any matter of special importance to discuss with her she was quite prepared to give me her attention. All this she had expressed with solemn literary perfection. I could think of no suitable reply, and with an 'at your service' I rose to go. Then, feeling that the interview had not been quite a success, she added, raising her voice 'Please come again when my breath has lost its smell.' I could not pretend I had not heard. I had however no intention of prolonging my visit, particularly as the odour was now becoming definitely unpleasant, and looking cross I recited the acrostic, 'On this night marked by the strange behaviour of the spider, how foolish to bid me come back tomorrow'[12] and calling over my shoulder, 'There is no excuse for you!' I ran out of the room. But she, following me, 'If night by night and every night we met, in daytime too I should grow bold to meet you face to face.' Here in the second sentence she had cleverly concealed the meaning, 'If I had had any reason to expect you, I should not have eaten garlic.'"

"What a revolting story," cried the young princes, and then, laughing, "He must have invented it."

"Such a woman is quite incredible; it must have been some sort of ogress. You have shocked us, Shikibu!" and they looked at him with disapproval.

"You must try to tell us a better story than that."

"I do not see how any story could be better," said Shikibu, and left the room.

"There is a tendency among men as well as women," said Uma no Kami, "so soon as they have acquired a little knowledge of some kind, to want to display it to the best advantage. To have mastered all the difficulties in the Three Histories and Five Classics is no road to amiability. But even a woman cannot afford to lack all knowledge of public and private affairs. Her best way will be without regular study to

---

[12] There is a reference to an old poem which says: "I know that tonight my lover will come to me. The spider's antics prove it clearly" Omens were drawn from the behaviour of spiders. There is also a pun on *hiru* "day" and *hiru* "garlic," so that an ordinary person would require a few moments" reflection before understanding the poem.

pick up a little here and a little there, merely by keeping her eyes and ears open. Then, if she has her wits at all about her, she will soon find that she has amassed a surprising store of information. Let her be content with this and not insist upon cramming her letters with Chinese characters which do not at all accord with her feminine style of composition, and will make the recipient exclaim in despair, 'If only she could contrive to be a little less mannish!' And many of these characters, to which she intended the colloquial pronunciation to be given, are certain to be read as Chinese, and this will give the whole composition an even more pedantic sound than it deserves. Even among our ladies of rank and fashion there are many of this sort, and there are others who, wishing to master the art of verse-making, in the end allow it to master them, and, slaves to poetry, cannot resist the temptation, however urgent the business they are about or however inappropriate the time, to make use of some happy allusion which has occurred to them, but must needs fly to their desks and work it up into a poem. On festival days such a woman is very troublesome. For example on the morning of the Iris Festival, when everyone is busy making ready to go to the temple, she will worry them by stringing together all the old tags about the 'matchless root'[13] or on the 9th day of the 9th month, when everyone is busy thinking out some difficult Chinese poem to fit the rhymes which have been prescribed, she begins making metaphors about the 'dew on the chrysanthemums,' thus diverting our attention from the far more important business which is in hand. At another time we might have found these compositions quite delightful; but by thrusting them upon our notice at inconvenient moments, when we cannot give them proper attention, she makes them seem worse than they really are. For in all matters we shall best commend ourselves if we study men's faces to read in them the 'Why so?' or the 'As you will' and do not, regardless of times and circumstances, demand an interest and sympathy that they have not leisure to give.

"Sometimes indeed a woman should even pretend to know less than she knows, or say only a part of what she would like to say. . ."

All this while Genji, though he had sometimes joined in the conversation, had in his heart of hearts been thinking of one person only, and the more he thought the less could he find a single trace

---

[13] The irises used for the Tango festival (5th day of 5th month) had to have nine flowers growing on a root.

of those shortcomings and excesses which, so his friends had declared, were common to all women.

"There is no one like her," he thought, and his heart was very full.

The conversation indeed had not brought them to a definite conclusion, but it had led to many curious anecdotes and reflections. So they passed the night, and at last, for a wonder, the weather had improved. After this long residence at the Palace Genji knew he would be expected at the Great Hall and set out at once. There was in Princess Aoi's air and dress a dignified precision which had something in it even of stiffness; and in the very act of reflecting that she, above all women, was the type of that single-hearted and devoted wife whom (as his friends had said last night) no sensible man would lightly offend, he found himself oppressed by the very perfection of her beauty, which seemed only to make all intimacy with her the more impossible.

He turned to Lady Chūnagon, to Nakatsukasa and other attendants of the common sort who were standing near and began to jest with them. The day was now very hot, but they thought that flushed cheeks became Prince Genji very well. Aoi's father came, and standing behind the curtain, began to converse very amiably. Genji, who considered the weather too hot for visits, frowned, at which the ladies-in-waiting tittered. Genji, making furious signs at them to be quiet, flung himself on to a divan. In fact, he behaved far from well.

It was now growing dark. Someone said that the position of the Earth Star[14] would make it unlucky for the Prince to go back to the Palace that night; and another: "You are right. It is now set dead against him."

"But my own palace is in the same direction!" cried Genji. "How vexing! Where then shall I go?" and promptly fell asleep.

The ladies-in-waiting however, agreed that it was a very serious matter and began discussing what could be done.

"There is Ki no Kami's house," said one. This Ki no Kami was one of Genji's gentlemen in waiting.

"It is in the Middle River," she went on; "and delightfully cool and shady, for they have lately dammed the river and made it flow right through the garden."

"That sounds very pleasant," said Genji, waking up, "besides they are

---

[14] The "Lord of the Centre," i.e. the planet Saturn.

the sort of people who would not mind one's driving right in at the front gate, if one had a mind to."[15]

He had many friends whose houses lay out of the unlucky direction. But he feared that if he went to one of them, Aoi would think that, after absenting himself so long, he was now merely using the Earth Star as an excuse for returning to more congenial company. He therefore broached the matter to Ki no Kami, who accepted the proposal, but stepping aside whispered to his companions that his father Iyo no Kami, who was absent on service, had asked him to look after his young wife.[16] "I am afraid we have not sufficient room in the house to entertain him as I could wish."

Genji overhearing this, strove to reassure him, saying, "It will be a pleasure to me to be near the lady. A visit is much more agreeable when there is a hostess to welcome us. Find me some corner behind her partition. . . !"

"Even then, I fear you may not find. . ." but breaking off Ki no Kami sent a runner to his house, with orders to make ready an apartment for the Prince.

Treating a visit to so humble a house as a matter of no importance, he started at once, without even informing the Minister, and taking with him only a few trusted body-servants. Ki no Kami protested against the precipitation, but in vain.

The servants dusted and aired the eastern side-chamber of the Central Hall and here made temporary quarters for the Prince. They were at pains to improve the view from his windows, for example by altering the course of certain rivulets. They set up a rustic wattled hedge and filled the borders with the choicest plants. The low humming of insects floated on the cool breeze; numberless fireflies wove inextricable mazes in the air. The whole party settled down near where the moat flowed under the covered bridge and began to drink wine.

Ki no Kami went off in a great bustle, saying that he must find them something to eat. Genji, quietly surveying the scene, decided this was one of those middle-class families which in last night's conversation had been so highly commended. He remembered that he had heard the lady who was staying in the house well spoken of and was curious to

---

[15] I.e. people with whom one can be quite at ease. It was usual to unharness one's bulls at the gate.

[16] Ki no Kami's stepmother.

see her. He listened and thought that there seemed to be people in the western wing. There was a soft rustling of skirts, and from time to time the sound of young and by no means disagreeable voices. They did not seem to be much in earnest in their efforts to make their whispering and laughter unheard, for soon one of them opened the sliding window. But Ki no Kami crying, "What are you thinking of?" crossly closed it again.

The light of a candle in the room filtered through a crack in the paper-window. Genji edged slightly closer to the window in the hope of being able to see through the crack, but found that he could see nothing. He listened for a while, and came to the conclusion that they were sitting in the main women's apartments, out of which the little front room opened. They were speaking very low, but he could catch enough of it to make out that they were talking about him.

"What a shame that a fine young Prince should be taken so young and settled down forever with a lady that was none of his choosing!"

"I understand that marriage does not weigh very heavily upon him," said another.

This probably meant nothing in particular, but Genji, who imagined they were talking about what was uppermost in his own mind, was appalled at the idea that his relations with Lady Fujitsubo were about to be discussed. How could they have found out? But the subsequent conversation of the ladies soon showed that they knew nothing of the matter at all, and Genji stopped listening. Presently he heard them trying to repeat the poem which he had sent with a nose-gay of morning-glory to Princess Asagao, daughter of Prince Momozono.[17] But they got the lines rather mixed up, and Genji began to wonder whether the lady's appearance would turn out to be on a level with her knowledge of prosody.

At this moment Ki no Kami came in with a lamp which he hung on the wall. Having carefully trimmed it, he offered Genji a tray of fruit. This was all rather dull and Genji by a quotation from an old folk-song hinted that he would like to meet Ki no Kami's other guests. The hint was not taken. Genji began to doze, and his attendants sat silent and motionless.

---

[17] We learn later that Genji courted this lady in vain from his seventeenth year onward. Though she has never been mentioned before, Murasaki speaks of her as though the reader already knew all about her. This device is also employed by Marcel Proust.

There were in the room several charming boys, sons of Ki no Kami, some of whom Genji already knew as pages at the Palace. There were also numerous sons of Iyo no Kami; with them was a boy of twelve or thirteen who particularly caught Genji's fancy. He began asking whose sons the boys were, and when he came to this one Ki no Kami replied, "He is the youngest son of the late Chūnagon, who loved him dearly, but died while this boy was still a child. His sister married my father and that is why he is living here. He is quick at his books, and we hope one day to send him to Court, but I fear that his lack of influence. . ."

"Poor child!" said Genji. "His sister, then, is your stepmother, is that not so? How strange that you should stand in this relationship with so young a girl! And now I come to think of it there was some talk once of her being presented at Court, and I once heard the Emperor asking what had become of her. How changeable are the fortunes of the world." He was trying to talk in a very grown-up way.

"Indeed, Sir," answered Ki no Kami, "her subsequent state was humbler than she had reason to expect. But such is our mortal life. Yes, yes, and such has it always been. We have our ups and downs—and the women even more than the men."

Genji, "But your father no doubt makes much of her?"

Ki no Kami, "Makes much of her indeed! You may well say so. She rules his house, and he dotes on her in so wholesale and extravagant a fashion that all of us (and I among the foremost) have had occasion before now to call him to order, but he does not listen."

Genji, "How comes it then that he has left her behind in the house of a fashionable young Courtier? For he looks like a man of prudence and good sense. But pray, where is she now?"

Ki no Kami, "The ladies have been ordered to retire to the common room, but they have not yet finished all their preparations."

Genji's followers, who had drunk heavily, were now all lying fast asleep on the verandah. He was alone in his room, but could not get to sleep. Having at last dozed for a moment, he woke suddenly and noticed that someone was moving behind the paper-window of the back wall. This, he thought, must be where she is hiding, and faintly curious he sauntered in that direction and stood listening.

"Where are you? I say. Where are you?" whispered someone in a quaint, hoarse voice, which seemed to be that of the boy whom Genji had noticed earlier in the evening.

"I am lying over here," another voice answered. "Has the stranger gone to sleep yet? His room must be quite close to this; but all the same how far off he seems!" Her sleepy voice was so like the boy's, that Genji concluded this must be his sister.

"He is sleeping in the wing, I saw him tonight. All that we have heard of him is true enough. He is as handsome as can be," whispered the boy.

"I wish it were tomorrow; I want to see him properly," she answered drowsily, her voice seeming to come from under the bed clothes. Genji was rather disappointed that she did not ask more questions about him. Presently he heard the boy saying, "I am going to sleep over in the corner room. How bad the light is," and he seemed to be trimming the lamp. His sister's bed appeared to be in the corner opposite the paper-window.

"Where is Chūjō?" she called. "I am frightened, I like to have someone close to me."

"Madam," answered several voices from the servants' room, "she is taking her bath in the lower house. She will be back presently."

When all was quiet again, Genji slipped back the bolt and tried the door. It was not fastened on the other side. He found himself in an ante-room with a screen at the end, beyond which a light glimmered. In the half-darkness he could see clothes boxes and trunks strewn about in great disorder. Quietly threading his way among them, he entered the inner room from which the voices had proceeded. One very minute figure was couched there who, to Genji's slight embarrassment, on hearing his approach pushed aside the cloak which covered her, thinking that he was the maid for whom she had sent.

"Madam, hearing you call for Chūjō[18] I thought that I might now put at your service the esteem in which I have long secretly held you."

The lady could make nothing of all this, and terrified out of her wits tried hard to scream. But no sound came, for she had buried her face in the bed clothes.

"Please listen," said Genji. "This sudden intrusion must of course seem to you very impertinent. You do not know that for years I have waited for an occasion to tell you how much I like and admire you, and if tonight I could not resist the temptation of paying this secret visit, pray take the strangeness of my behaviour as proof of my impatience to pay a homage that has long been due." He spoke so courteously and

---

[18] Chūjō means "Captain," which was Genji's rank at the time.

LADY MURASAKI SHIKIBU

gently and looked so kind that not the devil himself would have taken umbrage at his presence. But feeling that the situation was not at all a proper one for a married lady she said (without much conviction)

"I think you have made a mistake." She spoke very low. Her bewildered air made her all the more attractive, and Genji, enchanted by her appearance, hastened to answer:

"Indeed I have made no mistake; rather, with no guide but a long-felt deference and esteem, I have found my way unerringly to your side. But I see that the suddenness of my visit has made you distrust my purpose. Let me tell you then that I have no evil intentions and seek only for someone to talk with me for a while about a matter which perplexes me."

So saying he took her up in his arms (for she was very small) and was carrying her through the ante-room when suddenly Chūjō, the servant for whom she had sent before, entered the bedroom. Genji gave an astonished cry and the maid, wondering who could have entered the ante-room, began groping her way towards them. But coming closer she recognized by the rich perfume of his dress that this could be none other than the Prince. And though she was sorely puzzled to know what was afoot, she dared not say a word. Had he been an ordinary person, she would soon have had him by the ears.

"Nay," she thought, "even if he were not a Prince I should do best to keep my hands off him; for the more stir one makes, the more tongues wag. But if I should touch this fine gentleman. . . ," and all in a flutter she found herself obediently following Genji to his room. Here he calmly closed the door upon her, saying as he did so, "You will come back to fetch your mistress in the morning."

Utsusemi herself was vexed beyond measure at being thus disposed of in the presence of her own waiting-maid, who could indeed draw but one conclusion from what she had seen. But to all her misgivings and anxieties Genji, who had the art of improvising a convincing reply to almost any question, answered with such a wealth of ingenuity and tender concern, that for awhile she was content.

But soon becoming again uneasy, "This must all be a dream—that you, so great a Prince, should stoop to consider so humble a creature as I, and I am overwhelmed by so much kindness. But I think you have forgotten what I am. A Zuryō's wife! There is no altering that, and you. . . !"

Genji now began to realize how deeply he had distressed and disquieted her by his wild behaviour, and feeling thoroughly ashamed of himself he answered: "I am afraid I know very little about these questions of rank and precedence. Such things are too confusing to carry in one's head. And whatever you may have heard of me I want to tell you for some reason or other I have till this day cared nothing for gallantry nor ever practised it, and that even you cannot be more astonished at what I have done tonight than I myself am."

With this and a score of other speeches he sought to win her confidence. But she, knowing that if once their talk became a jot less formal, she would be hard put to it to withstand his singular charm, was determined, even at the risk of seeming stiff and awkward, to show him that in trying so hard to put her at her ease he was only wasting his time, with the result that she behaved very boorishly indeed. She was by nature singularly gentle and yielding, so that the effort of steeling her heart and despite her feelings, playing all the while the part of the young bamboo-shoot which though so green and tender cannot be broken, was very painful to her; and finding that she could not longer think of arguments with which to withstand his importunity, she burst into tears; and though he was very sorry for her, it occurred to him that he would not gladly have missed that sight. He longed however to console her, but could not think of a way to do so, and said at last, "Why do you treat me so unkindly? It is true that the manner of our meeting was strange, yet I think that Fate meant us to meet. It is harsh that you should shrink from me as though the World and you had never met."

So he chided her, and she: "If this had happened long ago before my troubles, before my lot was cast, perhaps I should have been glad to take your kindness while it lasted, knowing that you would soon think better of your strange condescension. But now that my course is fixed, what can such meetings bring me save misery and regret? *Tell none that you have seen my home,*" she ended, quoting the old song.[19]

"Small wonder that she is sad," thought Genji, and he found many a tender way to comfort her. And now the cock began to crow. Out in the courtyard Genji's men were staggering to their feet, one crying drowsily

"How I should like to go to sleep again," and another, "Make haste there, bring out his Honour's coach."

Ki no Kami came out into the yard, "What's all this hurry? It is only when there are women in his party that a man need hasten from

---

[19] *Kokinshū* 811, an anonymous love-poem.

a refuge to which the Earth star has sent him. Why is his Highness setting off in the middle of the night?"

Genji was wondering whether such an opportunity would ever occur again. How would he be able even to send her letters? And thinking of all the difficulties that awaited him, he became very despondent. Chūjō arrived to fetch her mistress. For a long while he would not let her go, and when at last he handed her over, he drew her back to him saying, "How can I send news to you? For Madam," he said raising his voice that the maid Chūjō might hear, "such love as mine, and such pitiless cruelty as yours have never been seen in the world before." Already the birds were singing in good earnest. She could not forget that she was no one and he a Prince. And even now, while he was tenderly entreating her, there came unbidden to her mind the image of her husband Iyo no Suke, about whom she generally thought either not at all or with disdain. To think that even in a dream he might see her now, filled her with shame and terror.

It was daylight. Genji went with her to the partition door. Indoors and out there was a bustle of feet. As he closed the door upon her, it seemed to him a barrier that shut him out from all happiness. He dressed, and went out on to the balcony. A blind in the western wing was hastily raised. There seemed to be people behind who were looking at him. They could only see him indistinctly across the top of a partition in the verandah. Among them was one, perhaps, whose heart beat wildly as she looked. . . ?

The moon had not set, and though with dwindled light still shone crisp and clear in the dawn. It was a daybreak of marvellous beauty. But in the passionless visage of the sky men read only their own comfort or despair; and Genji, as with many backward glances he went upon his way, paid little heed to the beauty of the dawn. He would send her a message? No, even that was utterly impossible. And so, in great unhappiness he returned to his wife's house.

He would gladly have slept a little, but could not stop trying to invent some way of seeing her again; or when that seemed hopeless, imagining to himself all that must now be going on in her mind. She was no great beauty, Genji reflected, and yet one could not say that she was ugly. Yes, she was in every sense a member of that Middle Class upon which Uma no Kami had given them so complete a dissertation.

He stayed for some while at the Great Hall, and finding that, try as he might, he could not stop thinking about her and longing for her, at last in despair he sent for Ki no Kami and said to him, "Why do you not let me have that boy in my service,—the Chūnagon's son, whom I saw at your house? He is a likely looking boy, and I might make him my body-servant, or even recommend him to the Emperor."

"I am sensible of your kindness," said Ki no Kami, "I will mention what you have said to the boy's sister."

This answer irritated Genji, but he continued: "And has this lady given you step-brothers my lord?"

"Sir, she has been married these two years, but has had no child. It seems that in making this marriage she disobeyed her father's last injunctions, and this has set her against her husband."

Genji said, "That is sad indeed. I am told that she is not ill-looking. Is that so?"

Ki no Kami replied, "I believe she is considered quite passable. But I have had very little to do with her. Intimacy between step-children and step-parents is indeed proverbially difficult."

Five or six days afterwards Ki no Kami brought the boy. He was not exactly handsome, but he had great charm and (thought Genji) an air of distinction. The Prince spoke very kindly to him and soon completely won his heart. To Genji's many questions about his sister he made such answers as he could, and when he seemed embarrassed or tongue-tied Genji found some less direct way of finding out what he wanted to know, and soon put the boy at his ease. For though he vaguely realized what was going on and thought it rather odd, he was so young that he made no effort to understand it, and without further question carried back a letter from Genji to his sister.

She was so much agitated by the sight of it that she burst into tears and, lest her brother should perceive them, held the letter in front of her face while she read it. It was very long. Among much else it contained the verse, *"Would that I might dream that dream again! Alas, since first this wish was mine, not once have my eyelids closed in sleep."*

She had never seen such beautiful writing, and as she read, a haze clouded her eyes. What incomprehensible fate had first dragged her down to be the wife of a Zuryō, and then for a moment raised her so high? Still pondering, she went to her room.

Next day, Genji again sent for the boy, who went to his sister saying, "I am going to Prince Genji. Where is your answer to his letter?"

"Tell him," she answered, "that there is no one here who reads such letters."

The boy burst out laughing.

"Why, you silly, how could I say such a thing to him. He told me himself to be sure to bring an answer."

It infuriated her to think that Genji should have thus taken the boy into his confidence and she answered angrily, "He has no business to talk to you about such things at your age. If that is what you talk about you had better not go to him anymore."

"But he sent for me," said the boy, and started off.

"I was waiting for you all yesterday," said Genji when the boy returned. "Did you forget to bring the answer? Did you forget to come?"

The child blushed and made no reply.

"And now?"

"She said there is no one at home who reads such letters."

"How silly, what can be the use of saying such things?" and he wrote another letter and gave it to the boy, saying:

I expect you do not know that I used to meet your sister before her marriage. She treats me in this scornful fashion because she looks upon me as a poor-spirited, defenceless creature. Whereas she has now a mighty Deputy Governor to look after her. But I hope that you will promise to be my child not his. For he is very old, and will not be able to take care of you for long.

The boy was quite content with this explanation, and admired Genji more than ever. The prince kept him always at his side, even taking him to the Palace. And he ordered his Chamberlain to see to it that he was provided with a little Court suit. Indeed he treated him just as though he were his own child.

Genji continued to send letters; but she, thinking that the boy, young as he was, might easily allow a message to fall into the wrong hands and that then she would lose her fair name to no purpose, feeling too (that however much he desired it) between persons so far removed in rank there could be no lasting union, she answered his letters only in the most formal terms.

Dark though it had been during most of the time they were together, she yet had a clear recollection of his appearance, and could not deny to herself that she thought him uncommonly handsome. But she very much doubted if he on his side really knew what she was like; indeed she felt sure that the next time they met he would think her very plain and all would be over.

Genji meanwhile thought about her continually. He was forever calling back to memory each incident of that one meeting, and every recollection filled him with longing and despair. He remembered how sad she had looked when she spoke to him of herself, and he longed to make her happier. He thought of visiting her in secret. But the risk of discovery was too great, and the consequences likely to be more fatal to her even than to himself.

He had been many days at the Palace, when at last the Earth Star again barred the road to his home. He set out at once, but on the way pretended that he had just remembered the unfavourable posture of the stars. There was nothing to do but seek shelter again in the house on the Middle River. Ki no Kami was surprised but by no means ill-pleased, for he attributed Genji's visit to the amenity of the little pools and fountains which he had constructed in his garden.

Genji had told the boy in the morning that he intended to visit the Middle River, and since he had now become the Prince's constant companion, he was sent for at once to wait upon him in his room. He had already given a message to his sister, in which Genji told her of his plan. She could not but feel flattered at the knowledge that it was on her account he had contrived this ingenious excuse for coming to the house. Yet she had, as we have seen, for some reason got it into her head that at a leisurely meeting she would not please him as she had done at that first fleeting and dreamlike encounter, and she dreaded adding a new sorrow to the burden of her thwarted and unhappy existence.

Too proud to let him think that she had posted herself in waiting for him, she said to her servants (while the boy was busy in Genji's room), "I do not care to be at such close quarters with our guest, besides I am stiff, and would like to be massaged; I must go where there is more room," and so saying she made them carry her things to the maid Chūjō's bedroom in the cross-wing.

Genji had purposely sent his attendants early to bed, and now that all was quiet, he hastened to send her a message. But the boy could not find her. At last when he had looked in every corner of the house, he tried the cross-wing, and succeeded in tracking her down to Chūjō's room. It was too bad of her to hide like this, and half in tears he gasped out, "Oh how can you be so horrid? What will he think of you?"

"You have no business to run after me like this," she answered angrily,

"It is very wicked for children to carry such messages. But—" she added, "you may tell him I am not well, that my ladies are with me, and I am going to be massaged. . ."

So she dismissed him; but in her heart of hearts she was thinking that if such an adventure had happened to her while she was still a person of consequence, before her father died and left her to shift for herself in the world, she would have known how to enjoy it. But now she must force herself to look askance at all his kindness. How tiresome he must think her! And she fretted so much at not being free to fall in love with him, that in the end she was more in love than ever. But then she remembered suddenly that her lot had long ago been cast. She was a wife. There was no sense in thinking of such things, and she made up her mind once and for all never again to let foolish ideas enter her head.

Genji lay on his bed, anxiously waiting to see with what success so young a messenger would execute his delicate mission. When at last the answer came, astonished at this sudden exhibition of coldness, he exclaimed in deep mortification, "This is a disgrace, a hideous disgrace," and he looked very rueful indeed."

For a while he said no more, but lay sighing deeply, in great distress. At last he recited the poem, "*I knew not the nature of the strange tree*[20] *that stands on Sono plain, and when I sought the comfort of its shade, I did but lose my road,*" and sent it to her.

She was still awake, and answered with the poem, "*Too like am I in these my outcast years to the dim tree that dwindles from the traveller's approaching gaze.*"

The boy was terribly sorry for Genji and did not feel sleepy at all, but he was afraid people would think his continual excursions very strange. By this time, however, everyone else in the house was sound asleep. Genji alone lay plunged in the blackest melancholy. But even while he was raging at the inhuman stubbornness of her new-found and incomprehensible resolve, he found that he could not but admire her the more for this invincible tenacity. At last he grew tired of lying awake; there was no more to be done. A moment later he had changed his mind again, and suddenly whispered to the boy, "Take me to where she is hiding!"

---

[20] The *hahakigi* or "broom-tree" when seen in the distance appears to offer ample shade; but when approached turns out to be a skimpy bush.

"It is too difficult," he said, "she is locked in and there are so many people there. I am afraid to go with you."

"So be it," said Genji, "but you at least must not abandon me," and he laid the boy beside him on his bed. He was well content to find himself lying by this handsome young Prince's side, and Genji, we must record, found the boy no bad substitute for his ungracious sister.

III

Utsusemi

Genji was still sleepless. "No one has ever disliked me before," he whispered to the boy. "It is more than I can bear. I am sick of myself and of the world, and do not want to go on living anymore."

This sounded so tragic that the boy began to weep. The smallness and delicacy of his build, even the way in which his hair was cropped, gave him an astonishing resemblance to his sister, thought Genji, who found his sympathy very endearing. At times he had half thought of creeping away from the boy's side and searching on his own account for the lady's hiding place; but soon abandoned a project which would only have involved him in the most appalling scandal. So he lay, waiting for the dawn. At last, while it was still dark, so full of his own thoughts that he quite forgot to make his usual parting speech to his young page, he left the house. The boy's feelings were very much hurt, and all that day he felt lonely and injured. The lady, when no answer came from Genji, thought that he had changed his mind, and though she would have been very angry if he had persisted in his suit, she was not quite prepared to lose him with so little ado.

But this was a good opportunity once and for all to lock up her heart against him. She thought that she had done so successfully, but found to her surprise that he still occupied an uncommonly large share of her thoughts. Genji, though he felt it would have been much better to put the whole business out of his head, knew that he had not the strength of mind to do so and at last, unable to bear his wretchedness any longer he said to the boy, "I am feeling very unhappy. I keep on trying to think of other things, but my thoughts will not obey me. I can struggle no longer. You must watch for a suitable occasion, and then contrive some way of bringing me into the presence of your sister." This worried the boy, but he was inwardly flattered at the confidence which Genji placed in him. And an opportunity soon presented itself.

Ki no Kami had been called away to the provinces, and there were only women in the house. One evening when dusk had settled upon the quiet streets the boy brought a carriage to fetch him. He knew that the lad would do his best, but not feeling quite safe in the hands of so young an accomplice, he put on a disguise, and then in his impatience, not waiting even to see the gates closed behind him, he drove off at top speed. They entered unobserved at a side-gate, and here he bade Genji descend. The brother knew that as he was only a boy, the watchman and gardeners would not pay any particular attention to his movements, and so he was not at all uneasy. Hiding Genji in the porch of the double-door of the eastern wing, he purposely banged against the sliding partition which separated this wing from the main part of the house, and that the maids might have the impression he did not mind who heard him enter he called out crossly, "Why is the door shut on a hot night like this?"

"'My lady of the West'[1] has been here since this morning, and she is playing *go* with my other lady."

Longing to catch sight of her, even though she were with a companion, Genji stole from his hiding place, and crept through a gap in the curtains. The partition door through which the boy had passed was still open, and he could see through it, right along the corridor into the room on the other side. The screen which protected the entrance of this room was partly folded, and the curtains which usually concealed the divan had, owing to the great heat, been hooked up out of the way, so that he had an excellent view.

The lady sitting near the lamp, half-leaning against the middle pillar must, he supposed, be his beloved. He looked closely at her. She seemed to be wearing an unlined, dark purple dress, with some kind of scarf thrown over her shoulders. The poise of her head was graceful, but her extreme smallness had the effect of making her seem somewhat insignificant. She seemed to be trying all the while to hide her face from her companion, and there was something furtive about the movements of her slender hands, which she seemed never to show for more than a moment.

Her companion was sitting right opposite him, and he could see her perfectly. She wore an underdress of thin white stuff, and thrown carelessly over it a cloak embroidered with red and blue flowers. The dress was not fastened in front, showing a bare neck and breast, showing even the little red sash which held up her drawers. She had indeed an engagingly free and easy air. Her skin was very white and delicate, she was rather plump, but tall and well built. The poise of her head and angle of her brow were faultless, the expression of her mouth and eyes

---

[1] Ki no Kami's sister, referred to later in the story as Nokiba no Ogi.

LADY MURASAKI SHIKIBU

was very pleasing and her appearance altogether most delightful. Her hair grew very thick, but was cut short so as to hang on a level with her shoulders. It was very fine and smooth. How exciting it must be to have such a girl for one's daughter! Small wonder if Iyo no Kami was proud of her. If she was a little less restless, he thought, she would be quite perfect.

The game was nearly over, she was clearing away the unwanted pieces. She seemed to be very excitable and was making a quite unnecessary commotion about the business. "Wait a little," said her companion very quietly, "here there is a stalemate. My only move is to counterattack over there. . ."

"It is all over," said the other impatiently, "I am beaten, let us count the score;" and she began counting, "ten, twenty, thirty, forty," on her fingers.

Genji could not help remembering the old song about the wash-house at Iyo ("eight tubs to the left, nine tubs to the right") and as this lady of Iyo, determined that nothing should be left unsettled, went on stolidly counting her losses and gains, he thought her for the moment slightly common. It was strange to contrast her with Utsusemi,[2] who sat silent, her face half-covered, so that he could scarcely discern her features. But when he looked at her fixedly, she, as though uneasy under this gaze of which she was not actually aware, shifted in her seat, and showed him her full profile. Her eyelids gave the impression of being a little swollen, and there was at places a certain lack of delicacy in the lines of her features, while her good points were not visible. But when she began to speak, it was as though she were determined to make amends for the deficiencies of her appearance and show that she had, if not so much beauty, at any rate more sense than her companion.

The latter was now flaunting her charms with more and more careless abandonment. Her continual laughter and high spirits were certainly rather engaging, and she seemed in her way to be a most entertaining person. He did not imagine that she was very virtuous, but that was far from being altogether a disadvantage.

It amused him very much to see people behaving quite naturally together. He had lived in an atmosphere of ceremony and reserve. This

---

[2] This name means 'cicada' and is given to her later in the story in reference to the scarf which she "discarded as a cicada sheds its husk." But at this point it becomes grammatically important that she should have a name and I therefore anticipate.

peep at everyday life was a most exciting novelty, and though he felt slightly uneasy at spying in this deliberate way upon two persons who had no notion that they were observed, he would gladly have gone on looking, when suddenly the boy, who had been sitting by his sister's side, got up, and Genji slipped back again into his proper hiding place. The boy was full of apologies at having left him waiting for so long: "But I am afraid nothing can be done today; there is still a visitor in her room."

"And am I now to go home again?" said Genji; "that is really too much to ask."

"No, no, stay here, I will try what can be done, when the visitor has gone."

Genji felt quite sure that the boy would manage to find some way of cajoling his sister, for he had noticed that though a mere child, he had a way of quietly observing situations and characters, and making use of his knowledge.

The game of *go* must now be over. A rustling of skirts and pattering of feet showed that the household was not retiring to rest.

"Where is the young master?" Genji heard a servant saying, "I am going to fasten this partition door," and there was the sound of bolts being slipped.

"They have all gone to bed," said Genji, "now is the time to think of a plan."

The boy knew that it would be no use arguing with his sister or trying beforehand in any way to bend her obstinate resolution. The best thing to be done under the circumstances was to wait till no one was about, and then lead Genji straight to her.

"Is Ki no Kami's sister still here?" asked Genji, "I should like just to catch a glimpse of her."

"But that is impossible," said the boy, "She is in my sister's room."

"Indeed," said Genji, affecting surprise. For though he knew very well where she was he did not wish to show that he had already seen her. Becoming very impatient of all these delays, he pointed out that it was growing very late, and there was no time to be lost.

The boy nodded, and tapping on the main door of the women's quarters, he entered. Everyone was sound asleep. "I am going to sleep in the ante-room," the boy said out loud; "I shall leave the door open so as to make a draught"; and so saying he spread his mattress on the ground, and for a while pretended to be asleep. Soon however, he got up and spread a screen as though to protect him from the light, and under its shadow Genji slipped softly into the room.

Not knowing what was to happen next, and much doubting whether any good would come of the venture, with great trepidation he followed the boy to the curtain that screened the main bedroom, and pulling it aside entered on tip-toe. But even in the drab garments which he had chosen for his disguise, he seemed to the boy to cut a terribly conspicuous figure as he passed through the midnight quietness of the house.

Utsusemi meanwhile had persuaded herself that she was very glad Genji had forgotten to pay his threatened visit. But she was still haunted by the memory of their one strange and dreamlike meeting, and was in no mood for sleep. But near her, as she lay tossing, the lady of the *go* party, delighted by her visit and all the opportunities it had afforded for chattering to her heart's content, was already asleep. And as she was young and had no troubles she slept very soundly. The princely scent which still clung to Genji's person reached the bed. Utsusemi raised her head, and fancied that she saw something move behind a part of the curtain that was only of one thickness. Though it was very dark she recognized Genji's figure. Filled with a sudden terror and utter bewilderment, she sprang from the bed, threw a fragile gauze mantle over her shoulders, and fled silently from the room.

A moment later Genji entered. He saw with delight that there was only one person in the room, and that the bed was arranged for two. He threw off his cloak, and advanced towards the sleeping figure. She seemed a more imposing figure than he had expected, but this did not trouble him. It did indeed seem rather strange that she should be so sound asleep. Gradually he realized with horror that it was not she at all.

"It is no use," thought Genji, "saying that I have come to the wrong room, for I have no business anywhere here. Nor is it worth while pursuing my real lady, for she would not have vanished like this if she cared a straw about me." What if it were the lady he had seen by the lamplight? She might not after all prove a bad exchange! But no sooner had he thought this than he was horrified at his own frivolity.

She opened her eyes. She was naturally somewhat startled, but did not seem to be at all seriously put out. She was a thoughtless creature in whose life no very strong emotion had ever played a part. Hers was the flippancy that goes with inexperience, and even this sudden visitation did not seem very much to perturb her.

He meant at first to explain that it was not to see her that he had come. But to do so would have been to give away the secret which Utsusemi so jealously guarded from the world. There was nothing for it, but to pretend that his repeated visits to the house, of which the lady was well aware, had been made in the hope of meeting her! This was a story which would not have withstood the most cursory examination; but, outrageous as it was, the girl accepted it without hesitation.

He did not by any means dislike her, but at that moment all his thoughts were busy with the lady who had so mysteriously vanished. No doubt she was congratulating herself in some safe hiding place upon the absurd situation in which she had left him. Really, she was the most obstinate creature in the world! What was the use of running after her? But all the same she continued to obsess him.

But the girl in front of him was young and gay and charming. They were soon getting on very well together.

"Is not this kind of thing much more amusing than what happens with people whom one knows?" asked Genji a little later. "Do not think unkindly of me. Our meeting must for the present remain a secret. I am in a position which does not always allow me to act as I please. Your people too would no doubt interfere if they should hear of it, which would be very tiresome. Wait patiently, and do not forget me."

These rather tepid injunctions did not strike her as at all unsatisfactory, and she answered very seriously, "I am afraid it will not be very easy for me even to write to you. People would think it very odd."

"Of course we must not let ordinary people into our secret," he answered, "but there is no reason why this little page should not sometimes carry a message. Meanwhile not a word to anyone!" And with that he left her, taking as he did so Utsusemi's thin scarf which had slipped from her shoulders when she fled from the room.

He went to wake his page who was lying not far away. The boy sprang instantly to his feet, for he was sleeping very lightly, not knowing when his help might be required. He opened the door as quietly as he could.

"Who is that?" someone called out in great alarm. It was the voice of an old woman who worked in the house.

"It is I," answered the boy uneasily.

"What are you walking about here for at this time of night?" and scolding as she came, she began to advance towards the door.

"Bother her," thought the boy, but he answered hastily, "It's all right, I am only going outside for a minute"; but just as Genji passed through the door, the moon of dawn suddenly emerged in all her brightness.

Seeing a grown man's figure appear in the doorway, "Whom have you got with you?" the old lady asked, and then answering her own question "Why it is Mimbu! What an outrageous height that girl has grown to!" and continuing to imagine that the boy was walking with Mimbu, a maid-servant whose lankiness was a standing joke in the house, "and you will soon be as big as she is, little Master!" she cried, and so saying came out through the door that they had just passed through. Genji felt very uncomfortable, and making no answer on the supposed Mimbu's behalf, he stood in the shadow at the end of the corridor, hiding himself as best he could.

"You have been on duty, haven't you dear?" said the old lady as she came towards them. "I have been terribly bad with the colic since yesterday and was lying up, but they were shorthanded last night, and I had to go and help, though I did feel very queer all the while." And then, without waiting for them to answer, "Oh, my pain, my poor pain," she muttered, "I can't stop here talking like this," and she hobbled past them without looking up.

So narrow an escape made Genji wonder more than ever whether the whole thing was worth while. He drove back to his house, with the boy riding as his postillion.

Here he told him the story of his evening's adventure. "A pretty mess you made of it!" And when he had finished scolding the boy for his incompetence, he began to rail at the sister's irritating prudishness. The poor child felt very unhappy, but could think of nothing to say in his own or his sister's defence.

"I am utterly wretched," said Genji. "It is obvious that she would not have behaved as she did last night unless she absolutely detested me. But she might at least have the decency to send civil answers to my letters. Oh, well, I suppose Iyo no Kami is the better man. . ." So he spoke, thinking that she desired only to be rid of him. Yet when at last he lay down to rest, he was wearing her scarf hidden under his dress. He had put the boy by his side, and after giving much vent to his exasperation, he said at last, "I am very fond of you, but I am afraid in future I shall always think of you in connection with this hateful business, and that will put an end to our friendship." He said it with such conviction that the boy felt quite forlorn.

For a while they rested, but Genji could not sleep, and at dawn he sent in haste for his ink-stone. He did not write a proper letter, but scribbled on a piece of folded paper, in the manner of a writing exercise, a poem in which he compared the scarf which she had dropped in her flight to the dainty husk which the cicada sheds on some bank beneath a tree.

The boy picked the paper up, and thrust it into the folds of his dress.

Genji was very much distressed at the thought of what the other lady's feelings must be; but after some reflection he decided that it would be better not to send any message.

The scarf, to which still clung the delicate perfume of its owner, he wore for long afterwards beneath his dress.

When the boy got home he found his sister waiting for him in very ill-humour. "It was not your doing that I escaped from the odious quandary in which you landed me! And even so pray what explanation can I offer to my friend?"

"A fine little clown the Prince must think you now. I hope you are ashamed of yourself."

Despite the fact that both parties were using him so ill, the boy drew the rescued verses from out the folds of his dress and handed them to her. She could not forbear to read them. What of this discarded mantle? Why should he speak of it? *The coat that the fishers of Iseo left lying upon the shore. . .*[3] those were the words that came into her mind, but they were not the clue. She was sorely puzzled.

Meanwhile the Lady of the West[4] was feeling very ill at ease. She was longing to talk about what had happened, but must not do so, and had to bear the burden of her impatience all alone. The arrival of Utsusemi's brother put her into a great state of excitement. No letter for her? she could not understand it at all, and for the first time a cloud settled upon her gay confiding heart.

Utsusemi, though she had so fiercely steeled herself against his love, seeing such tenderness hidden under the words of his message, again fell to longing that she were free, and though there was no undoing what was done she found it so hard to go without him that she took up the folded paper and wrote in the margin a poem in which she said that her sleeve, so often wet with tears, was like the cicada's dew-drenched wing.

---

[3] Allusion to the old poem, "Does he know that since he left me my eyes are wet as the coat that the fishers. . . left lying upon the shore?"

[4] The visitor.

IV

Yūgao

It was at the time when he was secretly visiting the lady of the Sixth Ward.[1] One day on his way back from the Palace he thought that he would call upon his foster mother who, having for a long while been very ill, had become a nun. She lived in the Fifth Ward. After many enquiries he managed to find the house; but the front gate was locked and he could not drive in. He sent one of his servants for Koremitsu, his foster-nurse's son, and while he was waiting began to examine the rather wretched looking by-street. The house next door was fenced with a new paling, above which at one place were four or five panels of open trellis-work, screened by blinds which were very white and bare. Through chinks in these blinds a number of foreheads could be seen. They seemed to belong to a group of ladies who must be peeping with interest into the street below.

At first he thought they had merely peeped out as they passed; but he soon realized that if they were standing on the floor they must be giants. No, evidently they had taken the trouble to climb on to some table or bed; which was surely rather odd!

He had come in a plain coach with no outriders. No one could possibly guess who he was, and feeling quite at his ease he leant forward and deliberately examined the house. The gate, also made of a kind of trellis-work, stood ajar, and he could see enough of the interior to realize that it was a very humble and poorly furnished dwelling. For a moment he pitied those who lived in such a place, but then he remembered the song, "*Seek not in the wide world to find a home; but where you chance to rest, call that your house*"; and again, "*Monarchs may keep their palaces of jade, for in a leafy cottage two can sleep.*"

There was a wattled fence over which some ivy-like creeper spread its cool green leaves, and among the leaves were white flowers with petals half unfolded like the lips of people smiling at their own thoughts. "They are called Yūgao, 'Evening Faces,'" one of his servants told him; "how strange to find so lovely a crowd clustering on this deserted wall!" And indeed

---

[1] Lady Rokujō. Who she was gradually becomes apparent in the course of the story.

it was a most strange and delightful thing to see how on the narrow tenement in a poor quarter of the town they had clambered over rickety eaves and gables and spread wherever there was room for them to grow. He sent one of his servants to pick some. The man entered at the half-opened door, and had begun to pluck the flowers, when a little girl in a long yellow tunic came through a quite genteel sliding door, and holding out towards Genji's servant a white fan heavily perfumed with incense, she said to him, "Would you like something to put them on? I am afraid you have chosen a wretched-looking bunch," and she handed him the fan.

Just as he was opening the gate on his way back, the old nurse's son Koremitsu came out of the other house full of apologies for having kept Genji waiting so long—"I could not find the key of the gate," he said. "Fortunately the people of this humble quarter were not likely to recognize you and press or stare; but I am afraid you must have been very much bored waiting in this hugger-mugger back street," and he conducted Genji into the house. Koremitsu's brother, the deacon, his brother-in-law Mikawa no Kami and his sister all assembled to greet the Prince, delighted by a visit with which they had not thought he was ever likely to honour them again.

The nun too rose from her couch: "For a long time I had been waiting to give up the world, but one thing held me back: I wanted you to see your old nurse just once again as you used to know her. You never came to see me, and at last I gave up waiting and took my vows. Now, in reward for the penances which my Order enjoins, I have got back a little of my health, and having seen my dear young master again, I can wait with a quiet mind for the Lord Amida's Light," and in her weakness she shed a few tears.

"I heard some days ago," said Genji, "that you were very dangerously ill, and was in great anxiety. It is sad now to find you in this penitential garb. You must live longer yet, and see me rise in the world, that you may be born again high in the ninth sphere of Amida's Paradise. For they say that those who died with longings unfulfilled are burdened with an evil Karma in their life to come."

People such as old nurses regard even the most blackguardly and ill-favoured foster children as prodigies of beauty and virtue. Small wonder then if Genji's nurse, who had played so great a part in his early life, always regarded her office as immensely honourable and important, and tears of pride came into her eyes while he spoke to her.

The old lady's children thought it very improper that their mother, having taken holy orders, should show so lively an interest in a human career. Certain that Genji himself would be very much shocked, they exchanged uneasy glances. He was on the contrary deeply touched.

"When I was a child," he said, "those who were dearest to me were early taken away, and although there were many who gave a hand to my upbringing, it was to you only, dear nurse, that I was deeply and tenderly attached. When I grew up I could not any longer be often in your company. I have not even been able to come here and see you as often as I wanted to. But in all the long time which has passed since I was last here, I have thought a great deal about you and wished that life did not force so many bitter partings upon us."

So he spoke tenderly. The princely scent of the sleeve which he had raised to brush away his tears filled the low and narrow room, and even the young people, who had till now been irritated by their mother's obvious pride at having been the nurse of so splendid a prince, found themselves in tears.

Having arranged for continual masses to be said on the sick woman's behalf, he took his leave, ordering Koremitsu to light him with a candle. As they left the house he looked at the fan upon which the white flowers had been laid. He now saw that there was writing on it, a poem carelessly but elegantly scribbled:

> *The flower that puzzled you was but the Yūgao, strange beyond knowing in its dress of shining dew.*

It was written with a deliberate negligence which seemed to aim at concealing the writer's status and identity. But for all that the hand showed a breeding and distinction which agreeably surprised him.

"Who lives in the house on the left?" he asked.

Koremitsu, who did not at all want to act as a go-between, replied that he had only been at his mother's for five or six days and had been so much occupied by her illness that he had not asked any questions about the neighbours.

"I want to know for a quite harmless reason," said Genji. "There is something about this fan which raises a rather important point. I positively must settle it. You would oblige me by making enquiries from someone who knows the neighbourhood."

Koremitsu went at once to the house next door and sent for the steward. "This house," the man said, "belongs to a certain Titular-Prefect.

He is living in the country, but my lady is still here; and as she is young and loves company, her brothers who are in service at the Court often come here to visit her."

"And that is about all one can expect a servant to know," said Koremitsu when he repeated this information. It occurred at once to Genji that it was one of these Courtiers who had written the poem. Yes, there was certainly a self-confident air in the writing. It was by someone whose rank entitled him to have a good opinion of himself. But he was romantically disposed; it was too painful to dismiss altogether the idea that, after all, the verses might really have been meant for him, and on a folded paper he wrote: "Could I but get a closer view, no longer would they puzzle me—the flowers that all too dimly in the gathering dusk I saw." This he wrote in a disguised hand and gave to his servant. The man reflected that though the senders of the fan had never seen Genji before, yet so well known were his features, that even the glimpse they had got from the window might easily have revealed to them his identity. He could imagine the excitement with which the fan had been despatched and the disappointment when for so long a time no answer came. His somewhat rudely belated arrival would seem to them to have been purposely contrived. They would all be agog to know what was in the reply, and he felt very nervous as he approached the house.

Meanwhile, lighted only by a dim torch, Genji quietly left his nurse's home. The blinds of the other house were now drawn and only the fire-fly glimmer of a candle shone through the gap between them.

When he reached his destination[2] a very different scene met his eyes. A handsome park, a well-kept garden; how spacious and comfortable it all was! And soon the magnificent owner of these splendours had driven from his head all thought of the wooden paling, the shutters and the flowers.

He stayed longer than he intended, and the sun was already up when he set out for home. Again he passed the house with the shutters. He had driven through the quarter countless times without taking the slightest interest in it; but that one small episode of the fan had suddenly made his daily passage through these streets an event of great importance. He looked about him eagerly, and would have liked to know who lived in all the houses.

---

[2] Lady Rokujō's house.

For several days Koremitsu did not present himself at Genji's palace. When at last he came, he explained that his mother was growing much weaker and it was very difficult for him to get away. Then drawing nearer, he said in a low voice, "I made some further enquiries, but could not find out much. It seems that someone came very secretly in June and has been living there ever since; but who she really is not even her own servants know. I have once or twice peeped through a hole in the hedge and caught a glimpse of some young women; but their skirts were rolled back and tucked in at their belts, so I think they must have been waiting-maids. Yesterday some while after sunset I saw a lady writing a letter. Her face was calm, but she looked very unhappy, and I noticed that some of her women were secretly weeping." Genji was more curious than ever.

Though his master was of a rank which brought with it great responsibilities, Koremitsu knew that in view of his youth and popularity the young prince would be thought to be positively neglecting his duty if he did not indulge in a few escapades, and that everyone would regard his conduct as perfectly natural and proper even when it was such as they would not have dreamed of permitting to ordinary people.

"Hoping to get a little further information," he said, "I found an excuse for communicating with her, and received in reply a very well-worded answer in a cultivated hand. She must be a girl of quite good position."

"You must find out more," said Genji; "I shall not be happy till I know all about her."

Here perhaps was just such a case as they had imagined on that rainy night: a lady whose outward circumstances seemed to place her in that "Lowest Class" which they had agreed to dismiss as of no interest; but who in her own person showed qualities by no means despicable.

But to return for a moment to Utsusemi. Her unkindness had not affected him as it would have affected most people. If she had encouraged him he would soon have regarded the affair as an appalling indiscretion which he must put an end to at all costs; whereas now he brooded continually upon his defeat and was forever plotting new ways to shake her resolution.

He had never, till the day of his visit to the foster-nurse, been interested in anyone of quite the common classes. But now, since that rainy night's conversation, he had explored (so it seemed to him) every corner of society, including in his survey even those categories which his friends had passed over as utterly remote and improbable. He thought of the lady who had, so to speak, been thrown into his life as an extra. With how confiding an air she had promised that she would wait! He was very sorry about her, but he was afraid that if he wrote to her Utsusemi might find out and that would prejudice his chances. He would write to her afterwards. . .

Suddenly at this point Iyo no Suke himself was announced. He had just returned from his province, and had lost no time in paying his respects to the prince. The long journey by boat had made him look rather swarthy and haggard.

"Really," thought Genji, "he is not at all an attractive man!" Still it was possible to talk to him; for if a man is of decent birth and breeding, however broken he may be by age or misfortune, he will always retain a certain refinement of mind and manners which prevent him from becoming merely repulsive. They were beginning to discuss the affairs of Iyo's province and Genji was even joking with him, when a sudden feeling of embarrassment came over him. Why should those recollections make him feel so awkward? Iyo no Suke was quite an old man, it had done him no harm.

"These scruples are absurd," thought Genji. However, she was right in thinking it was too queer, too ill-assorted a match; and remembering Uma no Kami's warnings, he felt that he had behaved badly. Though her unkindness still deeply wounded him, he was almost glad for Iyo's sake that she had not relented.

"My daughter is to be married," Iyo was saying, "And I am going to take my wife back with me to my province." Here was a double surprise. At all costs he must see Utsusemi once again. He spoke with her brother and the boy discussed the matter with her. It would have been difficult enough for anyone to have carried on an intrigue with the prince under such circumstances as these. But for her, so far below him in rank and beset by new restrictions, it had now become unthinkable. She could not however bear to lose all contact with him, and not only did she answer his letters much more kindly than before, but took pains, though they were written with apparent negligence, to add little touches that would give him pleasure and make him see that she still cared for him. All this he noticed, and though he was vexed that she would not relent towards him, he found it impossible to put her out of his mind.

As for the other girl, he did not think that she was at all the kind of person to go on pining for him once she was properly settled with a husband; and he now felt quite happy about her.

It was autumn. Genji had brought so many complications into his life that he had for some while been very irregular in his visits to the Great Hall, and was in great disgrace there. The lady[3] in the grand mansion was very difficult to get on with; but he had surmounted so many obstacles in his courtship of her that to give her up the moment he had won her seemed absurd. Yet he could not deny that the blind intoxicating passion which possessed him while she was still unattainable, had almost disappeared. To begin with, she was far too sensitive; then there was the disparity of their ages,[4] and the constant dread of discovery which haunted him during those painful partings at small hours of the morning. In fact, there were too many disadvantages.

It was a morning when mist lay heavy over the garden. After being many times roused Genji at last came out of Rokujō's room, looking very cross and sleepy. One of the maids lifted part of the folding-shutter, seeming to invite her mistress to watch the prince's departure. Rokujō pulled aside the bed-curtains and tossing her hair back over her shoulders looked out into the garden. So many lovely flowers were growing in the borders that Genji halted for a while to enjoy them. How beautiful he looked standing there, she thought. As he was nearing the portico the maid who had opened the shutters came and walked by his side. She wore a light green skirt exquisitely matched to the season and place; it was so hung as to show to great advantage the grace and suppleness of her stride. Genji looked round at her. "Let us sit down for a minute on the railing here in the corner," he said.

"She seems very shy," he thought, "but how charmingly her hair falls about her shoulders," and he recited the poem: "*Though I would not be thought to wander heedlessly from flower to flower, yet this morning's pale convolvulus I fain would pluck!*"

As he said the lines he took her hand and she answered with practised ease: "You hasten, I observe, to admire the morning flowers while the mist still lies about them," thus parrying the compliment by a verse which might be understood either in a personal or general sense. At this moment a very elegant page wearing the most bewitching baggy

---

[3] Rokujō.

[4] Genji was now seventeen; Rokujō twenty-four.

trousers came among the flowers brushing the dew as he walked, and began to pick a bunch of the convolvuli. Genji longed to paint the scene.

No one could see him without pleasure. He was like the flowering tree under whose shade even the rude mountain peasant delights to rest. And so great was the fascination he exercised that those who knew him longed to offer him whatever was dearest to them. One who had a favourite daughter would ask for nothing better than to make her Genji's handmaiden. Another who had an exquisite sister was ready for her to serve in his household, though it were at the most menial tasks. Still less could these ladies who on such occasions as this were privileged to converse with him and stare at him as much as they pleased, and were moreover young people of much sensibility—how could they fail to delight in his company and note with much uneasiness that his visits were becoming far less frequent than before?

"But where have I got to? Ah, yes." Koremitsu had patiently continued the enquiry with which Genji entrusted him.

"Who the mistress is," he said, "I have not been able to discover; and for the most part she is at great pains not to show herself. But more than once in the general confusion, when there was the sound of a carriage coming along past that great row of tenement houses, and all the maid-servants were peering out into the road, the young lady whom I suppose to be the mistress of the house slipped out along with them. I could not see her clearly, but she seemed to be very pretty.

"One day, seeing a carriage with outriders coming towards the house, one of the maids rushed off calling out 'Ukon, Ukon, come quickly and look. The Captain's carriage is coming this way.' At once a pleasant-faced lady no longer young, came bustling out. 'Quietly, quietly,' she said holding up a warning finger; 'how do you know it is the Captain? I shall have to go and look,' and she slipped out. A sort of rough drawbridge leads from the garden into the lane. In her excitement the good lady caught her skirt in it and falling flat on her face almost tumbled into the ditch: 'A bad piece of work His Holiness of Katsuragi[5] made here!' she grumbled; but her curiosity did not seem to be at all damped and she stared harder than ever at the approaching carriage. The visitor was dressed in a plain, wide cloak. He had attendants with him, whose names the excited servant-girls called out as one after another they came

[5] The god of bridges. He built in a single night the stone causeway which joins Mount Katsuragi and Mount Kombu.

near enough to be recognized; and the odd thing is that the names were certainly those of Tō no Chūjō's[6] grooms and pages."

"I must see that carriage for myself," said Genji. What if this should be the very lady whom Chūjō, at the time of that rainy night's conversation, despaired of rediscovering?"

Koremitsu, noting that Genji was listening with particular attention continued: "I must tell you that I too have reason to be interested in this house, and while making enquiries on my own account I discovered that the young lady always addresses the other girls in the house as though they were her equals. But when, pretending to be taken in by this comedy, I began visiting there, I noticed that though the older ladies played their part very well, the young girls would every now and then curtsey or slip in a 'My Lady' without thinking; whereupon the others would hasten to cover up the mistake as best they might, saying anything they could think of to make it appear that there was no mistress among them," and Koremitsu laughed as he recollected it.

"Next time I come to visit your mother," said Genji, "you must let me have a chance of peeping at them." He pictured to himself the queer, tumbled-down house. She was only living there for the time being; but all the same she must surely belong to that "bottom class" which they had dismissed as having no possible bearing on the discussion. How amusing it would be to show that they were wrong and that after all something of interest might be discovered in such a place!

Koremitsu, anxious to carry out his master's every wish and intent also on his own intrigue, contrived at last by a series of ingenious stratagems to effect a secret meeting between Genji and the mysterious lady. The details of the plan by which he brought this about would make a tedious story, and as is my rule in such cases I have thought it better to omit them.

Genji never asked her by what name he was to call her, nor did he reveal his own identity. He came very poorly dressed and—what was most unusual for him—on foot. But Koremitsu regarded this as too great a tribute to so unimportant a lady, and insisted upon Genji riding his horse, while he walked by his side. In doing so he sacrificed his own feelings; for he too had reasons for wishing to create a good impression in the house, and he knew that by arriving in this rather undignified way he would sink in the estimation of the inhabitants. Fortunately his

---

[6] Genji's brother-in-law.

discomfiture was almost unwitnessed, for Genji took with him only the one attendant who had on the first occasion plucked the flowers—a boy whom no one was likely to recognize; and lest suspicions should be aroused, he did not even take advantage of his presence in the neighbourhood to call at his foster-nurse's house.

The lady was very much mystified by all these precautions and made great efforts to discover something more about him. She even sent someone after him to see where he went to when he left her at day-break; but he succeeded in throwing his pursuer off the scent and she was no wiser than before. He was now growing far too fond of her. He was miserable if anything interfered with his visits; and though he utterly disapproved of his own conduct and worried a great deal about it, he soon found that he was spending most of his time at her house.

He knew that at sometime or another in their lives even the soberest people lose their heads in this way; but hitherto he had never really lost his, or done anything which could possibly have been considered very wrong. Now to his astonishment and dismay he discovered that even the few morning hours during which he was separated from her were becoming unendurable.

"What is it in her that makes me behave like a madman?" he kept on asking himself. She was astonishingly gentle and unassuming, to the point even of seeming rather apathetic, rather deficient perhaps in depth of character and emotion; and though she had a certain air of girlish inexperience, it was clear that he was not by any means her first lover; and certainly she was rather plebeian. What was it exactly that so fascinated him? He asked himself the question again and again, but found no answer.

She for her part was very uneasy to see him come to her thus in shabby old hunting-clothes, trying always to hide his face, leaving while it was still dark and everyone was asleep. He seemed like some demon-lover in an old ghost-tale, and she was half-afraid. But his smallest gesture showed that he was someone out of the ordinary, and she began to suspect that he was a person of high rank, who had used Koremitsu as his go-between. But Koremitsu obstinately pretended to know nothing at all about his companion, and continued to amuse himself by frequenting the house on his own account.

What could it mean? She was dismayed at this strange lovemaking with—she knew not whom. But about her too there was something fugitive, insubstantial. Genji was obsessed by the idea that, just as she

LADY MURASAKI SHIKIBU

had hidden herself in this place, so one day she would once more vanish and hide, and he would never be able to find her again. There was every sign that her residence here was quite temporary. He was sure that when the time came to move she would not tell him where she was going. Of course her running away would be proof that she was not worth bothering about anymore, and he ought, thankful for the pleasure they had had together, simply to leave the matter at that. But he knew that this was the last thing he would be likely to do.

People were already beginning to be suspicious, and often for several nights running he was unable to visit her. This became so intolerable that in his impatience he determined to bring her secretly to the Nijō-in.[7] There would be an appalling outcry if she were discovered; but that must be risked.

"I am going to take you somewhere very nice where no one will disturb us," he said at last.

"No, no," she cried; "your ways are so strange, I should be frightened to go with you."

She spoke in a tone of childish terror, and Genji answered smiling:

"One or the other of us must be a fox-in-disguise.[8] Here is a chance to find out which it is!" He spoke very kindly, and suddenly, in a tone of absolute submission, she consented to do whatever he thought best. He could not but be touched at her willingness to follow him in what must appear to her to be the most hazardous and bizarre adventure. Again he thought of Tō no Chūjō's story on that rainy night, and could not doubt that this must indeed be Chūjō's fugitive lady. But he saw that she had some reason for wishing to avoid all questions about her past, and he restrained his curiosity. So far as he could see she showed no signs of running away; nor did he believe that she would do so as long as he was faithful. Tō no Chūjō, after all, had for months on end left her to her own devices. But he felt that if for an instant she suspected him of the slightest leaning in any other direction it would be a bad business.

It was the fifteenth night of the eighth month. The light of an unclouded full-moon shone between the ill-fitting planks of the roof and flooded the room. What a queer place to be lying in! thought Genji, as he gazed round the garret, so different from any room he had ever

---

[7] His own palace.

[8] Foxes, dressed up as men, were believed to be in the habit of seducing and bewitching human beings.

known before. It must be almost day. In the neighbouring houses people were beginning to stir, and there was an uncouth sound of peasant voices: "Eh! How cold it is! I can't believe we shall do much with the crops this year."

"I don't know what's going to happen about my carrying-trade," said another; "things look very bad." Then (banging on the wall of another house), "Wake up, neighbour. Time to start. Did he hear, d'you think?" and they rose and went off each to the wretched task by which he earned his bread.

All this clatter and bustle going on so near her made the lady very uncomfortable, and indeed so dainty and fastidious a person must often in this miserable lodging have suffered things which would make her long to sink through the floor. But however painful, disagreeable or provoking were the things that happened, she gave no sign of noticing them. That being herself so shrinking and delicate in her ways she could yet endure without a murmur the exasperating banging and bumping that was going on in every direction, aroused his admiration, and he felt that this was much nicer of her than if she had shuddered with horror at each sound. But now, louder than thunder, came the noise of the threshing-mills, seeming so near that they could hardly believe it did not come from out of the pillow itself. Genji thought that his ears would burst. What many of the noises were he could not at all make out; but they were very peculiar and startling. The whole air seemed to be full of crashings and bangings. Now from one side, now from another, came too the faint thud of the bleacher's mallet, and the scream of wild geese passing overhead. It was all too distracting.

Their room was in the front of the house. Genji got up and opened the long, sliding shutters. They stood together looking out. In the courtyard near them was a clump of fine Chinese bamboos; dew lay thick on the borders, glittering here no less brightly than in the great gardens to which Genji was better accustomed. There was a confused buzzing of insects. Crickets were chirping in the wall. He had often listened to them, but always at a distance; now, singing so close to him, they made a music which was unfamiliar and indeed seemed far lovelier than that with which he was acquainted. But then, everything in this place where one thing was so much to his liking, seemed despite all drawbacks to take on a new tinge of interest and beauty. She was wearing a white bodice with a soft, grey cloak over it. It was a poor dress, but she looked charming and almost distinguished; even so, there was nothing very striking in her appearance—only a certain fragile grace and elegance. It was when she was speaking that she looked really beautiful, there was such pathos, such earnestness in her manner. If only she had a little more spirit! But even as she was he found her irresistible and longed to take her to some place where no one could disturb them: "I am going to take you somewhere not at all far away where we shall be able to pass the rest of the night in peace. We cannot go on like this, parting always at break of day."

"Why have you suddenly come to that conclusion?" she asked, but she spoke submissively. He vowed to her that she should be his love in this and in all future lives and she answered so passionately that she seemed utterly transformed from the listless creature he had known, and it was hard to believe that such vows were no novelty to her.

Discarding all prudence he sent for the maid Ukon and bade her order his servants to fetch a coach. The affair was soon known to all the household, and the ladies were at first somewhat uneasy at seeing their mistress carried off in this fashion; but on the whole they did not think he looked the sort of person who would do her any harm. It was now almost daylight. The cocks had stopped crowing. The voice of an old man (a pilgrim preparing for the ascent of the Holy Mountain) sounded somewhere not far away; and, as at each prayer he bent forward to touch the ground with his head, they could hear with what pain and difficulty he moved. What could he be asking for in his prayers, this old man whose life seemed fragile as the morning dew? Namu tōrai no dōshi, "Glory be to the Saviour that shall come": now they could hear the words.

"Listen," said Genji tenderly, "is not that an omen that our love shall last through many lives to come?" And he recited the poem: "*Do not prove false this omen of the pilgrim's chant: that even in lives to come our love shall last unchanged.*"

Then unlike the lovers in the "Everlasting Wrong" who prayed that they might be as the "twin birds that share a wing" (for they remembered that this story had ended very sadly) they prayed, "May our love last till Maitreya comes as a Buddha into the World." But she, still distrustful, answered his poem with the verse: "*Such sorrow have I known in this world that I have small hope of worlds to come.*" Her versification was still a little tentative.[9]

---

[9] We gather later that she was only nineteen.

She was thinking with pleasure that the setting moon would light them on their way, and Genji was just saying so when suddenly the moon disappeared behind a bank of clouds. But there was still great beauty in the dawning sky. Anxious to be gone before it was quite light, he hurried her away to the coach and put Ukon by her side.

They drove to an untenanted mansion which was not far off. While he waited for the steward to come out Genji noticed that the gates were crumbling away; dense shinobu-grass grew around them. So sombre an entrance he had never seen. There was a thick mist and the dew was so heavy that when he raised the carriage-blind his sleeve was drenched. "Never yet has such an adventure as this befallen me," said Genji; "so I am, as you may imagine, rather excited," and he made a poem in which he said that though love's folly had existed since the beginning of the world, never could man have set out more rashly at the break of day into a land unknown. "But to you this is no great novelty?"

She blushed and in her turn made a poem: "*I am as the moon that walks the sky not knowing what menace the cruel hills may hold in store; high though she sweeps, her light may suddenly be blotted out.*"

She seemed very depressed and nervous. But this he attributed to the fact that she had probably always lived in small houses where everything was huddled together, and he was amused at the idea that this large mansion should overawe her. They drove in, and while a room was being got ready they remained in the carriage which had been drawn up alongside of the balustrade. Ukon, looking very innocent all the while, was inwardly comparing this excursion with her mistress's previous adventures. She had noticed the tone of extreme deference with which this latest lover had been received by the steward, and had begun to draw her own conclusions.

The mist was gradually clearing away. They left the coach and went into the room which had been prepared for them. Though so quickly improvised, their quarters were admirably clean and well-provided, for the steward's son had previously been a trusted house-servant of Genji's and had also worked at the Great Hall. Coming now to their room he offered to send for some of Genji's gentlemen, "For," he said, "I cannot bear to see you going unattended."

"Do nothing of the kind," said Genji; "I have come here because I do not wish to be disturbed. No one but yourself is to know that I have used this house," and he exacted a promise of absolute secrecy. No regular meal had been prepared, but the steward brought them a little rice porridge. Then they lay down again to sleep together for the first time in this unfamiliar and so strangely different place.

The sun was high when they woke. Genji went and opened the shutters himself. How deserted the garden looked! Certainly here there was no one to spy upon them. He looked out into the distance: dense woods fast turning to jungle. And nearer the house not a flower or bush, but only unkempt, autumn grasslands, and a pond choked with weeds. It was a wild and desolate place. It seemed that the steward and his men must live in some outbuilding or lodge at a distance from the house; for here there was no sign or sound of life.

"It is, I must own, a strange and forsaken place to which we have come. But no ghost or evil fairy will dare molest you while *I* am here."

It pained her very much that he still was masked;[10] and indeed such a precaution was quite out of keeping with the stage at which they had now arrived. So at last, reciting a poem in which he reminded her that all their love down to this moment when "*the flower opened its petals to the evening dew*" had come from a chance vision seen casually from the street, half-turning his face away, for a moment he let her see him unmasked.

"What of the 'shining dew,'" he asked using the words that she had written on the fan.

"How little knew I of its beauty who had but in the twilight doubted and guessed. . . !"; so she answered his poem in a low and halting voice. She need not have feared, for to him, poor as the verses were, they seemed delightful. And indeed the beauty of his uncovered face, suddenly revealed to her in this black wilderness of dereliction and decay, surpassed all loveliness that she had ever dreamed of or imagined.

"I cannot wonder that while I still set this barrier between us, you did not choose to tell me all that I longed to know. But now it would be very unkind of you not to tell me your name."

"I am like the fisherman's daughter in the song,"[11] she said, "I have no name or home." But for all that she would not tell him who she was, she seemed much comforted that he had let her see him.

"Do as you please about it," said Genji at last; but for a while he was out of temper.

---

[10] I.e. covered part of his face with a scarf or the like, a practice usual with illicit lovers in mediæval Japan.

[11] *Shin Kokinshū*, 1701.

Soon they had made it up again; and so the day passed. Presently Koremitsu came to their quarters, bringing fruit and other viands. He would not come in, for he was frightened that Ukon would rate him mercilessly for the part he had played in arranging the abduction of her mistress. He had now come to the conclusion that the Lady must possess charms which he had wholly overlooked, or Genji would certainly never have taken all this trouble about her, and he was touched at his own magnanimity in surrendering to his master a prize which he might well have kept for himself. It was an evening of marvellous stillness. Genji sat watching the sky. The lady found the inner room where she was sitting depressingly dark and gloomy. He raised the blinds of the front room, and came to sit with her. They watched the light of the sunset glowing in each other's eyes, and in her wonder at his adorable beauty and tenderness she forgot all her fears. At last she was shy with him no longer, and he thought that the new-found boldness and merriment became her very well. She lay by his side till night. He saw that she was again wearing the plaintive expression of a frightened child; so quickly closing the partition-door he brought in the great lamp, saying: "Outwardly you are no longer shy with me; but I can see that deep down in your heart there is still some sediment of rancour and distrust. It is not kind to use me so," and again he was cross with her.

What were the people at the Palace thinking? Would he have been sent for? How far would the messengers pursue their search? He became quite agitated. Then there was the great lady in the Sixth Ward.[12] What a frenzy she must be in! This time, however, she really had good cause to be jealous. These and other unpleasant considerations were crowding into his head, when looking at the girl who lay beside him so trustfully, unconscious of all that was going on in his mind, he was suddenly filled with an overwhelming tenderness towards her. How tiresome the other was, with her eternal susceptibilities, jealousies and suspicions! For a while at any rate he would stop seeing her. As the night wore on they began sometimes to doze. Suddenly Genji saw standing over him the figure of a woman, tall and majestic:

"You who think yourself so fine, how comes it that you have brought to toy with you here this worthless common creature, picked up at random in the streets? I am astonished and displeased," and with this she made as though to drag the lady from his side. Thinking that this was some

---

[12] Lady Rokujō.

nightmare or hallucination, he roused himself and sat up. The lamp had gone out. Somewhat agitated he drew his sword and laid it beside him, calling as he did so for Ukon. She came at once, looking a good deal scared herself.

"Please wake the watchman in the cross-wing," he said, "and tell him to bring a candle."

"All in the dark like this? How can I?" she answered.

"Don't be childish," said Genji laughing and clapped his hands.[13] The sound echoed desolately through the empty house. He could not make anyone hear; and meanwhile he noticed that his mistress was trembling from head to foot. What should he do? He was still undecided, when suddenly she burst out into a cold sweat. She seemed to be losing consciousness.

"Do not fear, Sir," said Ukon, "all her life she has been subject to these nightmare fits."

He remembered now how tired she had seemed in the morning and how she had lain with her eyes turned upwards as though in pain.

"I will go myself and wake someone," he said; "I am tired of clapping with only echoes to answer me. Do not leave her!" and drawing Ukon towards the bed he went in the direction of the main western door. But when he opened it, he found that the lamp in the cross-wing had also gone out. A wind had risen. The few attendants he had brought with him were already in bed. There was indeed only the steward's son (the young man who had once been Genji's body-servant), and the one young courtier who had attended him on all his visits. They answered when he called and sprang to their feet.

"Come with a candle," he said to the steward's son, "and tell my man to get his bow and keep on twanging the string as loud as he can. I wonder anyone should sleep so soundly in such a deserted place. What has happened to Koremitsu?"

"He waited for sometime, but as you seemed to have no need of him, he went home, saying he would be back at daybreak."

Genji's man had been an Imperial Bowman, and making a tremendous din with his bow he strode towards the steward's lodge crying "Fire, fire," at the top of his voice. The twanging of the bow reminded Genji of the Palace. The roll call of night courtiers must be over; the Bowman's roll call must be actually going on. It was not so very late.

---

[13] To summon a servant.

He groped his way back into the room. She was lying just as he had left her, with Ukon face downwards beside her.

"What are you doing there?" he cried. "Have you gone mad with fright? You have heard no doubt that in such lonely places as this, fox-spirits sometimes try to cast a spell upon men. But, dear people, you need not fear. I have come back, and will not let such creatures harm you." And so saying he dragged Ukon from the bed.

"Oh, Sir," she said, "I felt so queer and frightened that I fell flat down upon my face; and what my poor lady must be going through I dare not think."

"Then try not to add to her fright," said Genji, and pushing her aside bent over the prostate form. The girl was scarcely breathing. He touched her; she was quite limp. She did not know him.

Perhaps some accursed thing, some demon had tried to snatch her spirit away; she was so timid, so childishly helpless. The man came with the candle. Ukon was still too frightened to move. Genji placed a screen so as to hide the bed and called the man to him. It was of course contrary to etiquette that he should serve Genji himself and he hesitated in embarrassment, not venturing even to ascend the dais.

"Come here," said Genji impatiently; "use your common sense." Reluctantly the man gave him the light, and as he held it towards the bed, he saw for a moment the figure which had stood there in his dream still hovering beside the pillow; suddenly it vanished. He had read in old tales of such apparitions and of their power, and was in great alarm. But for the moment he was so full of concern for the lady who now lay motionless on the bed, that he gave no thought to that menacing vision, and lying down beside her, began gently to move her limbs. Already they were growing cold. Her breathing had quite stopped. What could he do? To whom could he turn for help? He ought to send for a priest. He tried to control himself, but he was very young, and seeing her lying there all still and pale, he could contain himself no longer and crying, "Come back to me, my own darling, come back to life. Do not look at me so strangely!" He flung his arms about her. But now she was quite cold. Her face was set in a dull, senseless stare.

Suddenly Ukon, who had been so busy with her own fears, came to herself again, and set up the most dismal weeping. He disregarded her. Something had occurred to him. There was a story of how a certain minister was waylaid by a demon as he passed through the Southern Hall. The man, Genji remembered, had been prostrate with fear; but in the end he revived and escaped. No, she could not really be dead, and turning to Ukon he said firmly: "Come now, we cannot have you making such a hideous noise in the middle of the night." But he himself was stunned with grief, and though he gave Ukon distracted orders scarce knew what he was doing.

Presently he sent for the steward's son and said to him: "Someone here has had a fright and is in a very bad way. I want you to go to Koremitsu's house and tell him to come as quickly as he can. If his brother the priest is there too, take him aside and tell him quietly that I should like to see him at once. But do not speak loud enough for the nun their mother to hear; for I would not have her know of this excursion." But though he managed to say the words, his brain was all the while in a hideous turmoil. For added to the ghastly thought that he himself had caused her death there was the dread and horror with which the whole place now inspired him.

It was past midnight. A violent storm began to rise, sighing dismally as it swept the pine-trees that clustered round the house. And all the while some strange bird—an owl, he supposed—kept screeching hoarsely. Utter desolation on all sides. No human voice; no friendly sound. Why, why had he chosen this hideous place?

Ukon had fainted and was lying by her mistress's side. Was she too going to die of fright? No, no. He must not give way to such thoughts. He was now the only person left who was capable of action. Was there nothing he could do? The candle was burning badly. He lit it again. Over by the screen in the corner of the main room something was moving. There it was again, but in another corner now. There was a sound of footsteps treading cautiously. It still went on. Now they were coming up behind him. . .

If only Koremitsu would return! But Koremitsu was a rover and a long time was wasted in looking for him. Would it never be day? It seemed to him that this night was lasting a thousand years. But now, somewhere a long way off, a cock crowed.

Why had fate seen fit to treat him thus? He felt that it must be as a punishment for all the strange and forbidden amours into which in these last years he had despite himself been drawn, that now this unheard of horror had befallen him. And such things, though one may keep them secret for a time, always come out in the end. He minded most that the Emperor would be certain to discover sooner or later about this and all his other affairs. Then there was the general scandal. Everyone would know. The very gutter boys would make merry over him. Never, never must he do such things again, or his reputation would utterly collapse. . .

At last Koremitsu arrived. He prided himself on being always ready to carry out his master's wishes immediately at whatever hour of the night or day, and he thought it very provoking of Genji to have sent for him just on the one occasion when he was not to hand. And now that he had come his master did not seem able to give him any orders, but stood speechless in front of him.

Ukon, hearing Koremitsu's voice, suddenly came to herself and remembering what had happened, burst into tears. And now Genji, who while he alone was there had supported and encouraged the weeping maid-servant, relieved at last by Koremitsu could contain himself no longer, and suddenly realizing again the terrible thing that had befallen him he burst into uncontrollable weeping.

"Something horrible has happened here," he managed to say at last, "too dreadful to explain. I have heard that when such things as this suddenly befall, certain scriptures should be read. I would have this done, and prayers said. That is why I asked you to bring your brother. . ."

"He went up to the mountain yesterday," said Koremitsu. "But I see that there has been terrible work here afoot. Was it in some sudden fit of madness that you did this thing?" Genji shook his head.

So moved was Koremitsu at the sight of his master weeping, that he too began to sob. Had he been an older man, versed in the ways of the world, he might have been of some use in such a crisis, but both of them were young and both were equally perplexed. At last Koremitsu said: "One thing at least is clear. The steward's son must not know. For though he himself can be depended upon, he is the sort of person who is sure to tell all his relatives, and they might meddle disastrously in the affair. We had best get clear of this house as quietly as we can."

"Perhaps," said Genji; "but it would be hard to find a less frequented place than this."

"At any rate," Koremitsu continued, "we cannot take her to her own house; for there her gentlewomen, who loved her dearly, would raise such a weeping and wailing as would soon bring a pack of neighbours swarming around, and all would quickly be known. If only I knew of some mountain-temple—for there such things are customary[14] and pass almost unnoticed."

---

[14] The bringing of a corpse. Temples were used as mortuaries.

He paused and reflected, "there is a lady I once knew who has become a nun and now lives on the Higashi Yama. She was my father's wet-nurse and is now very old and bent. She does not of course live alone; but no outside people come there."

A faint light was already showing in the sky when Koremitsu brought the carriage in. Thinking that Genji would not wish to move the body himself, he wrapt it in a rush-mat and carried it towards the carriage. How small she was to hold! Her face was calm and beautiful. He felt no repulsion. He could find no way to secure her hair, and when he began to carry her it overflowed and hung towards the ground. Genji saw, and his eyes darkened. A hideous anguish possessed him.

He tried to follow the body, but Koremitsu dissuaded him, saying, "You must ride back to your palace as quickly as you can; you have just time to get there before the stir begins," and putting Ukon into the carriage, he gave Genji his horse. Then pulling up his silk trousers to the knee, he accompanied the carriage on foot. It was a very singular procession; but Koremitsu, seeing his master's terrible distress, forgot for the moment his own dignity and walked stolidly on. Genji, hardly conscious of what went on around him arrived at last in ghostly pallor at his house.

"Where do you come from, my Lord?"

"How ill you look." . . .

Questions assailed him, but he hurried to his room and lay behind his curtain. He tried to calm himself, but hideous thoughts tormented him. Why had he not insisted upon going with her? What if after all she were not dead and waking up should find that he had thus abandoned her? While these wild thoughts chased through his brain a terrible sensation of choking began to torment him. His head ached, his body seemed to be on fire. Indeed he felt so strange that he thought he too was about to die suddenly and inexplicably as she had done. The sun was now high, but he did not get up. His gentlemen, with murmurs of astonishment, tried every means to rouse him. He sent away the dainties they brought, and lay hour after hour plunged in the darkest thoughts. A messenger arrived from the Emperor: "His Majesty has been uneasy since yesterday when his envoys sought everywhere for your Highness in vain."

The young lords too came from the Great Hall. He would see none of them but Tō no Chūjō, and even him he made stand outside his curtain while he spoke to him: "My foster mother has been very ill since the fifth month. She shaved her head and performed other penances, in consequence of which (or so it seems) she recovered a little and got up, but is very much enfeebled. She sent word that she desired to see me once more before she died, and as I was very fond of her when I was a child, I could not refuse. While I was there a servant in the house fell ill and died quite suddenly. Out of consideration for me they removed the body at nightfall. But as soon as I was told of what had happened I remembered that the Fast of the Ninth Month was at hand and for this reason I have not thought it right to present myself to the Emperor my father. Moreover, since early morning I have had a cough and very bad headache, so you will forgive me for treating you in this way."

"I will give the Emperor your message. But I must tell you that last night when you were out he sent messengers to look for you and seemed, if I may venture to say so, to be in a very ill humour." Tō no Chūjō turned to go, but pausing a moment came back to Genji's couch and said quietly: "What really happened to you last night? What you told me just now cannot possibly be true."

"You need not go into details," answered Genji impatiently. "Simply tell him that unintentionally I became exposed to a pollution, and apologize to him for me as best you can." He spoke sharply, but in his heart there was only an unspeakable sadness; and he was very tired.

All day he lay hidden from sight. Once he sent for Tō no Chūjō's brother Kurōdo no Ben and gave him a formal message for the Emperor. The same excuse would serve for the Great Hall, and he sent a similar message there and to other houses where he might be expected.

At dusk Koremitsu came. The story of Genji's pollution had turned all visitors from the door, and Koremitsu found his palace utterly deserted. "What happened?" said Genji, summoning him, "you are sure that she is dead?" and holding his sleeve before his face he wept.

"All is over; of that there is no doubt," said Koremitsu, also in tears; "and since it is not possible for them to keep the body long, I have arranged with a very respectable aged priest who is my friend that the ceremony shall take place tomorrow, since tomorrow chances to be a good calendar day."

"And what of her gentlewoman?" asked Genji.

"I fear she will not live," said Koremitsu. "She cries out that she must follow her mistress and this morning, had I not held her, she would have cast herself from a high rock. She threatened to tell the servants at my lady's house, but I prevailed upon her to think the matter over quietly before she did this."

"Poor thing," said Genji, "small wonder that she should be thus distracted. I too am feeling strangely disordered and do not know what will become of me."

"Torment yourself no more," said Koremitsu. "All things happen as they must. Here is one who will handle this matter very prudently for you, and none shall be the wiser."

"Happen as they must. You are right," said Genji, "and so I try to persuade myself. But in the pursuit of one's own wanton pleasures to have done harm and to have caused someone's death—that is a hideous crime; a terrible load of sin to bear with me through the world. Do not tell even your sister; much less your mother the nun, for I am ashamed that she should even know I have ever done that kind of thing."[15]

"Do not fear," answered Koremitsu. "Even to the priests, who must to a certain extent be let into the secret, I have told a long made-up tale," and Genji felt a little easier in his mind.

The waiting-women of his palace were sorely puzzled; "First he says he has been defiled and cannot go to Court, and now he sits whispering and sighing." What could it all mean?

"Again I beg you," said Genji at last, "to see that everything is done as it should be." He was thinking all the time of the elaborate Court funerals which he had witnessed (he had, indeed, seen no others) and imagined Koremitsu directing a complicated succession of rituals.

"I will do what I can; it will be no such great matter," he answered and turned to go.

Suddenly Genji could bear no longer the thought that he should never see her again. "You will think it very foolish of me," he said, "but I am coming with you. I shall ride on horseback."

"If your heart is set upon it," said Koremitsu, "it is not for me to reason with you. Let us start soon, so that we may be back before the night is over." So putting on the hunting-dress and other garments in which he had disguised himself before, he left his room.

Already the most hideous anguish possessed him, and now, as he set out upon this strange journey, to the dark thoughts that filled his mind was added a dread lest his visit might rouse to some fresh fury the

---

[15] I.e. pursued illicit amours.

mysterious power which had destroyed her. Should he go? He hesitated; but though he knew that this way lay no cure for his sadness, yet if he did not see her now, never again perhaps in any life to come would he meet the face and form that he had loved so well. So with Koremitsu and the one same groom to bear him company he set out upon the road.

The way seemed endless. The moon of the seventeenth night had risen and lit up the whole space of the Kamo plain, and in the light of the outrunners' torches the countryside towards Toribeno now came dimly into sight. But Genji in his sickness and despair saw none of this, and suddenly waking from the stupor into which he had fallen found that they had arrived.

The nun's cell was in a chapel built against the wall of a wooden house. It was a desolate spot, but the chapel itself was very beautiful. The light of the visitors' torches flickered through the open door. In the inner room there was no sound but that of a woman weeping by herself; in the outer room were several priests talking together (or was it praying?) in hushed voices. In the neighbouring temples vespers were over and there was absolute stillness; only towards the Kiyomizu were lights visible and many figures seemed to throng the hillside.[16]

A senior priest, son of the aged nun, now began to recite the Scriptures in an impressive voice, and Genji as he listened felt the tears come into his eyes. He went in. Ukon was lying behind a screen; when she heard him enter, she turned the lamp to the wall. What terrible thing was she trying to hide from him? But when he came nearer he saw to his joy that the dead lady was not changed in any way whatsoever, but lay there very calm and beautiful; and feeling no horror or fear at all he took her hand and said, "Speak to me once again; tell me why for so short a while you came to me and filled my heart with gladness, and then so soon forsook me, who loved you so well?" and he wept long and bitterly by her side.

The priests did not know who he was, but they were touched by his evident misery and themselves shed tears. He asked Ukon to come back with him, but she answered: "I have served this lady since she was a little child and never once for so much as an hour have I left her. How can I suddenly part from one who was so dear to me and serve in another's house? And I must now go and tell her people what has become of her; for (such is the manner of her death) if I do not speak

---

[16] Pilgrimages to Kiyomizu Temple are made on the seventeenth day.

soon, there will be an outcry that it was I who was to blame, and that would be a terrible thing for me, Sir," and she burst into tears, wailing "I will lie with her upon the pyre; my smoke shall mingle with hers!"

"Poor soul," said Genji, "I do not wonder at your despair. But this is the way of the world. Late or soon we must all go where she has gone. Take comfort and trust in me." So he sought to console her, but in a moment he added: "Those, I know, are but hollow words. I too care no longer for life and would gladly follow her." So he spoke, giving her in the end but little comfort.

"The night is far spent," said Koremitsu; "we must now be on our way." And so with many backward looks and a heart full to bursting he left the house. A heavy dew had fallen and the mist was so thick that it was hard to see the road. On the way it occurred to him that she was still wearing his scarlet cloak, which he had lent her when they lay down together on the last evening. How closely their lives had been entwined!

Noting that he sat very unsteadily in his saddle, Koremitsu walked beside him and gave him a hand. But when they came to a dyke, he lost hold and his master fell to the ground. Here he lay in great pain and bewilderment. "I shall not live to finish the journey," he said; "I have not strength to go so far."

Koremitsu too was sorely troubled, for he felt that despite all Genji's insistence, he ought never to have allowed him, fever-stricken as he was, to embark upon this disastrous journey. In great agitation he plunged his hands in the river and prayed to Our Lady Kwannon of Kiyomizu. Genji too roused himself at last and forced himself to pray inwardly to the Buddha. And so they managed to start upon their journey again and in the end with Koremitsu's help he reached his palace.

This sudden journey undertaken so late at night had seemed to all his household the height of imprudence. They had noted for some while past his nightly wanderings grow more and more frequent; but though often agitated and preoccupied, never had he returned so haggard as that morning. What could be the object of these continual excursions? And they shook their heads in great concern. Genji flung himself upon his bed and lay there in fever and pain for several days. He was growing very weak. The news was brought to the Emperor who was greatly distressed and ordered continual prayers to be said for him in all the great temples; and indeed there were more special services and purification-ceremonies and incantations than I have room to rehearse. When it became known that this prince so famous for his great charm and beauty, was likely soon to die, there was a great stir in all the kingdom.

Sick though he was he did not forget to send for Ukon and have her enrolled among his gentlewomen. Koremitsu, who was beside himself with anxiety concerning his master, yet managed on her arrival to calm himself and give to Ukon friendly instruction in her new duties; for he was touched by the helpless plight in which she had been left. And Genji, whenever he felt a little better, would use her to carry messages and letters, so that she soon grew used to waiting upon him. She was dressed in deep black and though not at all handsome was a pleasant enough looking woman.

"It seems that the same fate which so early stayed your lady's course has willed that I too should be but little longer for this world. I know in what sore distress you are left by the loss of one who was for so many years your mistress and friend; and it was my purpose to have comforted you in your bereavement by every care and kindness I could devise. For this reason, indeed, it grieves me that I shall survive her for so short a time." So, somewhat stiltedly, he whispered to Ukon, and being now very weak he could not refrain from tears. Apart from the fact that his death would leave her utterly without resource, she had now quite taken to him and would have been very sorry indeed if he had died.

His gentlemen ran hither and thither, distracted; the Emperor's envoys thronged thick as the feet of the raindrops. Hearing of his father's distress and anxiety, Genji strove hard to reassure him by pretending to some slight respite or improvement. His father-in-law too showed great concern, calling everyday for news and ordering the performance of various rites and potent liturgies; and it was perhaps as a result of this, that having been dangerously ill for more than twenty days, he took a turn for the better, and soon all his symptoms began to disappear. On the night of his recovery the term of his defilement also ended and hearing that the Emperor was still extremely uneasy about him, he determined to reassure the Court by returning to his official residence at the Palace. His father-in-law came to fetch him in his own carriage and rather irritatingly urged upon him all sorts of remedies and precautions.

For some while everything in the world to which he had now returned seemed strange to him and he indeed scarce knew himself; but by the twentieth day of the ninth month his recovery was complete, nor did the pallor and thinness of his face become him by any means ill.

At times he would stare vacantly before him and burst into loud weeping, and seeing this there were not wanting those who said that he was surely possessed.

Often he would send for Ukon, and once when they had been talking in the still of the evening he said to her, "There is one thing which still puzzles me. Why would she never tell me who she was? For even if she was indeed, as she once said, 'a fisherman's child,' it was a strange perversity to use such reticence with one who loved her so well."

"You ask why she hid her name from you?" said Ukon. "Can you wonder at it? When could she have been expected to tell you her name (not that it would have meant much to you if you had heard it)? For from the beginning you treated her with a strange mistrust, coming with such secrecy and mystery as might well make her doubt whether you were indeed a creature of the waking world. But though you never told her she knew well enough who you were, and the thought that you would not be thus secret had you regarded her as more than a mere plaything or idle distraction was very painful to her."

"What a wretched series of misunderstandings," said Genji. "For my part I had no mind to put a distance between us. But I had no experience in such affairs as this. There are many difficulties in the path of such people as I. First and foremost I feared the anger of my father the Emperor; and then, the foolish jesting of the world. I felt myself hedged in by courtly rules and restrictions. But for all the tiresome concealments that my rank forced upon me, from that first evening I had so strangely set my heart upon her that though reason counselled me I could not hold back; and indeed it seems sometimes to me that an irresistible fate drove me to do the thing of which I now so bitterly and continually repent. But tell me more about her. For there can now be no reason for concealment. When on each seventh day I cause the names of the Buddhas to be written for her comfort and salvation, whom am I to name in my inward prayer?"

"There can be no harm in my telling you that," said Ukon, "and I should have done so before, did I not somehow feel it a shame to be prating to you now about things she would not have me speak of while she was alive. Her parents died when she was quite small. Her father, Sammi Chūjō, loved her very dearly, but felt always that he could not give her all the advantages to which her great beauty entitled her; and still perplexed about her future and how best to do his duty by her, he died. Soon afterwards some accident brought her into the company of

Tō no Chūjō[17] who was at that time still a lieutenant and for three years he made her very happy. But in the autumn of last year disquieting letters began to arrive from the Great Hall of the Right,[18] and being by nature prone to fits of unreasoning fear she now fell into a wild panic and fled to the western part of the town where she hid herself in the house of her old wet-nurse. Here she was very uncomfortable, and had planned to move to a certain village in the hills, when she discovered that it would be unlucky, owing to the position of the stars since the beginning of the year, to make a journey in that direction; and (though she never told me so) I think, Sir, it troubled her sorely that you should have come upon her when she was living in so wretched a place. But there was never anyone in the world like my lady for keeping things to herself; she could never bear that other people should know what was on her mind. I have no doubt, Sir, that she sometimes behaved very oddly to you and that you have seen all this for yourself."

Yes, this was all just as Tō no Chūjō had described.

"I think there was some mention of a child that Chūjō was vexed to have lost sight of," said Genji more interested than ever; "am I right?"

"Yes, indeed," she answered, "it was born in the spring of last year, a girl, and a fine child it was."

"Where is it now?" asked Genji. "Could you get hold of it and bring it to me here without letting anyone know where you were taking it? It would be a great comfort to me in my present misery to have some remembrance of her near me;" and he added, "I ought of course to tell Chūjō, but that would lead to useless and painful discussions about what has happened. Somehow or other I will manage to bring her up here in my palace. I think there can be no harm in that. And you will easily enough find some story to tell to whatever people are now looking after her."

"I am very glad that this has entered your head," said Ukon, "it would be a poor look-out for her to grow up in the quarter where she is now living. With no one properly belonging to her and in such a part of the town. . ."

In the stillness of the evening, under a sky of exquisite beauty, here and there along the borders in front of his palace some insect croaked its song; the leaves were just beginning to turn. And as he looked upon this pleasant picture he felt ashamed at the contrast between his surroundings and the little house where Yūgao had lived. Suddenly

---

[17] Chūjō means "Captain"; see above, p. 71.
[18] From Tō no Chūjō's wife, who was the daughter of the Minister of the Right.

somewhere among the bamboo groves the bird called iyebato uttered its sharp note. He remembered just how she had looked when in the gardens of that fatal house the same bird had startled her by its cry, and turning to Ukon, "How old was she?" he suddenly asked; "for though she seemed childlike in her diffidence and helplessness, that may only have been a sign that she was not long for this world."

"She must have been nineteen," said Ukon. "When my mother, who was her first wet-nurse, died and left me an orphan, my lady's father was pleased to notice me and reared me at my lady's side. Ah Sir, when I think of it, I do not know how I shall live without her; for kind as people here may be I do not seem to get used to them. I suppose it is that I knew her ways, poor lady, she having been my mistress for so many years."

To Genji even the din of the cloth-beaters' mallets had become dear through recollection, and as he lay in bed he repeated those verses of Po Chü-i, "*In the eighth month and ninth month when the nights are growing long A thousand times, ten thousand times the fuller's stick beats.*"

The young brother still waited upon him, but he no longer brought with him the letters which he had been used to bring. Utsusemi thought he had at last decided that her treatment of him was too unfriendly to be borne, and was vexed that he should feel so. Then suddenly she heard of his illness, and all her vexation turned to consternation and anxiety. She was soon to set out upon her long journey, but this did not much interest her; and to see whether Genji had quite forgotten her she sent him a message saying that she had been able to find no words in which to express her grief at hearing the news of his illness. With it she sent the poem: "*I did not ask for news and you did not ask why I was silent; so the days wore on and I remained in sorrow and dismay.*"

He had not forgotten her, no, not in all his trouble; and his answer came:

"*Of this life, fragile as the utsusemi's[19] shell, already I was weary, when your word came, and gave me strength to live anew.*"

The poem was written in a very tremulous and confused hand; but she thought the writing very beautiful and it delighted her that he had not forgotten how, cicada-like, she had shed her scarf. There could be no harm in this interchange of notes, but she had no intention of arranging a meeting. She thought that at last even he had seen that there could be no sense in that.

---

[19] Cicada.

As for Utsusemi's companion, she was not yet married, and Genji heard that she had become the mistress of Tō no Chūjō's brother Kurōdo no Shōshō; and though he feared that Shōshō might already have taken very ill the discovery that he was not first in the field, and did not at all wish to offend him, yet he had a certain curiosity about the girl and sent Utsusemi's little brother with a message asking if she had heard of his illness and the poem: *"Had I not once gathered for my pillow a handful of the sedge that grows upon the eaves,*[20] *not a dewdrop of pretext could my present message find."*

It was an acrostic with many hidden meanings. He tied the letter to a tall reed and bade him deliver it secretly; but was afterwards very uneasy at the thought that it might go astray.

"If it falls into Shōshō's hands," he thought, "he will at once guess that it was I who was before him." But after all Shōshō would probably not take that so very hard, Genji had vanity enough to think.

The boy delivered the message when Shōshō was at a safe distance. She could not help feeling a little hurt; but it was something that he had remembered her at all, and justifying it to herself with the excuse that she had had no time to do anything better, she sent the boy straight back with the verse: *"The faint wind of your favour, that but for a moment blew, with grief has part befrosted the small sedge of the eaves."* It was very ill-written, with all sorts of ornamental but misleading strokes and flourishes; indeed with a complete lack of style. However, it served to remind him of the face he had first seen that evening by the lamplight. As for the other who on that occasion had sat so stiffly facing her, what determination there had been in her face, what a steady resolution to give no quarter!

The affair with the lady of the sedge was so unintentional and so insignificant that though he regarded it as rather frivolous and indiscreet, he saw no great harm in it. But if he did not take himself in hand before it was too late he would soon again be involved in some entanglement which might finally ruin his reputation.

On the forty-ninth day after Yūgao's death a service in her memory was by his orders secretly held in the Hokedō on Mount Hiyei. The ritual performed was of the most elaborate kind, everything that was required being supplied from the Prince's own store; and even the decoration of the service books and images was carried out with

---

[20] 'Sedge upon the eaves' is *Nokiba no Ogi*, and it is by this name that the lady is generally known.

the utmost attention. Koremitsu's brother, a man of great piety, was entrusted with the direction of the ceremony, and all went well. Next Genji sent for his old writing-master, a doctor of letters for whom he had a great liking and bade him write the prayer for the dead.[21]

"Say that I commit to Amida the Buddha one not named whom I loved, but lost disastrously," and he wrote out a rough draft for the learned man to amend.

"There is nothing to add or alter," said the master, deeply moved. Who could it be, he wondered, at whose death the prince was so distressed? (For Genji, try as he might, could not hide his tears.)

When he was secretly looking through his store for largesse to give to the Hokedō priests, he came upon a certain dress and as he folded it made the poem: "*The girdle that today with tears I knot, shall we ever in some new life untie?*"

Till now her spirit had wandered in the void.[22]

But already she must be setting out on her new life-path, and in great solicitude, he prayed continually for her safety.

He met Tō no Chūjō and his heart beat violently, for he had longed to tell him about Yūgao's child and how it was to be reared. But he feared that the rest of the story would needlessly anger and distress him, and he did not mention the matter. Meanwhile the servants of Yūgao's house were surprised that they had had no news from her nor even from Ukon, and had begun to be seriously disquieted. They had still no proof that it was Genji who was her lover, but several of them thought that they had recognized him and his name was whispered among them. They would have it that Koremitsu knew the secret, but he pretended to know nothing whatever about Yūgao's lover and found a way to put off all their questions; and as he was still frequenting the house for his own purposes, it was easy for them to believe that he was not really concerned in their mistress's affairs. Perhaps after all it was some blackguard of a Zuryō's son who, frightened of Tō no Chūjō's interference, had carried her off to his province. The real owner of the house was a daughter of Yūgao's second wet-nurse, who had three children of her own. Ukon had been brought up with them, but they thought that it was perhaps

---

[21] *Gwammon.*

[22] For forty-nine days the spirit of the dead leads the intermediate existence so strangely described in the *Abhidharma Kośa Śāstra*; then it begins its new incarnation.

because she was not their own sister that Ukon sent them no news of their mistress, and they were in great distress.

Ukon who knew that they would assail her with questions which her promise to Genji forbade her to answer, dared not go to the house, not even to get news of her lady's child. It had been put out somewhere to nurse, but to her great sorrow she had quite lost sight of it.

Longing all the while to see her face once more though only in a dream, upon the night after the ceremony on Mount Hiyei, he had a vision very different from that for which he prayed. There appeared to him once more, just as on that fatal night, the figure of a woman in menacing posture, and he was dismayed at the thought that some demon which haunted the desolate spot might on the occasion when it did that terrible thing, also have entered into him and possessed him.

Iyo no Suke was to start early in the Godless Month and had announced that his wife would go with him. Genji sent very handsome parting presents and among them with special intent he put many very exquisite combs and fans. With them were silk strips to offer to the God of Journeys and, above all, the scarf which she had dropped, and, tied to it, a poem in which he said that he had kept it in remembrance of her while there was still hope of their meeting, but now returned it wet with tears shed in vain. There was a long letter with the poem, but this was of no particular interest and is here omitted. She sent no answer by the man who had brought the presents, but gave her brother the poem: *"That to the changed cicada you should return her summer dress shows that you too have changed and fills an insect heart with woe."*

He thought long about her. Though she had with so strange and inexplicable a resolution steeled her heart against him to the end, yet each time he remembered that she had gone forever it filled him with depression.

It was the first day of the tenth month, and as though in sign that winter had indeed begun heavy rain fell. All day long Genji watched the stormy sky. Autumn had hideously bereaved him and winter already was taking from him one whom he dearly loved:

> *Now like a traveller who has tried two ways in vain*
> *I stand perplexed where these sad seasons meet.*

Now at least we must suppose he was convinced that such secret adventures led only to misery.

I should indeed be very loth to recount in all their detail matters which he took so much trouble to conceal, did I not know that if you found I had omitted anything you would at once ask why, just because he was supposed to be an Emperor's son, I must needs put a favourable showing on his conduct by leaving out all his indiscretions; and you would soon be saying that this was no history but a mere made-up tale designed to influence the judgment of posterity. As it is I shall be called a scandal-monger; but that I cannot help.

V

Murasaki

He fell sick of an ague, and when numerous charms and spells had been tried in vain, the illness many times returning, someone said that in a certain temple on the Northern Hills there lived a wise and holy man who in the summer of the year before (the ague was then rife and the usual spells were giving no relief) was able to work many signal cures: "Lose no time in consulting him, for while you try one useless means after another the disease gains greater hold upon you." At once he sent a messenger to fetch the holy man, who however replied that the infirmities of old age no longer permitted him to go abroad.

"What is to be done?" said Genji; "I must go secretly to visit him"; and taking only four or five trusted servants he set out long before dawn. The place lay somewhat deep into the hills. It was the last day of the third month and in the Capital the blossoms had all fallen. The hill-cherry was not yet out; but as he approached the open country, the mists began to assume strange and lovely forms, which pleased him the more because, being one whose movements were tethered by many proprieties, he had seldom seen such sights before. The temples too delighted him. The holy man lived in a deep cave hollowed out of a high wall of rock. Genji did not send in his name and was in close disguise, but his face was well known and the priest at once recognized him.

"Forgive me," he said; "it was you, was it not, who sent for me the other day? Alas, I think no longer of the things of this world and I am afraid I have forgotten how to work my cures. I am very sorry indeed that you have come so far," and pretending to be very much upset, he looked at Genji, laughing. But it was soon apparent that he was a man of very great piety and learning. He wrote out certain talismans and administered them, and read certain spells. By the time this was over, the sun had risen, and Genji went a little way outside the cave and looked around him. From the high ground where he was standing he looked down on a number of scattered hermitages. A winding track led down to a hut which, though it was hedged with the same small brushwood as the rest, was more spaciously planned, having a pleasant roofed alley running out from it, and there were trim copses set around. He asked whose house it was and was told by one of his men that a certain abbot had been living there in retirement for two years.

"I know him well," said Genji on hearing the abbot's name; "I should not like to meet him dressed and attended as I am. I hope he will not hear. . ." Just then a party of nicely dressed children came out of the house and began to pluck such flowers as are used for the decoration of altars and holy images.

"There are some girls with them," said one of Genji's men. "We cannot suppose that His Reverence keeps them. Who then can they be?" and to satisfy his curiosity he went a little way down the hill and watched them.

"Yes, there are some very pretty girls, some of them grown up and others quite children," he came back and reported.

During a great part of the morning Genji was busy with his cure. When at last the ceremony was completed his attendants, dreading the hour at which the fever usually returned, strove to distract his attention by taking him a little way across the mountain to a point from which the Capital could be seen.

"How lovely," cried Genji, "are those distances half lost in haze, and that blur of shimmering woods that stretches out on every side. How could anyone be unhappy for a single instant who lived in such a place?"

"This is nothing," said one of his men. "If I could but show you the lakes and mountains of other provinces, you would soon see how far they excel all that you here admire"; and he began to tell him first of Mount Fuji and many another famous peak, and then of the West Country with all its pleasant bays and shores, till he quite forgot that it was the hour of his fever.

"Yonder, nearest to us," the man continued, pointing to the sea, "is the bay of Akashi in Harima. Note it well; for though it is not a very out-of-the-way place, yet the feeling one has there of being shut off from everything save one huge waste of sea makes it the strangest and most desolate spot I know. And there it is that the daughter of a lay priest who was once governor of the province presides over a mansion of quite disproportionate and unexpected magnificence. He is the descendant of a Prime Minister and was expected to cut a great figure in the world. But he is a man of very singular disposition and is averse to all society. For a time he was an officer in the Palace Guard, but he gave this up and accepted the province of Harima. However he soon quarrelled with the local people and, announcing that he had been badly treated and was going back to the Capital, he did nothing of the sort, but shaved his head and became a lay priest. Then instead of settling, as is usually done, on some secluded hillside, he built himself a house on the seashore, which may seem to you a very strange thing to do; but as a matter of fact, whereas in that province in one place or another a good many recluses have taken up their abode, the mountain-country is far more dull and lonely and would sorely have tried the patience of his young wife and child; and so as a compromise he chose the seashore. Once when I was travelling in the province of Harima I took occasion to visit his house and noted that, though at the Capital he had lived in a very modest style, here he had built on the most magnificent and lavish scale; as though determined in spite of what had happened (now that he was free from the bother of governing the province) to spend the rest of his days in the greatest comfort imaginable. But all the while he was making great preparations for the life to come and no ordained priest could have led a more austere and pious life."

"But you spoke of his daughter?" said Genji.

"She is passably good-looking," he answered, "and not by any means stupid. Several governors and officers of the province have set their hearts upon her and pressed their suit most urgently; but her father has sent them all away. It seems that though in his own person so indifferent to worldly glory, he is determined that this one child, his only object of care, should make amends for his obscurity, and has sworn that if ever she chooses against his will, and when he is gone flouts his set purpose and injunction to satisfy some idle fancy of her own, his ghost will rise and call upon the sea to cover her."

Genji listened with great attention.

"Why, she is like the vestal virgin who may know no husband but the King-Dragon of the Sea," and they laughed at the old ex-Governor's absurd ambitions. The teller of the story was a son of the present Governor of Harima, who from being a clerk in the Treasury had last year been capped an officer of the Fifth Rank. He was famous for his love-adventures and the others whispered to one another that it was with every intention of persuading the lady to disobey her father's injunctions that he had gone out of his way to visit the shore of Akashi.

"I fear her breeding must be somewhat countrified," said one; "it cannot well be otherwise, seeing that she has grown up with no other company than that of her old-fashioned parents,—though indeed it appears that her mother was a person of some consequence."

"Why, yes," said Yoshikiyo, the Governor's son, "and for this reason she was able to secure little girls and boys from all the best houses in the Capital, persuading them to pay visits to the sea-side and be playmates to her own little girl, who thus acquired the most polished breeding."

"If an unscrupulous person were to find himself in that quarter," said another, "I fear that despite the dead father's curse he might not find it easy to resist her."

The story made a deep impression upon Genji's imagination. As his gentlemen well knew, whatever was fantastic or grotesque both in people and situations at once strongly attracted him. They were therefore not surprised to see him listen with so much attention.

"It is now well past noon," said one of them, "and I think we may reckon that you will get safely through the day without a return of your complaint. So let us soon be starting for home."

But the priest persuaded him to stay a little longer: "The sinister influences are not yet wholly banished," he said; "it would be well that a further ritual should continue quietly during the night. By tomorrow morning, I think you will be able to proceed."

His gentlemen all urged him to stay; nor was he at all unwilling, for the novelty of such a lodging amused him.

"Very well then, at dawn," he said, and having nothing to do till bedtime which was still a long way off, he went out on to the hillside, and under cover of the heavy evening mist loitered near the brushwood hedge.

His attendants had gone back to the hermit's cave and only Koremitsu was with him. In the western wing, opposite which he was standing, was a nun at her devotions. The blind was partly raised. He thought she seemed to be dedicating flowers to an image. Sitting near the middle pillar, a sutra-book propped upon a stool by her side, was another nun. She was reading aloud; there was a look of great unhappiness in her face. She seemed to be about forty; not a woman of the common people. Her skin was white and very fine, and though she was much emaciated, there was a certain roundness and fulness in her cheeks, and her hair, clipped short on a level with her eyes, hung in so delicate a fringe across her brow that she looked, thought Genji, more elegant and even fashionable in this convent guise, than if her hair had been long. Two very well-conditioned maids waited upon her. Several little girls came running in and out of the room at play. Among them was one who seemed to be about ten years old. She came running into the room dressed in a rather worn white frock lined with stuff of a deep saffron colour. Never had he seen a child like this. What an astonishing creature she would grow into! Her hair, thick and wavy, stood out fanwise about her head. She was very flushed and her lips were trembling.

"What is it? Have you quarrelled with one of the other little girls?" The nun raised her head as she spoke and Genji fancied that there was some resemblance between her and the child. No doubt she was its mother.

"Inu has let out my sparrow—the little one that I kept in the clothesbasket," she said, looking very unhappy.

"What a tiresome boy that Inu is!" said one of the two maids. "He deserves a good scolding for playing such a stupid trick. Where can it have got to? And this after we had taken so much trouble to tame it nicely! I only hope the crows have not found it," and so saying she left the room. She was a pleasant-looking woman, with very long, wavy hair. The others called her Nurse Shōnagon, and she seemed to be in charge of the child.

"Come," said the nun to the little girl, "you must not be such a baby. You are thinking all the time of things that do not matter at all. Just fancy! Even now when I am so ill that any day I may be taken from you, you do not trouble your head about me, but are grieving about a sparrow. It is very unkind, particularly as I have told you I don't know how many times that it is naughty to shut up live things in cages. Come over here!" and the child sat down beside her. Her features were very exquisite; but it was above all the way her hair grew, in cloudy masses over her temples, but thrust back in childish fashion from her forehead, that struck him as marvellously beautiful. As he watched her and wondered what she would be like when she grew up it suddenly occurred to him that she bore no small resemblance to one whom he had loved with all his being,[1] and at the resemblance he secretly wept.

The nun, stroking the child's hair, now said to her: "It's a lovely mop, though you *are* so naughty about having it combed. But it worries me very much that you are still so babyish. Some children of your age are very different. Your dear mother was only twelve when her father died; yet she showed herself quite capable of managing her own affairs. But if I were taken from you now, I do not know what would become of you, I do not indeed," and she began to weep. Even Genji, peeping at

---

[1] Fujitsubo, who was indeed the child's aunt.

the scene from a distance, found himself becoming quite distressed. The girl, who had been watching the nun's face with a strange unchildish intensity, now dropped her head disconsolately, and as she did so her hair fell forward across her cheeks in two great waves of black. Looking at her fondly the nun recited the poem: "*Not knowing if any will come to nurture the tender leaf whereon it lies, how loath is the dewdrop to vanish in the sunny air.*" To which the waiting-woman replied with a sigh: "O dewdrop, surely you will linger till the young budding leaf has shown in what fair form it means to grow."

At this moment the priest to whom the house belonged entered the room from the other side: "Pray, ladies," he said, "are you not unduly exposing yourselves? You have chosen a bad day to take up your stand so close to the window. I have just heard that Prince Genji has come to the hermit yonder to be cured of an ague. But he has disguised himself in so mean a habit that I did not know him, and have been so near all day without going to pay my respects to him."

The nun started back in horror; "How distressing! He may even have passed and seen us. . ." and she hastened to let down the folding blind. "I am really very glad that I am to have an opportunity of visiting this Prince Genji of whom one hears so much. He is said to be so handsome that even austere old priests like myself forget in his presence the sins and sorrows of the life they have discarded and take heart to live a little longer in a world where so much beauty dwells. But you shall hear all about it. . ."

Before the old priest had time to leave the house Genji was on his way back to the hermit's cave. What an enchanting creature he had discovered! How right too his friends had been on that rainy night when they told him that on strange excursions such as this beauty might well be found lurking in unexpected quarters! How delightful to have strolled out by chance and at once made so astonishing a find! Whose could this exquisite child be? He would dearly love to have her always near him, to be able to turn to her at any moment for comfort and distraction, as once he had turned to the lady in the Palace.

He was already lying down in the hermit's cave when (everything being at very close quarters) he heard the voice of the old priest's disciple calling for Koremitsu.

"My master has just learnt," said this disciple, "that you were lodged so near at hand; and though it grieves him that you did not in passing honour him with a visit, he would at once have paid his respects to the Prince, had he not thought that Lord Genji could not be unaware of his presence in the neighbourhood of this hermitage, and might perhaps have refrained from visiting him only because he did not wish to disclose the motive of his present pilgrimage."

"But my master would remind you," continued the man, "that we too in our poor hut could provide you with straw beds to lie on, and should be sorry if you left without honouring us. . ."

"For ten days," answered Genji from within, "I have been suffering from an ague which returned so constantly that I was in despair, when someone advised me to consult the hermit of this mountain, whom I accordingly visited. But thinking that it would be very disagreeable for a sage of his repute if in such a case as mine it became known that his treatment had been unsuccessful, I was at greater pains to conceal myself than I should have been if visiting an ordinary wonder-worker. Pray ask your master to accept this excuse and bid him enter the cave." Thus encouraged, the priest presented himself.

Genji was rather afraid of him, for though an ecclesiastic he was a man of superior genius, very much respected in the secular world, and Genji felt that it was not at all proper to receive him in the shabby old clothes which he had used for his disguise. After giving some details of his life since he had left the Capital and come to live in retirement on this mountain, the priest begged Genji to come back with him and visit the cold spring which flowed in the garden of his hut. Here was an opportunity to see again the people who had so much interested him. But the thought of all the stories that the old priest might have told them about him made him feel rather uncomfortable. What matter? At all costs he must see that lovely child again and he followed the old priest back to his hut. In the garden the natural vegetation of the hillside had been turned to skilful use. There was no moon, and torches had been lit along the sides of the moat, while fairy lanterns hung on the trees. The front parlour was very nicely arranged. A heavy perfume of costly and exotic scents stole from hidden incense-burners and filled the room with a delicious fragrance. These perfumes were quite unfamiliar to Genji and he supposed that they must have been prepared by the ladies of the inner room, who would seem to have spent considerable ingenuity in the task.

The priest began to tell stories about the uncertainty of this life and the retributions of the life to come. Genji was appalled to think how heavy his own sins had already been. It was bad enough to think that he would have them on his conscience for the rest of his present life. But then there was also the life to come. What terrible punishments he had to look forward to! And all the while the priest was speaking Genji thought of his own wickedness. What a good idea it would be to turn hermit and live in some such place. . . But immediately his thoughts strayed to the lovely face which he had seen that afternoon and longing to know more of her.

"Who lives with you here?" he asked. "It interests me to know, because I once saw this place in a dream and was astonished to recognize it when I came here today."

At this the priest laughed: "Your dream seems to have come rather suddenly into the conversation," he said, "but I fear that if you pursue your enquiry, your expectations will be sadly disappointed. You have probably never heard of Azechi no Dainagon, he died so long ago. He married my sister, who after his death turned her back upon the world. Just at that time I myself was in certain difficulties and was unable to visit the Capital; so for company she came to join me here in my retreat."

"I have heard that Aseji no Dainagon had a daughter. Is that so?" said Genji at a venture; "I am sure you will not think I ask the question with any indiscreet intention. . ."

"He had an only daughter who died about ten years ago. Her father had always wanted to present her at Court. But she would not listen, and when he was dead and there was only my sister the nun to look after her, she allowed some wretched go-between to introduce her to Prince Hyōbukyō whose mistress she became. His wife, a proud, relentless woman, from the first pursued her with constant vexations and affronts; day in and day out this obstinate persecution continued, till at last she died of heartbreak. They say that unkindness cannot kill; but I shall never say so, for from this cause alone I saw my kinswoman fall sick and perish."

"Then the little girl must be this lady's child," Genji realized at last. And that accounted for her resemblance to the lady in the Palace.[2] He felt more drawn towards her than ever. She was of good lineage, which is never amiss; and her rather rustic simplicity would be an actual advantage when she became his pupil, as he was now determined she should; for it would make it the easier for him to mould her unformed tastes to the pattern of his own.

---

[2] Fujitsubo, who was Hyōbukyō's sister.

"And did the lady whose sad story you have told me leave no remembrance behind her?" asked Genji, still hoping to turn the conversation on to the child herself.

"She died only a short while after her child was born, and it too was a girl. The charge of it fell to my sister who is in failing health and feels herself by no means equal to such a responsibility."

All was now clear.

"You will think it a very strange proposal," said Genji, "but I feel that I should like to adopt this child. Perhaps you would mention this to your sister? Though others early involved me in marriage, their choice proved distasteful to me and having, as it seems, very little relish for society, I now live entirely alone. She is, I quite realize, a mere child, and I am not proposing. . ."

Here he paused and the priest answered: "I am very much obliged to you for this offer; but I am afraid it is clear that you do *not* at all realize that the child in question is a mere infant. You would not even find her amusing as a casual distraction. But it is true that a girl as she grows up needs the backing of powerful friends if she is to make her way in the world, and though I cannot promise you that anything will come of it, I ought certainly to mention the matter to her grandmother."

His manner had suddenly become somewhat cool and severe. Genji felt that he had been indiscreet and preserved an embarrassed silence.

"There is something which I ought to be doing in the Hall of Our Lord Amida," the priest presently continued, "so I must take leave of you for a while. I must also read my vespers; but I will rejoin you afterwards," and he set out to climb the hill.

Genji felt very disconsolate. It had begun to rain; a cold wind blew across the hill, carrying with it the sound of a waterfall,—audible till then as a gentle intermittent plashing, but now a mighty roar; and with it, somnolently rising and falling, mingled the monotonous chanting of the scriptures. Even the most unimpressionable nature would have been plunged into melancholy by such surroundings. How much the more so Prince Genji, as he lay sleepless on his bed, continually planning and counter-planning! The priest had spoken of "vespers," but the hour was indeed very late. It was clear however that the nun was still awake, for though she was making as little noise as possible, every now and then her rosary would knock with a faint click against the praying-stool. There was something alluring in the sound of this low, delicate tapping.

It seemed to come from quite close. He opened a small space between the screens which divided the living room from the inner chamber and rustled his fan. He had the impression that someone in the inner room after a little hesitation had come towards the screen as though saying to herself, "It cannot be so, yet I could have sworn I heard. . ." and then retreated a little, as though thinking "Well, it was only my fancy after all!" Now she seemed to be feeling her way in the dark, and Genji said aloud, "Follow the Lord Buddha and though your way lie in darkness yet shall you not go astray."

Suddenly hearing his clear young voice in the darkness, the woman had not at first the courage to reply. But at last she managed to answer: "In which direction, please, is he leading me? I am afraid I do not quite understand."

"I am sorry to have startled you," said Genji. "I have only this small request to make: that you will carry to your mistress the following poem: *Since first he saw the green leaf of the tender bush, never for a moment has the dew of longing dried from the traveller's sleeve.*"

"Surely you must know that there is no one here who understands messages of that kind," said the woman; "I wonder whom you mean?"

"I have a particular reason for wishing your mistress to receive the message," said Genji, "and I should be obliged if you would contrive to deliver it."

The nun at once perceived that the poem referred to her grandchild and supposed that Genji, having been wrongly informed about her age, was intending to make love to her. But how had he discovered her granddaughter's existence? For some while she pondered in great annoyance and perplexity, and at last answered prudently with a poem in which she said that, "*he who was but spending a night upon a traveller's dewy bed could know little of those whose home was forever upon the cold moss of the hillside.*" Thus she turned his poem to a harmless meaning.

"Tell her," said Genji when the message was brought back, "that I am not accustomed to carry on conversations in this indirect manner. However shy she may be, I must ask her on this occasion to dispense with formalities and discuss this matter with me seriously!"

"How can he have been thus misinformed?" said the nun, still thinking that Genji imagined her granddaughter to be a grown-up woman. She was terrified at being suddenly commanded to appear before this illustrious personage and was wondering what excuse she would make.

Her maids, however, were convinced that Genji would be grievously offended if she did not appear, and at last, coming out from the women's chamber, she said to him: "Though I am no longer a young woman, I very much doubt whether I ought to come like this. But since you sent word that you have serious business to discuss with me, I could not refuse. . ."

"Perhaps," said Genji, "you will think my proposal both ill-timed and frivolous. I can only assure you that I mean it very seriously. Let Buddha judge. . ." But here he broke off, intimidated by her age and gravity.

"You have certainly chosen a very strange manner of communicating this proposal to me. But though you have not yet said what it is, I am sure you are quite in earnest about it."

Thus encouraged, Genji continued: "I was deeply touched by the story of your long widowhood and of your daughter's death. I too, like this poor child, was deprived in earliest infancy of the one being who tenderly loved me, and in my childhood suffered long years of loneliness and misery. Thus we are both in like case, and this has given me so deep a sympathy for the child that I long to make amends for what she has lost. It was, then, to ask if you would consent to let me play a mother's part that at this strange and inconvenient hour I trespassed so inconsiderately upon your patience."

"I am sure that you are meaning to be very kind," said the nun, "but— forgive me—you have evidently been misinformed. There is indeed a girl living here under my charge; but she is a mere infant and could not be of the slightest interest to you in any way, so that I cannot consent to your proposal."

"On the contrary," said Genji, "I am perfectly conversant with every detail concerning this child; but if you think my sympathy for her exaggerated or misplaced, pray pardon me for having mentioned it." It was evident that he did not in the least realize the absurdity of what he had proposed, and she saw no use in explaining herself any further. The priest was now returning and Genji, saying that he had not expected she would at once fall in with his idea and was confident that she would soon see the matter in a different light, closed the screen behind her.

The night was almost over. In a chapel near by, the Four Meditations of the Law Flower were being practised. The voices of the ministrants who were now chanting the Litany of Atonement came floating on the gusty mountain-wind, and with this solemn sound was mingled the roar of hurrying waters.

Startled from my dream by a wandering gust of the mountain gale,
I heard the waterfall, and at the beauty of its music wept.

So Genji greeted the priest; and he in turn replied with the poem, *"At the noise of a torrent wherein I daily fill my bowl I am scarce likely to start back in wonder and delight."*

"I get so used to it," he added apologetically. A heavy mist covered the morning sky, and even the chirruping of the mountain-birds sounded muffled and dim. Such a variety of flowers and blossoming trees (he did not know their names) grew upon the hillside, that the rocks seemed to be spread with a many-coloured embroidery. Above all he marvelled at the exquisite stepping of the deer who moved across the slope, now treading daintily, now suddenly pausing; and as he watched them the last remnants of his sickness were dispelled by sheer delight. Though the hermit had little use of his limbs, he managed by hook or crook to perform the mystic motions of the Guardian Spell,[3] and though his aged voice was husky and faltering, he read the sacred text with great dignity and fervour. Several of Genji's friends now arrived to congratulate him upon his recovery, among them a messenger from the Palace. The priest from the hut below brought a present of strange-looking roots for which he had gone deep into the ravine. He begged to be excused from accompanying Genji on his way.

"Till the end of the year," he said, "I am bound by a vow which must deprive me of what would have been a great pleasure," and he handed Genji the stirrup-cup.

"Were I but able to follow my own desires," said Genji taking the cup, "I would not leave these hills and streams. But I hear that my father the Emperor is making anxious enquiry after me. I will come back before the blossom is over." And he recited the verse, *"I will go back to the men of*

---

[3] The Guardian Spell (*goshin*) is practised as follows:

The ministrant holds the palms of his hands together with middle fingers touching and extended, first fingers separated and bent, tips of thumbs and little fingers bunched together, and third fingers in line with middle fingers so as to be invisible from in front. With hands in this sacred pose (*mudrā*) he touches the worshipper on forehead, left and right shoulder, heart and throat. At each contact he utters the spell

ON · BASARA GONJI HARAJŪBATA · SOHAKA

which is corrupt Sanskrit and means "I invoke thee, thou diamond-fiery very majestic Star." The deity here invoked is Vairocana, favourite Buddha of the Mystic Sect.

the City and tell them to come quickly, lest the wild wind outstripping them should toss these blossoms from the cherry bough."

The old priest, flattered by Genji's politeness and captivated by the charm of his voice, answered with the poem: "*Like one who finds the aloe-tree in bloom, to the flower of the mountain-cherry I no longer turn my gaze.*"

"I am not after all quite so great a rarity as the aloe-flower," said Genji smiling.

Next the hermit handed him a parting-cup, with the poem, "*Though seldom I open the pine-tree door of my mountain-cell, yet have I now seen face to face the flower few live to see,*" and as he looked up at Genji, his eyes filled with tears.

He gave him, to keep him safe in future from all harm, a magical wand; and seeing this the nun's brother in his turn presented a rosary brought back from Korea by Prince Shōtoku. It was ornamented with jade and was still in the same Chinese-looking box in which it had been brought from that country. The box was in an open-work bag, and a five-leafed pine-branch was with it. He also gave him some little vases of blue crystal to keep his medicines in, with sprays of cherry-blossom and wistaria along with them, and such other presents as the place could supply. Genji had sent to the Capital for gifts with which to repay his reception in the mountain. First he gave a reward to the hermit, then distributed alms to the priests who had chanted liturgies on his behalf, and finally he gave useful presents to the poor villagers of the neighbourhood. While he was reading a short passage from the scriptures in preparation for his departure, the old priest went into his house and asked his sister the nun whether she had any message for the Prince.

"It is very hard to say anything at present," she said. "Perhaps if he still felt the same inclination four, or five years hence, we might begin to consider it."

"That is just what I think," said the priest.

Genji saw to his regret that he had made no progress whatever. In answer to the nun's message he sent a small boy who belonged to the priest's household with the following poem:

Last night indeed, though in the greyness of twilight only, I saw the lovely flower. But today a hateful mist has hidden it utterly from my sight.

The nun replied:

That I may know whether indeed it pains you so deeply
to leave this flower, I shall watch intently the motions of this
hazy sky.

It was written in a noteworthy and very aristocratic hand, but quite without the graces of deliberate artistry. While his carriage was being got ready, a great company of young lords arrived from the Great Hall, saying that they had been hard put to it to discover what had become of him and now desired to give him their escort. Among them were Tō no Chūjō, Sachū Ben, and other lesser lords, who had come out of affection for the Prince.

"We like nothing better than waiting upon you," they said, rather aggrieved, "it was not kind of you to leave us behind."

"But having come so far," said another, "it would be a pity to go away without resting for a while under the shadow of these flowering trees"; whereupon they all sat down in a row upon the moss under a tall rock and passed a rough earthenware wine-jar from hand to hand. Close by them the stream leaped over the rocks in a magnificent cascade. Tō no Chūjō pulled out a flute from the folds of his dress and played a few trills upon it. Sachū Ben, tapping idly with his fan, began to sing "The Temple of Toyora." The young lords who had come to fetch him were all persons of great distinction; but so striking was Genji's appearance as he sat leaning disconsolately against the rock that no eye was likely to be turned in any other direction. One of his attendants now performed upon the reed-pipe; someone else turned out to be a skilful *shō*⁴ player.

Presently the old priest came out of his house carrying a zithern, and putting it into Genji's hands begged him to play something, "that the birds of the mountain may rejoice." He protested that he was not feeling at all in the mood to play; but yielding to the priest's persuasion, he gave what was really not at all a contemptible performance. After that, they all got up and started for home. Everyone on the mountain, down to the humblest priest and youngest neophyte, was bitterly disappointed at the shortness of his stay, and there were many tears shed; while the old nun within doors was sorry to think that she had had but that one brief glimpse of him and might never see him again. The priest declared that for his part he thought the Land of the Rising Sun in her last degenerate days ill-deserved that such a Prince should be born to her,

---

⁴ A Chinese instrument; often translated "mouth-organ."

and he wiped his eyes. The little girl too was very much pleased with him and said he was a prettier gentleman than her own father.

"If you think so, you had better become his little girl instead," said her nurse. At which the child nodded, thinking that it would be a very good plan indeed; and in future the best-dressed person in the pictures she painted was called "Prince Genji" and so was her handsomest doll.

On his return to the Capital he went straight to the Palace and described to his father the experiences of the last two days. The Emperor thought him looking very haggard and was much concerned. He asked many questions about the hermit's magical powers, to all of which Genji replied in great detail.

"He ought certainly to have been made Master Magician long ago," said His Majesty. "His ministrations have repeatedly been attended with great success, but for some reason his services have escaped public acknowledgment," and he issued a proclamation to this effect. The Minister of the Left came to meet him on his way from the Presence and apologized for not having come with his sons to bring him back from the mountain.

"I thought," he said, "that as you had gone there secretly, you would dislike being fetched; but I very much hope that you will now come and spend a few days with us quietly; after which I shall esteem it a privilege to escort you to your palace."

He did not in the least want to go, but there was no escape. His father-in-law drove him to the Great Hall in his own carriage, and when the bullocks had been unyoked dragged it in at the gate with his own hands. Such treatment was certainly meant to be very friendly; but Genji found the Minister's attentions merely irritating.

Aoi's quarters had, in anticipation of Genji's coming, just been put thoroughly to rights. In the long interval since he last visited her many changes had been made; among other improvements, a handsome terrace had been built. Not a thing was out of its right place in this supremely well-ordered house. Aoi, as usual, was nowhere to be seen. It was only after repeated entreaties by her father that she at last consented to appear in her husband's presence. Posed like a princess in a picture she sat almost motionless. Beautiful she certainly was.

"I should like to tell you about my visit to the mountain, if only I thought that it would interest you at all or draw an answer from you. I hate to go on always like this. Why are you so cold and distant and proud? Year after year we fail to reach an understanding and you cut yourself off from me more completely than before. Can we not manage for a little while to be on ordinary terms? It seems rather strange, considering how ill I have been, that you should not attempt to enquire after my health. Or rather, it is exactly what I should expect; but nevertheless I find it extremely painful."

"Yes," said Aoi, "it is extremely painful when people do not care what becomes of one." She glanced back over her shoulder as she spoke, her face full of scorn and pride, looking uncommonly handsome as she did so.

"You hardly ever speak," said Genji, "and when you do, it is only to say unkind things and twist one's harmless words so that they seem to be insults. And when I try to find some way of helping you for a while at least to be a little less disagreeable, you become more hopelessly unapproachable than ever. Shall I one day succeed in making you understand. . . ?" and so saying he went into their bedroom. She did not follow him.

He lay for a while in a state of great annoyance and distress. But, probably because he did not really care about her very much one way or the other, he soon became drowsy and all sorts of quite different matters drifted through his head. He wanted as much as ever to have the little girl in his keeping and watch her grow to womanhood. But the grandmother was right; the child was too absurdly young, and it would be very difficult to broach the matter again. Would it not however be possible to contrive that she should be brought to the Capital? It would be easy then to find excuses for fetching her and she might, even through some such arrangement as that, become a source of constant delight to him. The father, Prince Hyōbukyō, was of course a man of very distinguished manners; but he was not at all handsome. How was it that the child resembled one of her aunts and was so unlike all the rest? He had an idea that Fujitsubo and Prince Hyōbukyō were children of the same mother, while the others were only half-sisters. The fact that the little girl was closely related to the lady whom he had loved for so long made him all the more set upon securing her, and he began again to puzzle his head for some means of bringing this about.

Next day he wrote his letter of thanks to the priest. No doubt it contained some allusion to his project. To the nun he wrote:

Seeing you so resolutely averse to what I had proposed, I refrained from justifying my intentions so fully as I could have wished. But should it prove that, even by the few words

I ventured to speak, I was able to convince you that this is no mere whim or common fancy, how happy would such news make me.

On a slip of paper folded small and tucked into the letter he wrote the poem:

Though with all my heart I tried to leave it behind me, never for a moment has it left me,—the fair face of that mountain-flower!

Though she had long passed the zenith of her years the nun could not but be pleased and flattered by the elegance of the note; for it was not only written in an exquisite hand, but was folded with a careless dexterity which she greatly admired. She felt very sorry for him, and would have been glad, had it been in her conscience, to have sent him a more favourable reply.

"We were delighted," she wrote, "that being in the neighbourhood you took occasion to pay us a visit. But I fear that when (as I very much hope you will) you come here purposely to visit us, I shall not be able to add anything to what I have said already. As for the poem which you enclose, do not expect her to answer it, for she cannot yet write her 'Naniwa Zu'[5] properly, even letter by letter. Let me then answer it for her: 'For as long as the cherry-blossoms remain unscattered upon the shore of Onoe where wild storms blow,—so long have you till now been constant!' For my part, I am very uneasy about the matter."

The priest replied to the same effect. Genji was very much disappointed and after two or three days he sent for Koremitsu and gave him a letter for the nun, telling him at the same time to find out whatever he could from Shōnagon, the child's nurse.

"What an impressionable character he is," thought Koremitsu. He had only had a glimpse of the child; but that had sufficed to convince him that she was a mere baby, though he remembered thinking her quite pretty. What trick would his master's heart be playing upon him next?

The old priest was deeply impressed by the arrival of a letter in the hands of so special and confidential a messenger. After delivering it, Koremitsu sought out the nurse. He repeated all that Genji had told him to say and added a great deal of general information about his

---

[5] A song the words of which were used as a first writing lesson.

master. Being a man of many words he talked on and on, continually introducing some new topic which had suddenly occurred to him as relevant. But at the end of it all Shōnagon was just as puzzled as everyone else had been to account for Genji's interest in a child so ridiculously young. His letter was very deferential. In it he said that he longed to see a specimen of her childish writing done letter by letter, as the nun had described. As before, he enclosed a poem:

> *Was it the shadows in the mountain well that told you my purpose was but jest?*[6]

To which she answered,

> Some perhaps that have drawn in that well now bitterly repent. Can the shadows tell me if again it will be so?

and Koremitsu brought a spoken message to the same effect, together with the assurance that so soon as the nun's health improved, she intended to visit the Capital and would then communicate with him again. The prospect of her visit was very exciting.

About this time Lady Fujitsubo fell ill and retired for a while from the Palace. The sight of the Emperor's grief and anxiety moved Genji's pity. But he could not help thinking that this was an opportunity which must not be missed. He spent the whole of that day in a state of great agitation, unable whether in his own house or at the Palace to think of anything else or call upon anyone. When at last the day was over, he succeeded in persuading her maid Ōmyōbu to take a message. The girl, though she regarded any communication between them as most imprudent, seeing a strange look in his face like that of one who walks in a dream, took pity on him and went. The Princess looked back upon their former relationship as something wicked and horrible and the memory of it was a continual torment to her. She had determined that such a thing must never happen again.

She met him with a stern and sorrowful countenance, but this did not disguise her charm, and as though conscious that he was unduly admiring her she began to treat him with great coldness and disdain.

---

[6] There is here a pun, and a reference to poem 3807 in the *Manyōshū*.

He longed to find some blemish in her, to think that he had been mistaken, and be at peace.

I need not tell all that happened. The night passed only too quickly. He whispered in her ear the poem: *"Now that at last we have met, would that we might vanish forever into the dream we dreamed tonight!"*

But she, still conscience-stricken: "Though I were to hide in the darkness of eternal sleep, yet would my shame run through the world from tongue to tongue."

And indeed, as Genji knew, it was not without good cause that she had suddenly fallen into this fit of apprehension and remorse. As he left, Ōmyōbu came running after him with his cloak and other belongings which he had left behind. He lay all day upon his bed in great torment. He sent a letter, but it was returned unopened. This had happened many times in the past, but now it filled him with such consternation that for two or three days he was completely prostrate and kept his room. All this while he was in constant dread lest his father, full of solicitude, should begin enquiring what new trouble had overtaken him. Fujitsubo, convinced that her ruin was accomplished, fell into a profound melancholy and her health grew daily worse. Messengers arrived constantly from the Court begging her to return without delay; but she could not bring herself to go. Her disorder had now taken a turn which filled her with secret foreboding, and she did nothing all day long but sit distractedly wondering what would become of her. When the hot weather set in she ceased to leave her bed at all. Three months had now passed and there was no mistaking her condition. Soon it would be known and everywhere discussed. She was appalled at the calamity which had overtaken her. Not knowing that there was any cause for secrecy, her people were astonished that she had not long ago informed the Emperor of her condition. Speculations were rife, but the question was one which only the Princess herself was in a position definitely to solve. Ōmyōbu and her old nurse's daughter who waited upon her at her toilet and in the bathhouse had at once noted the change and were somewhat taken aback. But Ōmyōbu was unwilling to discuss the matter. She had an uncomfortable suspicion that it was the meeting which she arranged that had now taken effect with cruel promptness and precision. It was announced in the Palace that other disorders had misled those about her and prevented them from recognizing the true nature of her condition. This explanation was accepted by everyone.

LADY MURASAKI SHIKIBU

The Emperor himself was full of tender concern, and though messengers kept him constantly informed, the gloomiest doubts and fancies passed continually through his mind. Genji was at this time visited by a most terrifying and extraordinary dream. He sent for interpreters, but they could make little of it. There were indeed certain passages to which they could assign no meaning at all; but this much was clear: the dreamer had made a false step and must be on his guard.

"It was not *my* dream," said Genji, feeling somewhat alarmed. "I am consulting you on behalf of someone else," and he was wondering what this "false step" could have been when news reached him of the Princess's condition.

This then was the disaster which his dream had portended! At once he wrote her an immense letter full of passionate self-reproaches and exhortations. But Ōmyōbu, thinking that it would only increase her agitation, refused to deliver it, and he could trust no other messenger. Even the few wretched lines which she had been in the habit of sending to him now and again had for some while utterly ceased.

In her seventh month she again appeared at Court. Overjoyed at her return, the Emperor lavished boundless affection upon her. The added fulness of her figure, the unwonted pallor and thinness of her face gave her, he thought, a new and incomparable charm. As before, all his leisure was spent in her company. During this time several Court festivals took place and Genji's presence was constantly required; sometimes he was called upon to play the *koto* or flute, sometimes to serve his father in other ways. On such occasions, strive as he might to show no trace of embarrassment or agitation, he feared more than once that he had betrayed himself; while to her such confrontations were one long torment.

The nun had somewhat improved in health and was now living in the Capital. He had enquired where she was lodging and sent messages from time to time, receiving (which indeed was all he expected) as little encouragement as before. In the last months his longing for the child had increased rather than diminished, but day after day went by without his finding any means to change the situation. As the autumn drew to its close, he fell into a state of great despondency. One fine moonlit night when he had decided, against his own inclination, to pay a certain secret visit,[7] a shower came on. As he had started from the Palace and the place to which he was going was in the suburbs of the Sixth Ward,

---

[7] To Lady Rokujō.

it occurred to him that it would be disagreeable to go so far in the rain. He was considering what he should do when he noticed a tumbled-down house surrounded by very ancient trees. He asked whose this gloomy and desolate mansion might be, and Koremitsu, who, as usual, was with him replied:

"Why that is the late Azechi no Dainagon's house. A day or two ago I took occasion to call there and was told that my Lady the nun has grown very weak and does not now know what goes on about her."

"Why did you not tell me this before?" said Genji deeply concerned; "I should have called at once to convey my sympathy to her household. Pray go in at once and ask for news."

Koremitsu accordingly sent one of the lesser attendants to the house, instructing him to give the impression that Genji had come on purpose to enquire. When the man announced that Prince Genji had sent him for news and was himself waiting outside, great excitement and consternation prevailed in the house. Their mistress, the servants said, had for several days been lying in a very parlous condition and could not possibly receive a visit. But they dared not simply send so distinguished a visitor away, and hastily tidying the southern parlour, they bustled him into it, saying, "You must forgive us for showing you into this untidy room. We have done our best to make it presentable. Perhaps, on a surprise visit, you will forgive us for conducting you to such an out-of-the-way closet. . ." It was indeed not at all the kind of room that he was used to.

"I have been meaning for a long while to visit this house," said Genji; "but time after time the proposals which I made in writing concerning a certain project of mine were summarily rejected and this discouraged me. Had I but known that your mistress's health had taken this turn for the worse. . ."

"Tell him that at this moment my mind is clear, though it may soon be darkened again. I am deeply sensible of the kindness he has shown in thus visiting my death-bed, and regret that I cannot speak with him face to face. Tell him that if by any chance he has not altered his mind with regard to the matter that he has discussed with me before, by all means let him, when the time has come, number her among the ladies of his household. It is with great anxiety that I leave her behind me and I fear that such a bond with earth may hinder me from reaching the life for which I have prayed."

Her room was so near and the partition so thin that as she gave

Shōnagon her message he could hear now and again the sound of her sad, quavering voice. Presently he heard her saying to someone, "How kind, how very kind of him to come. If only the child were old enough to thank him nicely!"

"It is indeed no question of kindness," said Genji to Shōnagon. "Surely it is evident that only some very deep feeling would have driven me to display so zealous a persistency! Since first I saw this child, a feeling of strange tenderness towards her possessed me, and it has grown to such a love as cannot be of this world only.[8] Though it is but an idle fancy, I have a longing to hear her voice. Could you not send for her before I go?"

"Poor little thing," said Shōnagon. "She is fast asleep in her room and knows nothing of all our troubles."

But as she spoke there was a sound of someone moving in the women's quarters and a voice suddenly was heard saying: "Grandmother, Grandmother! Prince Genji who came to see us in the mountains is here, paying a visit. Why do you not let him come and talk to you?"

"Hush, child, hush!" cried all the gentlewomen, scandalized.

"No, no," said the child; "Grandmother said that when she saw this prince it made her feel better at once. I was not being silly at all."

This speech delighted Genji; but the gentlewomen of the household thought the child's incursion painful and unseemly, and pretended not to hear her last remark. Genji gave up the idea of paying a real visit and drove back to his house, thinking as he went that her behaviour was indeed still that of a mere infant. Yet how easy and delightful it would be to teach her!

Next day he paid a proper visit. On his arrival he sent in a poem written on his usual tiny slip of paper:

> *Since first I heard the voice of the young crane, my boat shows a strange tendency to stick among the reeds!*

It was meant for the little girl and was written in a large, childish hand, but very beautifully, so that the ladies of the house said as soon as they saw it, "This will have to go into the child's copybook."

Shōnagon sent him the following note:

---

[8] Arises out of some connection in a previous existence.

My mistress, feeling that she might not live through the day, asked us to have her moved to the temple in the hills, and she is already on her way. I shall see to it that she learns of your enquiry, if I can but send word to her before it is too late.

The letter touched him deeply.

During these autumn evenings his heart was in a continual ferment. But though all his thoughts were occupied in a different quarter, yet owing to the curious relationship in which the child stood to the being who thus obsessed his mind, the desire to make the girl his own throughout this stormy time grew daily stronger. He remembered the evening when he had first seen her and the nun's poem, *"Not knowing if any will come to nurture the tender leaf. . ."* She would always be delightful; but in some respects she might not fulfil her early promise. One must take risks. And he made the poem: *"When shall I see it lying in my hand, the young grass of the moor-side that springs from purple[9] roots?"*

In the tenth month the Emperor was to visit the Suzaku-in for the Festival of Red Leaves. The dancers were all to be sons of the noblest houses. The most accomplished among the princes, courtiers and other great gentlemen had been chosen for their parts by the Emperor himself, and from the Royal Princes and State Ministers downward everyone was busy with continual practices and rehearsals. Genji suddenly realized that for a long while he had not enquired after his friends on the mountain. He at once sent a special messenger who brought back this letter from the priest:

"The end came on the twentieth day of last month. It is the common lot of mankind; yet her loss is very grievous to me!"

This and more he wrote, and Genji, reading the letter was filled with a bitter sense of life's briefness and futility. And what of the child concerning whose future the dead woman had shown such anxiety? He could not remember his own mother's death at all distinctly; but some dim recollection still floated in his mind and gave to his letter of condolence an added warmth of feeling. It was answered, not without a certain self-importance, by the nurse Shōnagon.

---

[9] Purple is *murasaki* in Japanese. From this poem the child is known as Murasaki; and hence the authoress derived the nickname by which she too is known.

After the funeral and mourning were over, the child was brought back to the Capital. Hearing of this he allowed a short while to elapse and then one fine, still night went to the house of his own accord. This gloomy, decaying, half-deserted mansion must, he thought, have a most depressing effect upon the child who lived there. He was shown into the same small room as before. Here Shōnagon told him between her sobs the whole tale of their bereavement, at which he too found himself strangely moved.

"I would send my little mistress to His Highness her father's," she continued, "did I not remember how cruelly her poor mother was used in that house. And I would do it still if my little lady were a child in arms who would not know where she had been taken to nor what the people there were feeling towards her. But she is now too big a girl to go among a lot of strange children who might not treat her kindly. So her poor dead grandmother was always saying down to her last day. You, Sir, have been very good to us, and it would be a great weight off my mind to know that she was coming to you even if it were only for a little while; and I would not worry you with asking what was to become of her afterwards. Only for her sake I am sorry indeed that she is not some years older, so that you might make a match of it. But the way she has been brought up has made her young even for her age."

"You need not so constantly remind me of her childishness," said Genji. "Though it is indeed her youth and helplessness which move my compassion, yet I realize (and why should I hide it from myself or from you?) that a far closer bond unites our souls. Let me tell her myself what we have just now decided," and he recited a poem in which he asked if, *like the waves that lap the shore where young reeds grow he must advance only to recede again.*

"Will she be too much surprised?" he added. Shōnagon, saying that the little girl should by all means be fetched, answered his poem with another in which she warned him that he must not expect her to "drift seaweed-like with the waves," before she understood his intention.

"Now, what made you think I should send you away without letting her see you?" she asked, speaking in an off-hand, familiar tone which he found it easy to pardon. His appearance, which the gentlewomen of the house studied with great care while he sat waiting for the child and singing to himself a verse of the song *Why so hard to cross the hill?* made a deep impression upon them, and they did not forget that moment for a long while after.

The child was lying on her bed weeping for her grandmother.

"A gentleman in a big cloak has come to play with you," said one of the women who were waiting upon her; "I wonder if it is your father." At this she jumped up and cried out:

"Nurse, where is the gentleman in a cloak? Is he my father?" and she came running into the room.

"No," said Genji, "it is not your father; but it is someone else who wants you to be very fond of him. Come. . ." She had learnt from the way people talked about him that Prince Genji was someone very important, and feeling that he must really be very angry with her for speaking of him as the "gentleman in a cloak" she went straight to her nurse and whispered, "Please, I am sleepy."

"You must not be shy of me anymore," said Genji. "If you are sleepy, come here and lie on my knee. Will you not even come and talk to me?"

"There," said Shōnagon, "you see what a little savage she is," and pushed the child towards him.

She stood listlessly by his side, passing her hand under her hair so that it fell in waves over her soft dress or clasping a great bunch of it where it stuck out thick around her shoulders. Presently he took her hand in his; but at once, in terror of this close contact with someone to whom she was not used, she cried out, "I said I wanted to go to bed," and snatching her hand away she ran into the women's quarters.

He followed her crying, "Dear one, do not run away from me! Now that your granny is gone, you must love me instead."

"Well!" gasped Shōnagon, deeply shocked. "No, that is too much! How can you bring yourself to say such a wicked thing to the poor child? And it is not much use *telling* people to be fond of one, is it?"

"For the moment, it may not be," said Genji. "But you will see that strange things happen if one's heart is set upon a thing as mine is now."

Hail was falling. It was a wild and terrible night. The thought of leaving her to pass it in this gloomy and half-deserted mansion immeasurably depressed him and snatching at this excuse for remaining near her: "Shut the partition-door!" he cried. "I will stay for a while and play the watchman here on this terrible night. Draw near to me, all of you!" and so saying, as though it were the most natural thing in the world, he picked up the child in his arms and carried her to her bed. The gentlewomen were far too astonished and confounded to budge from their seats; while Shōnagon, though his high-handed proceedings greatly agitated and alarmed her, had to confess to herself that there was no real reason to interfere, and could only sit moaning in her corner.

The little girl was at first terribly frightened. She did not know what he was going to do with her and shuddered violently. Even the feel of his delicate, cool skin when he drew her to him, gave her goose-flesh. He saw this; but none the less he began gently and carefully to remove her outer garments, and laid her down.

Then, though he knew quite well that she was still frightened of him, he began talking to her softly and tenderly: "How would you like to come with me one day to a place where there are lots of lovely pictures and dolls and toys?" And he went on to speak so feelingly of all the things she was most interested in that soon she felt almost at home with him. But for a long while she was restless and did not go properly to sleep. The storm still raged.

"Whatever should we have done if this gentleman had not been here," whispered one of the women; "I know that for my part I should have been in a terrible fright. If only our little lady were nearer to his age!" Shōnagon, still mistrustful, sat quite close to Genji all the while.

At last the wind began to drop. The night was far spent; but his return at such an hour would cause no surprise!

"She has become so dear to me," said Genji, "that, above all at this sad time in her life, I am loath to leave her even for a few short hours. I think I shall put her somewhere where I can see her whenever I wish. I wonder that she is not frightened to live in such a place as this."

"I think her father spoke of coming to fetch her," said Shōnagon; "but that is not likely to be till the Forty-nine Days are up."

"It would of course under ordinary circumstances be natural that her father should look after her," admitted Genji; "but as she has been brought up entirely by someone else she has no more reason to care for him than for me. And though I have known her so short a time, I am certainly far fonder of her than her father can possibly be." So saying he stroked the child's hair and then reluctantly, with many backward glances, left the room.

There was now a heavy white fog, and hoar-frost lay thick on the grass. Suddenly he found himself wishing that it were a real love-affair, and he became very depressed. It occurred to him that on his way home he would pass by a certain house which he had once familiarly frequented. He knocked at the door, but no one answered. He then ordered one of his servants who had a strong voice to recite the following lines: *"By my Sister's gate though morning fog makes all the world still dark as night, I could not fail to pause."*

When this had been sung twice, the lady sent an impertinent coxcomb of a valet to the door, who having recited the poem, *"If you disliked the hedge of fog that lies about this place, a gate of crazy wicker would not keep you standing in the street,*" at once went back again into the house. He waited; but no one else came to the door, and though he was in no mood to go dully home since it was now broad daylight, what else could be done? At his palace he lay for a long while smiling to himself with pleasure as he recollected the child's pretty speeches and ways. Towards noon he rose and began to write a letter to her; but he could not find the right words, and after many times laying his brush aside he determined at last to send her some nice pictures instead.

That day Prince Hyōbukyō paid his long-promised visit to the late nun's house. The place seemed to him even more ruinous, vast and antiquated than he remembered it years ago. How depressing it must be for a handful of persons to live in these decaying halls, and looking about him he said to the nurse: "No child ought to live in a place like this even for a little while. I must take her away at once; there is plenty of room in my house. You"—(turning to Shōnagon)—"shall be found a place as a Lady-in-Waiting there. The child will be very well off, for there are several other young people for her to play with."

He called the little girl to him and noticing the rich perfume that clung to her dress since Genji held her in his arms, the Prince said, "How nicely your dress is scented. But isn't it rather drab?" No sooner had he said this than he remembered that she was in mourning, and felt slightly uncomfortable.

"I used sometimes to tell her grandmother," he continued, "that she ought to let her come to see me and get used to our ways; for indeed it was a strange upbringing for her to live alone year in year out with one whose health and spirits steadily declined. But she for some reason was very unfriendly towards me, and there was in another quarter[10] too a reluctance which I fear even at such a time as this may not be wholly overcome. . ."

"If that is so," said Shōnagon, "dull as it is for her here, I do not think she should be moved till she is a little better able to shift for herself."

For days on end the child had been in a terrible state of grief, and not having eaten the least bite of anything she was grown very thin, but was none the less lovely for that. He looked at her tenderly and said: "You must not cry anymore now. When people die, there is no help for it and we must bear it bravely. But now all is well, for I have come instead. . ." But it was getting late and he could not stay any longer.

---

[10] His wife.

As he turned to go he saw that the child, by no means consoled at the prospect of falling under his care, was again crying bitterly. The Prince, himself shedding a few tears did his best to comfort her:

"Do not grieve so," he said, "today or tomorrow I will send for you to come and live with me," and with that he departed.

Still the child wept and no way could be found to distract her thoughts. It was not of course that she had any anxiety about her own future, for about such matters she had not yet begun to think at all; but only that she had lost the companion from whom for years on end she had never for a moment been separated. Young as she was, she suffered so cruelly that all her usual games were quite abandoned, and though sometimes during the day her spirits would a little improve, as night drew on she became so melancholy that Shōnagon began to wonder how much longer things would go on like this, and in despair at not being able to comfort her, would herself burst into tears.

Presently Koremitsu arrived with a message saying that Genji had intended to visit them, but owing to a sudden command from the Palace was unable to do so, and being very much perturbed at the little one's grievous condition had sent for further news. Having delivered this message Koremitsu brought in some of Genji's servants whom he had sent to mount guard over the house that night.

"This kindness is indeed ill-placed," said Shōnagon.

"It may not seem to him of much consequence that his gentlemen should be installed here; but if the child's father hears of it, we servants shall get all the blame for the little lady's being given away to a married gentleman. It was you who let it all begin, we shall be told. Now be careful," she said turning to her fellow-servants, "do not let her even mention these watchmen to her father." But alas, the child was quite incapable of understanding such a prohibition, and Shōnagon, after pouring out many lamentations to Koremitsu, continued:

"I do not doubt but that in due time she will somehow become his wife, for so their fate seems to decree. But now and for a long while there can be no talk of any such thing, and this, as he has roundly told me, he knows as well as the rest of us. So what he is after I cannot for the life of me imagine. Only today when Prince Hyōbukyō was here he bade me keep a sharp eye upon her and not let her be treated with any indiscretion. I confess when he said it I remembered with vexation certain liberties which I have allowed your master to take, thinking little enough of them at the time."

No sooner had she said this than she began to fear that Koremitsu would put a worse construction on her words than she intended, and shaking her head very dolefully she relapsed into silence. Nor was she far wrong, for Koremitsu was indeed wondering of what sort Genji's misdemeanours could have been.

On hearing Koremitsu's report Genji's heart was filled with pity for the child's state and he would like to have gone to her at once. But he feared that ignorant people would misunderstand these frequent visits and, thinking the girl older than she was, spread foolish scandals abroad. It would be far simpler to fetch her to his Palace and keep her there. All through the day he sent numerous letters, and at dusk Koremitsu again went to the house saying that urgent business had once more prevented Genji from visiting them, for which remissness he tendered his apologies. Shōnagon answered curtly that the girl's father had suddenly decided to fetch her away next day and that they were too busy to receive visits: "The servants are all in a fluster at leaving this shabby old house where they have lived so long and going to a strange, grand place. . ." She answered his further questions so briefly and seemed so intent upon her sewing, that Koremitsu went away.

Genji was at the Great Hall, but as usual he had been unable to get a word out of Aoi and in a gloomy mood he was plucking at his zithern and singing *"Why sped you across field and hill So fast upon this rainy night?"*[11]

The words of the song were aimed at Aoi and he sang them with much feeling. He was thus employed when Koremitsu arrived at the Great Hall. Genji sent for him at once and bade him tell his story. Koremitsu's news was very disquieting. Once she was in her father's palace it would look very odd that Genji should fetch her away, even if she came willingly. It would inevitably be rumoured abroad that he had made off with her like a child-snatcher, a thief. Far better to anticipate his rival and exacting a promise of silence from the people about her, carry her off to his own palace immediately.

"I shall go there at daybreak," he said to Koremitsu; "Order the carriage that I came here in, it can be used just as it is, and see to it that one or two attendants are ready to go with me." Koremitsu bowed and retired.

---

[11] The song is addressed by a girl to a suspicious lover; Genji reverses the sense.

Genji knew that whichever course he chose, there was bound to be a scandal so soon as the thing became known. Inevitably gossips would spread the report that, young though she was, the child by this time knew well enough why she had been invited to live with Prince Genji in his palace. Let them draw their own conclusions. That did not matter. There was a much worse possibility. What if Hyōbukyō found out where she was? His conduct in abducting another man's child would appear in the highest degree outrageous and discreditable. He was sorely puzzled, but he knew that if he let this opportunity slip he would afterwards bitterly repent it, and long before daybreak he started on his way. Aoi was cold and sullen as ever.

"I have just remembered something very important which I must see about at home," he said; "I shall not be away long," and he slipped out so quietly that the servants of the house did not know that he was gone.

His cloak was brought to him from his own apartments and he drove off attended only by Koremitsu who followed on horseback. After much knocking they succeeded in getting the gate opened, but by a servant who was not in the secret. Koremitsu ordered the man to pull in Genji's carriage as quietly as he could and himself went straight to the front door, which he rattled, coughing as he did so that Shōnagon might know who was there.

"My lord is waiting," he said when she came to the door.

"But the young lady is fast asleep," said Shōnagon; "his Highness has no business to be up and about at this time of night." She said this thinking that he was returning from some nocturnal escapade and had only called there in passing. "I hear," said Genji now coming forward, "that the child is to be moved to her father's and I have something of importance which I must say to her before she goes."

"Whatever business you have to transact with her, I am sure she will give the matter her closest attention," scoffed Shōnagon. Matters of importance indeed, with a child of ten! Genji entered the women's quarters.

"You cannot go in there," cried Shōnagon in horror; "several aged ladies are lying all undressed. . ."

"They are all fast asleep," said Genji. "See, I am only rousing the child," and bending over her: "The morning mist is rising," he cried, "it is time to wake!"

And before Shōnagon had time to utter a sound, he had taken the child in his arms and begun gently to rouse her. Still half-dreaming, she thought it was the prince her father who had come to fetch her.

"Come," said Genji while he put her hair to rights, "your father has sent me to bring you back with me to his palace." For a moment she was dazed to find that it was not her father and shrank from him in fright.

"Never mind whether it is your father or I," he cried; "it is all the same," and so saying he picked her up in his arms and carried her out of the inner room.

"Well!" cried out Koremitsu and Shōnagon in astonishment. What would he do next?

"It seems," said Genji, "that you were disquieted at my telling you I could not visit her here as often as I wished and would make arrangements for her to go to a more convenient place. I hear that you are sending her where it will be even more difficult for me to see her. Therefore. . . make ready one or the other of you to come with me."

Shōnagon, who now realized that he was going to make off with the child, fell into a terrible fluster. "O Sir," she said, "you could not have chosen a worse time. Today her father is coming to fetch her, and whatever shall I say to him? If only you would wait, I am sure it would all come right in the end. But by acting so hastily you will do yourself no good and leave the poor servants here in a sad pickle."

"If that is all," cried Genji, "let them follow as soon as they choose," and to Shōnagon's despair he had the carriage brought in. The child stood by weeping and bewildered. There seemed no way of preventing him from carrying out his purpose and gathering together the child's clothes that she had been sewing the night before, the nurse put on her own best dress and stepped into the carriage. Genji's house was not far off and they arrived before daylight. They drew up in front of the western wing and Genji alighted. Taking the child lightly in his arms he set her on the ground. Shōnagon, to whom these strange events seemed like a dream, hesitated as though still uncertain whether she should enter the house or no.

"There is no need for you to come in if you do not want to," said Genji. "Now that the child herself is safely here I am quite content. If you had rather go back, you have only to say so and I will escort you."

Reluctantly she left the carriage. The suddenness of the move was in itself enough to have upset her; but she was also worrying about what Prince Hyōbukyō would think when he found that his child had vanished. And indeed what *was* going to become of her? One way or another all her mistresses seemed to be taken from her and it was only when she became frightened of having wept for so long on end that she at last dried her eyes and began to pray.

The western wing had long been uninhabited and was not completely furnished; but Koremitsu had soon fitted up screens and curtains where they were required. For Genji makeshift quarters were soon contrived by letting down the side-wings of his screen-of-honour. He sent to the other part of the house for his night things and went to sleep. The child, who had been put to bed not far off, was still very apprehensive and ill at ease in these new surroundings. Her lips were trembling, but she dared not cry out loud.

"I want to sleep with Shōnagon," she said at last in a tearful, babyish voice.

"You are getting too big to sleep with a nurse," said Genji, who had heard her. "You must try and go to sleep nicely where you are."

She felt very lonely and lay weeping for a long while. The nurse was far too much upset to think of going to bed and sat up for the rest of the night in the servants' quarters crying so bitterly that she was unconscious of all that went on around her.

But when it grew light she began to look about her a little. Not only this great palace with its marvellous pillars and carvings, but the sand in the courtyard outside which seemed to her like a carpet of jewels made so dazzling an impression upon her that at first she felt somewhat overawed. However, the fact that she was now no longer in a household of women gave her an agreeable sense of security.

It was the hour at which business brought various strangers to the house. There were several men walking just outside her window and she heard one of them whisper to another: "They say that someone new has come to live here. Who can it be, I wonder? A lady of note, I'll warrant you."

Bath water was brought from the other wing, and steamed rice for breakfast. Genji did not rise till far on into the morning. "It is not good for the child to be alone," he said to Shōnagon, "so last night before I came to you I arranged for some little people to come and stay here," and so saying he sent a servant to "fetch the little girls from the eastern wing." He had given special orders that they were to be as small as possible and now four of the tiniest and prettiest creatures imaginable arrived upon the scene.

Murasaki was still asleep, lying wrapped in Genji's own coat. It was with difficulty that he roused her. "You must not be sad anymore," he said; "If I were not very fond of you, should I be looking after you like this? Little girls ought to be very gentle and obedient in their ways." And thus her education was begun.

She seemed to him, now that he could study her at leisure, even more lovely than he had realized and they were soon engaged in an affectionate conversation. He sent for delightful pictures and toys to show her and set to work to amuse her in every way he could. Gradually he persuaded her to get up and look about her. In her shabby dress made of some dark grey material she looked so charming now that she was laughing and playing, with all her woes forgotten, that Genji too laughed with pleasure as he watched her. When at last he retired to the eastern wing, she went out of doors to look at the garden. As she picked her way among the trees and along the side of the lake, and gazed with delight upon the frosty flower-beds that glittered gay as a picture, while a many-coloured throng of unknown people passed constantly in and out of the house, she began to think that this was a very nice place indeed. Then she looked at the wonderful pictures that were painted on all the panels and screens and quite lost her heart to them.

For two or three days Genji did not go to the Palace, but spent all his time amusing the little girl. Finally he drew all sorts of pictures for her to put into her copybook, showing them to her one by one as he did so. She thought them the loveliest set of pictures she had ever seen. Then he wrote part of the *Musashi-no* poem.[12] She was delighted by the way it was written in bold ink-strokes on a background stained with purple. In a smaller hand was the poem: "*Though the parent-root[13] I cannot see, yet tenderly I love its off-shoot,[14]—the dewy plant that grows upon Musashi Moor.*"

"Come," said Genji while she was admiring it, "you must write something too."

"I cannot write properly yet," she answered, looking up at him with a witchery so wholly unconscious that Genji laughed.

"Even if you cannot write properly it will never do for us to let you off altogether. Let me give you a lesson." With many timid glances towards him she began to write. Even the childish manner in which she grasped the brush gave him a thrill of delight which he was at a loss to explain.

---

[12] "Though I know not the place, yet when they told me this was the moor of Musashi, the thought flashed through my mind: 'What else indeed could it be, since all its grass is purple-dyed?'"

[13] Fujitsubo. The fuji flower is also purple (*murasaki*) in colour.

[14] The child Murasaki, who was Fujitsubo's niece. Musashi was famous for the purple dye extracted from the roots of a grass that grew there.

"Oh, I have spoiled it," she suddenly cried out and blushing hid from him what she had written. But he forced her to let him see it and found the poem:

I do not know what put Musashi into your head and am very puzzled. What plant is it that you say is a relative of mine?

It was written in a large childish hand which was indeed very undeveloped, but was nevertheless full of promise. It showed a strong resemblance to the late nun's writing. He felt certain that if she were given up-to-date copybooks she would soon write very nicely.

Next they built houses for the dolls and played so long at this game together that Genji forgot for a while the great anxiety[15] which was at that time preying upon his mind.

The servants who had been left behind at Murasaki's house were extremely embarrassed when Prince Hyōbukyō came to fetch her. Genji had made them promise for a time at any rate to tell no one of what had happened and Shōnagon had seemed to agree that this was best. Accordingly he could get nothing out of them save that Shōnagon had taken the child away with her without saying anything about where she was going. The Prince felt completely baffled. Perhaps the grandmother had instilled into the nurse's mind the idea that things would not go smoothly for the child at his palace. In that case the nurse with an excess of craftiness might, instead of openly saying that she feared the child would not be well treated under his roof, have thought it wiser to make off with her when opportunity offered. He went home very depressed, asking them to let him know instantly if they had any news, a request which again embarrassed them. He also made enquiries of the priest at the temple in the hills, but could learn nothing. She had seemed to him to be a most lovable and delightful child; it was very disappointing to lose sight of her in this manner. The princess his wife had long ago got over her dislike of the child's mother and was indignant at the idea that she was not to be trusted to do her duty by the child properly.

Gradually the servants from Murasaki's house assembled at her new home. The little girls who had been brought to play with her were delighted with their new companion and they were soon all playing together very happily.

---

[15] The pregnancy of Fujitsubo.

When her prince was away or busy, on dreary evenings she would still sometimes long for her grandmother the nun and cry a little. But she never thought about her father whom she had never been used to see except at rare intervals. Now indeed she had "a new father" of whom she was growing everyday more fond. When he came back from anywhere she was the first to meet him and then wonderful games and conversations began, she sitting all the while on his lap without the least shyness or restraint. A more charming companion could not have been imagined. It might be that when she grew older, she would not always be so trustful. New aspects of her character might come into play. If she suspected, for example, that he cared for someone else, she might resent it, and in such a case all sorts of unexpected things are apt to happen; but for the present she was a delightful plaything. Had she really been his daughter, convention would not have allowed him to go on much longer living with her on terms of such complete intimacy; but in a case like this he felt that such scruples were not applicable.

VI

The Saffron-Flower

Try as he might he could not dispel the melancholy into which Yūgao's sudden death[1] had cast him, and though many months had gone by he longed for her passionately as ever. In other quarters where he had looked for affection, coldness vied with coldness and pride with pride. He longed to escape once more from the claims of these passionate and exacting natures, and renew the life of tender intimacy which for a while had given him so great a happiness. But alas, no second Yūgao would he ever find. Despite his bitter experience he still fancied that one day he might at least discover some beautiful girl of humble origin whom he could meet without concealment, and he listened eagerly to any hint that was likely to put him upon a promising track. If the prospects seemed favourable he would follow up his enquiries by writing a discreet letter which, as he knew from experience, would seldom indeed meet with a wholly discouraging reply. Even those who seemed bent on showing by the prim stiffness of their answers that they placed virtue high above sensibility, and who at first appeared hardly conversant with the usages of polite society, would suddenly collapse into the wildest intimacy which would continue until their marriage with some commonplace husband cut short the correspondence.

There were vacant moments when he thought of Utsusemi with regret. And there was her companion too; sometime or other there would surely be an opportunity of sending her a surprise message. If only he could see her again as he had seen her that night sitting by the chess-board in the dim lamplight. It was not indeed in his nature ever to forget anyone of whom he had once been fond.

Among his old nurses there was one called Sayemon to whom, next after Koremitsu's mother, he was most deeply attached. She had a daughter called Taifu no Myōbu who was in service at the Palace. This girl was an illegitimate child of a certain member of the Imperial family who was then Vice-minister of the Board of War. She was a young person of very lively disposition and Genji often made use of her services. Her

---

[1] The events of this chapter are synchronous with those of the last.

mother, Genji's nurse, had afterwards married the governor of Echizen and had gone with him to his province, so the girl when she was not at the Palace lived chiefly at her father's.

She happened one day when she was talking with Genji to mention a certain princess, daughter of the late Prince Hitachi. This lady, she said, was born to the Prince when he was quite an old man and every care had been lavished upon her upbringing. Since his death she had lived alone and was very unhappy. Genji's sympathy was aroused and he began to question Myōbu about this unfortunate lady.

"I do not really know much either about her character or her appearance," said Myōbu; "she is extremely seclusive in her habits. Sometimes I have talked to her a little in the evening, but always with a curtain between us. I believe her zithern is the only companion in whom she is willing to confide."

"Of the Three Friends[2] one at least would in her case be unsuitable," said Genji. "But I should like to hear her play; her father was a great performer on this instrument and it is unlikely that she has not inherited some of his skill."

"Oh, I am afraid she is not worth your coming to hear," said Myōbu.

"You are very discouraging," he answered, "but all the same I shall hide there one of these nights when the full moon is behind the clouds and listen to her playing; and you shall come with me."

She was not best pleased; but just then even upon the busy Palace a springtime quiet seemed to have settled, and being quite at leisure she consented to accompany him. Her father's house was at some distance from the town and for convenience he sometimes lodged in Prince Hitachi's palace. Myōbo got on badly with her stepmother, and taking a fancy to the lonely princess's quarters she kept a room there.

It was indeed on the night after the full moon, in just such a veiled light as Genji had spoken of, that they visited the Hitachi palace.

"I am afraid," said Myōbu, "that it is not a very goodnight for listening to music; sounds do not seem to carry very well." But he would not be thus put off.

"Go to her room," he said, "and persuade her to play a few notes; it would be a pity if I went away without hearing her at all."

Myōbu felt somewhat shy of leaving him like this in her own little private room. She found the princess sitting by the window, her shutters

---

[2] Wine, zithern and song—in allusion to a poem by Po Chü-i.

not yet closed for the night; she was enjoying the scent of a blossoming plum-tree which stood in the garden just outside. It did indeed seem just the right moment.

"I thought how lovely your zithern would sound on such a night as this," she said, "and could not resist coming to see you. I am always in such a hurry, going to and from the Palace, that do you know I have never had time to hear you play. It is such a pity."

"Music of this sort," she replied, "gives no pleasure to those who have not studied it. What do they care for such matters *who all day long run hither and thither in the City of a Hundred Towers*?"[3] She sent for her zithern; but her heart beat fast. What impression would her playing make upon this girl? Timidly she sounded a few notes. The effect was very agreeable. True, she was not a great performer; but the instrument was a particularly fine one and Genji found her playing by no means unpleasant to listen to.

Living in this lonely and half-ruined palace after such an upbringing (full no doubt of antiquated formalities and restrictions) as her father was likely to have given her it would be strange indeed if her life did not for the most part consist of memories and regrets. This was just the sort of place which in an old tale would be chosen as the scene for the most romantic happenings. His imagination thus stirred, he thought of sending her a message. But perhaps she would think this rather sudden. For some reason he felt shy, and hesitated.

"It seems to be clouding over," said the astute Myōbu, who knew that Genji would carry away a far deeper impression if he heard no more for the present.

"Someone was coming to see me," she continued; "I must not keep him waiting. Perhaps someother time when I am not in such a hurry. . . Let me close your window for you," and with that she rejoined Genji, giving the princess no encouragement to play anymore.

"She stopped so soon," he complained, "that it was hardly worth getting her to play at all. One had not time to catch the drift of what she was playing. Really it was a pity!" That the princess was beautiful he made no doubt at all. "I should be very much obliged if you would arrange for me to hear her at closer quarters."

But Myōbu, thinking that this would lead to disappointment, told him that the princess who led so hermit-like an existence and seemed

---

[3] Evidently a quotation.

always so depressed and subdued would hardly welcome the suggestion that she should perform before a stranger.

"Of course," said Genji, "a thing of that kind could only be suggested between people who were on familiar terms or to someone of very different rank. This lady's rank, as I am perfectly well aware, entitles her to be treated with every consideration, and I would not ask you to do more than hint at my desire." He had promised to meet someone else that night and carefully disguising himself he was preparing to depart when Myōbu said laughing, "It amuses me sometimes to think how the Emperor deplores the too strict and domesticated life which he suffers you to lead. What would he think if he could see you disguising yourself like this?"

Genji laughed. "I am afraid," he said as he left the room, "that you are not quite the right person to denounce me. Those who think such conduct reprehensible in a man must find it even less excusable in a girl." She remembered that Genji had often been obliged to reproach her for her reckless flirtations, and blushing made no reply.

Still hoping to catch a glimpse of the zithern-player he crept softly towards her window. He was about to hide at a point where the bamboo-fence was somewhat broken down when he perceived that a man was already ensconced there. Who could it be? No doubt it was one of the princess's lovers and he stepped back to conceal himself in the darkness. The stranger followed him and turned out to be no other than Tō no Chūjō. That evening they had left the Palace together, but when they parted Genji (Chūjō had noticed) did not either go in the direction of the Great Hall nor back to his own palace. This aroused Chūjō's curiosity and, despite the fact that he too had a secret appointment that night, he decided first to follow Genji and discover what was afoot. So riding upon a strange horse and wearing a hunting-cloak, he had got himself up altogether so villainously that he was able to follow Genji without being recognized upon the road. Seeing him enter so unexpected a place, Chūjō was trying to imagine what business his friend could possibly have in such a quarter when the music began and he secreted himself with a vague idea of waylaying Genji when he came out. But the prince, not knowing who the stranger was and frightened of being recognized, stole on tip-toe into the shadow.

Chūjō suddenly accosted him: "Though you shook me off so uncivilly, I thought it my duty to keep an eye on you," he said, and recited the poem:
"Though together we left the great Palace hill, your setting-place you would not show me, Moon of the sixteenth night!" Thus he remonstrated; and Genji,

though at first he had been somewhat put out by finding that he was not alone, when he recognized Tō no Chūjō could not help being rather amused.

"This is indeed an unexpected attention on your part," he said, and expressed his slight annoyance in the answering verse: "*Though wheresoever it shines men marvel at its light, who has before thought fit to follow the full moon to the hill whereon it sets?*"

"It is most unsafe for you to go about like this," said Chūjō. "I really mean it. You ought always to have a bodyguard; then you are all right whatever happens. I wish you would always let me come with you. I am afraid that these clandestine expeditions may one day get you into trouble," and he solemnly repeated the warning. What chiefly worried Genji was the thought that this might not be the first occasion upon which Chūjō had followed him; but if it had been his habit to do so it was certainly very tactful of him never to have questioned Genji about Yūgao's child.[4]

Though each of them had an appointment elsewhere, they agreed not to part. Both of them got into Genji's carriage and the moon having vanished behind a cloud, beguiled the way to the Great Hall by playing a duet upon their flutes. They did not send for torch-bearers to see them in at the gates, but creeping in very quietly stole to a portico where they could not be seen and had their ordinary clothes brought to them there. Having changed, they entered the house merrily blowing their flutes as though they had just come back from the Palace.

Chūjō's father, who usually pretended not to hear them when they returned late at night, on this occasion brought out his flageolet, which was his favourite instrument, and began to play very agreeably. Aoi sent for her zithern and made all her ladies play on the instruments at which they excelled. Only Nakatsukasa, though she was known for her lute-playing, having thrown over Tō no Chūjō who had been her lover because of her infatuation for Genji with whom her sole intercourse was that she sometimes saw him casually when he visited the Great Hall,— only Nakatsukasa sat drooping listlessly; for her passion had become known to Aoi's mother and the rest, and they were being very unpleasant about it. She was thinking in her despair that perhaps it would be better if she went and lived in some place where she would never see Genji at all; but the step was hard to take and she was very unhappy.

---

[4] Chūjō's child by Yūgao.

The young princes were thinking of the music they had heard earlier in the evening, of those romantic surroundings tinged with a peculiar and inexplicable beauty. Merely because it pleased him so to imagine her, Tō no Chūjō had already endowed the occupant of the lonely mansion with every charm. He had quite decided that Genji had been courting her for months or even years, and thought impatiently that he for his part, if like Genji he were violently in love with a lady of this kind, would have been willing to risk a few reproaches or even the loss of a little reputation. He could not however believe that his friend intended to let the matter rest as it was much longer and determined to amuse himself by a little rivalry. From that time onwards both of them sent letters to the lady, but neither ever received any answer. This both vexed and puzzled them. What could be the reason? Thinking that such images were suitable to a lady brought up in these rustic surroundings, in most of the poems which they sent her they alluded to delicate trees and flowers or other aspects of nature, hoping sooner or later to hit on some topic which would arouse her interest in their suit. Though she was of good birth and education, perhaps through being so long buried away in her vast mansion she had not any longer the wits to write a reply. And what indeed did it matter whether she answered or not, thought Tō no Chūjō, who none the less was somewhat piqued.

With his usual frankness he said to Genji: "I wonder whether you have had any answer. I must confess that as an experiment I too sent a mild hint, but without any success, so I have not repeated it."

"So he too has been trying his hand," thought Genji smiling to himself.

"No," he answered aloud, "my letter did not need an answer, which was perhaps the reason that I did not receive one."

From this enigmatic reply Chūjō deduced that Genji had been in communication of some kind with the lady and he was slightly piqued by the fact that she had shown a preference between them. Genji's deeper feelings were in no way involved, and though his vanity was a little wounded he would not have pursued the matter farther had he not known the persuasive power of Chūjō's style, and feared that even now she might overcome her scruples and send him a reply. Chūjō would become insufferably cock-a-hoop if he got into his head the idea that the princess had transferred her affections from Genji to himself. He must see what Myōbu could be persuaded to do.

　　　　　　　　　　　　　　LADY MURASAKI SHIKIBU

"I cannot understand," he said to her, "why the princess should refuse to take any notice of my letters. It is really very uncivil of her. I suppose she thinks I am a frivolous person who intends to amuse himself a little in her company and then disappear. It is a strangely false conception of my character. As you know, my affections never alter, and if I have ever seemed to the world to be unfaithful it has always been because in reality my suit had met with some unexpected discouragement. But this lady is so placed that no opposition from parents or brothers can interrupt our friendship, and if she will but trust me she will find that her being alone in the world, so far from exposing her to callous treatment, makes her the more attractive."

"Come," answered Myōbu, "it will never do for you to run away with the idea that you can treat this great lady as a pleasant wayside distraction; on the contrary she is extremely difficult of access and her rank has accustomed her to be treated with deference and ceremony." So spoke Myōbu, in accordance indeed with her own experience of the princess.

"She has evidently no desire to be thought clever or dashing," said Genji; "for some reason I imagine her as very gentle and forgiving." He was thinking of Yūgao when he said this.

Soon after this he fell sick of his fever and after that was occupied by a matter of great secrecy; so that spring and summer had both passed away before he could again turn his attention to the lonely lady. But in the autumn came a time of quiet meditation and reflexion. Again the sound of the cloth-beaters' mallets reached his ears, tormenting him with memories and longings. He wrote many letters to the zithern-player, but with no more success than before. Her churlishness exasperated him. More than ever he was determined not to give in, and sending for Myōbu he scolded her for having been of so little assistance to him.

"What can be going on in the princess's mind?" he said; "such strange behaviour I have never met with before."

If he was piqued and surprised, Myōbu for her part was vexed that the affair had gone so badly. "No one can say that you have done anything so very eccentric or indiscreet, and I do not think she feels so. If she does not answer your letters it is only part of her general unwillingness to face the outer world."

"But such a way of behaving is positively barbarous," said Genji; "if she were a girl in her teens and under the care of parents or guardians, such timidity might be pardoned; but in an independent woman it is inconceivable. I would never have written had I not taken it for granted that she had some experience of the world. I was merely hoping that I had found someone who in moments of idleness or depression would respond to me sympathetically. I did not address her in the language of gallantry, but only begged for permission sometimes to converse with her in that strange and lonely dwelling-place. But since she seems unable to understand what it is I am asking of her, we must see what can be done without waiting for her permission. If you will help me, you may be sure I shall not disgrace you in any way."

Myōbu had once been in the habit of describing to him the appearance of people whom she had chanced to meet and he always listened to such accounts with insatiable interest and curiosity; but for a long while he had paid no attention to her reports. Now for no reason at all the mere mention of the princess's existence had aroused in him a fever of excitement and activity. It was all very unaccountable. Probably he would find the poor lady extremely unattractive when he saw her and she would be doing her a very poor service in effecting the introduction; but to give Genji no help in a matter to which he evidently attached so much importance, would seem very ill-natured.

Even in Prince Hitachi's lifetime visitors to this stiff, old-fashioned establishment had been very rare, and now no foot at all ever made its way through the thickets which were closing in around the house. It may be imagined then what the visit of so celebrated a person as Genji would have meant to the ladies-in-waiting and lesser persons of the household and with what urgency they begged their mistress to send a favourable reply. But the same desperate shyness still possessed her and Genji's letters she would not even read. Hearing this Myōbu determined to submit Genji's request to her at some suitable moment when she and the princess were carrying on one of their usual uneasy conversations, with the princess's screen-of-honour planted between them.

"If she seems displeased," thought Myōbu, "I will positively have nothing more to do with the matter; but if she receives him and some sort of an affair starts between them, there is fortunately no one connected with her to scold me or get me into trouble." As the result of these and other reflections, being quite at home in matters of this kind, she sensibly decided to say nothing about the business to anybody, not even to her father.

Late one night, soon after the twentieth day of the eighth month, the princess sat waiting for the moon to rise. Though the star-light shone clear and lovely the moaning of the wind in the pine-tree branches oppressed her with its melancholy, and growing weary of waiting she was with many tears and sighs recounting to Myōbu stories of bygone men and days.

Now was the time to convey Genji's message, thought Myōbu. She sent for him, and secretly as before he crept up to the palace. The moon was just rising. He stood where the neglected bamboo-hedge grew somewhat sparsely and watched. Persuaded by Myōbu the princess was already at her zithern. So far as he could hear it at this distance, he did not find the music displeasing; but Myōbu in her anxiety and confusion thought the tune very dull and wished it would occur to the princess to play something rather more up-to-date. The place where Genji was waiting was well screened from view and he had no difficulty in creeping unobserved into the house. Here he called for Myōbu, who pretending that the visit was a complete surprise to her said to the princess: "I am so sorry, here is Prince Genji come to see me. I am always getting into trouble with him for failing to secure him your favour. I have really done my best, but you do not make it possible for me to give him any encouragement, so now I imagine he has come to deal with the matter for himself. What am I to say to him? I can answer for it that he will do nothing violent or rash. I think that considering all the trouble he has taken you might at least tell him that you will speak to him through a screen or curtain." The idea filled the princess with consternation.

"I should not know what to say to him," she wailed and as she said the words bolted towards the far side of the room with a bashfulness so infantile that Myōbu could not help laughing.

"Indeed, Madam," she said, "it is childish of you to take the matter to heart in this way. If you were an ordinary young lady under the eye of stern parents and brothers, one could understand it; but for a person in your position to go on forever being afraid to face the world is fantastic."

So Myōbu admonished her and the princess, who could never think of any argument against doing what she was told to do, said at last: "If I have only to listen and need not say anything he may speak to me from behind the lattice-door, so long as it is well locked."

"I cannot ask him to sit on the servant's bench," said Myōbu. "You really need not be afraid that he will do anything violent or sudden."

Thus persuaded, the princess went to a hatch which communicated between the women's quarters and the strangers' dais and firmly locking it with her own hand stuffed a mattress against it to make sure that no chink was left unstopped. She was in such a terrible state of confusion that she had not the least idea what she should say to her visitor, if she had to speak to him, and had agreed to listen to him only because Myōbu told her that she ought to.

Several elderly serving-women of the wet-nurse type had been lying half-asleep in the inner room since dusk. There were however one or two younger maids who had heard a great deal about this Prince Genji and were ready to fall in love with him at a moment's notice. They now brought out their lady's handsomest dress and persuaded her to let them put her a little to rights; but she displayed no interest in these preparations. Myōbu meanwhile was thinking how well Genji looked in the picturesque disguise which he had elaborated for use on these night excursions and wished it were being employed in some quarter where it was more likely to be appreciated. Her only consolation was that so mild a lady was not likely to make inordinate demands upon him or pester him with jealousies and exactions. On the other hand, she was rather worried about the princess.

"What," thought Myōbu, "if she should fall in love with him and her heart be broken merely because I was frightened of getting scolded?"

Remembering her rank and upbringing, he was far from expecting her to behave with the lively pertness of an up-to-date miss. She would be langorous; yes, langorous and passionate. When, half-pushed by Myōbu, the princess at last took her stand near the partition where she was to converse with her visitor, a delicious scent of sandal-wood[5] invaded his nostrils, and this piece of coquetry at once raised his hopes. He began to tell her with great earnestness and eloquence how for almost a year she had continually occupied his thoughts. But not a word did she answer; talking to her was no better than writing! Irritated beyond measure he recited the verse: "*If with a Vow of Silence thus ten times and again my combat I renew, 'tis that against me at least no sentence of muteness has been passed.*"

"Speak at least one word of dismissal," he continued; "do not leave me in this bewilderment." There was among her ladies one called Jijū, the daughter of her old nurse. Being a girl of great liveliness and intelligence she could not bear to see her mistress cutting such a figure

---

[5] Used to scent clothes with.

as this and stepping to her side she answered with the poem: "*The bell*[6] *had sounded and for a moment silence was imposed upon my lips. To have kept you waiting grieves me, and there let the matter rest.*" She said the words in such a way that Genji was completely taken in and thought it was the princess who had thus readily answered his poem. He had not expected such smartness from an aristocratic lady of the old school; but the surprise was agreeable and he answered:

"Madam, you have won the day," adding the verse: "*Though well I know that thoughts unspoken count more than thoughts expressed, yet dumb-crambo is not a cheering game to play.*"

He went on to speak of one trifle or another as it occurred to him, doing his very best to entertain her; but it was no use. Thinking at last that silence might after all in this strange creature be merely a sign of deep emotion he could no longer restrain his curiosity and, easily pushing back the bolted door, entered the room. Myōbu, seeing with consternation that he had falsified all her assurances, thought it better to know nothing of what followed and without turning her head rushed away to her own apartments. Jijū and the other ladies-in-waiting had heard so much about Genji and were so anxious to catch sight of him that they were more than ready to forgive his uncivil intrusion. Their only fear was that their mistress would be at a loss how to deal with so unexpected a situation. He did indeed find her in the last extremity of bashfulness and embarrassment, but under the circumstances that, thought Genji, was natural. Much was to be explained by the strict seclusion in which she had been brought up. He must be patient with her.

As his eyes grew used to the dim light he began to see that she was not at all beautiful. Had she then not one quality at all to justify all these hopes and schemes? Apparently not one. It was late. What was the use of staying? Bitterly disappointed he left the house. Myōbu, intensely curious to know what would happen, had lain awake listening. She wanted however to keep up the pretence that she had not witnessed Genji's intrusion and though she plainly heard him leaving the house she did not go to see him off or utter a sound of any kind. Stealing away as quietly as possible he returned to the Nijō-in and lay down upon his bed. This time at least he thought he was on the right path. What a disillusionment! And the worst of it was that she was a princess, a great

---

[6] The bell which the Zen-master strikes when it is time for his pupils to fall into silent meditation.

lady. What a mess he was in! So he lay thinking, when Tō no Chūjō entered the room.

"How late you are!" he cried; "I can easily guess the reason."

Genji rose: "I was so comfortable sleeping here all alone that I overslept myself," he said. "Have you come here from the Palace?"

"Yes," said Chūjō, "I was on my way home. I heard yesterday that today they are choosing the dancers and musicians for the celebrations of the Emperor's visit to the Suzaku-in and I am going home to tell my father of this. I will look in here on my way back."

Seeing that Chūjō was in a hurry Genji said that he would go with him to the Great Hall. He sent at once for his breakfast, bidding them also serve the guest. Two carriages were drawn up waiting for them, but they both got into the same one. "You still seem very sleepy," said Chūjō in an aggrieved tone; "I am sure you have been doing something interesting that you do not want to tell me about."

That day he had a number of important duties to perform and was hard at work in the Palace till nightfall. It did not occur to him till a very late hour that he ought at least to send the customary letter. It was raining. Myōbu had only the day before reproached him for using the princess's palace as a "wayside refuge." Today however he had no inclination whatever to halt there.

When hour after hour went by and still no letter came Myōbu began to feel very sorry for the princess whom she imagined to be suffering acutely from Genji's incivility. But in reality the poor lady was still far too occupied with shame and horror at what had happened the night before to think of anything else, and when late in the evening Genji's note at last arrived she could not understand in the least what it meant. It began with the poem: "*Scarce had the evening mist lifted and revealed the prospect to my sight when the night rain closed gloomily about me.*"

"I shall watch with impatience for a sign that the clouds are breaking," the letter continued. The ladies of the household at once saw with consternation the meaning of this note: Genji did not intend ever to come again. But they were all agreed that an answer must be sent, and their mistress was for the time being in far too overwrought a condition to put brush to paper; so Jijū (pointing out that it was late and there was no time to be lost) again came to the rescue:

"Give a thought to the country folk who wait for moonlight on this cloudy night, though, while they gaze, so different their thoughts from yours!" This she dictated to her mistress who, under the joint direction of all her ladies, wrote it upon a piece of paper which had once been purple but was now faded and shabby. Her writing was coarse and stiff, very mediocre in style, the upward and downward strokes being of the same thickness. Genji laid it aside scarcely glancing at it; but he was very much worried by the situation. How should he avoid hurting her feelings? Such an affair was certain to get him into trouble of some kind. What was he to do? He made up his mind that at all costs he must go on seeing her. Meanwhile, knowing nothing of this decision, the poor lady was very unhappy.

That night his father-in-law called for him on the way back from the Palace and carried him off to the Great Hall.

Here in preparation for the coming festival all the young princes were gathered together, and during the days which followed everyone was busy practising the songs or dances which had been assigned to him. Never had the Great Hall resounded with such a continual flow of music. The recorder and the big flute were all the while in full blast; and even the big drum was rolled out on to the verandah, the younger princes amusing themselves by experimenting upon it. Genji was so busy that he had barely time to pay an occasional surreptitious visit even to his dearest friends, and the autumn passed without his returning to the Hitachi Palace. The princess could not make it out.

Just at the time when the music-practices were at their height Myōbu came to see him. Her account of the princess's condition was very distressing.

"It is sad to witness day by day as I do how the poor lady suffers from your unkind treatment," she said and almost wept as she told him about it. He was doubly embarrassed. What must Myōbu be thinking of him since she found out that he had so recklessly falsified all the assurances of good behaviour that she had made on his account? And then the princess herself. . . He could imagine what a pathetic figure she must be, dumbly buried in her own despondent thoughts and questionings.

"Please make it clear to her," he said, "that I have been extremely busy; that is really the sole reason that I have not visited her." But he added with a sigh, "I hope soon to have a chance of teaching her not to be quite so stiff and shy." He smiled as he said it, and because he was so young and charming Myōbu somehow felt that despite her indignation she must smile too.

At his age it was inevitable that he should cause a certain amount of suffering. Suddenly it seemed to her perfectly right that he should do as he felt inclined without thinking much about the consequences. When the busy festival time was over he did indeed pay several visits to the Hitachi Palace, but then followed his adoption of little Murasaki whose ways so entranced him that he became very irregular even in his visits to the Sixth Ward;[7] still less had he any inclination, though he felt as sorry for the princess as ever, to visit that desolate palace. For a long while he had no desire to probe the secret of her bashfulness, to drive her into the light of day. But at last the idea occurred to him that he had perhaps all the while been mistaken. It was only a vague impression gathered in a room so dark that one could hardly see one's hand in front of one's face. If only he could persuade her to let him see her properly? But she seemed frightened to submit herself to the ordeal of daylight. Accordingly one night when he knew that he should catch her household quite at its ease he crept in unobserved and peeped through a gap in the door of the women's apartments. The princess herself was not visible. There was a very dilapidated screen-of-honour at the end of the room, but it looked as if it had not been moved from where it stood for years and years. Four or five elderly gentlewomen were in the room. They were preparing their mistress's supper in Chinese vessels which looked like the famous "royal blue" ware,[8] but they were much damaged and the food which had been provided seemed quite unworthy of these precious dishes. The old ladies soon retired, presumably to have their own supper. In a closet opening out of the main road he could see a very chilly-looking lady in an incredibly smoke-stained white dress and dirty apron tied at the waist. Despite this shabbiness, her hair was done over a comb in the manner of Court servants in ancient days when they waited at their master's table, though it hung down untidily. He had sometimes seen figures such as this haunting the housekeeper's rooms in the Palace, but he had no idea that they could still actually be seen waiting upon a living person!

"O dear, O dear," cried the lady in the apron, "what a cold winter we are having! It was not worth living so long only to meet times like these," and she shed a tear. "If only things had but gone on as they were in the old Prince's time!" she moaned. "What a change! No discipline, no authority. To think that I should have lived to see such days!" and she quivered with horror like one who "were he a bird would take wing

[7] To Lady Rokujō.

[8] *Pi-sē*. See Hetherington, *Early Ceramic Wares of China*, pp. 71–73.

and fly away."[9] She went on to pour out such a pitiful tale of things gone awry that Genji could bear it no longer, and pretending that he had just arrived tapped at the partition-door. With many exclamations of surprise the old lady brought a candle and let him in. Unfortunately Jijū had been chosen with other young persons to wait upon the Vestal Virgin and was not at home. Her absence made the house seem more rustic and old-fashioned than ever, and its oddity struck him even more forcibly than before.

The melancholy snow was now falling faster and faster. Dark clouds hung in the sky, the wind blew fierce and wild. The big lamp had burnt out and it seemed to be no one's business to light it. He remembered the terrible night upon which Yūgao had been bewitched. The house indeed was almost as dilapidated. But it was not quite so large and was (to Genji's comfort) at least to some small degree inhabited. Nevertheless it was a depressing place to spend the night at in such weather as this. Yet the snow-storm had a beauty and fascination of its own and it was tiresome that the lady whom he had come to visit was far too stiff and awkward to join him in appreciating its wildness. The dawn was just breaking and lifting one of the shutters with his own hand, he looked out at the snow-covered flower-beds. Beyond them stretched great fields of snow untrodden by any foot. The sight was very strange and lovely, and moved by the thought that he must soon leave it:

"Come and look how beautiful it is out of doors," he cried to the princess who was in an inner room. "It is unkind of you always to treat me as though I were a stranger."

Although it was still dark the light of the snow enabled the ancient gentlewomen who had now returned to the room to see the freshness and beauty of Genji's face. Gazing at him with undisguised wonder and delight, they cried out to their mistress:

"Yes, madam, indeed you must come. You are not behaving as you should. A young lady should be all kindness and pretty ways."

Thus admonished, the princess who when told what to do could never think of any reasons for not doing it, giving her costume a touch here and there reluctantly crept into the front room. Genji pretended to be still looking out of the window, but presently he managed to glance back into the room. His first impression was that her manner, had it been a little less diffident, would have been extremely pleasing. What an absurd

---

[9] *Manyōshū*, 893.

mistake he had made. She was certainly very tall as was shown by the length of her back when she took her seat; he could hardly believe that such a back could belong to a woman. A moment afterwards he suddenly became aware of her main defect. It was her nose. He could not help looking at it. It reminded him of the trunk of Samantabhadra's[10] steed!

Not only was it amazingly prominent, but (strangest of all) the tip which drooped downwards a little was tinged with pink, contrasting in the oddest manner with the rest of her complexion which was of a whiteness that would have put snow to shame. Her forehead was unusually high, so that altogether (though this was partly concealed by the forward tilt of her head) her face must be hugely long. She was very thin, her bones showing in the most painful manner, particularly her shoulder-bones which jutted out pitiably above her dress. He was sorry now that he had exacted from her this distressing exhibition, but so extraordinary a spectacle did she provide that he could not help continuing to gaze upon her. In one point at least she yielded nothing to the greatest beauties of the Capital. Her hair was magnificent; she was wearing it loose and it hung a foot or more below the skirt of her gown. A complete description of people's costumes is apt to be tedious, but as in stories the first thing that is said about the characters is invariably *what they wore*, I shall once in a way attempt such a description. Over a terribly faded bodice of imperial purple she wore a gown of which the purple had turned definitely black with age. Her mantle was of sable-skins heavily perfumed with scent. Such a garment as this mantle was considered very smart several generations ago, but it struck him as the most extraordinary costume for a comparatively young girl. However as a matter of fact she looked as though without this monstrous wrapping she would perish with cold and he could not help feeling sorry for her. As usual she seemed quite devoid of conversation and her silence ended by depriving Genji also of the power of speech. He felt however that he must try again to conquer her religious muteness and began making a string of casual remarks. Overcome with embarrassment she hid her face with her sleeve. This attitude, together with her costume, reminded him so forcibly of queer pompous old officials whom he had sometimes seen walking at funeral pace in state processions, hugging their emblems of office to their breasts, that he could not help laughing. This he felt to be very rude. Really he was very sorry for her and longing to put a quick end to her embarrassment he rose to go.

---

[10]The Bodhisattva Samantabhadra rides on a white elephant with a red trunk.

"Till I began to look after you there was no one in whom you could possibly have confided. But henceforward I think you must make up your mind to be frank with me and tell me all your secrets. Your stern aloofness is very painful to me," and he recited the verse: *"Already the icicle that hangs from the eaves is melting in the rays of the morning sun. How comes it that these drippings to new ice should turn?"*

At this she tittered slightly. Finding her inability to express herself quite unendurable he left the house. Even in the dim light of early morning he noticed that the courtyard gate at which his carriage awaited him was shaky on its posts and much askew; daylight, he was sure, would have revealed many other signs of dilapidation and neglect. In all the desolate landscape which stretched monotonously before him under the bleak light of dawn only the thick mantle of snow which covered the pine-trees gave a note of comfort and almost of warmth.

Surely it was such a place as this, sombre as a little village in the hills, that his friends had thought of on that rainy night when they had spoken of the gate "deep buried in green thickets." If only there were really hidden behind *these* walls some such exquisite creature as they had imagined. How patiently, how tenderly he would court her! He longed for some experience which would bring him respite from the anguish with which a certain hopeless and illicit passion was at that time tormenting him. Alas, no one could have been less likely to bring him the longed-for distraction than the owner of this romantic mansion. Yet the very fact that she had nothing to recommend her made it impossible for him to give her up, for it was certain that no one else would ever take the trouble to visit her. But why, why had it fallen to him of all people to become her intimate? Had the spirit of the departed Prince Hitachi, unhappy at the girl's friendless plight, chosen him out and led him to her?

At the side of the road he noticed a little orange-tree almost buried in snow. He ordered one of his attendants to uncover it. As though jealous of the attention that the man was paying to its neighbour a pine-tree near by shook its heavily laden branches, pouring great billows of snow over his sleeve. Delighted with the scene Genji suddenly longed for some companion with whom he might share this pleasure; not necessarily someone who loved such things as he did, but one who at least responded to them in an ordinary way.

The gate through which his carriage had to pass in order to leave the grounds was still locked. When at last the man who kept the key had been discovered he turned out to be immensely old and feeble. With him was a big, awkward girl who seemed to be his daughter or grand-daughter. Her dress looked very grimy in contrast with the new snow amid which she was standing. She seemed to be suffering very much from the cold, for she was hugging a little brazier of some kind with a stick or two of charcoal burning none too brightly in it. The old man had not the strength to push back the door, and the girl was dragging at it as well. Taking pity on them one of Genji's servants went to their assistance and quickly opened it. Genji remembered the poem in which Po Chü-i describes the sufferings of villagers in wintry weather and he murmured the lines "*The little children run naked in the cold; the aged shiver for lack of winter clothes.*" All at once he remembered the chilly appearance which that unhappy bloom had given to the princess's face and he could not help smiling. If ever he were able to show her to Tō no Chūjō, what strange comparison, he wondered, would Chūjō use concerning it? He remembered how Chūjō had followed him on the first occasion. Had he continued to do so? Perhaps even at this minute he was under observation. The thought irritated him.

Had her defects been less striking he could not possibly have continued these distressing visits. But since he had actually seen her in all her tragic uncouthness pity gained the upper hand, and henceforward he kept in constant touch with her and showed her every kindness. In the hope that she would abandon her sables he sent her presents of silk, satin and quilted stuffs. He also sent thick cloth such as old people wear, that the old man at the gate might be more comfortably dressed. Indeed he sent presents to everyone on the estate from the highest to the lowest. She did not seem to have any objection to receiving these donations, which under the circumstances was very convenient as it enabled him for the most part to limit their very singular friendship to good offices of this kind.

Utsusemi too, he remembered, had seemed to him far from handsome when he had peeped at her on the evening of her sudden flight. But she at least knew how to behave and that saved her plainness from being obtrusive. It was hard to believe that the princess belonged to a class so far above that of Utsusemi. It only showed how little these things have to do with birth or station. For in idle moments he still regretted the loss of Utsusemi and it rankled in him yet that he had in the end allowed her unyielding persistency to win the day.

And so the year drew to its close. One day when he was at his apartments in the Emperor's Palace, Myōbu came to see him. He liked to have her to do his hair and do small commissions for him. He was not in the least in love with her; but they got on very well together and he found her conversation so amusing that even when she had no duty to perform at the Palace he encouraged her to come and see him whenever she had any news.

"Something so absurd has happened," she said, "that I can hardly bring myself to tell you about it. . . ," and she paused smiling.

"I can hardly think," answered Genji, "that there can be anything which you are frightened of telling to me."

"If it were connected with my own affairs," she said, "you know quite well that I should tell you at once. But this is something quite different. I really find it very hard to talk about." For a long while he could get nothing out of her, and only after he had scolded her for making so unnecessary a fuss she at last handed him a letter. It was from the princess.

"But this," said Genji taking it, "is the last thing in the world that you could have any reason to hide from me."

She watched with interest while he read it. It was written on thick paper drenched with a strong perfume; the characters were bold and firm. With it was a poem:

> *Because of your hard heart, your hard heart only, the sleeves of this*
> *my Chinese dress are drenched with tears.*

The poem must, he thought, refer to something not contained in the letter.

He was considering what this could be, when his eye fell on a clumsy, old-fashioned clothes-box wrapped in a painted canvas cover. "Now," said Myōbu, "perhaps you understand why I was feeling rather uncomfortable. You may not believe it, but the princess means you to wear this jacket on New Year's Day. I am afraid I cannot take it back to her; that would be too unkind. But if you like I will keep it for you and no one else shall see it. Only please, since it was to you that she sent, just have one look at it before it goes away."

"But I should hate it to go away," said Genji; "I think it was so kind of her to send it."

It was difficult to know what to say. Her poem was indeed the most unpleasant jangle of syllables that he had ever encountered. He now realized that the other poems must have been dictated to her, perhaps by

Jijū or one of the other ladies. And Jijū too it must surely be who held the princess's brush and acted as writing-master. When he considered what her utmost poetic endeavour would be likely to produce he realized that these absurd verses were probably her masterpiece and should be prized accordingly. He began to examine the parcel; Myōbu blushed while she watched him. It was a plain, old-fashioned, buff-coloured jacket of finely woven material, but apparently not particularly well cut or stitched. It was indeed a strange present, and spreading out her letter he wrote something carelessly in the margin. When Myōbu looked over his shoulder she saw that he had written the verse:

How comes it that with my sleeve I brushed this saffron-flower[11] that has no loveliness either of shape or hue?

What, wondered Myōbu, could be the meaning of this outburst against a flower? At last turning over in her mind the various occasions when Genji had visited the princess she remembered something[12] which she had herself noticed one moonlit night, and though she felt the joke was rather unkind, she could not help being amused. With practised ease she threw out a verse in which she warned him that in the eyes of a censorious world even this half-whimsical courtship might fatally damage his good name. Her impromptu poem was certainly faulty; but Genji reflected that if the poor princess had even Myōbu's very ordinary degree of alertness it would make things much easier; and it was quite true that to tamper with a lady of such high rank was not very safe.

At this point visitors began to arrive. "Please put this somewhere out of sight," said Genji pointing to the jacket; "could one have believed that it was possible to be presented with such an object?" and he groaned.

"Oh why ever did I show it to him?" thought Myōbu. "The only result is that now he will be angry with me as well as with the princess," and in very low spirits she slipped out of his apartments.

Next day she was in attendance upon the Emperor and while she was waiting with other gentlewomen in the ladies' commonroom Genji came up saying: "Here you are. The answer to yesterday's letter. I am afraid it is rather far-fetched," and he flung a note to her. The curiosity of the other gentlewomen was violently aroused. Genji left the room humming "The

[11] *Suyetsumuhana*, by which name, the princess is subsequently alluded to in the story.
[12] I.e. the redness of the princess's nose.

Lady of Mikasa Hill,"[13] which naturally amused Myōbu very much. The other ladies wanted to know why the prince was laughing to himself. Was there some joke. . . ?

"Oh, no," said Myōbu; "I think it was only that he had noticed someone whose nose was a little red with the morning cold. The song he hummed was surely very appropriate."

"I think it was very silly," said one of the ladies. "There is no one here today with a red nose. He must be thinking of Lady Sakon or Higo no Uneme." They were completely mystified. When Myōbu presented Genji's reply, the ladies of the Hitachi Palace gathered round her to admire it. It was written negligently on plain white paper but was none the less very elegant. "Does your gift of a garment mean that you wish a greater distance than ever to be kept between us?"[14]

On the evening of the last day of the year he sent back the box which had contained his jacket, putting into it a court dress which had formerly been presented to him, a dress of woven stuff dyed grape-colour and various stuffs of yellow-rose colour and the like. The box was brought by Myōbu. The princess's ancient gentlewomen realized that Genji did not approve of their mistress's taste in colours and wished to give her a lesson.

"Yes," they said grudgingly, "that's a fine deep red while its new, but just think how it will fade. And in Madam's poem too, I am sure, there was much more good sense. In his answer he only tries to be smart." The princess shared their good opinion of her poem. It had cost her a great deal of effort and before she sent it she had been careful to copy it into her note-book.

Then came the New Year's Day celebrations; and this year there was also to be the New Year's mumming, a band of young noblemen going round dancing and singing in various parts of the Palace. After the festival of the White Horse on the seventh day Genji left the Emperor's presence at nightfall and went to his own apartments in the Palace as though intending to stay the night there. But later he adjourned to the Hitachi Palace which had on this occasion a less forbidding appearance than usual. Even the princess was rather more ordinary and amenable. He was hoping that like the season she too had begun anew, when he

---

[13] A popular song about a lady who suffered from the same defect as the princess.

[14] Genji's poem is an allusion to a well-known *uta* which runs: "Must we who once would not allow even the thickness of a garment to part us be now far from each other for whole nights on end?"

saw that sunlight was coming into the room. After hesitating for a while, he got up and went out into the front room. The double doors at the end of the eastern wing were wide open, and the roof of the verandah having fallen in, the sunshine poured straight into the house. A little snow was still falling and its brightness made the morning light yet more exquisitely brilliant and sparkling. She watched a servant helping him into his cloak. She was lying half out of the bed, her head hanging a little downwards and her hair falling in great waves to the floor. Pleased with the sight he began to wonder whether she would not one day outgrow her plainness. He began to close the door of the women's apartments, but suddenly feeling that he owed her amends for the harsh opinion of her appearance which he had formed before, he did not quite shut the door, but bringing a low stool towards it sat there putting his disordered head-dress to rights. One of the maids brought him an incredibly battered mirror-stand, Chinese combs, a box of toilet articles and other things. It amused him to discover that in this household of women a little male gear still survived, even in so decrepit a state.

He noticed that the princess, who was now up and dressed, was looking quite fashionable. She was in fact wearing the clothes which he had sent her before the New Year, but he did not at first recognize them. He began however to have a vague idea that her mantle, with its rather conspicuous pattern, was very like one of the things he had given her.

"I do hope," he said presently, "that this year you will be a little more conversational. I await the day when you will unbend a little towards me more eagerly than the poet longs for the first nightingale. If only like the year that has changed you too would begin anew!" Her face brightened. She had thought of a remark and trembling from head to foot with a tremendous effort she brought out the quotation, *"When plovers chirp and all things grow anew."*

"Splendid," said Genji, "this is a sign that the new year has indeed begun," and smiling encouragingly at her he left the house, she following him with her eyes from the couch on which she lay. Her face as usual was half covered by her arm; but the unfortunate flower still bloomed conspicuously.

"Poor thing, she really *is* very ugly," thought Genji in despair.

When he returned to the Nijō-in he found Murasaki waiting for him. She was growing up as handsome a girl as one could wish, and promised well for the future. She was wearing a plain close-fitting dress of cherry colour; above all, the unstudied grace and ease of her movements charmed and delighted him as he watched her come to meet him. In accordance with the wishes of her old-fashioned grandmother

her teeth were not blackened, but her eyebrows were delicately touched with stain. "Why, when I might be playing with a beautiful child, do I spend my time with an ugly woman?" Genji kept on asking himself in bewilderment while they sat together playing with her dolls. Next she began to draw pictures and colour them. After she had painted all sorts of queer and amusing things.

"Now I am going to do a picture for you," said Genji and drawing a lady with very long hair he put a dab of red on her nose. Even in a picture, he thought pausing to look at the effect, it gave one a most uncomfortable feeling. He went and looked at himself in the mirror and as though dissatisfied with his own fresh complexion he suddenly put on his own nose a dab of red such as he had given to the lady in the picture. He looked at himself in the mirror. His handsome face had in an instant become ridiculous and repulsive. At first the child laughed.

"Should you go on liking me if I were always as ugly as this?" he asked. Suddenly she began to be afraid that the paint would not come off.

"Oh why did you do it?" she cried. "How horrible!"

He pretended to rub it without effect. "No," he said ruefully, "it will not come off. What a sad end to our game! I wonder what the Emperor will say when I go back to the Palace?" He said it so seriously that she became very unhappy, and longing to cure him dipped a piece of thick soft paper in the water-jug which stood by his writing-things, and began scrubbing at his nose.

"Take care," he cried laughing, "that you do not serve me as Heichū[15] was treated by his lady. I would rather have a red nose than a black one." So they passed their time, making the prettiest couple.

In the gentle spring sunshine the trees were already shimmering with a haze of new-grown buds. Among them it was the plum-trees that gave the surest promise, for already their blossoms were uncurling, like lips parted in a faint smile. Earliest of them all was a red plum that grew beside the covered steps. It was in full colour. "Though fair the tree on which it blooms, this red flower fills me with a strange misgiving,"[16] sang Genji with a deep sigh.

We shall see in the next chapter what happened in the end to all these people.

---

[15] He used to splash his cheeks with water from a little bottle in order that she might think he was weeping at her unkindness. She exposed this device by mixing ink with the water.

[16] The reference of course is to the princess. "Though fair the tree" refers to her high birth.

VII

THE FESTIVAL OF RED LEAVES

The imperial visit to the Red Sparrow Court was to take place on the tenth day of the Godless Month. It was to be a more magnificent sight this year than it had ever been before and the ladies of the Palace were very disappointed that they could not be present.[1] The Emperor too could not bear that Fujitsubo should miss the spectacle, and he decided to hold a grand rehearsal in the Palace. Prince Genji danced the "Waves of the Blue Sea." Tō no Chūjō was his partner; but though both in skill and beauty he far surpassed the common run of performers, yet beside Genji he seemed like a mountain fir growing beside a cherry-tree in bloom. There was a wonderful moment when the rays of the setting sun fell upon him and the music grew suddenly louder. Never had the onlookers seen feet tread so delicately nor head so exquisitely poised; and in the song which follows the first movement of the dance his voice was sweet as that of Kalavinka[2] whose music is Buddha's Law. So moving and beautiful was this dance that at the end of it the Emperor's eyes were wet, and all the princes and great gentlemen wept aloud. When the song was over and, straightening his long dancer's sleeves, he stood waiting for the music to begin again and at last the more lively tune of the second movement struck up,—then indeed, with his flushed and eager face, he merited more than ever his name of Genji the Shining One.

The Princess Kōkiden[3] did not at all like to see her stepson's beauty arousing so much enthusiasm and she said sarcastically, "He is altogether too beautiful. Presently we shall have a god coming down from the sky to fetch him away."[4]

Her young waiting-ladies noticed the spiteful tone in which the remark was made and felt somewhat embarrassed. As for Fujitsubo, she kept on telling herself that were it not for the guilty secret which

[1] They were not allowed to leave the palace.
[2] The bird that sings in Paradise.
[3] See above p. 19.
[4] In allusion to a boy-prince of seven years old whom the jealous gods carried off to the sky. See the *Ōkagami*.

was shared between them the dance she was now witnessing would be filling her with wonder and delight. As it was, she sat as though in a dream, hardly knowing what went on around her.

Now she was back in her own room. The Emperor was with her.

"At today's rehearsal," he said, "The 'Waves of the Blue Sea' went perfectly." Then, noticing that she made no response, "What did you think of it?"

"Yes, it was very good," she managed to say at last. "The partner did not seem to me bad either," he went on; "there is always something about the way a gentleman moves and uses his hands which distinguishes his dancing from that of professionals. Some of our crack dancing-masters have certainly made very clever performers of their own children; but they never have the same freshness, the same charm as the young people of our class. They expended so much effort on the rehearsal that I am afraid the festival itself may seem a very poor affair. No doubt they took all this trouble because they knew that you were here at the rehearsal and would not see the real performance."

Next morning she received a letter from Genji:

What of the rehearsal? How little the people who watched me knew of the turmoil that all the while was seething in my brain!

And to this he added the poem:

When sick with love I yet sprang to my feet and capered with the rest, knew you what meant the fevered waving of my long dancing-sleeve?

Next he enjoined secrecy and prudence upon her, and so his letter ended. Her answer showed that despite her agitation she had not been wholly insensible to what had fascinated all other eyes:

"Though from far off a man of China waved his long dancing-sleeves, yet did his every motion fill my heart with wonder and delight."

To receive such a letter from her was indeed a surprise. It charmed him that her knowledge should extend even to the Court customs of a land beyond the sea. Already there was a regal note in her words. Yes, that was the end to which she was destined. Smiling to himself with pleasure he spread the letter out before him, grasping it tightly in both hands as a priest holds the holy book, and gazed at it for a long while.

On the day of the festival the royal princes and all the great gentlemen of the Court were in attendance. Even the Heir Apparent went with the procession. After the music-boats had rowed round the lake dance upon dance was performed, both Korean and of the land beyond the sea. The whole valley resounded with the noise of music and drums. The Emperor insisted upon treating Genji's performance at the rehearsal as a kind of miracle or religious portent, and ordered special services to be read in every temple. Most people thought this step quite reasonable; but Princess Kōkiden said crossly that she saw no necessity for it. The Ring[5] was by the Emperor's order composed indifferently of commoners and noblemen chosen out of the whole realm for their skill and grace. The two Masters of Ceremony, Sayemon no Kami and Uyemon no Kami, were in charge of the left and right wings of the orchestra. Dancing-masters and others were entrusted with the task of seeking out performers of unusual merit and training them for the festival in their own houses. When at last under the red leafage of tall autumn trees forty men stood circle-wise with their flutes and to the music that they made a strong wind from the hills sweeping the pine-woods added its fierce harmonies, while from amid a wreckage of whirling and scattered leaves the Dance of the Blue Waves suddenly broke out in all its glittering splendour,—a rapture seized the onlookers that was akin to fear.

The maple-wreath that Genji wore had suffered in the wind and thinking that the few red leaves which clung to it had a desolate air the Minister of the Left[6] plucked a bunch of chrysanthemums from among those that grew before the Emperor's seat and twined them in the dancer's wreath.

At sunset the sky clouded over and it looked like rain. But even the weather seemed conscious that such sights as this would not for a long while be seen again, and till all was over not a drop fell. His Exit Dance, crowned as he was with this unspeakably beautiful wreath of many coloured flowers, was even more astonishing than that wonderful moment on the day of the rehearsal and seemed to the thrilled onlookers like the vision of another world. Humble and ignorant folk sitting afar

---

[5] Those who stand in a circle round the dancers while the latter change their clothes.

[6] Reading "Sadaijin," not "Sadaishō."

on tree-roots or beneath some rock, or half-buried in deep banks of fallen leaves—few were so hardened that they did not shed a tear. Next came the "Autumn Wind" danced by Lady Jōkyōden's son[7] who was still a mere child. The remaining performances attracted little attention, for the audience had had its fill of wonders and felt that whatever followed could but spoil the recollection of what had gone before.

That night Genji was promoted to the First Class of the Third Rank and Tō no Chūjō was promoted to intermediate standing between the First and Second Classes of the Fourth Rank. The gentlemen of the court were all promoted one rank. But though they celebrated their good fortune with the usual rejoicings they were well aware that they had only been dragged in Genji's wake and wondered how it was that their destinies had come to be linked in this curious way with those of the prince who had brought them this unexpected piece of good fortune.

Fujitsubo now retired to her own house and Genji, waiting about for a chance of visiting her, was seldom at the Great Hall and was consequently in very ill odour there. It was soon after this that he brought the child Murasaki to live with him. Aoi heard a rumour of this, but it reached her merely in the form that someone was living with him at his palace and she did not know that it was a child. Under these circumstances it was quite natural that she should feel much aggrieved. But if only she had flown into an honest passion and abused him for it as most people would have done, he would have told her everything and put matters right. As it was, she only redoubled her icy aloofness and thus led him to seek those very distractions of which it was intended as a rebuke. Not only was her beauty so flawless that it could not fail to win his admiration, but also the mere fact that he had known her since so long ago, before all the rest, made him feel towards her a tenderness of which she seemed quite unaware. He was convinced however that her nature was not at bottom narrow and vindictive, and this gave him some hope that she would one day relent.

Meanwhile as he got to know little Murasaki better he became the more content both with her appearance and her character. She at least gave him her whole heart. For the present he did not intend to reveal her identity even to the servants in his own palace. She continued to use the somewhat outlying western wing which had now been put into

---

[7] Another illegitimate son of the Emperor; Genji's step-brother.

excellent order, and here Genji constantly came to see her. He gave her all kinds of lessons, writing exercises for her to copy and treating her in every way as though she were a little daughter who had been brought up by foster parents, but had now come to live with him. He chose her servants with great care and gave orders that they should do everything in their power to make her comfortable; but no one except Koremitsu knew who the child was or how she came to be living there. Nor had her father discovered what had become of her.

The little girl still sometimes thought of the past and then she would feel for a while very lonely without her grandmother. When Genji was there she forgot her sorrow; but in the evening he was very seldom at home. She was sorry that he was so busy and when he hurried every evening to some strange place or other she missed him terribly; but she was never angry with him. Sometimes for two or three days on end he would be at the Palace or the Great Hall and when he returned he would find her very tearful and depressed. Then he felt just as though he were neglecting some child of his own, whose mother had died and left it in his keeping, and for a while he grew uneasy about his night excursions.

The priest was puzzled when he heard that Genji had taken Murasaki to live with him, but saw no harm in it and was delighted that she should be so well cared for. He was gratified too when Genji begged that the services in the dead nun's memory should be celebrated with special pomp and magnificence.

When he went to Fujitsubo's palace, anxious to see for himself whether she was keeping her health, he was met by a posse of waiting-women (Myōbus, Chūnagons, Nakatsukasas and the like) and Fujitsubo herself showed, to his great disappointment, no sign of appearing. They gave a good account of her, which somewhat allayed his anxiety, and had passed on to general gossip when it was announced that Prince Hyōbukyō[8] had arrived. Genji at once went out to speak to him. This time Genji thought him extremely handsome and there was a softness, a caressing quality in his manner (Genji was watching him more closely than he knew) which was feminine enough to make his connection with Fujitsubo and Murasaki at once uppermost in the mind of his observer. It was, then, as the brother of the one and the father of the other that the new-comer at once created a feeling of intimacy, and

---

[8] Fujitsubo's brother; Murasaki's father.

they had a long conversation. Hyōbukyō could not fail to notice that Genji was suddenly treating him with an affection which he had never displayed before. He was naturally very much gratified, not realizing that Genji had now, in a sense, become his son-in-law. It was getting late and Hyōbukyō was about to join his sister in another room. It was with bitterness that Genji remembered how long ago the Emperor had brought her to play with him. In those days he ran in and out of her room just as he chose; now he could not address her save in precarious messages. She was as inaccessible, as remote as one person conceivably could be from another, and finding the situation intolerable, he said politely to Prince Hyōbukyō:

"I wish I saw you more often; unless there is some special reason for seeing people, I am lazy about it. But if you ever felt inclined to send for me, I should be delighted. . ." and he hurried away.

Ōmyōbu, the gentlewoman who had contrived Genji's meeting with Fujitsubo, seeing her mistress relapse into a steady gloom and vexed at her belated caution was all the time doing her best to bring the lovers together again; but days and months went by and still all her efforts were in vain; while they, poor souls, strove desperately to put away from them this love that was a perpetual disaster.

At Genji's palace Shōnagon, the little girl's nurse, finding herself in a world of unimagined luxuries and amenities, could only attribute this good fortune to the success of the late nun's prayers. The Lord Buddha to whose protection the dying lady had so fervently recommended her granddaughter had indeed made handsome provision for her. There were of course certain disadvantages. The haughtiness of Aoi was not only in itself to be feared, but it seemed to have the consequence of driving Prince Genji to seek distractions right and left, which would be very unpleasant for the little princess so soon as she was old enough to realize it. Yet so strong a preference did he show for the child's company that Shōnagon did not altogether lose heart.

It being then three months since her grandmother died Murasaki came out of mourning at the end of the Godless Month. But it was thought proper since she was to be brought up as an orphan that she should still avoid patterned stuffs, and she wore a little tunic of plain red, brown or yellow, in which she nevertheless looked very smart and gay.

He came to have a look at her before going off to the New Year's Day reception at Court. "From today onwards you are a grown-up lady," he said, and as he stood smiling at her he looked so charming and friendly that she could not bear him to go, and hoping that he would stay and play with her a little while longer she got out her toys. There was a doll's kitchen only three feet high but fitted out with all the proper utensils, and a whole collection of little houses which Genji had made for her. Now she had got them all spread out over the floor so that it was difficult to move without treading on them.

"Little Inu broke them yesterday," she explained, "when he was pretending to drive out the Old Year's demons, and I am mending them." She was evidently in great trouble.

"What a tiresome child he is," said Genji. "I will get them mended for you. Come, you must not cry on New Year's Day," and he went out. Many of the servants had collected at the end of the corridor to see him starting out for the Court in all his splendour. Murasaki too went out and watched him. When she came back she put a grand dress on one of her dolls and did a performance with it which she called "Prince Genji visiting the Emperor."

"This year," said Shōnagon, looking on with disapproval, "you must really try not to be such a baby. It is time little girls stopped playing with dolls when they are ten years old, and now that you have got a kind gentleman wanting to be your husband you ought to try and show him that you can behave like a nice little grown-up lady or he will get tired of waiting." She said this because she thought that it must be painful for Genji to see the child still so intent upon her games and be thus reminded that she was a mere baby. Her admonishment had the effect of making Murasaki for the first time aware that Genji was to be her husband. She knew all about husbands. Many of the maid-servants had them, but such ugly ones! She was very glad that hers was so much younger and handsomer. Nevertheless the mere fact that she thought about the matter at all showed that she was beginning to grow up a little. Her childish ways and appearance were by no means so great a misfortune as Shōnagon supposed, for they went a long way towards allaying the suspicions which the child's presence might otherwise have aroused in Genji's somewhat puzzled household.

When he returned from Court he went straight to the Great Hall. Aoi was as perfect as ever, and just as unfriendly. This never failed to wound Genji.

"If only you had changed with the New Year, had become a little less cold and forbidding, how happy I should be!" he exclaimed.

But she had heard that someone was living with him and had at once made up her mind that she herself had been utterly supplanted and put aside. Hence she was more sullen than ever; but he pretended not to notice it and by his gaiety and gentleness at last induced her to answer when he spoke. Was it her being four years older than him that made her seem so unapproachable, so exasperatingly well-regulated? But that was not fair. What fault could he possibly find in her? She was perfect in every respect and he realized that if she was sometimes out of humour this was solely the result of his own irregularities. She was after all the daughter of a Minister, and of the Minister who above all others enjoyed the greatest influence and esteem. She was the only child of the Emperor's sister and had been brought up with a full sense of her own dignity and importance. The least slight, the merest hint of disrespect came to her as a complete surprise. To Genji all these pretensions naturally seemed somewhat exaggerated and his failure to make allowances for them increased her hostility.

Aoi's father was vexed by Genji's seeming fickleness, but so soon as he was with him he forgot all his grievances and was always extremely nice to him. When Genji was leaving next day his father-in-law came to his room and helped him to dress, bringing in his own hands a belt which was an heirloom famous far and wide. He pulled straight the back of Genji's robe which had become a little crumpled, and indeed short of bringing him his shoes performed in the friendliest way every possible small service.

"This," said Genji handing back the belt, "is for Imperial banquets or other great occasions of that kind."

"I have others much more valuable," said the Minister, "which I will give you for the Imperial banquets. This one is not of much account save that the workmanship of it is rather unusual," and despite Genji's protests he insisted upon buckling it round him. The performance of such services was his principal interest in life. What did it matter if Genji was rather irregular in his visits? To have so agreeable a young man going in and out of one's house at all was the greatest pleasure he could imagine.

Genji did not pay many New Year's visits. First he went to the Emperor, then the Heir Apparent and the Ex-Emperor, and after that to Princess Fujitsubo's house in the Third Ward. As they saw him enter the servants of the house noticed how much he had grown and altered in the last year.

"Look how he has filled out," they said, "even since his last visit!"

Of the Princess herself he was only allowed a distant glimpse. It gave him many forebodings. Her child had been expected in the twelfth month and her condition was now causing some anxiety. That it would at any rate be born sometime during the first weeks of the New Year was confidently assumed by her own people and had been stated at Court. But the first month went by and still nothing happened. It began to be rumoured that she was suffering from some kind of possession or delusion. She herself grew very depressed; she felt certain that when the event at last happened she would not survive it and she worried so much about herself that she became seriously ill. The delay made Genji more certain than ever of his own responsibility and he arranged secretly for prayers on her behalf to be said in all the great temples. He had already become firmly convinced that whatever might happen concerning the child Fujitsubo was herself utterly doomed when he heard that about the tenth day of the second month she had successfully given birth to a boy. The news brought great satisfaction both to the Emperor and the whole court.

The Emperor's fervent prayers for her life and for that of a child which she knew was not his, distressed and embarrassed her; whereas, when the maliciously gloomy prognostications of Kōkiden and the rest were brought to her notice, she was at once filled with a perverse desire to disappoint their hopes and make them look ridiculous in the eyes of those to whom they had confided their forebodings. By a great effort of will she threw off the despair which had been weighing down upon her and began little by little to recover her usual vigour.

The Emperor was impatient to see Fujitsubo's child and so too (though he was forced to conceal his interest in the matter) was Genji himself. Accordingly he went to her palace when there were not many people about and sent in a note offering as the Emperor was in such a state of impatience to see the child and etiquette forbade him to do so for several weeks, to look at the child himself and report upon its appearance to the Emperor. She replied that she would rather he saw it on a day when it was less peevish; but in reality her refusal had nothing to do with the state of the child's temper; she could not bear the idea of his seeing it at all. Already it bore an astonishing resemblance to him; of that she was convinced. Always there lurked in her heart the torturing demon of fear. Soon others would see the child and instantly know with absolute certainty the secret of her swift transgression. What charity towards such a crime as this would a world have that gossips if a single hair is awry? Such thoughts continually tormented her and she again became weary of her life.

From time to time he saw Ōmyōbu, but though he still implored her to arrange a meeting none of his many arguments availed him. He also pestered her with so many questions about the child that she exclaimed at last: "Why do you go on plaguing me like this? You will be seeing him for yourself soon, when he is shown at Court."

But though she spoke impatiently she knew quite well what he was suffering and felt for him deeply. The matter was not one which he could discuss except with Fujitsubo herself, and it was impossible to see her. Would he indeed ever again see her alone or communicate with her save through notes and messengers? And half-weeping with despair he recited the verse: "*What guilty intercourse must ours have been in some life long ago, that now so cruel a barrier should be set between us?*"

Ōmyōbu seeing that it cost her mistress a great struggle to do without him was at pains not to dismiss him too unkindly and answered with the verse: "*Should you see the child my lady would be in torment; and because you have not seen it you are full of lamentations. Truly have children been called a black darkness that leads the parents heart astray!*" And coming closer she whispered to him, "Poor souls, it is a hard fate that has overtaken you both."

Thus many times and again he returned to his house desperate. Fujitsubo meanwhile, fearing lest Genji's continual visits should attract notice, began to suspect that Ōmyōbu was secretly encouraging him and no longer felt the same affection for her. She did not want this to be noticed and tried to treat her just as usual; but her irritation was bound sometimes to betray itself and Ōmyōbu, feeling that her mistress was estranged from her and at a loss to find any reason for it, was very miserable.

It was not till its fourth month that the child was brought to the Palace. It was large for its age and had already begun to take a great interest in what went on around it. Its extraordinary resemblance to Genji was not remarked upon by the Emperor who had an idea that handsome children were all very much alike at that age. He became intensely devoted to the child and lavished every kind of care and attention upon it. For Genji himself he had always had so great a partiality that, had it not been for popular opposition, he would certainly have installed him as Heir Apparent. That he had not been able to do so constantly distressed him. To have produced so magnificent a son and be obliged to watch him growing up a mere nobleman had always been galling to him. Now in his old age a son had been born to him who promised to be equally handsome and had not the tiresome disadvantage of a plebeian mother, and upon this flawless pearl he expended his whole affection. The mother saw little chance of this rapture continuing and was all this while in a state of agonized apprehension.

One day, when as he had been wont to do before, Genji was making music for her at the Emperor's command, His Majesty took the child in his arms saying to Genji: "I have had many children, but you were the only other one that I ever behaved about in this fashion. It may be my fancy, but it seems to me this child is exactly like what you were at the same age. However, I suppose all babies are very much alike while they are as small as this," and he looked at the fine child with admiration. A succession of violent emotions—terror, shame, pride and love—passed through Genji's breast while these words were being spoken, and were reflected in his rapidly changing colour. He was almost in tears. The child looked so exquisitely beautiful as it lay crowing to itself and smiling that, hideous as the situation was, Genji could not help feeling glad it was thought to be like him. Fujitsubo meanwhile was in a state of embarrassment and agitation so painful that a cold sweat broke out upon her while she sat by. For Genji this jarring of opposite emotions was too much to be borne and he went home. Here he lay tossing on his bed and, unable to distract himself, he determined after a while to go to the Great Hall. As he passed by the flower-beds in front of his house he noticed that a faint tinge of green was already filming the bushes and under them the *tokonatsu*[9] were already in bloom. He plucked one and sent it to Ōmyōbu with a long letter and an acrostic poem in which he said that he was touched by the likeness of this flower to the child, but also hinted that he was perturbed by the child's likeness to himself.

"In this flower," he continued despondently, "I had hoped to see your beauty enshrined. But now I know that being mine yet not mine it can bring me no comfort to look upon it."

After waiting a little while till a favourable moment should arise Ōmyōbu showed her mistress the letter, saying with a sigh, "I fear that your answer will be but dust to the petals of this thirsting flower." But Fujitsubo, in whose heart also the new spring was awakening a host of tender thoughts, wrote in answer the poem:

---

[9] Another name for the *nadeshiko*, "Child-of-my-heart," see p. 58.

LADY MURASAKI SHIKIBU

Though it alone be the cause that these poor sleeves are wet with dew,
yet goes my heart still with it, this child-flower of Yamato Land.

This was all and it was roughly scribbled in a faint hand, but it was a comfort to Ōmyōbu to have even such a message as this to bring back. Genji knew quite well that it could lead to nothing. How many times had she sent him such messages before! Yet as he lay dejectedly gazing at the note, the mere sight of her handwriting soon stirred in him a frenzy of unreasoning excitement and delight. For a while he lay restlessly tossing on his bed. At last unable to remain any longer inactive he sprang up and went, as he had so often done before, to the western wing to seek distraction from the agitated thoughts which pursued him. He came towards the women's apartments with his hair loose upon his shoulders, wearing a queer dressing gown and, in order to amuse Murasaki, playing a tune on his flute as he walked. He peeped in at the door. She looked as she lay there for all the world like the fresh dewy flower that he had so recently plucked. She was growing a little bit spoilt and having heard some while ago that he had returned from Court she was rather cross with him for not coming to see her at once. She did not run to meet him as she usually did, but lay with her head turned away. He called to her from the far side of the room to get up and come to him, but she did not stir.

Suddenly he heard that she was murmuring to herself the lines *"Like a sea-flower that the waters have covered when a great tide mounts the shore."* They were from an old poem[10] that he had taught her, in which a lady complains that she is neglected by her lover. She looked bewitching as she lay with her face half-sullenly, half-coquettishly buried in her sleeve.

"How naughty," he cried. "Really you are becoming too witty. But if you saw me more often perhaps you would grow tired of me."

Then he sent for his zithern and asked her to play to him. But it was a big Chinese instrument[11] with thirteen strings; the five slender strings in the middle embarrassed her and she could not get the full sound out of them. Taking it from her he shifted the bridge, and tuning it to a lower pitch played a few chords upon it and bade her try again. Her sullen mood was over. She began to play very prettily; sometimes, when there was a gap too long for one small hand to stretch, helping herself

---

[10] *Shū-i Shū* 967.
[11] A sō no koto.

out so adroitly with the other hand that Genji was completely captivated and taking up his flute taught her a number of new tunes. She was very quick and grasped the most complicated rhythms at a single hearing. She had indeed in music as in all else just those talents with which it most delighted him that she should be endowed. When he played the Hosoroguseri (which in spite of its absurd name is an excellent tune) she accompanied him though with a childish touch, yet in perfect time.

The great lamp was brought in and they began looking at pictures together. But Genji was going out that night. Already his attendants were assembled in the courtyard outside. One of them was saying that a storm was coming on. He ought not to wait any longer. Again Murasaki was unhappy. She was not looking at the pictures, but sat with her head on her hands staring despondently at the floor. Stroking the lovely hair that had fallen forward across her lap Genji asked her if she missed him when he was away. She nodded.

"I am just the same," he said. "If I miss seeing you for a single day I am terribly unhappy. But you are only a little girl and I know that whatever I do you will not think harsh thoughts about me; while the lady that I go to see is very jealous and angry so that it would break her heart if I were to stay with you too long. But I do not at all like being there and that is why I just go for a little while like this. When you are grown up of course I shall never go away at all. I only go now because if I did not she would be so terribly angry with me that I might very likely die[12] and then there would be no one to love you and take care of you at all."

He had told her all he could, but still she was offended and would not answer a word. At last he took her on his knee and here to his great embarrassment she fell asleep.

"It is too late to go out now," he said after a while, turning to the gentlewomen who were in attendance. They rose and went to fetch his supper. He roused the child.

"Look," he said, "I did not go out after all." She was happy once more and they went to supper together. She liked the queer, irregular meal, but when it was over she began again to watch him uneasily.

"If you are really not going out," she said, "why do you not go to sleep at once?" Leaving her at such a moment to go back to his room he felt

---

[12] That hate kills is a fundamental thesis of the book.

all the reluctance of one who is setting out upon a long and perilous journey.

It constantly happened that at the last minute he thus decided to stay with her. It was natural that some report of his new pre-occupation should leak out into the world and be passed on to the Great Hall.

"Who can it be?" said one of Aoi's ladies. "It is really the most inexplicable business. How can he have suddenly become entirely wrapped up in someone whom we had never heard the existence of before? It cannot in any case be a person of much breeding or self-respect. It is probably some girl employed at the Palace whom he has taken to live with him in order that the affair may be hushed up. No doubt he is circulating the story that she is a child merely in order to put us off the scent." And this opinion was shared by the rest.

The Emperor too had heard that there was someone living with Genji and thought it a great pity. "You are treating the Minister very badly," he said. "He has shown the greatest possible devotion to you ever since you were a mere baby and now that you are old enough to know better you behave like this towards him and his family! It is really most ungrateful."

Genji listened respectfully, but made no reply. The Emperor began to fear that his marriage with Aoi had proved a very unhappy one and was sorry that he had arranged it. "I do not understand you," he said. "You seem to have no taste for gallantry and do not, so far as I can see, take the slightest interest in any of the ladies-in-waiting whom one might expect you to find attractive, nor do you bother yourself about the various beauties who in one part of the town or another are now in request; but instead you must needs pick up some creature from no one knows where and wound the feelings of others by keeping her as your mistress!"

Though he was now getting on in years the Emperor had himself by no means ceased to be interested in such matters. He had always seen to it that his ladies-in-waiting and palace-servants should be remarkable both for their looks and their intelligence, and it was a time when the Court was full of interesting women. There were few among them whom Genji could not by the slightest word or gesture have made his own. But, perhaps because he saw too much of them, he did not find them in the least attractive. Suspecting this, they would occasionally experiment upon him with some frivolous remark. He answered so staidly that they saw a flirtation would be impossible and some of them came to the conclusion that he was rather a dull, prudish young man.

There was an elderly lady-of-the-bedchamber who, though she was an excellent creature in every other way and was very much liked and respected, was an outrageous flirt. It astonished Genji that despite her advancing years she showed no sign of reforming her reckless and fantastic behaviour. Curious to see how she would take it he one day came up and began joking with her. She appeared to be quite unconscious of the disparity between their ages and at once counted him as an admirer. Slightly alarmed, he nevertheless found her company rather agreeable and often talked with her. But, chiefly because he was frightened of being laughed at if anyone found out, he refused to become her lover, and this she very much resented. One day she was dressing the Emperor's hair. When this was over his Majesty sent for his valets and went with them into another room. Genji and the elderly lady were left alone together. She was fuller than ever of languishing airs and poses, and her costume was to the last degree stylish and elaborate.

"Poor creature," he thought, "How little difference it all makes!" and he was passing her on his way out of the room when suddenly the temptation to give a tug at her dress became irresistible.

She glanced swiftly round, eyeing him above the rim of a marvellously painted summer-fan. The eyelids beneath which she ogled at him were blackened and sunken; wisps of hair projected untidily around her forehead. There was something singularly inappropriate about this gawdy, coquettish fan. Handing her his own instead, he took it from her and examined it. On paper coated with a red so thick and lustrous that you could see yourself reflected in it a forest of tall trees was painted in gold. At the side of this design, in a hand which though out-of-date was not lacking in distinction was written the poem about the Forest of Oaraki.[13] He made no doubt that the owner of the fan had written it in allusion to her own advancing years and was expecting him to make a gallant reply. Turning over in his mind how best to divert the extravagant ardour of this strange creature he could, to his own amusement, think only of another poem[14] about the same forest; but to this it would have been ill-bred to allude. He was feeling very uncomfortable lest someone should come in and see them together.

---

[13] "So withered is the grass beneath its trees that the young colt will not graze there and the reapers do not come."

[14] "So sweet is its shade that all the summer through its leafy avenues are thronged," alluding to the lady's many lovers.

She however was quite at her ease and seeing that he remained silent she recited with many arch looks the poem:

"*Come to me in the forest and I will cut pasture for your horse, though it be but of the under leaf whose season is past.*"

"Should I seek your woodland," he answered, "my fair name would be gone, for down its glades at all times the pattering of hoofs is heard," and he tried to get away; but she held him back saying: "How odious you are! That is not what I mean at all. No one has ever insulted me like this before," and she burst into tears.

"Let us talk about it someother time," said Genji; "I did not mean. . ." and freeing himself from her grasp he rushed out of the room, leaving her in great dudgeon. She felt indeed after his repulse prodigiously old and tottering. All this was seen by His Majesty who, his toilet long ago completed, had watched the ill-assorted pair with great amusement from behind his Imperial screen.

"I am always being told," he said, "that the boy takes no interest in the members of my household. But I cannot say that he seems to me unduly shy," and he laughed. For a moment she was slightly embarrassed; but she felt that any relationship with Genji, even if it consisted of being rebuffed by him in public, was distinctly a feather in her cap, and she made no attempt to defend herself against the Emperor's raillery. The story soon went the round of the Court. It astonished no one more than Tō no Chūjō who, though he knew that Genji was given to odd experiments, could not believe that his friend was really launched upon the fantastic courtship which rumour was attributing to him. There seemed no better way of discovering whether it was conceivably possible to regard the lady in such a light than to make love to her himself.

The attentions of so distinguished a suitor went a long way towards consoling her for her late discomfiture. Her new intrigue was of course carried on with absolute secrecy and Genji knew nothing about it. When he next met her she seemed to be very cross with him, and feeling sorry for her because she was so old he made up his mind that he must try to console her. But for a long while he was completely occupied by tiresome business of one kind and another. At last one very dismal rainy evening when he was strolling in the neighbourhood of the Ummeiden[15] he heard this lady playing most agreeably on her lute. She

---

[15] The headquarters of the Ladies of the Bedchamber.

was so good a performer that she was often called upon to play with the professional male musicians in the Imperial orchestra. It happened that at this moment she was somewhat downcast and discontented, and in such a mood she played with even greater feeling and verve. She was singing the "Melon-grower's Song"[16]; admirably, he thought, despite its inappropriateness to her age. So must the voice of the mysterious lady at O-chou have sounded in Po Chü-i's ears when he heard her singing on her boat at night[17]; and he stood listening. At the end of the song the player sighed heavily as though quite worn out by the passionate vehemence of her serenade.

Genji approached softly humming the "Azumaya": "*Here in the portico of the eastern house rain splashes on me while I wait. Come, my beloved, open the door and let me in.*"

Immediately, indeed with an unseemly haste, she answered as does the lady in the song, "*Open the door and come in,*"[18] adding the verse: "*In the wide shelter of that portico no man yet was ever splashed with rain,*" and again she sighed so portentously that although he did not at all suppose that he alone was the cause of this demonstration he felt it in any case to be somewhat exaggerated and answered with the poem: "*Your sighs show clearly that, despite the song, you are another's bride, and I for my part have no mind to haunt the loggias of your eastern house.*"

He would gladly have passed on, but he felt that this would be too unkind, and seeing that someone else was coming towards her room he stepped inside and began talking lightly of indifferent subjects, in a style which though it was in reality somewhat forced she found very entertaining.

It was intolerable, thought Tō no Chūjō, that Genji should be praised as a quiet and serious young man and should constantly rebuke him for his frivolity, while all the time he was carrying on a multiplicity of interesting intrigues which out of mere churlishness he kept entirely hidden from all his friends. For a long while Chūjō had been waiting for an opportunity to expose this sanctimonious imposture, and when he saw Genji enter the gentlewoman's apartment you may be sure he was

---

[16] An old folk-song the refrain of which is "At the melon-hoeing he said he loved me and what am I to do, what am I to do?"

[17] The poem referred to is not the famous *Lute Girl's Song*, but a much shorter one (*Works* x. 8) on a similar theme. O-chou is the modern Wu-chang in Hupeh.

[18] In the song the lady says: "The door is not bolted or barred. Come quickly and talk to me. Am I another's bride, that you should be so careful and shy?"

delighted. To scare him a little at such a moment would be an excellent way to punish him for his unfriendliness. He slackened his pace and watched. The wind sighed in the trees. It was getting very late. Surely Genji would soon begin to doze? And indeed he did now look as though he had fallen asleep. Chūjō stole on tip-toe into the room; but Genji who was only half dreaming instantly heard him, and not knowing that Chūjō had followed him got it into his head that it was a certain Commissioner of Works who years ago had been supposed to be an admirer of the lady. The idea of being discovered in such a situation by this important old gentleman filled him with horror. Furious with his companion for having exposed him to the chance of such a predicament:

"This is too bad," he whispered, "I am going home. What possessed you to let me in on a night when you knew that someone else was coming?"

He had only time to snatch up his cloak and hide behind a long folding screen before Chūjō entered the room and going straight up to the screen began in a business-like manner to fold it up. Though she was no longer young the lady did not lose her head in this alarming crisis. Being a woman of fashion she had on more than one occasion found herself in an equally agitating position, and now despite her astonishment, after considering for a moment what had best be done with the intruder, she seized him by the back of his coat and with a practised though trembling hand pulled him away from the screen. Genji had still no idea that it was Chūjō. He had half a mind to show himself, but quickly remembered that he was oddly and inadequately clad, with his head-dress all awry. He felt that if he ran for it he would cut much too strange a figure as he left the room, and for a moment he hesitated. Wondering how much longer Genji would take to recognize him Chūjō did not say a word but putting on the most ferocious air imaginable drew his sword from the scabbard. Whereupon the lady crying "Gentlemen! Gentlemen!" flung herself between them in an attitude of romantic supplication. They could hardly refrain from bursting into laughter. It was only by day when very carefully painted and bedizened that she still retained a certain superficial air of youth and charm. But now this woman of fifty-seven or eight, disturbed by a sudden brawl in the midst of her amours, created the most astonishing spectacle as she knelt at the feet of two young men in their 'teens beseeching them not to die for her. Chūjō however refrained from showing the slightest sign of amusement and continued to look as alarming and ferocious as he could. But he was now in full view and Genji realized in a moment that Chūjō had all the while known who he was and had been amusing himself at his expense. Much relieved at this discovery he grabbed at the scabbard from which Chūjō had drawn the sword and held it fast lest his friend should attempt to escape and then, despite his annoyance at having been followed, burst into an uncontrollable fit of laughter.

"Are you in your right mind?" said Genji at last. "This is really a very poor sort of joke. Do you mind letting me get into my cloak?" Whereupon Chūjō snatched the cloak from him and would not give it back.

"Very well then," said Genji; "if you are to have my cloak I must have yours," and so saying he pulled open the clasp of Chūjō's belt and began tugging his cloak from his shoulders. Chūjō resisted and a long tussle followed in which the cloak was torn to shreds.

"Should you now get it in exchange for yours, this tattered cloak will but reveal the secrets it is meant to hide," recited Tō no Chūjō; to which Genji replied with an acrostic poem in which he complained that Chūjō with whom he shared so many secrets should have thought it necessary to spy upon him in this fashion.

But neither was really angry with the other and setting their disordered costumes to rights they both took their departure. Genji discovered when he was alone that it had indeed upset him very much to find his movements had been watched, and he could not sleep. The lady felt utterly bewildered. On the floor she found a belt and a buckle which she sent to Genji next day with a complicated acrostic poem in which she compared these stranded properties to the weeds which after their straining and tugging the waves leave upon the shore. She added an allusion to the crystal river of her tears. He was irritated by her persistency but distressed at the shock to which she had been subjected by Chūjō's foolish joke, and he answered with the poem: *"At the antics of the prancing wave you have good cause to be angry; but blameless indeed is the shore on whose sands it lashed."*

The belt was Chūjō's; that was plain for it was darker in colour than his own cloak. And as he examined his cloak he noticed that the lower half of one sleeve was torn away. What a mess everything was in! He told himself with disgust that he was becoming a rowdy, a vulgar night-brawler. Such people, he knew, were always tearing their clothes and making themselves ridiculous. It was time to reform.

The missing sleeve soon arrived from Chūjō's apartments with the message:

Had you not better have this sewn on before you wear your cloak?

How had he managed to get hold of it? Such tricks were very tiresome and silly. But he supposed he must now give back the belt, and wrapping it in paper of the same colour he sent it with a riddling poem in which he said that he would not keep it lest he should make trouble between Chūjō and the lady.

"You have dragged her away from me as in the scuffle you snatched from me this belt," said Chūjō in his answering poem, and added, "Have I not good reason to be angry with you?"

Later in the morning they met in the Presence Room. Genji wore a solemn and abstracted air. Chūjō could not help recollecting the absurd scene of their last meeting, but it was a day upon which there was a great deal of public business to dispatch and he was soon absorbed in his duties. But from time to time each would catch sight of the other's serious face and heavy official bearing, and then they could not help smiling. In an interval Chūjō came up to Genji and asked him in a low voice whether he had decided in future to be a little more communicative about his affairs.

"No, indeed," said Genji; "but I feel I owe you an apology for preventing you from spending a happy hour with the lady whom you had come to visit. Everything in life seems to go wrong."

So they whispered and at the end each solemnly promised the other not to speak of the matter to anybody. But to the two of them it furnished a constant supply of jokes for a long while to come, though Genji took the matter to heart more than he showed and was determined never to get mixed up with such a tiresome creature again. He heard however that the lady was still much ruffled, and fearing that there might be no one at hand to comfort her he had not the heart quite to discontinue his visits.

Chūjō, faithful to his promise, did not mention the affair to anyone, not even to his sister, but kept it as a weapon of self-defence should Genji ever preach high morality to him again.

Such marked preference did the Emperor show in his treatment of Genji that even the other princes of the Blood Royal stood somewhat in awe of him. But Tō no Chūjō was ready to dispute with him on any subject, and was by no means inclined always to let him have his own way. He and Aoi were the only children of the Emperor's sister. Genji, it is true, was the Emperor's son; but though Chūjō's father was only a Minister his influence was far greater than that of his colleagues, and as the son of such a man by his marriage with a royal princess he was used to being treated with the greatest deference. It had never so much as occurred to him that he was in any way Genji's inferior; for he knew that as regards his person at least he had no reason to be dissatisfied; and with most other qualities, whether of character or intelligence, he believed himself to be very adequately endowed. Thus a friendly rivalry grew up between the two of them and led to many diverting incidents which it would take too long to describe.

In the seventh month two events of importance took place. An empress was appointed[19] and Genji was raised to the rank of Counsellor. The Emperor was intending very soon to resign the Throne. He would have liked to proclaim his new-born child as Heir Apparent in place of Kōkiden's son. This was difficult, for there was no political function which would have supported such a choice. Fujitsubo's relations were all members of the Imperial family[20] and Genji, to whom he might have looked for help owing to his affiliation with the Minamoto clan, unfortunately showed no aptitude for political intrigue. The best he could do was at any rate to strengthen Fujitsubo's position and hope that later on she would be able to exert her influence. Kōkiden heard of his intentions, and small wonder if she was distressed and astounded. The Emperor tried to quiet her by pointing out that in a short time her son would succeed to the Throne and that she would then hold the equally important rank of Empress Mother. But it was indeed hard that the mother of the Heir Apparent should be passed over in favour of a concubine aged little more than twenty. The public tended to take Kōkiden's side and there was a good deal of discontent. On the night when the new Empress was installed Genji, as a Counsellor, was among those who accompanied her to the Middle Palace. As daughter of a previous Empress and mother of an exquisite prince she enjoyed a consideration at Court beyond that which her new rank would have alone procured for her. But if it was with admiring devotion that the other great lords of her train attended her that day, it may be imagined with what fond yet agonized thoughts Prince Genji followed the litter

---

[19] The rank of Empress was often not conferred till quite late in a reign. It was of course Fujitsubo whom the Emperor chose in this case.

[20] And therefore debarred from taking part in political life.

LADY MURASAKI SHIKIBU

in which she rode. She seemed at last to have been raised so far beyond his reach that scarce knowing what he did he murmured to himself the lines: "*Now upon love's dark path has the last shadow closed; for I have seen you carried to a cloud-land whither none may climb.*"

As the days and months went by the child grew more and more like Genji. The new Empress was greatly distressed, but no one else seemed to notice the resemblance. He was not of course so handsome; how indeed should he have been? But both were beautiful, and the world was content to accept their beauty without troubling to compare them, just as it accepts both moon and sun as lovely occupants of the sky.

VIII

The Flower Feast

About the twentieth day of the second month the Emperor gave a Chinese banquet under the great cherry-tree of the Southern Court. Both Fujitsubo and the Heir Apparent were to be there. Kōkiden, although she knew that the mere presence of the Empress was sufficient to spoil her pleasure, could not bring herself to forego so delightful an entertainment. After some promise of rain the day turned out magnificent; and in full sunshine, with the birds singing in every tree, the guests (royal princes, noblemen and professional poets alike) were handed the rhyme words which the Emperor had drawn by lot, and set to work to compose their poems. It was with a clear and ringing voice that Genji read out the word "Spring" which he had received as the rhyme-sound of his poem.

Next came Tō no Chūjō who, feeling that all eyes were upon him and determined to impress himself favourably on his audience, moved with the greatest possible elegance and grace; and when on receiving his rhyme he announced his name, rank, and titles, he took great pains to speak pleasantly as well as audibly. Many of the other gentlemen were rather nervous and looked quite pale as they came forward, yet they acquitted themselves well enough. But the professional poets, particularly owing to the high standard of accomplishment which the Emperor's and Heir Apparent's lively interest in Chinese poetry had at that time diffused through the Court, were very ill at ease; as they crossed the long space of the garden on their way to receive their rhymes they felt utterly helpless.

A simple Chinese verse is surely not much to ask of a professional poet; but they all wore an expression of the deepest gloom. One expects elderly scholars to be somewhat odd in their movements and behaviour, and it was amusing to see the lively concern with which the Emperor watched their various but always uncouth and erratic methods of approaching the Throne. Needless to say a great deal of music had been arranged for. Towards dusk the delightful dance known as the Warbling of Spring Nightingales was performed, and when it was over the Heir Apparent, remembering the Festival of Red Leaves, placed a wreath on Genji's head and pressed him so urgently that it was impossible for him to refuse. Rising to his feet he danced very quietly a fragment of the sleeve-turning passage in the Wave Dance. In a few moments he was seated again, but even into this brief extract from a long dance he managed to import an unrivalled charm and grace. Even his father-in-law who was not in the best of humour with him was deeply moved and found himself wiping away a tear.

"And why have we not seen Tō no Chūjō?" said the Heir Apparent. Whereupon Chūjō danced the Park of Willow Flowers, giving a far more complete performance than Genji, for no doubt he knew that he would be called upon and had taken trouble to prepare his dance. It was a great success and the Emperor presented him with a cloak, which everyone said was a most unusual honour. After this the other young noblemen who were present danced in no particular order, but it was now so dark that it was impossible to discriminate between their performances.

Then the poems were opened and read aloud. The reading of Genji's verses was continually interrupted by loud murmurs of applause. Even the professional poets were deeply impressed, and it may well be imagined what pride the Emperor, to whom at times Genji was a source of consolation and delight, watched him upon such an occasion as this. Fujitsubo, when she allowed herself to glance in his direction, marvelled that even Kōkiden could find it in her heart to hate him. "It is because he is fond of me; there can be no other reason," she decided at last and the verse, "*Were I but a common mortal who now am gazing at the beauty of this flower, from its sweet petals not long should I withhold the dew of love,*" framed itself on her lips, though she dared not utter it aloud.

It was now very late and the banquet was over. The guests had scattered. The Empress and the Heir Apparent had both returned to the Palace—all was still. The moon had risen very bright and clear, and Genji, heated with wine, could not bear to quit so lovely a scene. The people at the Palace were probably all plunged in a heavy sleep. On such a night it was not impossible that some careless person might have left some door unfastened, some shutter unbarred. Cautiously and stealthily he crept towards Fujitsubo's apartments and inspected them. Every bolt was fast. He sighed; here there was evidently nothing to be done. He was passing the loggia of Kōkiden's palace when he noticed that the shutters of the third arch were not drawn. After the banquet Kōkiden herself had gone straight to the Emperor's rooms. There did not seem to be anyone about. A door leading from the loggia into the house was standing open, but he could hear no sound within.

"It is under just such circumstances as this that one is apt to drift into compromising situations," thought Genji. Nevertheless he climbed quietly on to the balustrade and peeped. Everyone must be asleep. But no; a very agreeable young voice with an intonation which was certainly not that of any waiting-woman or common person was softly humming the last two lines of the *Oborozuki-yo*.[1] Was not the voice coming towards him? It seemed so, and stretching out his hand he suddenly found that he was grasping a lady's sleeve.

"Oh, how you frightened me," she cried.

"Who is it?"

"Do not be alarmed," he whispered. "That both of us were not content to miss the beauty of this departing night is proof more clear than the half-clouded moon that we were meant to meet," and as he recited the words he took her gently by the hand and led her into the house, closing the door behind them. Her surprised and puzzled air fascinated him.

"There is someone there," she whispered tremulously, pointing to the inner room.

"Child," he answered, "I am allowed to go wherever I please and if you send for your friends they will only tell you that I have every right to be here. But if you will stay quietly here. . ."

It was Genji. She knew his voice and the discovery somewhat reassured her. She thought his conduct rather strange, but she was determined that he should not think her prudish or stiff. And so because he on his side was still somewhat excited after the doings of the evening, while she was far too young and pliant to offer any serious resistance, he soon got his own way with her.

Suddenly they saw to their discomfiture that dawn was creeping into the sky. She looked, thought Genji, as though many disquieting reflections were crowding into her mind. "Tell me your name," he said. "How can I write to you unless you do? Surely this is not going to be our only meeting?"

She answered with a poem in which she said that names are of this world only and he would not care to know hers if he were resolved that their love should last till worlds to come. It was a mere quip and

---

[1] A famous poem by Ōye no Chisato (ninth century): "What so lovely as a night when the moon though dimly clouded is never wholly lost to sight."

Genji, amused at her quickness, answered, "You are quite right. It was a mistake on my part to ask." And he recited the poem, *"While still I seek to find on which blade dwells the dew, a great wind shakes the grasses of the level land."*

"If you did not repent of this meeting," he continued, "you would surely tell me who you are. I do not believe that you want. . ." But here he was interrupted by the noise of people stirring in the next room. There was a great bustle and it was clear that they would soon be starting out to fetch Princess Kōkiden back from the Palace. There was just time to exchange fans in token of their new friendship before Genji was forced to fly precipitately from the room. In his own apartments he found many of his gentlemen waiting for him. Some were awake, and these nudged one another when he entered the room as though to say, "Will he never cease these disreputable excursions?"

But discretion forbade them to show that they had seen him and they all pretended to be fast asleep.

Genji too lay down, but he could not rest. He tried to recall the features of the lady with whom he had just spent so agreeable a time. Certainly she must be one of Kōkiden's sisters. Perhaps the fifth or sixth daughter, both of whom were still unmarried. The handsomest of them (or so he had always heard) were Prince Sochi's wife and the fourth daughter, the one with whom Tō no Chūjō got on so badly. It would really be rather amusing if it did turn out to be Chūjō's wife. The sixth was shortly to be married to the Heir Apparent. How tiresome if it were she! But at present he could think of no way to make sure. She had not behaved at all as though she did not want to see him again. Why then had she refused to give him any chance of communicating with her? In fact he worried about the matter so much and turned it over in his mind with such endless persistency that it soon became evident he had fallen deeply in love with her. Nevertheless no sooner did the recollection of Fujitsubo's serious and reticent demeanour come back to his mind than he realized how incomparably more she meant to him than this light-hearted lady.

That day the after-banquet kept him occupied till late at night. At the Emperor's command he performed on the thirteen-stringed zithern and had an even greater success than with his dancing on the day before. At dawn Fujitsubo retired to the Emperor's rooms. Disappointed in his hope that the lady of last night would somewhere or somehow make her appearance on the scene, he sent for Yoshikiyo and Koremitsu with whom all his secrets were shared and bade them keep watch upon the lady's family. When he returned next day from duty at the Palace they reported that they had just witnessed the departure of several coaches which had been drawn up under shelter in the Courtyard of the Watch. "Among a group of persons who seemed to be the domestic attendants of those for whom the coaches were waiting two gentlemen came threading their way in a great hurry. These we recognized as Shii no Shōshō and Uchūben,[2] so there is little doubt that the carriages belonged to Princess Kōkiden. For the rest we noted that the ladies were by no means ill looking and that the whole party drove away in three carriages."

Genji's heart beat fast. But he was no nearer than before to finding out which of the sisters it had been. Supposing her father, the Minister of the Right, should hear anything of this, what a to-do there would be! It would indeed mean his absolute ruin. It was a pity that while he was about it he did not stay with her till it was a little lighter. But there it was! He did not know her face, but yet he was determined to recognize her. How? He lay on his bed devising and rejecting endless schemes. Murasaki too must be growing impatient. Days had passed since he had visited her and he remembered with tenderness how low-spirited she became when he was not able to be with her. But in a moment his thoughts had returned to the unknown lady. He still had her fan. It was a folding fan with ribs of hinoki-wood and tassels tied in a splice-knot. One side was covered with silverleaf on which was painted a dim moon, giving the impression of a moon reflected in water. It was a device which he had seen many times before, but it had agreeable associations for him, and continuing the metaphor of the "grass on the moor" which she had used in her poem he wrote on the fan—"*Has mortal man ever puzzled his head with such a question before as to ask where the moon goes to when she leaves the sky at dawn?*" And he put the fan safely away. It was on his conscience that he had not for a long while been to the Great Hall; but fearing that Murasaki too might be feeling very unhappy he first went home to give her her lessons. Everyday she was improving not only in looks, but also in amiability of character. The beauty of her disposition was indeed quite out of the common. The idea that so perfect a nature was in his hands, to train and cultivate as he thought best, was very attractive to Genji. It might however have been objected

---

[2] Kōkiden's brothers.

that to receive all her education from a young man is likely to make a girl somewhat forward in her manner.

First there was a great deal to tell her about what had happened at the Court entertainments of the last few days. Then followed her music lesson, and already it was time to go. "Oh why must he always go away so soon?" she wondered sadly, but by now she was so used to it that she no longer fretted as she had done a little while ago.

At the Great Hall he could, as usual, scarcely get a word out of Aoi. The moment that he sat idle a thousand doubts and puzzles began to revolve in his mind. He took up his zithern and began to sing:

> *Not softlier pillowed is my head*
> *That rests by thine, unloving bride,*
> *Than were those jagged stones my bed*
> *Through which the falls of Nuki stride.*

At this moment Aoi's father came by and began to discuss the unusual success of the recent festivities. "Old as I am," he said, "and I may say that I have lived to see four illustrious sovereigns occupy the Throne, I have never taken part in a banquet which produced verses so spirited or dancing and music so admirably performed. Talent of every description seems at present to exist in abundance; but it is creditable to those in authority that they knew how to make good use of it. For my part I enjoyed myself so much that had I but been a few years younger I would positively have joined in the dancing!"

"No special steps were taken to discover the musicians," answered Genji. "We merely used those who were known to the government in one part of the country and another as capable performers. If I may say so, it was Chūjō's Willow Dance that made the deepest impression and is likely always to be remembered as a remarkable performance. But if you, Sir, had indeed honoured us a new lustre would have been added to my Father's reign." Aoi's brothers now arrived and leaning against the balustrade gave a little concert, their various instruments blending delightfully.

Fugitive as their meeting had been it had sufficed to plunge the lady whose identity Prince Genji was now seeking to establish into the depths of despair; for in the fourth month she was to become the Heir Apparent's wife. Turmoil filled her brain. Why had not Genji visited her again? He must surely know whose daughter she was. But how should he know which daughter? Besides, her sister Kōkiden's house was not a place where, save under very strange circumstances, he was likely to feel at all at his ease. And so she waited in great impatience and distress; but of Genji there was no news.

About the twentieth day of the third month her father, the Minister of the Right, held an archery meeting at which most of the young noblemen and princes were present. It was followed by a wistaria feast. The cherry blossom was for the most part over, but two trees, which the Minister seemed somehow to have persuaded to flower later than all the rest, were still an enchanting sight. He had had his house rebuilt only a short time ago when celebrating the initiation of his granddaughters, the children of Kōkiden. It was now a magnificent building and not a thing in it but was of the very latest fashion. He had invited Genji when he had met him at the Palace only a few days before and was extremely annoyed when he did not appear. Feeling that the party would be a failure if Genji did not come, he sent his son Shii no Shōshō to fetch him, with the poem: *"Were my flowers as those of other gardens never should I have ventured to summon you."* Genji was in attendance upon the Emperor and at once showed him the message.

"He seems very pleased with himself and his flowers," said his Majesty with a smile; adding "as he has sent for you like this, I think you had better go. After all your half-sisters are being brought up at his house, and you ought not to treat him quite as a stranger." He went to his apartments and dressed.

It was very late indeed when at last he made his appearance at the party. He was dressed in a cloak of thin Chinese fabric, white outside but lined with yellow. His robe was of a deep wine-red colour with a very long train. The dignity and grace with which he carried this fancifully regal[3] attire in a company where all were dressed in plain official robes were indeed remarkable, and in the end his presence perhaps contributed more to the success of the party than did the fragrance of the Minister's boasted flowers. His entry was followed by some very agreeable music. It was already fairly late when Genji, on the plea that the wine had given him a headache, left his seat and went for a walk. He knew that his two step-sisters, the daughters of Kōkiden, were in

---

[3] He had no right to such a costume; for though a son of the Emperor, he had been affiliated to the Minamoto clan and no longer counted as a member of the Imperial family.

the inner apartments of the palace. He went to the eastern portico and rested there. It was on this side of the house that the wistaria grew. The wooden blinds were raised and a number of ladies were leaning out of the window to enjoy the blossoms. They had hung bright-coloured robes and shawls over the window-sill just as is done at the time of the New Year dancing and other gala days and were behaving with a freedom of allure which contrasted very oddly with the sober decorum of Fujitsubo's household.

"I am feeling rather overpowered by all the noise and bustle of the flower-party" Genji explained. "I am very sorry to disturb my sisters, but I can think of nowhere else to seek refuge. . ." and advancing towards the main door of the women's apartments he pushed back the curtain with his shoulder.

"Refuge indeed!" cried one of the ladies laughing at him. "You ought to know by now that it is only poor relations who come to seek refuge with the more successful members of their family. What pray have you come to bother us for?"

"Impertinent creatures!" he thought but nevertheless there was something in their manner which convinced him they were persons of some consequence in the house and not, as he at first supposed, mere waiting-women. A scent of costly perfumes pervaded the room; silken skirts rustled in the darkness. There could be little doubt that these were Kōkiden's sisters and their friends. Deeply absorbed, as indeed was the whole of this family, in the fashionable gaieties of the moment, they had flouted decorum and posted themselves at the window that they might see what little they could of the banquet which was proceeding outside. Little thinking that his plan could succeed, yet led on by delightful recollections of his previous encounter he advanced towards them chanting in a careless undertone the song:

At Ishikawa, Ishikawa
A man from Koma[4] *took my belt away. . .*

But for "belt" he substituted "fan" and by this means he sought to discover which of the ladies was his friend.

"Why, you have got it wrong! I never heard of *that* Korean," one of them cried. Certainly it was not she. But there was another who though

---

[4] Korea.

she remained silent seemed to him to be sighing softly to herself. He stole towards the curtain-of-state behind which she was sitting and taking her hand in his at a venture he whispered the poem: *"If on this day of shooting my arrow went astray, 'twas that in dim morning twilight only the mark had glimmered in my view."*

And she, unable any longer to hide that she knew him, answered with the verse: *"Had it been with the arrows of the heart that you had shot, though from the moon's slim bow no brightness came would you have missed your mark?"* Yes, it was her voice. He was delighted, and yet. . .

IX

Aoi

The accession of the new Emperor was in many ways unfavourable to Genji's position. His recent promotion[1] too brought with it heavy responsibilities which sadly interrupted the course of his hidden friendships, so that complaints of desertion or neglect were soon heaped upon him from more than one quarter; while, as though Fate wished to turn the tables upon him, the one being on earth for whose love he longed in vain had now utterly abandoned him. Now that the Emperor was free to live as he chose she was more constantly than ever at his side, nor was her peace any longer disturbed by the presence of a rival, for Kōkiden resenting the old Emperor's neglect now seldom left her son's Palace. A constant succession of banquets and entertainments, the magnificence of which became the talk of the whole country, helped to enliven the ex-Emperor's retirement and he was on the whole very well content with his new condition. His only regret concerned the Heir Apparent[2] whose position, unsupported by any powerful influence outside the Palace, he regarded as extremely insecure. He constantly discussed the matter with Genji, begging him to enlist the support of the Minamoto clan. Such conversations tended to be somewhat embarrassing, but they gave Genji pleasure in so far as they enabled him to take measures for the boy's welfare.

An unexpected event now occurred. Lady Rokujō's daughter by her late husband Prince Zembō was chosen to be the new Vestal Virgin at Ise.[3] Her mother, who at the time when the appointment was first announced happened to be particularly aggrieved at Genji's treatment of her, at once determined to make her daughter's extreme youth a pretext for leaving the Capital and settling permanently at Ise. Being at the moment, as I have said, very much out of humour, she discussed

---

[1] We learn in Chapter XXXIV that he was made Commander of the Bodyguard at the age of twenty-one. He is now twenty-two.

[2] Genji's son by Fujitsubo (supposed by the world to be the Emperor's child) had been made Heir Apparent.

[3] An Emperor upon his succession was obliged to send one unmarried daughter or granddaughter to the Shintō Temple at Ise, another to the Shintō Temple at Kamo. See Appendix II.

the matter openly, making no secret of her real reasons for wishing to leave the City. The story soon reached the ex-Emperor's ears, and sending for Genji he said to him, "The late Prince my brother was, as you probably know, regarded with the utmost affection and esteem and I am profoundly grieved to hear that your reckless and inconsiderate conduct has cast a slur upon his family. For his daughter indeed I feel as much responsible as if she were of my own children. I must trouble you in future to safeguard to the utmost of your power the reputation of these unfortunate ladies. If you do not learn to keep better control over your frivolous inclinations you will soon find yourself becoming extremely unpopular." Why should his father be so much upset over the matter? And Genji, smarting under the rebuke, was about to defend himself when it occurred to him that the warning was not at all ill-merited and he maintained a respectful silence.

"Affairs of this kind," the ex-Emperor continued, "must be managed so that the woman, no matter who she is, need not feel that she has been brought into a humiliating position or treated in a cynical and off-hand way. Forget this rule, and she will soon make you feel the unpleasant consequences of her resentment."

"Wicked as he thinks me already," said Genji to himself while this lecture was going on, "there is a much worse enormity of which he as yet knows nothing." And stupefied with horror at the thought of what would ensue should his father ever discover this hideous secret, he bowed and left the room.

What the ex-Emperor had said about ruining other people's reputations cut him to the quick. He realized that Rokujō's rank and widowed position entitled her to the utmost consideration. But after all it was not he who had made public property of the affair; on the contrary he had done everything in his power to prevent its becoming known. There had always been a certain condescension in her treatment of him, arising perhaps from the inequality of their ages,[4] and his estrangement from her was solely due to the coldness with which she had for a long time received him. That their private affairs were now known not only to the ex-Emperor but also presumably to the whole Court showed a lack of reticence which seemed to him deplorable.

---

[4] She was seven years older than Genji.

Among others who heard of the business was Princess Asagao.[5] Determined that she at least would not submit herself to such treatment she ceased to answer his letters even with the short and guarded replies that she had been in the habit of sending to him. Nevertheless he found it hard to believe that so gentle-mannered a creature was thinking unkindly of him and continued to regard her with devoted admiration.

Princess Aoi when the story reached her ears was of course distressed by this new instance of his fickleness; but she felt that it was useless, now that his infidelity was open and unabashed, to protest against one particular injury, and to his surprise she seemed to take the matter rather lightly. She was suffering much inconvenience from her condition and her spirits were very low. Her parents were delighted and at the same time surprised to hear of what was to come. But their pleasure and that of all her friends was marred by grave forebodings, and it was arranged that prayers for her health and special services of intercession should be recited in all the temples. At such a time it was impossible for Genji to leave her and there were many who though his feelings had not in reality cooled towards them felt that they were being neglected.

The Vestal Virgin of Kamo still remained to be selected. The choice fell upon Kōkiden's daughter, San no Miya. She was a great favourite both with her brother the new Emperor and with the Empress Mother. Her retirement from the world was a bitter blow to them; but there was no help for it since she alone of all the royal princesses fulfilled the prescribed conditions.

The actual ritual of investiture could not be altered, but the Emperor saw to it that the proceedings should be attended with the utmost Pomp and splendour; while to the customary ritual of the Kamo Festival he added so many touches that it became a spectacle of unparalleled magnificence. All this was due to his partiality for the Virgin Elect.

On the day of her purification the Virgin is attended by a fixed number of noblemen and princes. For this retinue the Emperor was at pains to choose the best built and handsomest of the young men at Court; he settled what coloured gowns they were to wear, what pattern was to be on their breeches, and even on what saddles they should ride. By a special decree he ordered that Prince Genji should join this retinue, and so great was everyone's desire to get a good view of the procession that long beforehand people were getting ready special carriages with

---

[5] a Daughter of Prince Momozono. See above, p. 68.

which to line the route. The scene along the highroad of the First Ward was one of indescribable excitement. Dense crowds surged along the narrow space allotted to them, while the stands which with a wealth of ingenious fancy had been constructed all along the route of the procession, with gay cloaks and shawls hung over the balustrades, were in themselves a spectacle of astonishing beauty.

It had never been Aoi's practice to be present at such occasions as this and in her present state of health she would not have dreamt of doing so had not her gentlewomen pressed round her saying, "Come Madam! It will be no fun for us to go by ourselves and be hidden away in some corner. It is to see Prince Genji that all these people have come today. Why, all sorts of queer wild men from the mountains are here, and people have brought their wives and children from provinces ever so far away. If all these people who are nothing to do with him have taken the trouble to come so far, it will be too bad if you, his own lady, are not there!"

Overhearing this Aoi's mother joined in. "You are feeling much better just now," she said; "I think you ought to make the effort. It will be so disappointing for your gentlewomen. . ." At the last minute Aoi changed her mind and announced that she was going.

It was now so late that there was no time to put on gala clothes. The whole of the enclosure allotted for this purpose was already lined with coaches which were packed so close that it was quite impossible to find space for the large and numerous carriages of Aoi and her train. A number of grand ladies began to make room for her, backing their coaches away from a suitable space in the reserved enclosure. Conspicuous among the rest were two basket-work carriages of a rather old-fashioned pattern but with curtains such as are used by persons of quality, very discreetly decked with draperies that barely showed beneath the curtains, yet these draperies (whether sleeve-favour, skirt or scarf) all of the handsomest colours. They seemed to belong to some exalted personage who did not wish to be recognized. When it was their turn to move, the coachmen in charge of them would not lift a finger.

"It is not for such as we to make way," they said stiffly and did not stir. Among the attendants on both sides there was a number of young grooms who were already the worse for liquor. They were longing for a scuffle and it was impossible to keep them in hand. The staid and elderly outriders tried to call them back, but they took no notice.

The two carriages belonged to Princess Rokujō who had come secretly to the festival hoping for a while to find distraction from her troubles. Despite the steps which she had taken to conceal her identity, it was at once suspected by some of Aoi's gentlemen and they cried to the grooms that this was not an equipage which could be dealt with so high-handedly or it would be said that their lady was abusing her position as wife of the Lord Commander. But at this moment a number of Genji's servants mingled in the fray. They knew Rokujō's men by sight, but after a moment's embarrassment they decided not to give assistance to the enemy by betraying his identity.

Thus reinforced Aoi's side won the day and at length her coach and those of all her ladies were drawn up along the front row, while Rokujō's was pushed back among a miscellaneous collection of carts and gigs where she could see nothing at all. She was vexed beyond measure not only at missing what she had come to see but also that despite all her precautions she had been recognized and (as she was convinced) deliberately insulted. Her shaft-rest and other parts of her coach as well were damaged and she was obliged to prop it up against some common person's carriage wheels. Why, she vainly asked herself, had she come among these hateful crowds? She would go home at once. What sense was there in waiting for the procession to come? But when she tried to go, she found that it was impossible to force a way through the dense crowds. She was still struggling to escape when the cry went up that the procession was in sight. Her resolution weakened. She would wait till Genji had passed by. He did not see her. How should he, for the crowds flashed by him like the hurrying images that a stream catches and breaks. She realized this, yet her disappointment was none the less.

The carriages that lined the route, decked and garlanded for this great day, were crammed to overflowing with excited ladies who though there was no room for them would not consent to be left behind. Peeping out under the blinds of their coaches they smiled at the great personages who were passing quite regardless of whether their greetings were acknowledged. But every now and then a smile would be rewarded by a quick glance or the backward turn of a head. Aoi's party was large and conspicuous. He wheeled round as he passed and saluted its members attentively. Rider after rider again as the procession went by would pause in front of Aoi's coach and salute her with the deepest respect. The humiliation of witnessing all this from an obscure corner was more than Rokujō could bear, and murmuring the lines, *"Though I saw him but as a shadow that falls on hurrying waters yet knew I that at last my hour of utmost misery was come,"* she burst into tears. It was hideous that her servants should see her in this state. Yet even while she struggled with her tears she could not find it in her heart to regret that she had seen him in all his glory.

The riders in the procession were indeed all magnificently apparelled, each according to his own rank; in particular the young noblemen chosen by the Emperor cut so brilliant a figure that only the lustre of Genji's beauty could have eclipsed their splendour. The Commander of this Bodyguard is not generally allotted a Palace-Officer as his special attendant, but as the occasion was of such importance the Imperial Treasurer[6] rode at Genji's side. It seemed to those who saw so many public honours showered upon him that no flower of fortune could resist the favouring gale which blew towards his side. There were among the crowd women of quite good birth who had dressed in walking-skirts and come a long way on foot. There were nuns and other female recluses who, though in order to see anything of the procession they were obliged to endure being constantly pushed off their feet, and though they commonly regarded all such spectacles with contempt and aversion, were today declaring that they would not have missed it for anything.

There were old men grinning through toothless gums, strange-looking girls with their hair poked away under ragged hoods and stolid peasant boys standing with hands raised as though in prayer, whose uncouth faces were suddenly transfigured with wonder and joy as the procession burst into sight. Even the daughters of remote provincial magistrates and governors who had no acquaintances whatever in the City had expended as much coquetry upon the decoration of their persons and coaches as if they were about to submit themselves to a lover's inspection, and their equipages made a bright and varied show. If even these strangers were in such a taking, it may be imagined with what excitement, scattered here and there among the crowd, those with whom Genji was in secret communication watched the procession go by and with how many hidden sighs their bosoms heaved.

Prince Momozono[7] had a seat in one of the stands. He was amazed to see his nephew grown up into such a prodigiously handsome young man and was alarmed lest soon the gods should cast an envious eye upon him. Princess Asagao could not but be touched by the rare persistency with which year after year Genji had pressed his suit. Even had he been

---

[6] We learn later that he was a son of Iyo no Kami.

[7] Father of Princess Asagao; brother of the ex-Emperor and therefore Genji's paternal uncle.

positively ugly she would have found it hard to resist such importunity; so small wonder if seeing him ride by in all his splendour she marvelled that she had held out so long. But she was determined to know him much better before she committed herself. The young waiting-women who were with her were careful to belaud him in extravagant terms. To the festival itself[8] Aoi did not go. The affray between her servants and those of Rokujō was soon reported to Genji. It vexed him beyond measure that such a thing should have occurred. That the exquisitely well-bred Aoi should have been in any way responsible for this outburst of insolent ruffianism he did not for a moment believe; it must be the work of rough under-servants who, though they had no actual instructions, had imbibed the notion that all was not well between the two houses and imagined that they would get credit for espousing their mistress's cause. He knew well enough the unusual vanity and susceptibility of the affronted lady. Distressed to think of the pain which this incident must have caused her he hastened to her house. But her daughter, the Virgin Elect of Ise, was still in the house, and she made this a plea for turning him away after the exchange of a few formal words. He had the greatest possible sympathy for her; but he was feeling rather tired of coping with injured susceptibilities.

He could not face the idea of going straight back to the Great Hall. It was the day of the Kamo festival and going to his own palace he ordered Koremitsu to get his coach ready. "Look at her!" he cried smiling fondly at Murasaki when she appeared in all her finery surrounded by the little children whom he had given her for playmates, "She must needs bring her dames to wait upon her!" and stroking her lovely hair which today Shōnagon had dressed with more than usual care.

"It is getting rather long," he said; "today would not be a bad[9] time to have it cut," and sending for his astrologer he bade him consult his books.

"The maids-of-honour first!" he cried, nodding at the pretty troupe of babes, and their dainty tresses were trimmed so as to hang neatly over their diapered holiday gowns.

"I am going to cut yours myself," he said to Murasaki. "What a lot of it there is! I wonder how much longer it would have grown." Really it was quite hard work.

<hr>

[8] The clash of coaches took place at the Purification. The actual *matsuri* (Festival) takes place some days later.
[9] I.e. astrologically.

"People with very long hair ought to wear it cut rather short over the temples," he said at last; "but I have not the heart to crop you any closer," and he laid the knife down. Shōnagon's gratification knew no bounds when she heard him reciting the prayer with which the ceremony of hair-cutting should conclude. There is a seaweed called *miru* which is used in the dressing of ladies' hair and playing upon this word (which also means "to see") he recited a poem in which he said that the miru-weed which had been used in the washing of her hair was a token that he would forever fondly watch it grow. She answered that like the sea-tides which visit the *miru* in its cleft he came but went away, and often her tresses unwatched by him would like the hidden seaweed grow. This she wrote very prettily on a slip of paper and though the verse had no merit in it but the charm of a childish mind it gave him great delight. Today the crowds were as thick as ever. With great difficulty he managed to wedge in his carriage close to the Royal Stables. But here they were surrounded by somewhat turbulent young noblemen and he was looking for a quieter place when a smart carriage crammed full of ladies drew up near by and someone in it beckoned with a fan to Genji's servants.

"Will you not come over where we are?" said one of the ladies. "We will gladly make room for you." Such an offer was perhaps somewhat forward, but the place she had indicated was such a good one that Genji at once accepted the invitation.

"I am afraid it is very unfair that we should take your place like this. . ." Genji was beginning to say politely, when one of the ladies handed him a fan with the corner bent down. Here he found the poem:

This flower-decked day of meeting when the great god unfolds his portents in vain have I waited, for alas another is at thy side.

Surely the handwriting was familiar. Yes, it was that of the ancient lady-of-the-bedchamber. He felt that it was time she should give up such pranks as this and answered discouragingly:

"Not ours this day of tryst when garlanded and passionate the Eighty Tribes converge."

This put the lady out of countenance and she replied: "Now bitterly do I repent that for this cheating day my head is decked with flowers; for in name only is it a day of meeting."

Their carriages remained side by side, but Genji did not even draw up the side-curtains, which was a disappointment to more persons than one. The magnificence of his public appearance a few days ago was contrasted by everyone with the unobtrusive manner in which he now mingled with the crowd. It was agreed that his companion, whoever she might be, must certainly be some very great lady. Genji was afraid that his neighbour was going to prove troublesome. But fortunately some of her companions had more discretion than their mistress, and out of consideration for the unknown sharer of Genji's coach persuaded the voluble lady to restrain herself.

Lady Rokujō's sufferings were now far worse than in previous years. Though she could no longer endure to be treated as Genji was treating her, yet the thought of separating from him altogether and going so far away agitated her so much that she constantly deferred her journey. She felt too that she would become a laughingstock if it was thought that she had been spurred to flight by Genji's scorn; yet if at the last moment she changed her plans and stayed behind everyone would think her conduct extremely ill-balanced and unaccountable. Thus her days and nights were spent in an agony of indecision and often she repeated to herself the lines, *"My heart like the fishers' float on Ise shore is danced from wave to wave."*[10] She felt herself indeed swirled this way and that by paroxysms that sickened her but were utterly beyond her control.

Genji, though it pained him that she should feel it necessary to go so far away did not attempt to dissuade her from the journey.

"It is quite natural," he wrote, "that tiresome creature as I am you should want to put me altogether out of your head. I only beg that even though you see no use in it, you will let me see you once more before you go. Were we to meet, you would soon realize that I care for your happiness far more than you suppose." But she could not forget how when at the River of cleansing she sought a respite from the torture of her own doubt and indecision, rough waves had dashed her against the rocks,[11] and she brooded more and more upon this wrong till there was room for no other thought in all her heart.

Meanwhile Princess Aoi became strangely distraught, and it seemed at times as though some hostile spirit had entered into her. The whole household was plunged into such a state of anxiety and gloom that Genji had not the heart to absent himself for more than a few hours. It was only very occasionally that he got even as far as his own palace.

---

[10] *Kokinshū* 509.

[11] The clash of the chariots at the Festival of Purification. Probably a quotation.

After all, she was his wife; moreover, despite all the difficulties that had risen between them he cared for her very much indeed. He could no longer disguise from himself that there was something wrong with her in addition to the discomfort which naturally accompanied her condition, and he was in a state of great distress. Constant rituals of exorcism and divination were performed under his direction, and it was generally agreed that all the signs indicated possession by the spirit of some living person. Many names were tried but to none of them did the spirit respond, and it seemed as though it would be impossible to shift it. Aoi herself felt that some alien thing had entered into her, and though she was not conscious of any one definite pain or dread the sense that the thing was there never for a moment left her. The greatest healers of the day were powerless to eject it and it became apparent that this was no ordinary case of "possession": some tremendous accumulation of malice was discharging itself upon her. It was natural that her friends should turn over in their minds the names of those whom Genji had most favoured. It was whispered that only with Lady Rokujō and the girl at the Nijō-in was he on terms of such intimacy that their jealousy would be at all likely to produce a fatal effect. But when the doctors attempted to conjure the spirit by the use of these names, there was no visible response. She had not in all the world any enemy who might be practising conscious[12] witchcraft against her. Such indispositions were sometimes attributed to possession by the spirit of some dead retainer or old family-nurse; or again the malice of someone whom the Minister, Aoi's father, had offended might, owing to her delicate condition, have fastened upon her instead of him. Conjecture after conjecture was accepted and then falsified. Meanwhile she lay perpetually weeping. Constantly, indeed, she would break out into fits of sobbing so violent that her breath was stopped, while those about her, in great alarm for her safety, stood by in misery not knowing what to do.

The ex-Emperor enquired after her continually. He even ordered special services to be said on her behalf, and these attentions served to remind her parents in what high estimation she was held at the Court. Not among her friends only but throughout the whole country the news of her illness caused great distress. Rokujō heard of her sufferings with deep concern. For years they had been in open rivalry for Genji's favours, but even after that wretched affair of the coaches (though it

---

[12] The jealous person is unconscious of the fatal effects which his jealousy is producing.

must be admitted that this had greatly incensed her) she had never gone so far as to wish evil against the Princess. She herself was very unwell. She began to feel that the violent and distracting emotions which continually assailed her had in some subtle way unhinged her mind and she determined to seek spiritual assistance at a place some miles distant from her home. Genji heard of this and in great anxiety concerning her at once set out for the house where she was reported to be staying. It lay beyond the City precincts and he was obliged to go with the greatest secrecy.[13] He begged her to forgive him for not having come to see her for so long. "I have not been having a very cheerful time," he said and gave her some account of Aoi's condition. He wanted to make her feel that if he had stayed away it had been from a melancholy necessity and not because he had found more amusing company elsewhere. "It is not so much my own anxiety that unnerves me as the spectacle of the appalling helplessness and misery into which her illness has plunged her wretched parents, and it was in the hope of forgetting for a little while all these sickroom horrors that I came to see you here today. If only just for this once you could overlook all my offences and be kind to me. . ."

His pleading had no effect. Her attitude was more hostile than before. He was not angry with her, nor indeed was he surprised. Day was already breaking when, unsolaced, he set out for home. But as she watched him go his beauty suddenly made havoc of all her resolutions and again she felt that it was madness to leave him. Yet what had she to stay for? Aoi was with child and this could only be a sign that he had made his peace with her. Henceforward he could lead a life of irreproachable rectitude and if once in a way he came to make his excuse as he had come today, what purpose would that serve, save to keep ever fresh the torment of her desires? Thus when his letter came next day it found her more distraught than before:

> The sick woman who for a few days past had shown some improvement is again suffering acutely and it is at present impossible for me to leave her.

Certain that this was a mere excuse she sent in reply the poem,

---

[13] Members of the Imperial family were not allowed to leave the Capital without the consent of the Emperor.

The fault is mine and the regret, if careless as the peasant girl who stoops too low amid the sprouting rice I soiled my sleeve in love's dark road.

At the end of her letter she reminded him of the old song:

Now bitterly do I repent that ever I brought my pitcher to the mountain well where waters were but deep enough to soil my sleeve.

He looked at the delicate handwriting. Who was there, even among women of her high lineage and breeding, that could rival the ineffable grace and elegance with which this small note was penned? That one whose mind and person alike so strongly attracted him must now by his own act be lost to him forever, was a bitter thought.

Though it was almost dark, he sat down and wrote to her:

Do not say that the waters have but wetted your sleeve. For the shallowness is in your comparison only; not in my affections!

And to this he added the poem:

'Tis you, you only who have loitered among the shallow pools: while I till all my limbs were drenched have battled through the thickets of love's dark track.

And he ended with the words:

Had but a ray of comfort lighted the troubles of this house, I should myself have been the bearer of this note.

Meanwhile Aoi's possession had returned in full force; she was in a state of pitiable torment. It reached Lady Rokujō's ears that the illness had been attributed by some to the operation of her "living spirit." Others, she was told, believed that her father's ghost was avenging the betrayal of his daughter. She brooded constantly upon the nature of her own feelings towards Aoi, but could discover in herself nothing but intense unhappiness. Of hostility towards Aoi she could find no trace at all. Yet she could not be sure whether somewhere in the depths of a soul consumed by anguish some spark of malice had not lurked. Through all the long years during which she had loved and suffered, though it had often seemed to her that greater torment could not anywhere in the world exist, her whole being had never once been so utterly bruised and shattered as in these last days. It had begun with that hateful episode of the coaches. She had been scorned, treated as though she had no right to exist. Yes, it was true that since the Festival of Purification her mind had been buffeted by such a tempest of conflicting resolutions that sometimes it seemed as though she had lost all control over her own thoughts. She remembered how one night she had suddenly, in the midst of agonizing doubts and indecisions, found that she had been dreaming. It seemed to her that she had been in a large magnificent room, where lay a girl whom she knew to be the Princess Aoi. Snatching her by the arm she had dragged and mauled the prostrate figure, with an outburst of brutal fury such as in her waking life would have been utterly foreign to her. Since then she had had the same dream several times.

How terrible! It seemed then that it was really possible for one's spirit to leave the body and break out into emotions which the waking mind would not countenance. Even where someone's actions are all but irreproachable (she reflected) people take a malicious delight in saying nothing about the good he has done and everything about the evil. With what joy would they seize upon such a story as this! That after his death a man's ghost should pursue his enemies is a thing which seems to be of constant occurrence, yet even this is taken as a sign that the dead man was of a fiendishly venomous and malignant character and his reputation is utterly destroyed.

"What then will become of me if it is thought that while still alive I have been guilty of so hideous a crime?" She must face her fate. She had lost Genji forever. If she were to keep any control at all over her own thoughts she must first of all find some way of putting him wholly out of mind. She kept on reminding herself not to think of him, so that this very resolve led her in the end to think of him but the more.

The Virgin of Ise should by rights have entered upon her duties before the end of the year, but difficulties of various kinds arose and it was not till the autumn of the next year that she could at last be received. She was to enter the Palace in-the-Fields[14] in the ninth month, but this was decided

---

[14] A temporary building erected afresh for each new Virgin a few miles outside Kyoto. She spent several years there before proceeding to Ise.

so late that the arrangements for her second Purification had to be made in great haste. It was very inconvenient that at this crisis her mother, so far from superintending the preparations, spent hour after hour lying dazed and helpless upon her bed. At last the priests arrived to fetch the girl away. They took a grave view of the mother's condition and gave her the benefit of their presence by offering up many prayers and incantations. But week after week she remained in the same condition, showing no symptom which seemed actually dangerous, yet all the time (in some vague and indefinite way) obviously very ill. Genji sent constantly to enquire after her, but she saw clearly that his attention was occupied by quite other matters. Aoi's delivery was not yet due and no preparations for it had been made, when suddenly there were signs that it was close at hand. She was in great distress, but though the healers recited prayer upon prayer their utmost efforts could not shift by one jot the spiteful power which possessed her. All the greatest miracle-workers of the land were there; the utter failure of their ministrations irritated and perplexed them. At last, daunted by the potency of their incantations, the spirit that possessed her found voice and, weeping bitterly, she was heard to say:

"Give me a little respite; there is a matter of which Prince Genji and I must speak."

The healers nodded at one another as though to say, "Now we shall learn something worth knowing."

For they were convinced that the "possession" was speaking through the mouth of the possessed, and they hurried Genji to her bedside. Her parents thinking that, her end being near, she desired to give some last secret injunction to Genji, retired to the back of the room. The priests too ceased their incantations and began to recite the *Hokkekyo*[15] in low impressive tones. He raised the bed-curtain. She looked lovely as ever as she lay there, very big with child, and any man who saw her even now would have found himself strangely troubled by her beauty. How much the more then Prince Genji, whose heart was already overflowing with tenderness and remorse! The plaited tresses of her long hair stood out in sharp contrast to her white jacket.[16] Even to this loose, sick-room garb her natural grace imparted the air of a fashionable gown! He took her hand.

---

[15] The Chinese version of the Sanskrit *Saddharma Pundarika Sutra*; see *Sacred Books of the East*, Vol. 21.

[16] The lying-in jacket.

"It is terrible," he began, "to see you looking so unhappy. . ." he could say no more. Still she gazed at him, but through his tears he saw that there was no longer in her eyes the wounded scorn that he had come to know so well, but a look of forbearance and tender concern; and while she watched him weep her own eyes brimmed with tears. It would not do for him to go on crying like this. Her father and mother would be alarmed; besides, it was upsetting Aoi herself, and meaning to cheer her he said:

"Come, things are not so bad as that! You will soon be much better. But even if anything should happen, it is certain that we shall meet again in worlds to come. Your father and mother too, and many others, love you so dearly that between your fate and theirs must be some sure bond that will bring you back to them in many, many lives that are to be." Suddenly she interrupted him:

"No, no. That is not it. But stop these prayers awhile. They do me great harm," and drawing him nearer to her she went on "I did not think that you would come. I have waited for you till all my soul is burnt with longing."

She spoke wistfully, tenderly; and still in the same tone recited the verse, *"Bind thou, as the seam of a skirt is braided, this shred, that from my soul despair and loneliness have sundered."*

The voice in which these words were said was not Aoi's; nor was the manner hers. He knew someone whose voice was very like that. Who was it? Why, yes; surely only she,—the Lady Rokujō. Once or twice he had heard people suggest that something of this kind might be happening; but he had always rejected the idea as hideous and unthinkable, believing it to be the malicious invention of some unprincipled scandalmonger, and had even denied that such "possession" ever took place. Now he had seen one with his own eyes. Ghastly, unbelievable as they were, such things did happen in real life.

Controlling himself at last he said in a low voice: "I am not sure who is speaking to me. Do not leave me in doubt. . ." Her answer proved only too conclusively that he had guessed aright.

To his horror her parents now came back to the bed, but she had ceased to speak, and seeing her now lying quietly her mother thought the attack was over, and was coming towards the bed carrying a basin of hot water when Aoi suddenly started up and bore a child. For the moment all was gladness and rejoicing; but it seemed only too likely that the spirit which possessed her had but been temporarily dislodged; for a fierce fit of terror was soon upon her, as though the thing (whatever it was) were angry at having been put to the trouble of shifting, so that there was still grave anxiety about the future. The Abbot of Tendai and the other great ecclesiastics who were gathered together in the room attributed her easy delivery to the persistency of their own incantations and prayers, and as they hastily withdrew to seek refreshment and repose they wiped the sweat from their brows with an expression of considerable self-satisfaction. Her friends who had for days been plunged in the deepest gloom now began to take heart a little, believing that although there was no apparent improvement yet now that the child was safely born she could not fail to mend. The prayers and incantations began once more, but throughout the house there was a new feeling of confidence; for the amusement of looking after the baby at least gave them some relief from the strain under which they had been living for so many days. Handsome presents were sent by the ex-Emperor, the Royal Princes and all the Court, forming an array which grew more dazzling each night.[17] The fact that the child was a boy made the celebrations connected with his birth all the more sumptuous and elaborate.

The news of this event took Lady Rokujō somewhat aback. The last report she had heard from the Great Hall was that the confinement was bound to be very dangerous. And now they said that there had not been the slightest difficulty. She thought this very peculiar. She had herself for a long while been suffering from the most disconcerting sensations. Often she felt as though her whole personality had in some way suddenly altered. It was as though she were a stranger to herself. Recently she had noticed that a smell of mustard-seed incense for which she was at a loss to account was pervading her clothes and hair. She took a hot bath and put on other clothes; but still the same odour of incense pursued her. It was bad enough even in private to have this sensation of being as it were estranged from oneself. But now her body was playing tricks upon her which her attendants must have noticed and were no doubt discussing behind her back. Yet there was not one person among those about her with whom she could bring herself to discuss such things and all this pent-up misery seemed only to increase the strange process of dissolution which had begun to attack her mind.

Now that Genji was somewhat less anxious about Aoi's condition the recollection of his extraordinary conversation with her at the crisis

---

[17] These presents (*ubuyashinai*) were given on the third, fifth and ninth nights.

of her attack kept on recurring in his mind, and it made so painful an impression upon him that though it was now a long time since he had communicated with Rokujō and he knew that she must be deeply offended, he felt that no kind of intimacy with her would ever again be possible. Yet in the end pity prevailed and he sent her a letter. It seemed indeed that it would at present be heartless to absent himself at all from one who had just passed through days of such terrible suffering and from her friends who were still in a state of the gravest anxiety, and all his secret excursions were abandoned. Aoi still remained in a condition so serious that he was not allowed to see her. The child was as handsome an infant as you could wish to see. The great interest which Genji took in it and the zest with which he entered into all the arrangements which were made for its welfare delighted Aoi's father, inasmuch as they seemed signs of a better understanding between his daughter and Genji; and though her slow recovery caused him great anxiety, he realized that an illness such as that through which she had just passed must inevitably leave considerable traces behind it and he persuaded himself that her condition was less dangerous than one might have supposed. The child reminded Genji of the Heir Apparent and made him long to see Fujitsubo's little son again. The desire took such strong hold upon him that at last he sent Aoi a message in which he said:

It is a very long time since I have been to the Palace or indeed have paid any visits at all. I am beginning to feel the need of a little distraction, so today I am going out for a short while and should like to see you before I go. I do not want to feel that we are completely cut off from one another.

So he pleaded, and he was supported by her ladies who told her that Prince Genji was her own dear Lord and that she ought not to be so proud and stiff with him. She feared that her illness had told upon her looks and was for speaking to him with a curtain between, but this too her gentlewomen would not allow. He brought a stool close to where she was lying and began speaking to her of one thing or another. Occasionally she put in a word or two, but it was evident that she was still very weak. Nevertheless it was difficult to believe that she had so recently seemed almost at the point of death. They were talking quietly together about those worst days of her illness and how they now seemed like an evil dream when suddenly he recollected the extraordinary conversation he had had with her when she was lying apparently at her last gasp and filled with a sudden bitterness, he said to her:

"There are many other things that I must one day talk to you about. But you seem very tired and perhaps I had better leave you." So saying he arranged her pillows, brought her warm water to wash in and in fact played the sick-nurse so well that those about her wondered where he had acquired the art. Still peerlessly beautiful but weak and listless she seemed as she lay motionless on the bed at times almost to fade out of existence. He gazed at her with fond concern. Her hair, every ringlet still in its right place, was spread out over the pillow. Never before had her marvellous beauty so strangely impressed him. Was it conceivable that year after year he should have allowed such a woman to continue in estrangement from him? Still he stood gazing at her.

"I must start for the Palace," he said at last; "but I shall not be away long. Now that you are better you must try to make your mother feel less anxious about you when she comes presently; for though she tries hard not to show it, she is still terribly distressed about you. You must begin now to make an effort and sit up for a little while each day. I think it is partly because she spoils you so much that you are taking so long to get well."

As he left the room, robed in all the magnificence of his court attire she followed him with her eyes more fixedly than ever in her life before. The attendance of the officers who took part in the autumn session was required, and Aoi's father accompanied Genji to the Palace, as did also her brother who needed the Minister's assistance in making their arrangements for the coming political year. Many of their servants went too and the Great Hall wore a deserted and melancholy aspect. Suddenly Aoi was seized with the same choking-fit as before and was soon in a desperate condition. This news was brought to Genji in the Palace and breaking off his Audience he at once made for home.

The rest followed in hot haste and though it was Appointment Evening[18] they gave up all thought of attending the proceedings, knowing that the tragic turn of affairs at the Great Hall would be considered a sufficient excuse. It was too late to get hold of the abbot from Mount Tendai or any of the dignitaries who had given their assistance before. It was appalling that just when she seemed to have taken a turn for the better she should so suddenly again be at the point of death, and

---

[18] The ceremony of investing the newly elected officials.

the people at the Great Hall felt utterly helpless and bewildered. Soon the house was full of lackeys who were arriving from every side with messages of sympathy and enquiry; but from the inhabitants of that stricken house they could obtain no information, for they seemed to do nothing but rush about from one room to another in a state of frenzy which it was terrifying to behold.

Remembering that several times already her "possession" had reduced her to a trance-like state, they did not for sometime attempt to lay out the body or even touch her pillows, but left her lying just as she was. After two or three days however it became clear that life was extinct.

Amid the general lamentations which ensued Genji's spirit sank with the apathy of utter despair. Sorrow had followed too fast upon sorrow; life as he saw it now was but a succession of futile miseries. The messages of condolence which poured in from all the most exalted quarters in the Court and City merely fatigued and exasperated him.

The warmth of the old ex-Emperor's messages and his evident personal distress at Aoi's death were indeed very flattering and mingled a certain feeling of gratification with her father's perpetual weeping. At the suggestion of a friend various drastic means were resorted to in the hope that it might yet be possible to kindle some spark of life in the body. But it soon became evident, even to their reluctant eyes, that all this was too late, and heavy at heart they took the body to Toribeno. Here, in the great flat cremation-ground beyond the town, the horrors that they had dreaded were only too swiftly begun. Even in this huge open space there was scarcely room for the crowds of mourners who had come from all the great palaces of the City to follow behind the bier and for the concourses of priests who, chanting their liturgies, flocked from the neighbouring temples. The ex-Emperor was of course represented; so were the Princess Kōkiden and the Heir Apparent; while many other important people came in person and mingled with the crowd. Never had any funeral aroused so universal a demonstration of interest and sympathy. Her father was not present:

"Now in my declining years to have lost one who was so young and strong is a blow too staggering. . ." he said and he could no longer check the tears which he was striving to conceal. His grief was heart-rending. All night long the mournful ceremonies proceeded, but at last only a few pitiful ashes remained upon the pyre and in the morning the mourners returned to their homes. It was in fact, save for its grandeurs, much like any other funeral; but it so happened that save in one case only death had not yet come Genji's way and the scenes of that day haunted him long afterwards with hideous persistency.

The ceremony took place in the last week of the eighth month. Seeing that from Aoi's father all the soft brightness of this autumn morning was hid in the twilight of despair and well knowing what thoughts must be passing through his mind, Genji came to him and pointing to the sky whispered the following verse: *"Because of all the mists that wreathe the autumn sky I know not which ascended from my lady's bier, henceforth upon the country of the clouds from pole to pole I gaze with love."*

At last he was back in his room. He lay down, but could not sleep. His thoughts went back over the years that he had known her. Why had he been content lazily to assume that in the end all would go right and meanwhile amused himself regardless of her resentment? Why had he let year after year go by without managing even at the very end to establish any real intimacy, any sympathy between them? The bitterest remorse now filled his heart; but what use was it? His servants brought him his light grey mourner's dress and the strange thought floated into his mind.

"What if I had died instead and not she? She would be getting into the woman-mourner's deep-dyed robe," and he recited the poem: *"Though light in hue the dress which in bereavement custom bids me wear, yet black my sorrow as the gown thou wouldst have worn"*; and as thus clad he told his rosary those about him noted that even the dull hues of mourning could not make him look peaked or drab.

He read many sūtras in a low voice, among them the liturgy to Samantabhadra as Dispenser of the Dharmadhātu Samādhi, which he recited with an earnestness more impressive in its way than the dexterous intonation of the professional cleric. Next he visited the new-born child and took some comfort in the reflection that she had at least left behind her this memorial of their love. Genji did not attempt to go even for the day to the Nijō-in, but remained buried in recollections and regrets with no other occupation save the ordering of masses for her soul. He did however bring himself to write a few letters, among them one to Rokujō. The Virgin Elect was already in charge of the Guardsmen of the Gate and would soon be passed on by them to the Palace-in-the-Fields. Rokujō accordingly made her daughter's situation an excuse for sending no reply.[19] He was now so weary of life and its

---

[19] Had she corresponded with someone who was in mourning, she would herself have become unclean and been disqualified from attending upon her daughter the Vestal

LADY MURASAKI SHIKIBU

miseries that he seriously contemplated the taking of priestly vows, and might perhaps have done so, had there not been a new bond which seemed to tie him irrevocably to the world. But stay, there was the girl Murasaki too, waiting for him in the wing of his palace. How unhappy she must have been during all this long time! That night lying all alone within his royal curtains, though watchmen were going their rounds not far away, he felt very lonely and remembering that "autumn is no time to lie alone," he sent for the sweetest voiced among the chaplains of the palace. His chanting mingled with the sounds of early dawn was indeed of almost unendurable beauty. But soon the melancholy of late autumn, the murmur of the rising wind took possession of him, and little used to lonely nights he found it hard to keep his bed till morning. Looking out he saw that a heavy mist lay over the garden beds; yet despite the mist it was clear that something was tied to the stem of a fine chrysanthemum not far away. It was a letter written on dark blue paper.[20] The messenger had left it there and gone away.

"What a charming idea!" he was thinking when he suddenly recognized the hand. It was from Rokujō. She began by saying she did not think, having regard to her daughter's situation, that he would be surprised at her long delay in answering his previous note. She added an acrostic poem in which, playing upon the word chrysanthemum (*kiku*) she told him of her distress at hearing (*kiku*) of his bereavement.

"The beauty of the morning," she ended, "turned my thoughts more than ever towards you and your sorrow; that is why I could not choose but answer you." It was written even more elegantly than usual; but he tossed it aside. Her condolences wounded him, for after what he had seen he knew that they could not be sincere. Nevertheless he felt that it would be too harsh to break off all communication with her; that he should do so would in fact tend to incriminate her, and this was the last thing he desired. After all, it was probably not *that* at all which had brought about the disaster; maybe Aoi's fate was sealed in any case. If only he had chanced never to see or hear the fatal operation of her spirit! As it was, argue with himself as he might, he doubted whether he would ever be able to efface the impression of what had been revealed to him at that hideous scene.

Virgin.

[20] Used in writing to people who were in mourning.

He had the excuse that he was still in deep mourning and that to receive a letter from him would inconvenience her at this stage of her daughter's Purification. But after turning the matter over in his mind for a long while, he decided that it would be unfeeling not to answer a letter which had evidently been written with the sole object of giving him pleasure and on a paper lightly tinted with brown he wrote:

> Though I have let so many days slip by, believe me that you
> have not been absent from my thoughts. If I was reluctant
> to answer your letter, it was because, as a mourner, I was
> loath to trespass upon the sanctity which now surrounds your
> home, and this I trusted that you would understand. Do not
> brood overmuch upon what has happened; for "go we late
> or soon, more frail our lives than dew-drops hanging in the
> morning light." For the present, think of it no more. I say
> this now, because it is not possible for us to meet.

She received the letter at her daughter's place of preparation, but did not read it till she was back in her own house. At a glance she knew at what he was hinting. So he too accused her! And at last the hideous conviction of her own guilt forced itself upon her acceptance. Her misery increased tenfold.

If even Genji had reason to believe in her guilt, her brother-in-law, the ex-Emperor, must already have been informed. What was he thinking of her? Her dead husband, Prince Zembō, had been the brother whom he had loved best. He had accepted the guardianship of the little girl who was now about to be consecrated and at his brother's earnest entreaty had promised to undertake her education and indeed treat her as though she were his own child. The old Emperor had constantly invited the widowed lady and her daughter to live with him in the Palace, but she was reluctant to accept this offer, which indeed was somewhat impracticable. Meanwhile she allowed herself to listen to Genji's youthful addresses and was soon living in constant torment and agitation lest her indiscretion should be discovered.

During the whole period of this escapade she was in such a state of mingled excitement and apprehension that she scarcely knew what she was doing. In the world at large she had the reputation of being a great beauty and this, combined with her exalted lineage, brought to the Palace-in-the-Fields, so soon as it was known that she had repaired thither with her daughter, a host of frivolous dandies from the Court, who made it their business to force upon her their fashionable attentions morning, noon and night. Genji heard of this and did not blame them. He could only think it was a thousand pities that a woman endowed with every talent and charm, should take it into her head that she had done with the world and prepare to remove herself to so remote a place. He could not help thinking that she would find Ise extremely dull when she got there.

Though the masses for Aoi's soul were now over, he remained in retirement till the end of the seven weeks. He was not used to doing nothing and the time hung heavy on his hands. Often he sent for Tō no Chūjō to tell him all that was going on in the world, and among much serious information Chūjō would often seek to distract him by discussing the strange escapades in which they had sometimes shared.

On one of these occasions he indulged in some jokes at the expense of the ancient lady-of-the-bedchamber with whom Genji had so indiscreetly become involved.

"Poor old lady!" Genji protested; "it is too bad to make fun of her in this way. Please do not do it." But all the same he had to admit to himself that he could never think of her without smiling. Then Chūjō told him the whole story of how he had followed and watched him on that autumn night, the first after the full moon,[21] and many other stories besides of his own adventures and other people's. But in the end they fell to talking of their common loss, and agreeing that taken all in all life was but a sad business they parted in tears.

Some weeks afterwards on a gloomy wet evening Chūjō strode into the room looking somewhat self-conscious in the light grey winter cloak and breeches which he was today wearing for the first time.[22] Genji was leaning against the balustrade of the balcony above the main western door. For a long while he had been gazing at the frost-clad gardens which surrounded the house. A high wind was blowing and swift showers dashed against the trees.

Near to tears he murmured to himself the line, *"Tell me whether her soul be in the rain or whether in the clouds above!"*[23]

---

[21] See p. 182.

[22] Winter clothes are begun on the first day of the tenth month.

[23] From a poem to a dead lady, by Liu Yü-hsi (A.D. 772–842).

I saw you first standing at the window of Yü Liang's tower;
Your waist was slender as the willow-trees that grow

And as Chūjō watched him sitting there, his chin resting upon his hand, he thought the soul of one who had been wedded to so lovely a youth would not indeed have borne quite to renounce the scene of her earthly life and must surely be hovering very near him. Still gazing with eager admiration Chūjō came to Genji's side. He noticed now that though his friend had not in any other way abated the plainness of his dress, he had today put on a coloured sash. This streak of deep red showed up against his grey cloak (which though still a summer one[24] was of darker colour than that which he had lately been wearing) in so attractive a way that though the effect was very different from that of the magnificent attires which Genji had affected in happier days, yet Chūjō could not for a long while take his eyes off him. At last he too gazed up at the stormy sky, and remembering the Chinese verse which he had heard Genji repeat he recited the poem:

"*Though to rain her soul be turned, yet where in the clouded vault of heaven is that one mist-wreath which is she?*"

And Genji answered: "Since she whom once we knew beyond the country of the clouds is fled, two months of storm and darkness now have seared the wintry earth below."

The depth of Genji's feeling was evident. Sometimes Chūjō had thought it was merely dread of the old Emperor's rebukes—coupled with a sense of obligation towards Aoi's father whose kindness had always been so marked and also towards the Princess her mother, who had cherished him with an unfailing patience and fondness—that had made it difficult for him to break off a relationship which was in fact becoming very irksome. Often indeed Genji's apparent indifference to Aoi had been very painful to him. Now it was evident to him that she had never ceased to hold an important place in his affections, and this made him deplore more bitterly than ever the tragedy of her early death. Whatever he did and wherever he went he felt that a light was gone out of his life and he was very despondent.

Among the withered undergrowth in the garden Genji found to his delight a few gentians still blossoming and after Chūjō was gone he

---

at Wu-ch'ang.
My finding you and losing you were both like a dream;
Oh tell me if your soul dwells in the rain, or whether in
the clouds above!

[24] A husband in mourning may not wear winter clothes. The mourning lasts for three months.

plucked some and bade the wet-nurse Saisō give them to the child's grandmother, together with the verse: "*This gentian flower that lingered amid the withered grasses of the hedge I send you in remembrance of the autumn that is passed.*"

"To you," he added, "it will seem a poor thing in contrast to the flowers that are gone."

The Princess looked at her grandson's innocent smiling face and thought that in beauty he was not far behind the child she had lost. Already her tears were pouring faster than a stormy wind shakes down the dry leaves from a tree, and when she read Genji's message they flowed faster still. This was her answer: "New tears, but tears of joy it brings,—this blossom from a meadow that is now laid waste."

Still in need of some small employment to distract his thoughts, though it was already getting dark he began a letter to Princess Asagao who, he felt sure, must long ago have been told of his bereavement. Although it was a long time since he had heard from her he made no reference to their former friendship; his letter was indeed so formal that he allowed the messenger to read it before he started. It was written on Chinese paper tinted sky-blue. With it was the poem, "*When I look back upon an autumn fraught with diverse sorrows I find no dusk dimmed with such tears as I tonight have shed.*" He took great pains with his handwriting and her ladies thought it a shame that so elegant a note should remain unanswered. In the end she reached the same conclusion.

"Though my heart goes out towards you in your affliction," she answered, "I see no cause to abandon my distrust." And to this she added the poem, "*Since I heard that the mists of autumn had vanished and left desolate winter in your house, I have thought often of you as I watched the streaming sky.*" This was all, and it was written hastily, but to Genji, who for so long had received no news from her, it gave as much pleasure as the longest and most ingenious epistle.

It is in general the unexplored that attracts us, and Genji tended to fall most deeply in love with those who gave him least encouragement. The ideal condition for the continuance of his affection was that the beloved, much occupied elsewhere, should grant him no more than an occasional favour. There was one[25] who admirably fulfilled these conditions, but unfortunately her high rank and conspicuous position in society brought with them too many material difficulties. But little Murasaki was different.

---

[25] Fujitsubo.

There was no need to bring her up on this principle. He had not during the long days of his mourning ever forgotten her and he knew that she must be feeling very dull without him. But he regarded her merely as an orphan child whose care he had undertaken and it was a comfort to him to think that here at least was someone he could leave for a little while without anxiously wondering all the time whether he would get into trouble.

It was now quite dark, and gathering the people of the house round the great lamp he got them to tell him stories. There was among them a gentlewoman named Chūnagon with whom he had for years been secretly in love. He still felt drawn towards her, but at such a time there could of course be no thought of any closer tie. Seeing now that he was looking despondent she came over to him and when they had talked for a while of various matters at large, Genji said to her: "During these last weeks, when all has been quiet in the house, I have grown so used to the company of you gentlewomen that if a time comes when we can no longer meet so frequently, I shall miss you very much. That was why I was feeling particularly depressed; though indeed whichever way I turn my thoughts I find small matter for consolation!" Here he paused and some of the ladies shed a few tears.

At last one of them said: "I know, my Lord, how dark a cloud has fallen upon your life and would not venture to compare our sorrow with yours. But I would have you remember what it must mean to us that henceforward you will never. . ."

"Do not say never," answered Genji kindly. "I do not forget my friends so easily as that. If there are any among you who, mindful of the past, wish still to serve in this house, they may count upon it that so long as I live I shall never desert them." And as he sat gazing into the lamplight, with tears a-glitter in his eyes, they felt they were fortunate indeed in having such a protector.

There was among these gentlewomen a little orphan girl who had been Aoi's favourite among all her maids. Well knowing how desolate the child must now be feeling he said to her kindly:

"Whose business is it now but mine to look after little Miss Até?" The girl burst into tears. In her short tunic, darker than the dresses the others were wearing, with black neckerchief and dark blue breeches she was a charming figure.

"I hope," continued Genji "that there are some who despite the dull times they are likely to have in this house will choose, in memory of the past, to devote themselves to the care of the little prince whom I am

LADY MURASAKI SHIKIBU

leaving behind. If all who knew his mother are now to be dispersed his plight will be more wretched than before." Again he promised never to forget them, but they knew well enough that his visits would be few and far between, and felt very despondent.

That night he distributed among these waiting-ladies and among all the servants at the Great Hall according to their rank and condition various keepsakes and trifles that had belonged to their young mistress, giving to each whatever he thought most likely to keep her memory alive, without regard to his own preferences and dislikes in the household.

He had determined that he could not much longer continue this mode of life and must soon return to his own palace. While his servants were dragging out his coach and his gentlemen assembling in front of his rooms, as though on purpose to delay him a violent rainstorm began, with a wind that tore the last leaves from the trees and swept them over the earth with wild rapidity. The gentlemen who had assembled in front of the house were soon drenched to the skin. He had meant to go to the Palace, then to the Nijō-in and return to sleep at the Great Hall. But on such a night this was impossible, and he ordered his gentlemen to proceed straight to the Nijō-in where he would join them subsequently. As they trooped off each of them felt (though none of them was likely to be seeing the Great Hall for by any means the last time) that today a chapter in his life was closed. Both the Minister and his wife, when they heard that Genji was not returning that night, also felt that they had reached a new and bitter stage in the progress of their affliction. To Aoi's mother he sent this letter:

> The ex-Emperor has expressed a strong desire to see me and I feel bound to go to the Palace. Though I shall not be absent for many days, yet it is now so long a time since I left this house that I feel dazed at the prospect of facing the great world once more. I could not go without informing you of my departure, but am in no condition to pay you a visit.

The Princess was still lying with closed eyes, her thoughts buried in the profoundest gloom. She did not send a reply. Presently Aoi's father came to Genji's apartments. He found it very hard to bear up, and during the interview clung fast to his son-in-law's sleeve with an air of dependence which was pathetic to witness.

After much hesitation he began at last to say: "We old men are prone to tears even when small matters are amiss; you must not wonder then that under the weight of so terrible a sorrow I sometimes find myself breaking into fits of weeping which I am at a loss to control. At such moments of weakness and disarray I had rather be where none can see me, and that is why I have not as yet ventured even to pay my respects to his Majesty your good father. If opportunity offers, I beg you to explain this to him. To be left thus desolate in the last years of life is a sore trial, a very sore trial indeed. . ."

The effort which it cost him to say these words was distressing for Genji to watch and he hastened to assure the old Minister that he would make matters right at the Court.

"Though I do not doubt," he added, "that my father has already guessed the reason of your absence." As it was still raining heavily the Minister urged him to start before it grew quite dark. But Genji would not leave the house till he had taken a last look at the inner rooms. His father-in-law followed him. In the space beyond Aoi's curtained seat, packed away behind a screen, some thirty gentlewomen all clad in dark grey weeds were huddled together, forlorn and tearful.

"These hapless ladies," said the Minister, turning to Genji, "though they take some comfort in the thought that you are leaving behind you one whose presence will sometimes draw you to this house, well know that it will never again be your rightful home, and this distresses them no less than the loss of their dear mistress. For years they had hoped against hope that you and she would at last be reconciled. Consider then how bitter for them must be the day of this, your final departure."

"Let them take heart," said Genji; "for whereas while my lady was alive I would often of set purpose absent myself from her in the vain hope that upon my return I should find her less harshly disposed towards me, now that she is dead I have no longer any cause to shun this house, as soon you shall discover."

When he had watched Genji drive away, Aoi's father went to her bedroom. All her things were just as she had left them. On a stand in front of the bed writing materials lay scattered about. There were some papers covered with Genji's handwriting, and these the old man clasped with an eagerness that made some of the gentlewomen who had followed him smile even in the midst of their grief. The works that Genji had written out were all masterpieces of the past, some Chinese, some Japanese; some written in cursive, some in full script; they constituted indeed an astonishing display of versatile penmanship. The Minister gazed with an almost religious awe at these specimens of Genji's skill, and the thought that he must henceforth regard the young man whom he adored as no longer a member of his household and family must at that moment have been very painful to him.

Among these manuscripts was a copy of Po Chü-i's *Everlasting Wrong*[26] and beside the words "The old pillow, the old coverlet with whom shall he now share?" Genji had written the poem: *"Mournful her ghost that journeying now to unfamiliar realms must flee the couch where we were wont to rest."* While beside the words "The white petals of the frost" he had written: *"The dust shall cover this bed; for no longer can I bear to brush from it the nightly dew of my tears."*

Aoi's ladies were gathered together in groups of two or three in each of which some gentlewoman was pouring out her private griefs and vexations. "No doubt, as his Excellency the Minister told us, Prince Genji will come to us sometimes, if only to see the child. But for my part I doubt whether he will find much comfort in such visits. . ." So one of them was saying to her friends. And soon there were many affecting scenes of farewell between them, for it had been decided that for the present they were all of them to go back to their homes.

Meanwhile Genji was with his father in the Palace. "You are very thin in the face," said the ex-Emperor as soon as he saw him. "I am afraid you have overtaxed your strength by too much prayer and fasting," and in a state of the deepest concern he at once began pressing all kinds of viands and cordials upon him, showing with regard to his health and indeed his affairs in general a solicitude by which Genji could not help feeling touched.

Late that night he at last arrived at the Nijō-in. Here he found everything garnished and swept; his men-servants and maids were waiting for him at the door. All the gentlewomen of the household at once presented themselves in his apartments. They seemed to have vied with one another which should look the gayest and smartest, and their finery contrasted pleasantly with the sombre and dispiriting attire of the unfortunate ladies whom he had left behind him at the Great Hall.

---

[26] Murasaki quotes the line in the form in which it occurs in Japanese MSS. of Po Chü-i's poem. The Chinese editions have a slightly different text. Cf. Giles's translation, *History of Chinese Literature*, p. 172.

Having changed out of his court dress, he went at once to the western wing. Not only was Murasaki's winter costume most daintily designed, but her pretty waiting-maids and little companions were so handsomely equipped as to reflect the greatest credit on Shōnagon's management; and he saw with satisfaction that such matters might with perfect safety be left in her hands. Murasaki herself was indeed exquisitely dressed.

"How tall you have grown since last I saw you!" he said and pulled up her little curtain-of-honour. He had been away so long that she felt shy with him and turned her head aside. But he would not for the world have had her look otherwise than she looked at that moment, for as she sat in profile with the lamplight falling upon her face he realized with delight that she was becoming the very image of her whom from the beginning he had loved best.

Coming closer to her side he whispered to her: "Sometime or other I want to tell you about all that has been happening to me since I went away. But it has all been very terrible and I am too tired to speak of it now, so I am going away to rest for a little while in my own room. From tomorrow onwards you will have me to yourself all day long; in fact, I expect you will soon grow quite tired of me."

"So far, so good," thought Shōnagon when she heard this speech. But she was still very far from easy in her mind. She knew that there were several ladies of very great influence with whom Genji was on terms of friendship and she feared that when it came to choosing a second wife, he would be far more likely to take one of these than to remember her own little mistress; and she was not at all satisfied.

When Genji had retired to the eastern wing, he sent for a certain Lady Chūjō to rub his limbs and then went to bed. Next morning he wrote to the nurses of Aoi's child and received from them in reply a touching account of its beauty and progress; but the letter served only to awaken in him useless memories and regrets. Towards the end of the day he felt very restless and the time hung heavily on his hands, but he was in no mood to resume his secret rovings and such an idea did not even occur to him. In Murasaki none of his hopes had been disappointed; she had indeed grown up into as handsome a girl as you could wish to see, nor was she any longer at an age when it was impossible for him to become her lover. He constantly hinted at this, but she did not seem to understand what he meant.

He still had plenty of time on his hands, and the whole of it was now spent in her society. All day long they played together at draughts or word-picking, and even in the course of these trivial pursuits she showed a quickness of mind and beauty of disposition which continually delighted him; but she had been brought up in such rigid seclusion from the world that it never once occurred to her to exploit her charms in anymore adult way.

Soon the situation became unendurable, and though he knew that she would be very much upset he determined somehow or another to get his own way.

There came a morning when the gentleman was already up and about, but the young lady was still lying a-bed. Her attendants had no means of knowing that anything out of the ordinary had happened, for it had always been Genji's habit to go in and out of her room just as he chose. They naturally assumed that she was not feeling well and were glancing at her with sympathy when Genji arrived carrying a writing-box which he slipped behind the bed curtains. He at once retired, and the ladies also left the room. Seeing that she was alone Murasaki slowly raised her head. There by her pillow was the writing-box and tied to it with ribbon, a slender note. Listlessly she detached the note and unfolding it read the hastily scribbled poem:

Too long have we deferred this new emprise, who night by night till now have lain but with a shift between.

That *this* was what Genji had so long been wanting came to her as a complete surprise and she could not think why he should regard the unpleasant thing that had happened last night as in some way the beginning of a new and more intimate friendship between them.

Later in the morning he came again. "Is something the matter with you?" he asked. "I shall be very dull today if you cannot play draughts with me." But when he came close to her she only buried herself more deeply than ever under the bedclothes. He waited till the room was empty and then bending over her he said, "Why are you treating me in this surly way? I little expected to find you in so bad a humour this morning. The others will think it very strange if you lie here all day," and he pulled aside the scarlet coverlet beneath which she had dived. To his astonishment he found that she was bathed in sweat; even the hair that hung across her cheeks was dripping wet.

"No! This is too much," he said; "what a state you have worked yourself up into!" But try as he would to coax her back to reason he could not get a word out of her, for she was really feeling very vexed with him indeed.

"Very well then," he said at last, "if that is how you feel I will never come to see you again," and he pretended to be very much mortified and humiliated. Turning away, he opened the writing-box to see whether she had written any answer to his poem, but of course found none. He understood perfectly that her distress was due merely to extreme youth and inexperience, and was not at all put out. All day long he sat near her trying to win back her confidence, and though he had small success he found even her rebuffs in a curious way very endearing.

At nightfall, it being the Day of the Wild Boar, the festival cakes[27] were served. Owing to Genji's bereavement no great display was made, but a few were brought round to Murasaki's quarters in an elegant picnic-basket. Seeing that the different kinds were all mixed up together Genji came out into the front part of the house and calling for Koremitsu said to him: "I want you to take these cakes away and bring me some more tomorrow evening; only not nearly so many as this, and all of one kind.[28] This is not the right evening for them." He smiled as he said these words and Koremitsu was quick-witted enough at once to guess what had happened. He did not however think that it would be discreet to congratulate his master in so many words, and merely said: "It is true enough that if you want to make a good beginning you must eat your cakes on the proper day. The day of the Rat is certainly very much to the purpose.[29] Pray how many am I to bring?" When Genji answered, "Divide by three[30] and you will get the answer," Koremitsu was no longer in any doubt, and hastily retired, leaving Genji amused at the practised air with which he invariably handled matters of this kind. He said nothing to anyone, but returning to his private house made the cakes there with his own hands.

---

[27] On the Day of the Boar in the tenth month it was the custom to serve little cakes of seven different kinds, to wit: Large bean, mungo, dolicho, sesamun, chestnut, persimmon, sugar-starch.

[28] On the third night after the first cohabitation it was the custom to offer up small cakes (all of one kind and colour) to the god Izanagi and his sister Izanami.

[29] First, because the Rat comes at the beginning of the series of twelve animal signs; secondly, because "Rat" is written with a character that also means "baby."

[30] The phrase which I have translated "Divide by three" also means "One of three" i.e. of the Three Mysteries (Birth, *Marriage*, Death). That is why Koremitsu was "no longer in any doubt." But many other explanations of the passage have been given. It is indeed one of the three major difficulties enumerated by the old-fashioned Genji teachers.

LADY MURASAKI SHIKIBU

Genji was beginning to despair of ever restoring her confidence and good humour. But even now, when she seemed as shy of him as on the night when he first stole her from her home, her beauty fascinated him and he knew that his love for her in past days had been but a particle compared with what he had felt since yesterday.

How strange a thing is the heart of man! For now it would have seemed to him a calamity if even for a single night he had been taken from Murasaki's side; and only a little while ago. . .

Koremitsu brought the cakes which Genji had ordered very late on the following night. He was careful not to entrust them to Shōnagon, for he thought that such a commission might embarrass a grown woman. Instead, he sent for her daughter Miss Ben and putting all the cakes into one large perfume-box he bade her take them secretly to her mistress.

"Be sure to put them close by her pillow, for they are lucky cakes and must not be left about the house. Promise me not to do anything silly with them."

Miss Ben thought all this very odd, but tossing her head she answered, "When, pray, did you ever know me to be silly," and she walked off with the box. Being quite a young girl and completely innocent as regards matters of this kind she marched straight up to her mistress's bed and, remembering Koremitsu's instructions, pushed the box through the curtains and lodged it safely by the pillow. It seemed to her that there was someone else there as well as Murasaki. "No doubt," thought she "Prince Genji has come as usual to hear her repeat her lessons."

As yet no one in the household save Koremitsu had any knowledge of the betrothal. But when next day the box was found by the bed and brought into the servant's quarters some of those who were in closest touch with their master's affairs at once guessed the secret. Where did these little dishes come from, each set on its own little carved stand? and who had been at such pains to make these dainty and ingenious cakes? Shōnagon, though she was shocked at this casual way of slipping into matrimony, was overjoyed to learn that Genji's strange patronage of her young mistress had at last culminated in a definite act of betrothal, and her eyes brimmed with tears of thankfulness and delight. All the same, she thought he might at least have taken the trouble to inform her old nurse, and there was a good deal of grumbling in the household generally at an outside retainer such as Koremitsu having got wind of the matter first.

During the days that followed he grudged even the short hours of attendance which he was obliged to put in at the Palace and in his father's rooms, discovering (much to his own surprise) that save in her presence he could no longer enjoy a moment's peace. The friends whom he had been wont to visit showed themselves both surprised and offended by this unexplained neglect, but though he had no wish to stand ill with them he now found that even a remote prospect of having to absent himself from his palace for a single night was enough to throw him quite out of gear; and all the time he was away his spirits were at the very lowest ebb and he looked for all the world as though he were sickening from some strange illness. To all invitations or greetings he invariably replied that he was at present in no fit mood for company (which was naturally taken as an allusion to his recent loss) or that he must now be gone, for someone with whom he had business was already awaiting him.

The Minister of the Right was aware that his youngest daughter[31] was still pining for Prince Genji and he said one day to Princess Kōkiden: "While his wife was alive we were bound of course to discourage her friendship with him in every way we could. But the position is now quite changed and I feel that as things are there would be much to be said for such a match." But Kōkiden had always hated Genji and having herself arranged that her sister should enter the Palace,[32] she saw no reason why this plan should suddenly be abandoned. Indeed from this moment onwards she became obstinately determined that the girl should be given to the Emperor and to no one else. Genji indeed still retained a certain partiality towards her; but though it grieved him to hear that he had made her unhappy he had not at present any spare affection to offer her. Life, he had come to the conclusion, was not long enough for diversions and experiments; henceforward he would concentrate. He had moreover received a terrible warning of the dangers which might accrue from such jealousies and resentments as his former way of life had involved. He thought with great tenderness and concern of Lady Rokujō's distress; but it was clear to him that he must beware of ever again allowing her to regard him as her true haven of refuge. If however she would renew their friendship in quite new terms, permitting him to enjoy her company and conversation at such times

<hr />

[31] Oborozukiyo. See above, p. 242.

[32] I.e. become a concubine of the Emperor.

as he could conveniently arrange to do so, he saw no reason why they should not sometimes meet.

Society at large knew that someone was living with him, but her identity was quite unknown. This was of no consequence; but Genji felt that sooner or later he ought to let her father Prince Hyōbukyō know what had become of her and decided that before he did so it would be best to celebrate her Initiation. This was done privately, but he was at pains that every detail of the ceremony should be performed with due splendour and solemnity, and though the outside world was not invited it was as magnificent an affair as it well could be. But ever since their betrothal Murasaki had shown a certain shyness and diffidence in his presence. She could not help feeling sorry that after all the years during which they had got on so well together and been such close friends he should suddenly take this strange idea into his head, and whenever her eyes met his she hastily averted them. He tried to make a joke of the matter, but to her it was very serious indeed and weighed heavily upon her mind. Her changed attitude towards him was indeed somewhat comic; but it was also very distressing, and one day he said: "Sometimes it seems as though you had forgotten all the long years of our friendship and I had suddenly become as new to you as at the start"; and while thus he scolded her the year drew to a close. On New Year's Day he paid the usual visits of ceremony to his father, to the Emperor and to the Heir Apparent. Next he visited the Great Hall. The old Minister made no reference to the new year, but at once began to speak of the past. In the midst of his loneliness and sorrow he was so deeply moved even by this hasty and long deferred visit that though he strove hard to keep his composure it was more than he could compass to do. Looking fondly at his son-in-law he thought that the passage of each fresh year did but add new beauty to this fair face. They went together into the inner rooms, where his entry surprised and delighted beyond measure the disconsolate ladies who had remained behind. Next they visited the little prince who was growing into a fine child; his merry face was indeed a pleasure to see. His resemblance to the Heir Apparent was certainly very striking and Genji wondered whether it had been noticed.

Aoi's things were still as she had left them. His New Year clothes had as in former years been hung out for him on the clothes-frame. Aoi's clothes-frame which stood empty beside it wore a strangely desolate air. A letter from the Princess her mother was now brought to him:

"Today," she said, "our bereavement was more than ever present to my mind, and though touched at the news of your visit, I fear that to see you would but awaken unhappy recollections."

"You will remember," she continued, "that it was my custom to present you with a suit of clothes on each New Year's Day. But in these last months my sight has been so dimmed with tears that I fear you will think I have matched the colours very ill. Nevertheless I beg that though it be for today only you will suffer yourself to be disfigured by this unfashionable garb. . ." and a servant held out before him a second[33] suit, which was evidently the one he was expected to wear today. The under-stuff was of a most unusual pattern and mixture of colours and did not at all please him; but he could not allow her to feel that she had laboured in vain, and at once put the suit on. It was indeed fortunate that he had come to the Great Hall that day, for he could see that she had counted on it. In his reply he said: "Though I came with the hope that you would be the first friend I should greet at this new springtide, yet now that I am here too many bitter memories assail me and I think it wiser that we should not meet." To this he added an acrostic poem in which he said that with the mourning dress which he had just discarded so many years of friendship were cast aside that were he to come to her[34] he could but weep. To this she sent in answer an acrostic poem in which she said that in this new season when all things else on earth put on altered hue, one thing alone remained as in the months gone by—her longing for the child who like the passing year had vanished from their sight.

But though hers may have been the greater grief we must not think that there was not at that moment very deep emotion on both sides.

To Be Continued in *The Sacred Tree*.

---

[33] In addition to the one hanging on the frame.

[34] *Kiteba*, "were he to come," also means "should he wear it."

Appendix I

A.D. 978 (?)	Murasaki born.
A.D. 994 (?)	Marries Fujiwara no Nobutaka.
A.D. 1001	Nobutaka dies.
A.D. 1005 (?)	She becomes lady-in-waiting to the Empress Akiko, then a girl of sixteen.
A.D. 1007–1010	Keeps a diary, which survives.
A.D. 1008	Book I of the *Tale of Genji* read to the Emperor.
A.D. 1025	Murasaki still at Court.
A.D. 1031	Murasaki no longer at Court and perhaps dead.

Appendix II

The Vestal Virgins of Ise and Kamo.

So important a part do these ladies play in the Tale of Genji that the reader may perhaps wish to know exactly what they were. I may say at the outset that I have used the term "vestal" merely for convenience. These Virgins were not guardians of a sacred fire.

Ise.—Upon the accession of a new Emperor, a princess of the Imperial House (preferably a daughter of the Emperor) was sent to be priestess of the great Shintō shrines at Ise. According to the *Nihongi* (Bk. V; Emperor Sūjin 6th year[1]) "The gods Amaterasu and Ōkunidama were formerly both worshipped in the Emperor's Palace Hall. But the Emperor Sūjin was frightened of having so much divine power concentrated in one place. Accordingly he entrusted the worship of Amaterasu to the Princess Toyosuku-iri, bidding her carry it out in the village of Kasanui in Yamato." Subsequently Amaterasu expressed a desire to be moved to Ise.

The Virgin was usually about twelve years old at the time of her appointment. Cases however are recorded in which she was an infant of one year old; or again, a woman of twenty-eight. Her office lasted till

(1) The Emperor died or resigned
(2) She herself died or became disabled
(3) Either of her parents died
(4) She misconducted herself.

Thus in A.D. 541 the Vestal, a certain Princess Iwane, misconducted herself with Prince Mubaragi and was replaced. The process of preparing the Virgin for her office lasted three years. She was first of all, after a preliminary purification in running water handed over to the City guards. Meanwhile, just outside the Capital, a special place of purification was built for her, called the Palace-in-the-Fields. After a second River Purification she took up her residence in this temporary Palace and stayed there till the time came for her to settle at Ise. Before the journey to Ise she was again purified in the River, and she appeared at the Imperial

---

[1] 92 B.C. according to the usual chronology, which is however purely fictitious.

Palace to receive at the Emperor's hands the "Comb of Parting." No Virgin of Ise was appointed after 1342.

Kamo.—The Virgin of Kamo, first instituted in A.D. 818 was a replica of the Ise Virgin. She too had her Palace-in-the-Fields, three years of purification, etc. The practice of sending a Virgin to Kamo was discontinued in 1204.

Upon both Virgins curious speech-taboos were imposed. Thus they called

> death, "recovery"
> illness, "taking a rest"
> weeping, "dropping salt water"
> blood, "sweat"
> to strike, "to fondle"
> a tomb, "an earth heap"
> meat, "vegetables"

All words connected with Buddhism were taboo. Thus Buddha himself was called "The Centre"; Buddhist scriptures were called "stained paper"; a pagoda, "araragi" (meaning unknown); a temple, "a tile-covered place"; a priest (ironically), "hair-long"; a nun, "female hair-long"; fasting, "partial victuals."

To both Virgins was attached an important retinue of male officials. These were appointed by the Emperor and no doubt acted as his agents and informers in the districts of Ise and Kamo.

Probably the Ise Virgin was a very ancient institution which later proved useful for political ends. The Virgin of Kamo, who does not appear on the scene till the ninth century, was presumably instituted simply as a means of spreading Court influence.

A Note About the Author

Lady Murasaki Shikibu (c. 973–c. 1014 or 1925) was a Japanese novelist, poet and lady-in-waiting. Born in in Heian-kyō, Japan, Shikibu was a part of the Fujiwara clan. While Heian women were traditionally excluded from learning Chinese, Shikibu was able to become proficient in classical Chinese by listening in on her brother's lessons. With his further assistance, she was also instructed in traditional subjects such as music, calligraphy and Japanese poetry. At the age of twenty-five, Shikibu entered into marriage with a friend of her father's, Fujiwara no Nobutaka, and it was because of this marriage that Shikibu was allowed ample leisure time to read and eventually, write. Shikibu would produce at least three books: a diary (*The Diary of Lady Murasaki*), a volume of poetry (*Poetic Memoirs*), and the groundbreaking novel, *The Tale of Genji*.

A Note from the Publisher

Spanning many genres, from non-fiction essays to literature classics to children's books and lyric poetry, Mint Edition books showcase the master works of our time in a modern new package. The text is freshly typeset, is clean and easy to read, and features a new note about the author in each volume. Many books also include exclusive new introductory material. Every book boasts a striking new cover, which makes it as appropriate for collecting as it is for gift giving. Mint Edition books are only printed when a reader orders them, so natural resources are not wasted. We're proud that our books are never manufactured in excess and exist only in the exact quantity they need to be read and enjoyed.

Discover more of your favorite classics with Bookfinity™.

- Track your reading with custom book lists.
- Get great book recommendations for your personalized Reader Type.
- Add reviews for your favorite books.
- AND MUCH MORE!

Visit **bookfinity.com** and take the fun Reader Type quiz to get started.

Enjoy our classic and modern companion pairings!